"...an outstanding commentary on our time. ...well-developed characters and a compelling, page-turning plot. ...the finest treatment of the classic battle between good and evil that I have read in a long time. It is encouraging to come across a writer who can so clearly and yet engagingly portray moral truth with conviction, excitement and flair.

"Fred Schott is a delightful new author who will bring marvelous depth and insight into some of the least attractive, yet most compelling, parts of our culture. Watch for Fred Schott!"

—REV. MARTHA L. FREEMAN,

NORTH PARK THEOLOGICAL UNIVERSITY
SR. PASTOR, COMMUNITY COVENANT CHURCH, OMAHA, NE

"Fred Schott captures a battle being waged for control over the youth of the inner city. This battle is too frequently fought in our country's cities.

"He also explores the personal conflicts of people dealing with addictions, failed careers, loss of loved ones and, even more thought-provoking, the possibility of redemption.

"The story builds to a dramatic and surprising conclusion. Readers will enjoy the ride. I'm already looking forward to Fred's next release!"

—DICK KIZER,

CHAIRMAN AND PRESIDENT,
CENTRAL STATES HEALTH & LIFE COMPANY OF OMAHA

W H E N
SPARROWS
FALL

Moore—
for all
you do for our kids!
Fred Scott

WHEN SPARROWS FALL

A MYSTERY

FRED SCHOTT

BOOKPARTNERS
INCORPORATED

Library of Congress Cataloging-in-Publication Data

Schott, Fred W.
  When sparrows fall / Fred W. Schott
    p. cm.
  ISBN 1-58151-068-3 (alk. paper)
    1. Boys & Girls Clubs of America--Fiction. 2. Teenage boys--
Fiction. 2. Middle
    West--Fiction. 4. Gangs--Fiction. I. Title.
  PS3569.C52827 W48 2001
  813'.54--dc21

                                                      2001025448

Cover art by Kara Richardson
Cover design by Aimee Genter
Text design by Aimee Genter

This book may not be reproduced in whole or in part, by
electronic or any other means which exist or may yet be
developed, without permission of:

BookPartners, Inc.
P.O. Box 922
Wilsonville, OR 97070
www.bookpartners.com

BookPartners books are available at special discounts when purchased in bulk for premiums and
sales promotions, as well as for fund-raising or educational use. Special editions or book excerpts
can also be created for specification. For details, contact the Sales Director at the address above.

AUTHOR'S NOTE
LOVE THAT
CLUB

This is a work of fiction. All the characters are pure invention as is Parkland, the neighborhood where the story unfolds. But the Club was real for me and millions of other kids growing up in poor neighborhoods around the country. Thankfully, the Club remains a reality for even more kids today.

Boys & Girls Clubs of America has a unique legacy of success. With special emphasis on the nation's most disadvantaged youth, for nearly a century and a half, local Clubs have been filling the gaps in the lives of kids. Today, there are some 2,600 neighborhood-based facilities that more than three million girls and boys simply refer to as the Club.

Over 11,000 trained full-time youth professionals work in the Clubs. They are supported by another 40,000 trained part-time staff and over 200,000 community leaders who volunteer, serve on boards and contribute money to their local Club.

For more information or to learn how you can become involved with the largest and fastest growing youth organization in the country, contact:

Boys & Girls Clubs of America
1230 W. Peachtree Street
Atlanta, Georgia 30309
www.bgca.org

To Mom

Who faithfully escorted me to church
and let me go to the Club across the street.

So don't be afraid:

You are worth more than many sparrows.

PROLOGUE

PARKLAND

Parkland slumbers in the brittle stillness of a cold Midwestern spring. The wide meandering river mingles and dances softly with the reflection of her bright city lights and the twinkling stars of the clear crisp night. In the distance, storm clouds gather and the approaching thunder rumbles ominously.

On the edge of the city, itself a constellation of old and new, Parkland stubbornly clings to its old neighborhood identity. Its proud residents bravely resist the creeping of urban decay at one end, and the encroaching downtown development on the other. The residents sleep soundly, but are always vigilant. Parkland's sentinels—the hearty souls who work the graveyard shift at the all-night diner near downtown, at the nursing home, the small radio station, and at the new convenience store that borders the North Side—are all on duty, tenacious and watchful.

The people of Parkland are proud of their diversity, the mix of new and remodeled homes, refurbished apartments and fashionable condos, old-fashioned family-owned and high-tech businesses, and of its rich amalgam of people—souls who have steadfastly refused to melt into any identifiable kind of urban pot. These folks are proudest of the Club because the Club symbolizes Parkland's dedication and commitment to the children of the entire city, not just their own.

1

DISOWNED

1

The smack, which landed flush on the cheek, was hard. It caught the boy by surprise, knocking him backward.

"Look at me when I talk to you."

The boy looked up slowly, and bravely straightened and squared his shoulders. Unclouded by tears, he unwaveringly stared into the man's eyes. His heart pounded. Fear choked him and isolated him from the other boys who lined the walls. Most of the other boys were black, like their leader, but there were white and brown children in the mix as well. Their street-hardened looks could not mask the fear they felt for the foolish defiant one. It was too late—the boy would have to see it through. He knew what he had to do to end it—one way or another.

No one goes by their real names on the street. The boy couldn't remember when or how he'd gotten the name Hotchie. It was just what he was called. The man who was terrorizing him was called Juice.

"You push me too far, Li'l Bro. You got to start earning your keep. You hear what I say?"

Hotchie's resolve grew stronger as his tormentor closed the distance between them in the middle of the dark, musty living room that was nearly void of furniture. Juice wasn't all that big. It wasn't his size or strength that he used to intimidate people. Juice was dark and handsome, with clear smooth skin and perfect white teeth that he was now baring menacingly at the boy.

"You think you too good to work a corner? Too good to sell candy any-more?" Juice pointed at an older boy who was taking obvious satisfaction in his leader's diatribe. "You too good to take orders from my man? You costin'

3

me money, Hotchie. You make me come out here, after midnight, back to the street, maybe blow my cover, boy? I can't be havin' that, don't matter who you are, don't matter that you Momma's boy."

Hotchie neither answered nor flinched as Juice reached over his shoulder and slowly and deliberately removed the younger boy's brand new baseball cap that sat perched backwards on his head.

"Everybody else in here buy they own clothes, boy, with the money they make from my operation—good money." The man smiled and examined the cap. "But, you? You *owe* me money. Momma buys your clothes, boy, with the money I give her." With a sudden backhanded motion he used the hat to smack the boy across the other cheek. The tension in the room ratcheted even higher.

The button on top of the cap hurt as it scraped across the boy's face. A long, angry welt began to emerge under his eye. But Hotchie resisted the reflex to rub it and quickly resumed his stare. Juice threw the cap at the boy's feet.

"Momma buy those Nikes on your feet, Momma fix you breakfast everyday, Momma tuck you in at night. Momma give you lunch money. Momma get all her money from *me*, Hotchie. You and Angela been gettin' a free ride, Bro." Juice took two handfuls of the boy's coat and pulled him up, until only Hotchie's toes were touching the floor. They were almost nose to nose.

"Time to go to work, Momma's boy," Juice spat out as he roughly flung the boy across the room. Hotchie tried, almost comically, to stay on his feet. He finally rolled to a stop near the door that led to a side room. Three mattresses lay on the floor. They were covered and surrounded by rubbish and debris and smelled sharply of urine and feces.

As if on signal, the entire room erupted. From the middle of the room Juice conducted a crescendo of taunting laughter. Hotchie shot to his feet and screeched over the laughter, "Me and Angela ain't workin' for you no more. Never again. Never!"

The room went deathly silent and Juice took a few slow ominous steps toward the furious boy. In a sudden frenzy, Hotchie tore off the oversized jacket Juice had used to grab him. He threw it at him and yelled, "I seen what happens to people who work for Juice Johnson." The boy frantically untied the bandanna on his belt. "They end up in prison or as some dude's hole—or dead." He threw the bandanna in Juice's face who didn't flinch but took a step closer. "Me and Angela through—it don't matter that you our big brother—we done!"

Juice moved in closer. The boy quit yelling as he looked up at Juice towering over him. Hotchie was beyond afraid. He knew it was over, but he had promised his older sister, Angela, that he would quit working for Juice, too, like she had. He'd promised.

Juice didn't yell. His words came out slow, in a raspy whisper. "You dis me, boy? Nobody dis me. Specially you and Angela. Angela be back on the job tomorrow or… you hear me? Nobody dis me, it don't matter you Momma's boy."

"Burn in hell… *Bro!*"

The blow was a vicious, violent eruption—a full-fisted roundhouse right on the jaw. Hotchie was lifted off his feet by the strike which slammed him hard against the wall. His head snapped against the doorframe. As Hotchie slid down the wall, he nearly lost consciousness. It was not the first blow administered by his older brother, but it was one of the hardest. Juice was in his face now. Hotchie could hear his brother's rapid breathing, could smell his stale breath, even while tasting his own blood.

"Look at me. You little light-skinned bastard."

Hotchie ran out of courage. He did not say what came to mind. *We're all bastards, you, me, and Angela, too. You just too stupid to know what the word means. Just because our daddies was white, you hate us. Thas fine, cause I hate you, and my daddy. I ain't ever seen him and I wish I'd never laid eyes on you. I'm gonna bring you down, too, Juice—count on it—I'm gonna to bring you down.*

Instead, Hotchie looked up into the eyes of a big brother, who once upon a time, like in a fairy tale, he had loved, and wanted to be like. Angela was right. Juice didn't love them anymore. All Juice wanted was to use them, just like he uses everybody else. He had gotten bad, real bad, since they moved to Parkland. Momma wasn't able to protect them anymore. Angela was probably right about dying, too. If Juice did kill them, heaven would definitely be a better place to be. Hotchie didn't wince. He stared straight into the eyes of evil.

"Okay, okay then." It was as if Juice had read the younger boy's mind and accepted the conclusion. "You're no longer my brother. Get out. But, stay clear of me. Don't let me catch you at Momma's house. Don't cross me on the street. I *will* kill you, boy. Probably ought to just do it now."

Hotchie felt the hand on his throat, felt the iron fingers slowly begin to tighten. Stars shot in from the periphery of his vision. He thought of Angela, of Momma. Then suddenly, release. The rancid air made him rasp as he sucked it in.

"For Momma, I won't. But cross me? You dead. You hear that?"

Hotchie tried to speak, but ended up just nodding his head.

Juice let go. "Get out!"

Hotchie stumbled getting up, and Juice screamed, "Get that little pile of shit out of here!"

Two sets of hands grabbed Hotchie by the arms and tossed him out into the hallway. He tripped and fell down the steps to the first landing where the smell of fresh urine made its final brutal assault on his senses. Hotchie passed out. When he came to, he thought for a second that he had died. He was afraid to open his eyes, but the smells clearly told him he was back to hell on earth. Slowly, he rose to his feet and staggered down the rest of the steps and out the front door.

The thunderclaps were rolling closer, and it had begun to rain. Just a few months ago, fifty degrees would have seemed like a heat wave. But tonight a strong wind made the rain feel like cold needles against his cheeks. It was bone-chilling. Hotchie walked fast, wanting to put some serious distance between himself and the gang's headquarters. His head throbbed with each step he took, but it also began to clear. He began to assess his situation. His jaw ached terribly and was starting to swell. There was already a lump the size of a golf ball on the back of his head, but Hotchie felt exhilarated. Juice had disowned him. Juice meant it, too. He wasn't bluffing. They were no longer brothers. Someday he would grieve this loss, but not now, in a strange way, Hotchie, at not quite fifteen years of age, felt free. He also knew Juice wasn't bluffing. Juice *would* kill him. Hotchie had seen his older half-brother kill another boy last year, in D.C., and he had heard about others. Hotchie would have to steer clear of Juice. *I got to find a place to stay tonight. I can't go home—not tonight.*

At the corner, he looked up and down the tree-lined street. In the reflections of the street lights, the fresh green of spring competed with piles of decaying junk strewn liberally across unkept yards and vacant lots that dotted what had once been, long ago, a nice neighborhood. He heard voices behind him, then car doors slamming. *Gotta find a place to stay.* Better to be on a busy street should Juice change his mind and come after him. He ran as fast as he could in the other direction, away from the sound of the engine starting, south, past the storefronts and vacant shops, toward a traffic light two blocks away—toward Parkland.

SPRING STORMS

2

Jacob Riddler lay on his back, held the exhaust pipe in place with one hand and felt around beside him for his socket wrench with the other. *Secure this in place and I can go home and go to bed.*

"Jacob."

He ignored the summons, brushed the blond lock from his pale blue eyes and continued to grope for the wrench he thought lay at his side on the concrete floor.

"Hey, Mister I-didn't-know-you-was-such-a-handyman!"

This time Jacob forsook the search for his wrench and slid his lean six-foot-two-inch frame from under the car.

Evelyn was an attractive heavy set, black woman with beautiful rich coffee-and-cream complexion that offered a striking contrast to her large sparkling brown eyes. She stood, hand on one hip, her Aretha Franklin imitation demanding r-e-s-p-e-c-t. She feigned impatience and tapped water from the umbrella in her other hand. Then she broke into a broad smile as she looked down at him. He wasn't hard to look at even with grease smeared under one eye.

He smiled back. "Yeah?"

"Telephone. You got to be the only one in Parkland without a cell phone or a pager."

"Who is it?"

"It's the secretary down at the radio station."

Jacob sat up and began to wipe his hands on his jeans while looking around.

7

Reading his mind, Evelyn said, "Go ahead and finish up. I told her you'd call her back from here before you left, bein' you don't even have a phone at your house, I hear."

Jacob managed a half smile, enough to flash his perfect teeth, but he only shrugged.

"So, come on in when you get done. I just didn't want you to slip away without getting the message," Evelyn said in her most business-like voice.

"Thanks, Evelyn, I'm about done here. I'll be there in a minute."

"No problem. I'll put on a fresh pot of coffee," she said over her shoulder as she moved back across the old two-story garage. Like many of the fine old homes on the boulevard, ninety years or so ago the garage had been a carriage house.

"No, Evelyn, that's okay, I need..."

Evelyn dismissed him with her hand. "Maryann will want some when she gets back from her morning appointments. Come in the kitchen door when you get done." She exited the side door to the garage and opened the umbrella for the return trip across the backyard.

A few minutes later, Evelyn had just pushed the "on" button on the coffee maker to begin the brewing process when she saw Jacob throw his tool box into the front seat of his old blue truck and walk tentatively through the rain and toward the house. She quickly moved to open the sliding glass door that led to the screened-in back porch. The beautifully remodeled kitchen was stylishly decorated with large bay windows over-looking the side yard. It had floor-to-ceiling custom-made cabinetry and a huge center island.

"Come in this way, Jacob," she called as she unlatched the screen door and then turned for him to follow. "Ever been in Maryann's house?"

"No, it's beautiful," he said, looking around.

"There's a bathroom right there. I laid out some soap and an old towel for you." She motioned to the hallway at the other end of the kitchen as she closed the sliding door behind him. "Then just down the hallway are our business offices. You may use my phone. Punch either button and dial, no need to push nine."

By the time Jacob returned, he found Evelyn sitting in the breakfast nook drinking a steaming mug of coffee with another placed across the table from her. The aroma was wonderful. The cold concrete floor of the garage had chilled him. He slid into the bench across from Evelyn and raised the mug to his lips, but before drinking said, "Thanks, even though this will probably keep me awake and I need to get to bed. I'm volunteering at the Club tonight."

"Did you fix Ruth's car?"

He savored his coffee before answering. "Not yet. It needs a new tail pipe. I'll pick one up today and then come back Friday afternoon to put it on."

"So, auto mechanic is another talent of yours?"

"Not really, just something I've picked up over the years. I really enjoyed restoring Old Blue." Jacob smiled and nodded out the window. "That's the name I gave my old truck. But, that was probably a one-time deal. I'm way too busy with other things right now. But, when Ruth asked if I could fix her car, I said sure."

"Don't matter," said Evelyn. "Ruth don't know this yet, but her mother has already bought her a new car for graduation. Maryann is sure proud of that girl. Graduating from college this weekend—hard to believe. Seems like yesterday—she was just ten, eleven years old when I first started working with Maryann."

"Maryann should be proud of her. Ruth's wonderful—smart, kind, tough." Jacob raised an eyebrow. Evelyn thought he looked like a handsome actor. Except Jacob wasn't acting as he sincerely continued the list of Ruth's attributes. "Pretty, inside and out, hard-working, dedicated... I'm amazed at the way she relates to those kids at the Club. Not just the little kids, but the teenagers, too—black, white, Asian, Hispanic—all of them."

"Ruth is her mother's girl. Everything you said also applies to Maryann—tough, kind, smart and very good-looking." Evelyn smiled and returned the raised eyebrow.

Jacob nodded and looked around the kitchen again. "Maryann has sure done well. This kitchen is beautiful and your offices are very attractively done. Is the rest of the house this nice?"

"Yes, I think it's the nicest house on the boulevard. Your landlady has a nice house, too."

Jacob nodded in agreement. "But not much has been done on it since Mr. Carlson died over twenty years ago. It's too much house for her. Mrs. Carlson will be eighty next month. I try to help her keep it up, but..." He looked around the kitchen again. "This is really nice, though. I'll bet it was fun remodeling it."

"So, Mrs. Carlson takes all your phone messages?"

"Yeah, it gives me an excuse to look in on her a couple of times a day. She's very serious about it, takes detailed notes, asks a lot of questions. She's still really sharp," Jacob smiled. "I think it's good for her."

"Let me ask you something," Evelyn said seriously and leaned forward, both elbows on the table holding her mug with both hands. Her amber-brown eyes seemed to dance in the steam that rose from the hot coffee.

"Sure."

"I thought you earned your degree while you were away?"

"I did."

"A white man with a degree... multiple talents, nice, pleasant and also very good-looking." Her eyes glinted with mischief. "Why you working the midnight shift at that dinky little radio station?"

Jacob smiled, then took another drink before answering. "Degree or not, there's not a lot of opportunities for a guy like me. When I got here, I needed a job. Preacher Nate put me in touch with Bob Wilson to see if I could work in one of his businesses. Bob's an old friend from high school. Some people don't like him, but I think he's a good man. He was willing to give me a chance."

Evelyn made a face and rolled her big eyes at the notion that Bob Wilson was a good man, but chose to challenge something else. "It's been three years and I've heard you..."

"I know, but I enjoy the work. The station's perfect for me. I've learned a lot and I don't mind the crazy hours. It allows me to work on Old Blue and other projects during the day. I like the peace and quiet and the flexibility." He took a last swig of coffee and began to rise from the table. "Like I said, tonight I'm volunteering at the Club, so, I've got to get home and hit the hay." He took his cup to the kitchen sink.

Evelyn remained seated and said, "Maryann's going to be disappointed."

Jacob paused on his way to the door and asked warily, "Why? About what?"

Evelyn's eyes glinted again. "She called right after you got here. When she found out you were out here fixing Ruth's car, she said she'd hurry back after her appointments and fix you a sandwich for lunch. She'll be here any minute."

Jacob said nothing, but the look on his face said, *You're putting me on.*

"She likes you again." Evelyn raised both eyebrows, cocked her head and smiled.

Jacob leaned against the kitchen island and folded his arms across his chest. "Yeah, right. Maryann hates me, Evelyn, and for good reason."

"Not anymore. She told me just now on the phone that when you moved back to Parkland three years ago, she had her doubts. But, she's seen you at church and her kids tell her how good you are with the children down at the Club. Mark might like you even more than his big sister Ruth does."

"She has two great kids."

"Yes, she does, and she's a wonderful mother. Maryann says you visit your mom every single day—that right?"

Jacob nodded and then his attention was seized by something else. He walked to an antique icebox in the opposite corner of the large kitchen. The icebox was beautifully restored and covered with an assortment of picture frames, a photographic history of Maryann Bethel's family.

"These sure bring back memories." Jacob bent with both hands on his knees and looked over the gallery of pictures. He reached carefully into the collection and pulled one out, showing it to Evelyn. "Joe and Maryann sure looked like a happy couple."

"They were, and they were as nice as they were good-looking, too." Evelyn leaned across the table to better see the picture he held. "That one was taken just before Joe was diagnosed with cancer. The young professionals—they were on top of the world."

"Were you working for her then?"

"Oh, yes. I've been with Maryann for twelve years. She'd just quit teaching school and started her insurance agency and I had just graduated from high school. She takes care of the insurance sales and the real estate deals, I handle all the office stuff. Only job I've ever had. From day one she treated me like a partner, not an employee. We built this business together. We're a good team, except that I gained weight after each of my four kids and she looks the same as she did the first day I met her. We've been through a lot together."

Jacob returned the picture to its spot. "Well, she's done well. You've both done well." He pointed to another at the front corner of the collection and looked back at Evelyn. "You have a nice looking family, Evelyn."

"Thank you, I agree. Russell and I sure enjoy those kids. He's a good daddy, too. Watching Maryann suffer through the loss of Joe made me appreciate what we have."

Jacob cautiously picked up another frame. Cradling it almost reverently, he turned and held it out for Evelyn to see. "Do you know who this is?"

Evelyn nodded. "That's Maryann's mom and dad and your mom and dad, before either of you were born. That had to be back in the fifties. Let's see, Maryann's got one more year until the big 4-0," she teased. "That got to make you forty already."

"Forty-one." Jacob smiled, continuing to take in the picture.

"Maryann says your daddy died before you were born?"

"That's true. I never knew him."

"How is your mom, Jacob?"

Jacob smiled wistfully as he studied the picture of the two happy couples. "About the same. No improvement. The doctors don't expect her to regain consciousness. It was a severe stroke."

"I'm sorry," Evelyn said sincerely. "We all love her, especially Maryann and her kids. Your mom even watched my kids from time to time, whenever my sitter was sick."

Jacob nodded and carefully returned the picture. "Well, I've got to get going."

"Aren't you staying for lunch?" Evelyn quickly rose from her seat and took her cup to the sink.

"Ah… no, no thanks. Tell Maryann I appreciate it, but I really do have to go. I have to pick up some things for my class at the Club tonight.

"Not good to disappoint Maryann…"

Jacob smiled. "Gotta go, Evelyn. Thanks."

When Jacob stepped outside again the light blinded him. In the short time he spent talking to Evelyn, the rain had stopped and the skies had turned a brilliant blue, making it look like spring had chosen that moment to finally burst through in full glory. Jacob noticed, for the first time it seemed, that the trees were fully leafed and that the grass was rich, full and green. Everything smelled fresh and clean after last night's storm that brought the cleansing rain. He felt great. *Life is good,* he thought.

• • • • •

A few minutes later, Old Blue, Jacob's 1979 Chevy pickup truck, idled smoothly at a stoplight. Jacob was surrounded by the light rock sound that filled the cab and he bounced slightly with the beat. Keeping time, his fingers moved lightly on the steering wheel. The new CD system had been the latest part of Old Blue's loving restoration.

The light changed and Jacob turned onto Parkland Avenue and began to look for a parking spot. This was the business section of Parkland, near downtown. The Parkland Cafe, little shops, antique stores, and other small businesses lined both sides of the avenue for more than four blocks. Suddenly, out of the corner of his eye Jacob saw a kid running desperately. As he ran he looked back over his shoulder. Old Blue's brakes squealed. The startled kid turned, but he couldn't stop and ran smack into the truck.

Jacob was looking into the deep dark eyes of the startled kid who was now sprawled over Old Blue's hood. He saw more than surprise and more than fear—he saw sheer terror. More tires squealed as a late model Buick stopped inches from Old Blue's front bumper. Both doors of the Buick flew open and two young men lurched toward the boy who eluded their grasp and dashed past Jacob toward the rear of the truck. Jacob opened his door and started out. As an afterthought, he grabbed his toolbox and wedged it against the horn. Later, Jacob could not recall grabbing the long-handled crescent wrench before he joined the chase.

Up ahead, he saw the boy turn into an alley, his pursuers on his heels. Jacob dashed into the alley in time to see the boy fall and immediately the two gang-bangers pounced, one kicking and the other using his fists. Jacob saw the kicker trying to undo the chain at his waist and closed the distance quickly.

"Leave the boy alone!" Jacob hadn't raised his voice in anger in years and the sound of it surprised him. The boy's attackers turned to face him. Though their look was hard and the one with the bandanna tied tightly above his eyes showed no fear, Jacob could see they were little more than boys themselves, maybe still in their teens.

The assailants both cursed, shouting over the blare of Old Blue's horn in the background. They yelled at Jacob telling him if he didn't want to get hurt to mind his own business and turned to resume beating the younger boy. Jacob waded in. With the wrench in his right hand, he used his left to grab the kicker by the back of his neck. At the same instant, Jacob hit him hard in the back of the knee with the wrench. The kicker screamed and folded. Jacob looked up just in time to see Bandanna coming at him with a knife. Without thinking, Jacob swung the pipe wrench. Bandanna screamed, grabbed his wrist and fell to his knees. The boy they had been chasing scrambled to retrieve the fallen knife.

Jacob was sure the young man's wrist was broken. He took a step toward him. "I'm sorry about that, Bandanna. You left me…"

"Look out!"

Jacob spun around to face the kicker who had stopped in his tracks. Kicker now held the chain in his hand and waved it menacingly. Through a mask of rage the young gangster glared first at his prey, who was still afraid, but now held Bandanna's knife, then at the man who held the wrench. Jacob was afraid that the kicker might have a gun. Old Blue's horn continued to blare from a block-and-a-half away.

Bandanna writhed on the ground in pain. Tears rolled down his face. "It's broke, man. He broke my wrist."

Amid a string of vile curses and incoherent shouting at the boy, at Jacob, and each other, the two gang-bangers gathered themselves. Kicker helped Bandanna to his feet. Kicker limped and Bandanna hunched over his broken wrist as they quickly retreated.

At the entrance to the alley, Kicker stopped to yell, "You're dead, Hotchie. Juice sent us to give you one more chance, but you a dead man, now."

Hotchie looked at Jacob, eyes wide. "Thanks, mister."

Jacob looked him over. He was a good-looking kid. Dark loose curls atop a light brown face that, tattered and bruised as it was, revealed soft, attractive features.

"You okay?"

"Yeah, that was close. Thanks."

"You want to hand me that?" Jacob reached out and gestured. Hotchie looked down at the open blade in his hand, as if discovering it for the first time. His eyes came back up to Jacob, then back to the knife.

"I don't know, man. I might need it for protection. You know?" He looked up again. Something told him the man would not be put off. "Sure," he said and handed the knife to Jacob.

Jacob took the knife, closed it and put it in his pocket. "Come on, before Old Blue's battery dies."

They got to Old Blue ignoring a handful of curious onlookers. Jacob opened the passenger door and gestured to Hotchie. "Jump in."

Jacob loped around the back of the truck, took the toolbox off the horn and tossed it into the bed. He looked across the seat to where the boy still stood in the open door.

"Come on, hop in."

"Where we going?" Hotchie asked warily.

"Don't know. We'll talk in the cab. Get in."

As Hotchie settled in, Jacob started the engine and then pulled the truck over to the curb.

"Come on, man. Let's go. Somebody might have called the cops."

"That's why I left the horn blowing. Don't you want the cops to know what those guys did to you?"

"Fuck no! That's the last thing I need. Let's go!" Hotchie said as he looked around nervously and then reached for the door handle.

Jacob glanced up. *Lord, help me.* He sighed, then took a deep breath. "Okay, kid, okay, relax. Put on your seat belt and we'll go someplace to talk." Jacob manually shifted Old Blue into first gear and pulled away from the curb back onto the four-lane business section of Parkland Avenue. After he shifted into second, he extended his hand across the cab. "My name is Jacob—Jacob Riddler."

Hotchie paused, then gave Jacob's hand a couple of quick shakes. But Jacob did not let go. When Hotchie looked up. Jacob caught his eye and asked before looking back to the street, "And, your name is?"

"Andre Fitzgerald, but people call me Hotchie."

Jacob nodded but still held his gaze. When Hotchie looked up Jacob said, "Can we get one thing straight?" The grip was hard and Hotchie was becoming afraid. He nodded.

"When you're around me, especially when you're in my truck..." In between words Jacob switched his gaze back and forth, from the traffic on Parkland Avenue to Hotchie. He drove slowly and looked into the boy's big brown eyes. "Don't cuss," he said firmly, checked the traffic again and still held his grip on Hotchie's hand. This time when he looked back, he smiled. "Old Blue, she especially don't like the f-word. Okay?"

Relieved, but also a little surprised, Hotchie said, "Sure, no problem... sorry."

Jacob released Hotchie's hand and shifted Old Blue into third gear. "So, what do you want to be called?"

Hotchie looked up, surprised, "Huh?"

"You said people call you Hotchie. Do you prefer Hotchie or Andre?"

"Hotchie... I guess. My friends call me Hotchie." Hotchie looked around the cab. "Nice, dude. You fix this up yourself?"

"Uh-hu," Jacob nodded.

"Monster, 'cept that music you playing is weak, man."

Jacob smiled and reached over to advance the CD carriage to number six. A new sound filled the cab.

"How's that?" Jacob asked.

Hotchie smiled and swayed, "Sweet. Who is it?"

"Who is it?" Jacob laughed. "You don't know who that is? That's Billie Holiday, she's the greatest blues singer who ever lived."

Out of curiosity, Hotchie opened the glove compartment and nonchalantly rifled through its contents. "You ever been to one of her concerts?"

"Wow, you got a lot to learn, kid." Jacob pointed up the street and said, "I hear Taco Bell has a great breakfast. You hungry?"

Hotchie nodded eagerly, his eyes wide.

After his third breakfast burrito, Hotchie finally sat up and then fell back against the booth's bench.

"Thanks, man. That was good."

Jacob nodded and took a drink of coffee. He wasn't going to get much sleep today. He liked this kid, his spirit and his zest for life, even his strange high-pitched voice.

"I've seen you before, Hotchie. Right?"

Hotchie nodded. "Yeah, at the Club."

"That's what I thought. Why don't we swing by there?"

"It don't open till three o'clock."

"That's true," Jacob looked at his watch, "but it's almost eleven. If he's not out to lunch or at a meeting, Mr. Livingston will be there. Ruth might even be there by now. She'll know how to handle this, whether you should file a complaint with the police and..."

Hotchie's head snapped up. "Fu... I mean, no! No police, man."

"...What to do about you not being in school." Jacob raised an eyebrow and Hotchie squirmed. "...and where she can take you to have that messed-up face of yours looked at."

"I'm okay," the boy protested, feeling his jaw. "Just take me someplace... like a park or something. I can hang out there till three and then walk over to the Club."

• • • • •

It had taken Hotchie a couple of months after moving to town to find the Club. Last week when he finally decided to check it out, he got off on the wrong foot with Ruth because he didn't want to check his bandanna, chain, jacket and hat at the door. Ruth firmly told him he was welcome and that they wanted him to join. It was only five dollars for a whole year's membership. But she would not budge. No one came into the Club wearing any kind of gang colors, identity clothing or jewelry. She made him choose.

After a few days he realized that from three in the afternoon until nine-thirty at night, for six-and-a-half crucial hours during the day, he could be safe. Juice's gang-bangers couldn't get to him when he was in the Club. It gave him courage. Plus, the Club was fun. There were a lot of staff members around, and they were cool. He was able to shower before going swimming or after using the gym. Sometimes, he could even grab a nap in one of the soft chairs in the teen lounge. They served a hot meal every day in a clean cafeteria and the food wasn't bad. After the Club closed, he hid out somewhere in Parkland. Just before dawn, he'd sneak back to the North Side to his house, when most gangbangers were finally asleep, to get ready for school and to make plans with Angela. Angela was almost eighteen and only had one more week before graduating from Central High School. Angela wanted Hotchie to move with her to another city, but Hotchie said he couldn't leave their mother.

One night, after the Club had closed, Hotchie spent the night with Ruth's little brother, Mark. Mark was bigger, but about his age and was pretty cool. Hotchie made Mark laugh and they hit it off fairly well. Mark had a monster house and a big bedroom. His mom, Mrs. Bethel, was really nice, too. She fixed them a big breakfast and then drove him by his house early in the morning. Momma was asleep and couldn't talk to Mrs. Bethel. Then three days ago, Juice started spending the night at Momma's house so Hotchie couldn't take the chance of sneaking home. On the first two mornings, when Hotchie saw his older brother's Lexus in front of the house, he hid in a vacant house across the street. He waited and watched for Angela to leave for school, but she never came out of the house. Yesterday, he waited and looked for her outside the high school, but didn't see her. When he called the school from a phone booth, he learned she hadn't been to school for three days. Last night, when the Club closed, some gangbangers were waiting for him around the corner. They dragged him to the gang's apartment on the North Side for his appointment with Juice.

• • • • •

"What about home?" asked Jacob. "Why don't I take you...."

"No. Not now... not yet."

"Hotchie? Right now, you need a friend. I'll be your friend, okay?" Jacob waited for Hotchie to look up. When Hotchie nodded, Jacob continued. "But, the best friends you can have right now are Ruth Bethel and Mr. Livingston at the Club. You know Ruth?"

"Yeah, she's Mark's older sister. She's tough, man. I mean she talk sweet and all, and she's pretty, but that lady is one tough..."

Jacob smiled. "Yes, she is. So is Mr. Livingston. But, they care about kids. It's their job to help kids like you, kids in a tough situation. You are in a tough situation, right?"

Hotchie just looked down.

"Let's go see if Mr. Livingston or Ruth are in. They'll know what to do, okay?"

"Okay."

PARKLAND

FRIDAY, MAY 17, LATE MORNING

Maryann turned south onto Parkland Avenue. Parkland is a grand old neighborhood, her neighborhood, the neighborhood where she and Joe were born and raised—where they went to school and church, had married, bought a home and started their family. Maryann pulled up in front of the Parkland Avenue Boys & Girls Club. She turned off the ignition. She needed to talk to her daughter Ruth, the newly-appointed program director at the Club. Maryann was halted momentarily by a wave of memories and a rush of emotion.

The Parkland Boys Club was built in the early 1950s. Some of the kids who attend every day are second and even third generation Club members. In the late eighties it became the Parkland Boys & Girls Club. The original facility has disappeared, absorbed over the years by numerous additions and remodeling efforts. The Club and its outdoor playgrounds and athletic fields occupy an entire city block. The facilities provide a wonderful safe haven for children, and the quality of its staff and their programs attract children from all over the metropolitan area.

The Club is located at the northern end of Parkland Avenue, directly across the street from the small white-framed Antioch Church. Twelve blocks away, at the southern end of the avenue, just north of downtown, is a stately three-story brick building that is home to the ministries and broadcast studios of the interdenominational Community Church. Parkland Boulevard begins three blocks east of Community Church. The boulevard meanders along Riverside Park, which follows the twists and turns of the wide river, at its northern end, and is located fifteen blocks

19

from Antioch. The pie-shaped neighborhood, formed by the avenue and the boulevard and anchored by the two churches—each over one hundred years old, is a wonderfully diverse community.

A few rich families and quite a few well-to-do, up-and-coming folks live throughout Parkland. A few, like Maryann, live in the wonderful newly-restored homes on the boulevard opposite Riverside Park, from which Parkland derives its name. Most of the more well-to-do residents live in new condominiums and restored apartments, clustered toward Community Church and downtown. Without fanfare, about ten years ago, as Maryann's insurance agency prospered, she and Joe began to buy and restore old homes for sale and apartment houses to rent. In fact, Maryann became one of three or four individuals primarily responsible for the restoration of Parkland's old neighborhoods. For Joe and Maryann it was more a labor of love, than a desire to make money. But Maryann had done quite well financially—better than she had ever dreamed possible. Parkland's affluent residents smugly enjoyed the urban setting that is convenient to the city's financial hub and to the trendy shops and restaurants of The Old Market area that has developed in the old warehouse district.

The not-so-silent majority of middle class folks and poor people tend to live in apartments and older, smaller homes, bunched closer to Antioch and the Club at the northern border of Parkland. The North Side has not fared nearly so well as Parkland, suffering the inescapable plagues of urban life. For decades, the Club and Antioch have been allied advocates for both the Parkland and North Side communities, especially on behalf of their children.

The sight of her daughter in the rear view mirror stirred Maryann from her nostalgia. Like many of the neighborhood fitness enthusiasts, Ruth frequently jogged the five- and-three-quarter-miles around Parkland's perimeter. Ruth was finishing up her run with a final burst of speed. As she turned the corner, seeing her mother waiting in front of the Club was a pleasant surprise. She waved and flashed the smile that had warmed Maryann's heart since Ruth was a baby.

"Mom, you finally got to put the top down." Ruth called as she jogged up to the driver's door, leaned over and pecked her mom on the check. "You're lookin' good, lady."

Mother and daughter both looked good. Maryann certainly didn't look her thirty-nine years. Tall, graceful and perpetually tan, Maryann was an indigo-eyed beauty with a lovely mane of raven black hair. Even when Maryann tackled her days as the consummate professional in a tailored gray suit, she radiated with natural beauty. Ruth, having just turned twenty-one, was not quite as tall as her mother and was more athletic and finely tuned than graceful. Ruth was fair with bright blue eyes and thick blond hair that she kept short. Their full lips and broad smiles offered the best evidence that Maryann and Ruth were related—high-powered, genuine smiles that they now turned on each other.

Maryann had to admit that she thought she looked good in her car, too. She loved her new black Chrysler Sebring convertible with beige leather sports seats. Joe would have loved the sight of her in it. She had ordered it last September as a reward to herself for an exceptionally good year. It was loaded with all the extras. By the time it arrived, the weather had turned. Today was the first day that it was warm enough to put the top down.

"I thought spring would never get here." Maryann beamed, raising her hand to the bright blue skies. "Not even eleven o'clock and it's already seventy-five degrees. The sun feels great. Did you have a good run?"

Ruth nodded. "Yep—went around twice. I haven't done that in a long time."

"Twice? Are you training for another Marathon?"

Ruth laughed. "No, oh no. That was a once in a lifetime thing, part of my grieving process, I think. No, I'm just celebrating finally being finished with college."

Joe Bethel had struggled hard to stay alive, to hold off the cancer that had ravaged his body just long enough to see his little girl graduate from high school. Her high school commencement four years ago was the last social event he had ventured out to before passing away.

"Your dad is proud of you, Ruth. I sensed his presence at the graduation the other night."

Ruth's smile took a peaceful turn as she responded, "I know, I sensed it, too."

Maryann patted the passenger seat and extended an enthusiastic invitation. "Want a ride?"

"Sure!" Ruth quickly moved to the passenger side and got in. "I was going to run on home to my apartment, but I'll ride the rest of the way with you. I don't have to be back here till two. I need to meet with Dennis

when he's through playing basketball." She waved her hand dismissively.
"Nothing interferes with Friday noon hoops, you know. Someday one of
those old guys is going to have a heart attack."

Maryann laughed and shook her head. "Well it won't be Nathan. It
doesn't matter how often or how early I get to the health club, Nathan is
already there working up a sweat."

"He's in great shape and is a good player, too. How old is Preacher
Nate, anyway?" Ruth asked as she settled into the passenger seat and put
on her seatbelt.

"I'd say he's in his early fifties," answered Maryann. As she pulled
away from the curb, she pointed across the street and jovially comment-
ed, "Check it out, I can't wait to hear *that* sermon. Rather provocative
title, don't you think?"

Across the street, in the front yard of Antioch the signboard read:

ANTIOCH CHURCH

NATHAN WESLEY FRYE
SR. PASTOR
REV. JILL THOMAS
PASTOR
WORSHIP SERVICE
10:00 AM

THIS WEEK'S SERMON,
NAKED GRACE

Ruth gave a hearty laugh that sounded a lot like Maryann's. "One
never knows what Preacher Nate's going to come up with. I'm surprised
that Jill let him get away with that one."

"He always makes you think, but he's the best preacher I've ever
heard," said Maryann. "He's sure been there for us over the years."

"Do you have time for lunch, Mom?"

"Just what I was thinking. I don't have another appointment until this
afternoon. Why don't we go to your place? I'll check in with Evelyn at
the office while you clean up and then we can have lunch at the Diner."
Maryann glanced at the expensive gold wristwatch a grateful insurance

company had recently awarded her for her outstanding sales results. "If we get there by eleven-thirty, we should be able to get a table right away. I need to talk to you anyway, about your brother Mark's new friend."

"Oh, Andre Fitzgerald... 'but my friends call me Hotchie,'" she mimicked in a high-pitched squeaky voice. "He's a character. He's new. Moved here from Washington D.C. a few weeks ago, I think. He's taken to the Club. He's in a sad situation."

"How so?"

"He's been coming to the Club every day for better than a week. But yesterday Jacob rescued him and brought him by the Club before noon."

"Rescued him?"

Ruth nodded and told Maryann the story. A few minutes later, they pulled into the parking lot of an attractive grouping of four new condominiums called The Parkland Arms. Maryann owned The Parkland Arms and Ruth managed it for her in exchange for the rent on her condo. Maryann turned off the ignition and removed the keys, but made no move to get out. She turned slightly toward Ruth and slid her skirt up exposing her long legs to the balmy rays of the sun. Ruth laid her head back on the seat and closed her eyes. Mother and daughter both sighed, content to bask for a few minutes in the warmth while they talked.

"They beat the boy so badly that you had to take him to the clinic?" asked Maryann.

Without opening her eyes, Ruth nodded and said, "He had to have a few stitches above his eye and on the back of his head. They took x-rays of his jaw, and fortunately there were no fractures. This morning the school nurse said the swelling has gone down, but his eye has gotten even blacker than yesterday."

"I thought we'd done a pretty good job of running the gangs out of town...."

"You never run them out completely. There's just too much money to be made in cocaine, especially crack, and now there are the meth labs springing up everywhere. There are always the local wannabees, and every now and then someone a little older with street clout and connections or distribution contacts will move in from Kansas City or Chicago or somewhere and try to get something going again. Most of the street action, the gang-type activity, is on the North Side, not Parkland, but...."

Concerned for her son, Maryann asked, "And Hotchie is involved with the gangs somehow?"

Ruth faced her mom again and shrugged. "Andre's trying to get out, but he's not telling us everything. He's scared, Mom. It's dangerous to leave a gang."

"So, you call him Andre instead of Hotchie?"

Ruth nodded. "We don't make a big deal of it, but Dennis says nicknames have taken on a new meaning with the gangs. Unless a wannabee objects, the staff call them by their real names. It's a subtle, but powerful tool to help them make the break."

"So, Andre is involved with gangs?"

"I'm sure of it, but I don't think he had much choice up until now— it will be especially hard for Andre to break away."

"Why?"

Ruth sighed. "A couple of times he has mentioned someone named Juice who is evidently the new Top Rank in town. Dennis thinks Juice is Andre's older brother."

"No!" said Maryann. "You're kidding."

"We think so. I took Andre by his house yesterday to pick up his mom before we went to the clinic. She was livid when she saw how beat up he was. The first thing she said was, 'Did Juice do this to you?'" Ruth shook her head. "But, then there was this strange look between them, like they had a family secret or something."

"What does Andre say?" asked Maryann.

"He's talked more to Dennis than to me. Like I said, he's not telling us everything. Andre insisted that the boys Jacob drove off were the only ones involved. He said their names were Juwan and Anthony, but that's all he knew. LaTisha, that's Andre's mom, says he didn't come home Wednesday night, either."

"Well, he spent Tuesday night with Mark," said Maryann. "I tried to call his house and ended up having to leave a message. The next morning that woman couldn't even get out of bed to talk to me when I took him by there before school," Maryann said indignantly. She had little patience for people who did not care properly for their kids.

"She's a mess, Mom," said Ruth remembering the difficulty LaTisha seemed to have just getting ready to leave the house yesterday. "She's either got her own drug problem, or she's mentally ill. Maybe it's depression or possibly both. I don't know, but from what I could see, she's barely hanging on. She has an older daughter named Angela. Seems Angela has run away just a week before she was supposed to graduate from high school."

"Well, that woman… what's her name…LaTisha? She needs to start paying closer attention to her son, he's still a child," said Maryann, but the edge in her voice had softened.

"I told LaTisha about Antioch's counseling programs. In fact, she has an appointment at two-thirty. I may go get her—otherwise, she might just blow it off."

"She's meeting with Jill?" asked Maryann. "That's good."

"Actually, it's with Preacher Nate. Jill is at a conference today. But, Preacher Nate said he'd do the intake and then turn her over to Jill or one of the other volunteers."

Maryann nodded, then said thoughtfully, "Andre's… I don't know," she pondered. "You can't help but like that boy." She smiled broadly. "He has this contagious… energy, or something."

"He's a wonderful little oddball," Ruth agreed. Then she smiled mischievously at her mother. "You're not going to believe this either."

"What, believe what?"

"Thursday night, when he didn't go home… Andre slept in your garage."

"Our garage! You're not serious?"

Ruth enjoyed her mother's shock and said nothing, just tilted her head and bit her lower lip, trying to suppress her smile.

"You are! He spent the night in our garage?"

Ruth smiled, nodded and continued the story, "Andre said he came by to see if he could spend the night with Mark again, but all the lights in the house were off already. The side door to the garage was open so he slept in the hayloft. Can you believe that? He was there the whole time Jacob was trying to fix my car."

"Why didn't he go home?" asked Maryann.

"He was afraid that gang members would be waiting for him there. Maybe he's afraid of this Juice character."

"Oh, my. That poor kid," said Maryann.

Ruth checked her watch. "Hey, come on. We'd better hurry if we're going to get lunch."

It was just before two when they pulled up again in front of the Club.

"There's Preacher Nate," said Ruth cheerily. She jumped out of the car and moved quickly to meet her friend, who was halfway down the front steps, his gym bag hung over his shoulder. Ruth had changed into khaki pants, a polo shirt with the Club logo on the front pocket, and a pair of comfortable walking shoes.

• • • • •

Nathan Wesley Frye, known on the street and to his flock as Preacher Nate, was the long-time pastor of Antioch Church. Having just turned fifty, the preacher was a little over six-foot, a solid hundred and ninety-five pounds, with slightly reddish, but mostly white hair and a beard that he kept trimmed short. The preacher has a commanding presence everywhere he goes—not just in the pulpit where he is most at home.

Preacher Nate can be especially compelling in one-on-one situations. He is anything but handsome. In fact, until one gets to know him, he is not easy to look upon. His blotchy complexion is that of a fair-skinned person who has spent too much time in the sun, and he has a large scar indented at the hairline above his right eye. When greeting Preacher Nate, depending on the depth of your relationship, you'll either have to contend with a warm bear hug, like the one he now gave Ruth on the stairs in front of the Club, or having your hand being totally swallowed up by his mammoth paw.

Over the years, Nathan has skillfully honed his ability to flow naturally with the harmonies of small talk. He's able to quickly put people at ease. He is flexible and wise, always knowing when to disappear into the crowd, or the moment. Once people came to know him, Nathan appeared handsome, especially to the ladies of Parkland with whom he maintains a mutual love and respect that most husbands and boyfriends do not find threatening.

His eyes are another story. Anyone who has serious business with Nathan Wesley Frye, has to, at some point, confront those eyes. Almost fluorescent blue, the Preacher's eyes can gently pull one into a pool of love and compassion. But, they can also look all the way into the soul and detect lies, producing a look of righteous anger, that makes people squirm. For those who do not plan to be serious, it is wise to steer clear of his counsel and his church.

During a thundering sermon, those soul-searching blue eyes usually make their cycle several times. And sometimes, especially when he moves to the side of the pulpit and pauses, it seems as if he's speaking directly at one of his parishioners. The goal of this mammoth man is simple—to lift the soul, lighten the load, and help others find joy and peace in the midst of their pain. As a result, over the years, many have heard him speak, but more than a few who kept coming, have had their lives changed.

• • • • •

"Um, you smell good," teased Ruth as she pulled away from the friendly hug. "Is Dennis in there?"

"Yep, we just walked out of the locker room together. He's in his office."

"Good." Ruth took a step toward the door, then stopped. "Oh, Preacher Nate, if I can borrow your car in a few minutes, I want to go over and pick up LaTisha Johnson for her intake session with you at two-thirty."

"Sure." Nathan dug into his pocket and tossed her the keys. The old beat-up Chevy was clearly visible in its usual spot in the church parking lot across the street. Ruth waved and took the remaining steps two at a time as she entered the Club.

"Nathan, how are you?"

"Fine, Maryann, just fine. And you?" he asked sincerely as he leaned with one hand on the corner of the convertible's windshield.

"I'm wonderful, thank you."

Nathan looked back over his shoulder toward the front door of the Club before commenting, "She's always so cheerful, but she seems especially so today."

Maryann smiled. "We just came from Roy Smith Ford, where she picked out a two-year-old-Mustang in real nice condition, low miles and a good price. It was Ruth's graduation gift."

"Ah," said Nathan nodding and smiling approvingly. "Well deserved, she's worked hard."

"Yes she has. I tried to talk her into going away to school, but she insisted on going to the University and working at the Club, just like her father. Now, I'm glad she did. I missed her when she moved into an apartment two years ago, and I hate to think how much I would have missed her if she'd gone hundreds of miles away to school."

"Well, she's done great work. The promotion to program director was long overdue. Dennis just had to wait until she earned her degree."

Maryann nodded. "She's always been such an appreciative kid, Nathan. She must have thanked me thirty times already for her new car."

"I hear the prices at Wilson Super Auto Mart are hard to beat. How come you went to Roy Smith's?"

"Why else? He's a big contributor and supporter of the Club. Plus, Ruth said if she had to buy a car from Wilson, she'd go back to riding a bike."

Nathan roared his infectious laugh.

"Who won the game?" Maryann asked. "No heart attacks today?"

"Jacob's team won. Jacob's team always wins. When we choose sides, everyone always tries to get on Jacob's team."

"So, he's still that good?" she asked, a faraway look in her eyes.

"He's a great basketball player. I hear he was pretty good in high school."

Maryann nodded. "They were state champs during their junior and senior years. He and Joe and Bob Wilson were hard to beat."

"He's still good—plays hard, never complains, still runs hard and he can really jump."

"Where is Jacob?" asked Maryann. "I need to ask him something."

"He's at your house, probably. He didn't shower after the game. He said he needed to finish putting a tailpipe on Ruth's car. Said he might as well do that first, then he'd go home and shower."

"Nathan," Maryann's tone was serious and Nathan immediately picked up on the shift. He just made eye contact and nodded. Maryann asked, "Is Jacob really the changed man he appears to be?"

"Yes, Maryann, he really is," Nathan assured her.

Maryann smiled at the Preacher and cocked her head. "Are you sure? Nathan, you've been known to adopt some pretty lost characters."

Nathan's laughter roared again. "That I have, Maryann. That I have. But, I'd stake my life on this one. Jacob Riddler is a changed man."

THE REUNION

4

When Jacob was rummaging through Maryann's garage looking for the tools he needed, he ran across an old photograph of Joe and Maryann with Ruth who looked to be about five or six years old. Joe must have stapled the photo to the wall above the workshop just after they moved from their first house around the corner from the Club. Jacob figured the picture must have been taken shortly before Joe and Maryann had adopted the racially mixed infant whom they had named Mark Andrew. The young family looked so happy—in spite of himself, Jacob couldn't help but wonder about what might have been. He quickly suppressed the reflection, found the tools he needed and got on with his work.

Just two days ago, the garage had been damp and cold. Now as he slid under Ruth's car, it was hot and steamy. He was sticky and still sweating from the hour of full-court basketball. The dirt and dust stuck to him as he worked and he had to continually wipe sweat from his eyes.

As he lay on his back on the garage floor under Ruth's old car, the regrets and memories would not leave him alone.

• • • • •

"Jacob, no, please, don't." Maryann squeezed her thighs together and pushed his hand away. But he came right back, more determined than ever.

"Come on, Maryann—we love each other—we're going to get married as soon as you graduate. Come on. Don't you love me?"

She pushed him away, hard. "Stop it!" She almost screamed.

He sat up angrily, and moved all the way to the other side of the car's back seat.

She refastened her bra and started to button her blouse. "We've already gone farther than we agreed to." She looked at him and said angrily, "You promised, Jacob! You promised." She straightened her skirt and they sat in steely silence until Maryann finally reached over and tried to take his hand. He jerked away and stared out the frosty window. He could see ice floating in the river below.

"Jacob, please." Again she tried and again he would not let her take his hand. "I'm sorry. It's Sunday night. We just came from church. I feel... so..." She began to cry. She lowered her head into her hands and sobbed.

Jacob scooted back across the seat and took her into his arms, comforting her.

"Don't cry, Honey. Don't cry."

"I'm sorry, I'm so sorry," she said. Then she looked up at him; her face contorted in pain, her dark eyes overflowing, tears rolling down her cheeks. She said, "Jacob, I love you so much."

"I love you, too."

"I want to marry you. I want to live the rest of my life with you, but.... My parents are so... old... you know... old fashioned and they trust me, Jacob. They trust you, too."

He gently wiped away her tears with his thumb. "If we love each other, it's not wrong, Honey. If we love each other and promise to stay together for the rest of our lives, it's not wrong, Maryann. It can't be."

"Jacob, I don't know. We're so young—"

"I'm almost twenty and you're almost eighteen! I'm not asking you to use drugs or do something illegal. All I'm asking is for you to love me—really love me."

"I know, I know," she said. "But, I have a year of school left and you still have three years of college to finish."

"And as soon as you graduate, we'll get married. My basketball scholarship covers everything but room and board. You can get a job. I love you, Maryann. Nobody anymore, even good church people, wait until they're formally married...."

"Jacob... I don't know. It's still..."

"Hell, you think all those people in church tonight were virgins when they walked down the aisle?"

"Probably not, but that doesn't..."

"We'll be married, Maryann. In the eyes of God, we'll be married.

The wedding is just a formality, a piece of paper. That's all. I love you. I thought you loved me."

"*I do, Jacob, it's just...*"

"*Read your Bible.*"

"*What?*" *she said, almost laughing.*

"*A bunch of times it says something like, 'and he took her into his tent and he knew her and she became his wife.'*"

She smiled at him.

"*Seriously, it's in there. I just want to know you.*" *He was teasing now, making her laugh. He growled,* "*Really know you.*"

That night she gave herself to him completely, without reservation, trusting him so totally that it scared him and intimidated him. From that night on, for over a year, she was an eager and adventuresome lover. She became their teacher and if she ever felt another pang of guilt he did not recognize it. And, no matter how shabbily he treated her, she loved him.

• • • • •

Maryann kicked at the garage door with her foot and then used her hip to open it wider. She walked into the garage with a large glass of iced tea in each hand. She found Jacob still on his back, his head and shoulders under Ruth's car. His sweaty tank top had rolled up revealing his hard, muscular stomach. Her eyes followed the row of curly wet hair that contrasted sharply with the pale, white skin of his belly, and snaked around his navel disappearing under his gym shorts. His legs too, were hard and muscular. Maryann couldn't help herself. Jacob was more than attractive. She had noticed that more than a few times over the last couple of years. He seemed more healthy and fit than she remembered, even during that brief time when he was the local college basketball star. Except now he seemed content, at peace with himself.

Jacob heard footsteps on the dirty concrete floor as he made the last turn with the wrench. He prepared to have a little fun with Evelyn as he slid out from under the car, but his sly smile vanished the second he looked up into Maryann's dark eyes. So dark and so beautiful, wiser and deeper now, but it was the old twinkle that disconcerted him. But when he looked away, it was her feet in their spaghetti-strap sandals that awed him. How could feet be so pretty? His eyes took on a mind of their own as they slowly traveled up over her long, smooth legs until they lost their way under the baggy black shorts that did not quite hang to mid-thigh. Suddenly embarrassed, Jacob scrambled to his feet. He felt himself blushing all over. Awkwardly he blurted out; "Maryann!" as if he were a child caught in the act of doing something bad. "I just finished up," he said, trying to recover. "All done."

She laughed and held out a glass of tea. "I'd invite you into the house, but you are one dirty, smelly mess, fella."

Jacob felt the blush return, then looked down at himself and back up at Maryann who still held out the offering of tea.

"I guess I am, aren't I?" And they shared the laughter for a few wonderful seconds.

"Thanks," he said as he reached out for the glass of cold tea.

She watched his sweat-drenched neck as he drank more than half of the tea. When he finally lowered the glass she said, "The season's first sun tea." Then she raised her own glass in kind of a toast. "Thanks to Evelyn."

Jacob raised his glass in return and took another, smaller drink. "It's wonderful," he said, smacking his lips. "That's when I knew summer was really here as a kid, when Mom made the first pitcher of iced tea."

Jacob still held one of the wrenches in his left hand. "Hope you don't mind my using your… Joe's tools."

"Not at all, they're probably old and rusty. Evelyn said you had a large toolbox full of brand new tools the other day. Did you leave them at home?"

Jacob shook his head. "Somebody stole them."

"Stole them! When? Where?"

"I'm not sure." He placed the almost empty tea glass on the workbench and began gathering up the tools he had used and returned them to the bench. "I think I left them in the back of my truck last night. But, I can't remember. I must have, because the truck wasn't broken into or anything."

"You don't seem to be too upset," she said quizzically.

"They're only tools," he said, "and it doesn't do much good to get upset about it."

"Jacob… I've been wanting to talk to you."

Jacob leaned against the bench while he used a rag soaked with lubricant to wipe down the rusty tools. He said nothing, but looked into her eyes.

"I'd like to ask a favor," she said.

He continued to wipe the tools and said, "Sure, anything. Anything at all."

"First though," she took a drink then stared for a few seconds into the glass. She searched for the words she needed to say. She looked up again and the calm she saw on his face gave her the courage she needed.

"Jacob, I've owed you an apology for three years."

Shocked, Jacob quit wiping down the tool in his hand. He opened his mouth to object, but she waved him off before he could utter the first word.

"Yes, I do. I owe you an apology. When you showed up out of the blue at church three years ago... I wasn't prepared for that. Then when you approached me that first Sunday in church... Jacob, I had no right to talk to you the way I did. And, I had no right to be so cold for months after that. I don't know. It was a difficult time. I was grieving pretty hard. And..."

"I understand," began Jacob. Maryann tried to interrupt, but this time Jacob charged ahead. "I do, I do understand. You couldn't understand why Joe had to die... instead of me. I know. I've asked myself the same question. I'm so sorry, Maryann. Joe was such a good person. Of all of us, at school and at church, he was the Christian, maybe the only real Christian I... I'm so sorry."

"Thank you, Jacob. That is what I was thinking back then. But I was wrong to treat you so. It hit me during one of Nathan's sermons. Cut me to the quick. I have no right to continue to question God or his ways. I still do, but..."

"I know," said Jacob. "Me too, but I'm learning not to let it bother me so much, to just trust, you know?"

Maryann nodded, then looked up and her smile warmed his heart. "The last two years, every time after church, or at a potluck or something, I tried to speak to you or make my way over to you, but you avoided me like the plague." She laughed.

Jacob said, "I'm sorry, I guess I was afraid. I didn't know what to say. I still don't know what to say to you, Maryann." After another awkward pause, Jacob continued, "I guess I've owed you an apology for what— over twenty years now?"

"It was twenty-two years ago this month in fact, that you cut out on me, Jacob Riddler," she smiled with mock indignation. "What do you have to say for yourself?"

Jacob shook his head sadly. "I don't know, Maryann. I don't even know that guy anymore."

Maryann nodded, then smiled again and said, "Well, I forgive you if you forgive me."

Jacob chuckled. "Not quite an even trade, but I'll take it."

"I'd ah… give you hug, to seal the deal, but…" Maryann looked him over from head to toe and shrugged her shoulders."

"Yeah, right—but, I'll take a rain check." He smiled at the prospect. "Now what's that favor you need?"

Maryann moved over next to Jacob and also leaned one hip against the bench, facing him. Jacob started to step back, afraid of how he smelled, but pleased to have her so close. She asked, "I see you run by the house sometimes. Do you run every day?"

"Just about, except Fridays. On Fridays I…"

Maryann waved her hand and teased, "I know, you play basketball. Everybody knows about the Friday noon ball game. You, Dennis, Preacher Nate and what… seven to ten other businessmen? In Parkland, people know better than to plan anything from twelve to one-thirty on Fridays."

"Our reputation's that bad, uh? Okay, but just about every other day, I get off work at about seven, drop by the nursing home to see Mom and then I run. Saturdays I sleep in a little, but I run on Saturdays, too. Why?"

"Would you invite Ruth to run with you?"

"Sure, I'd be glad to. I've seen her run. Ruth runs a mean pace, but…."

Maryann nodded, acknowledging she owed him an explanation. "She worries me, Jacob. She's been so busy with school and her work at the Club, that she sometimes runs late at night. She's fearless and doesn't see why it concerns me. Parkland's safe, I think, but there's that stretch down the avenue and then along the North Side. And, you know… a lot can happen. She told me how you rescued Andre yesterday. I hear about the gangs, and this character, Juice…"

"You're right. I'll talk to her."

"No." Maryann held up her palm. "I mean, yes. But, if it comes across like you're worried, like you're trying to talk some sense into her, she's so stubborn. Especially if she knew I had asked you. Just *invite* her to run with you in the mornings. She thinks the world of you, Jacob. The summer schedule at the Club will be starting soon and it will be a good routine for her."

Jacob smiled. He had seen Ruth's stubborn streak himself. "You're right. I'll stop by the Club tonight right after my AA meeting and I'll invite her to start running with me."

"Thanks, Jacob."

"Maryann, thank you. Thanks for asking, for trusting me."

"You don't drink at all anymore, Jacob?"

"Not at all. I'll soon celebrate seven years of sobriety."

"That's good, Jacob. That's very good."

"Yeah, well, it's always one day at a time, just one day at a time."

CONFRONTATION
AT THE
CLUB
5

$\mathbf{T}$he AA group had been meeting in the basement fellowship hall at Antioch for over twenty years. It was originally organized by Antioch's fiery young associate pastor at the time, Nathan Wesley Frye. Many years ago, Nathan turned over the leadership of the group to others, choosing instead to just participate.

For over twenty years, regardless of the leader, the meetings began the same way. Twenty to thirty people pulled folding chairs across the tile floor into a circle and took their seats. Some held styrofoam cups of steaming coffee that they would refill several times during the next hour. Some brought giant plastic convenience store cups of Coca-Cola or other soft drinks. After some preliminary comments and housekeeping items or announcements, the leader begins:

"Hello, my name is Ruby and I'm an alcoholic and a drug addict."

"Hi, Ruby!" the group responds in unison.

"Hello, my name is Jacob and I'm an alcoholic and a drug addict."

"Hi, Jacob!"

"Hello, my name is Nathan and I'm an alcoholic."

"Hi, Preacher Nate!"

And so it goes, until the entire group had been introduced. There are the young and old, married, single, straight, and gay. There are business tycoons, waitresses, yuppies and union laborers; those who walked or rode the bus and those with fancy cars or hogs in the church parking lot. Over the years, people of all races and backgrounds have attended. This group included clergy, a police officer, a county judge, a couple of ex-cons and a convicted felon awaiting sentencing, a teenager and a deadbeat parent. All are welcome, and no questions are asked. There are no last names used here. They all abide by the solemn pledge—everything said here stays here. They simply share their stories and find comfort and strength from others who have walked the same path they have walked and who must fight the same demons.

A few, like Nathan, attend more from a need to give back than anything else. A few others were there because they were hanging on, knowing that the group was their best chance for survival. They were there because if they didn't come, they would die.

Tonight, Jacob, the quiet one, held their attention with his story.

"So, my experience with this kid everyone calls Hotchie just brought it all crashing in on me the last several days—the memories, the could-have-been, the regret."

"You got to give that shit up," said a well-intentioned group member.

Jacob nodded. "I know, but he reminds me so much of myself, except he's finding the Club at about the age that I started drifting away from it. In those days, the Club wasn't as good at hanging on to its teen members as it is today. And the staff in those days weren't trained to recognize child abuse and chemical addiction. I hope Andre sticks with the Club. It's his best chance. The odds are really stacked against him. I suppose he's over there now. I hope so. I'll never forget my first day at the Club. I was only eight."

• • • • •

"Come on, Jacob. Get your coat on." Momma's hands trembled. She looked around, not sure whether she was lost or looking for something. "Oh my, your gloves, where are your gloves and hat, Jacob?"

"Right here, Momma. I've got them all right here." Jacob quickly put on his coat. "Here, Momma, here's your coat, and your scarf, too. It's really windy out today. Where are we going, Momma?"

"Someplace special," she smiled and touched his cheek. Her hands always quivered a bit, but today they were real shaky. "Hurry, it's a short walk over to the avenue."

Jacob's heart leaped with excitement and nervousness when he real-ized Momma was taking him to the Parkland Boys Club. Several of his classmates were members of the Club. They had told him all about it, about all the fun they were having playing games, learning to swim and playing dodgeball in the gym. Jacob had mentioned the Club to his mother several days ago. When you turned eight, you could join and it was only one dollar a year, but she didn't seem to understand what he was talking about. Now she took him by the hand and they walked up the stairs together. Other boys, most of them older were excitedly rushing past them through the front doors.

Momma paused and took a deep breath. She straightened up as if trying to pull herself together. She looked down at Jacob and smiled. Then they walked through the door hand-in-hand. From that day on until about age sixteen when he became active in high school sports, the Club became Jacob's home away from home. Everyday, he went straight to the Club after school. Since most of the boys lived in the neighborhood, the Club closed from five to six every evening so they could go home for supper with their families. Jacob was always the first in line when the Club re-opened again at six and he stayed until the Club closed at nine-thirty.

That first day they met George Kinley, the Physical Education Director. He was a friendly guy who immediately made Jacob feel welcome and at ease. He usually had a fat cigar in his mouth. For years after he left town, whenever Jacob smelled cigar smoke he thought of George and the Club.

After Momma struggled through filling out the application for membership, George personally gave Momma and Jacob a tour. The Club was a place of wonder and excitement and Momma kept saying, as if she couldn't believe it, "And only a dollar a year?" George asked Momma about her black eye and the other bruises on her face. Jacob, even at eight years old, sensed that George did not believe her story about falling down the rickety old basement steps, but he let it pass. With Momma's relieved blessing the Club proved to be a safe haven, a refuge, for Jacob over the next eight years. Momma wasn't so lucky.

• • • • •

As Jacob told his story, across the street at the Club, the action was heavy. The Club was for both boys and girls now and they had a special after school program for six-year-olds. Smoking by staff and older boys had been banned anywhere in the building many years ago. Programs and activities throughout the facility were hopping with eager children and teenagers. Fridays seemed to increase the energy level of both the kids and staff. Well over three hundred children had joined the Club. They began to arrive just after school. Many walked in from Parkland or the North Side, but they also arrived from other parts of town, some in buses provided by the United Way. Parents from other neighborhoods organized carpools for their kids. Even kids from some of the outlying new affluent suburbs found the Club a great place to be.

As they did everyday, excited children showed their membership cards at the front entrance and fanned out through the large facility. Some went directly to the library or to the computer lab where they got help with homework. Some went to the arts and crafts area or to the photo lab. Some, depending on their ages, hung out at one of the two game rooms. Many activities and classes were organized according to age or ability, especially in the gym and pool.

In offices and meeting rooms throughout the facility small groups of children met with staff or trained volunteers in special programs designed to help kids make smart choices. A lot of one-on-one counseling and even some family therapy took place every day at the Club. A hot meal was served in the cafeteria from five to six o'clock. The cost was fifty cents, but no child was ever denied.

The programs were carefully organized and conducted by highly trained staff members dedicated to making the Club a haven from the streets. All of the professional staff were college educated; some with masters degrees in psychology, social work or health and physical education. College students, many on scholarships from the Club assisted the professional staff. A few high school kids, like Mark Bethel, sometimes helped teach classes or maintain order. They wore T-shirts identifying them as Jr. Staff. All of this activity was held together by its talented Executive Director, Dennis Livingston.

Ten years ago, Ruth's dad, Joe Bethel, was promoted to the position of Executive Director. At thirty-two, Joe was the youngest executive director of a large urban Boys & Girls Club in the country. Dennis was the first person Joe hired as the Club's guidance counselor. Joe's intuition and judgment was unerring. Dennis was ten years older, with impeccable credentials. He was big, handsome, black and proud. Joe was not at all threatened by the talent or the man. After a period of getting to know and trust each other, the two became genuine partners, united by their passion for kids.

Ruth was eleven when her father hired Dennis. She was at the Club every day. Some people claimed the reason Joe worked so hard to allow girls at the Club, was to accommodate Ruth's desire to be there and participate. They were at least partially right. When Joe died four years ago, even though he too was devastated, Dennis was the person Ruth permitted herself to lean on. In some ways they worked through their grief together. Dennis understood that Ruth's obsessive, undaunted commitment to her job as Program Director at the Club was a tribute to the dad she adored and still desperately missed.

Since becoming Executive Director, community relations, board development and fund raising filled Dennis' days. Several times in recent years he was offered much more lucrative positions with major corporations. He never seriously considered them, sometimes not trusting offers from powerful white men who seemed surprised at how well he ran the Club. The Club is where he belonged. He loved it. He worked hard, driven by the same passion for kids that he had as a counselor.

When his devoted secretary arrived just before eight each morning there was usually an hour's worth of work already waiting for her. Dennis generally did not work evenings, trusting Ruth and the staff they had assembled and trained. But tonight, his wife was out of town visiting one of their grown daughters, so he just dropped in to see how things were going.

• • • • •

Andre had only been a spectator at senior gym because it was for guys sixteen to eighteen years old. But, his new friend Mark played basketball so well it didn't matter. Andre liked this dude. Like Andre, Mark had a light complexion and tight black curls. Mark carried himself with confidence and got along well with others. Mark was several inches taller and almost a year older than Andre, but it didn't seem to matter to Mark that Andre wasn't a "jock."

The college girl supervising the gym had allowed Andre to sit in and watch the pick-up games as a favor to Mark. Andre volunteered to sweep the gym floor following the session and was waiting for Mark outside the locker room. Mark came through the door, his black curls still glistening from the shower.

"Hey, Hotch, let's go find Ruth and see if she can give you a ride home after the Club closes."

"Okay, man, but let me show you something." Andre looked around to make sure no one was watching. He pulled Mark into the hallway outside the double doors to the gym. He looked around again and then reached behind the thirty-gallon trashcan in the corner.

"Look at these Nikes, the latest Air Jordan's. Last week, these babies were sellin' at Crossroads Mall for a hundred and sixty-five. Know what I'm saying?" He proudly handed his loot over for Mark's inspection.

First confusion, then a smile came over Mark's face as he examined the shoes and realized what Andre was saying. "Awright, Hotchie! Come on," said Mark excitedly as he made a U-turn.

"Mark, we better leave them here till…"

But, Mark was already turning the corner. Andre jumped up and started after him. No sooner had they turned the corner, than three of the senior club members were coming out of the locker room. Andre took a step back, preparing to run.

"Eric, my man," said Mark to a tall white boy with red hair and rugged features. "Better check your gym bag. I think you're missing something." Mark smiled mischievously, as he held up Andre's find.

Eric looked at the shoes, then at Mark. He frantically unzipped his gym bag and saw the place where his shoes should have been.

"Hey! Where'd you get those?" Eric suspiciously eyed the new kid, the one with the black eye and the fat jaw who had been watching their game.

Mark reached back, put his arm around Andre's shoulders and pulled him up even with him.

"My main man, Hotchie—he found them." Mark squeezed Andre's shoulder. "He saw some little kids hiding them behind the trash can in the back hallway."

"Oh, wow," said Eric. "Thanks a lot, Hotchie. I just bought them, man, this afternoon. This was the first time I used them. I can't believe this… thanks, man."

The two black teens in the group cackled as Eric put the new shoes in his gym bag.

One teased, "No kidding, man. He would've had to work six more months at Taco Bell to pay for a new pair."

"Them old ones was so stinky, he was banned from the court, man," added the other.

A third teen, a white kid, jived, "So, he ought to give you a taco, large fries, large coke and an ice cream for rescuing his shoes, man."

Good-natured, with a toothy smile that covered most of his face, Eric looked at Andre and said, "Hey, little man. No problem. Pinhead there has a great idea. Stop by the Taco Bell at Twenty-fourth and Cummings anytime—on me. Whatever you want."

"Great," said Andre. "That's not far from my mom's crib anyway."

As the other boys walked away, Mark asked, "That is what happened. Right?"

"Yeah, right. Right."

Mark smiled a crooked, knowing smile, "That's good. You certainly don't need the other jaw broken."

"That is what happened, man."

"Who messed you up like that, Hotchie? Who broke your jaw?"

"It ain't broke, man. Your sister took me straight to the clinic when I got here yesterday. They checked me out. Not broke," Andre rubbed the side of his face. "But I'm going to be sore for awhile."

"I guess so. So, who did that to…"

"Mark. Mark!" Eric burst back through the front door. "Your sister, man. Looks like some real bad dudes are giving her a hard time out front."

"What? Go find Dennis. Quick!"

"Okay! Don't worry, Mark. The fellas are backing her up." Eric headed down the hall toward Dennis' office.

As he pushed through the front door of the Club, Andre right behind him, Mark heard, "Get out the way. We gonna play some hoops and you can't stop us. We got a right to be here too."

Andre froze in his tracks and retreated to the back of the crowd when he recognized Juwan's voice and saw the cast on his arm. Mark joined the group of four eighteen-year-olds with whom he'd just finished playing ball and who were now standing defiantly behind Ruth.

When Ruth did not budge Juwan said, "I'll hurt you, bitch. Get out the way."

There were six of the bad guys, all wearing gang colors, pants four sizes too big, with heavy key chains hanging from their belts, and black baseball hats turned backwards. They were all agitated. Mark had seen a couple of them in the neighborhood. Two whom he recognized used to come to the Club. They all looked mean and ready to create trouble. *Probably got guns, too*, he thought.

"Sir," said Ruth, too cool for her own good, "you can undoubtedly hurt me. But, in the long run you're the one who would be hurt. So, just go on home. You are not coming in. Even if you're under eighteen, you are gangbangers. Gangbangers are not welcome, at any time, under any circumstances at the Parkland Boys & Girls Club. You're exactly the kind of parasitic scum this place is designed to protect our children from. Go crawl back under the rock you came from."

Oh Ruth, thought Mark. *Don't antagonize this goon*. As if on a silent signal Juwan and his party all took a step toward Ruth and her backups.

• • • • •

As soon as the AA meeting concluded, desperate smokers made a beeline for the parking lot. Nathan, Jacob and several others were standing near the exit when someone called down the steps, "Preacher Nate, something's brewing across the street at the Club." With only a glance passing between them Nathan and Jacob took the steps three at a time. They quickly moved through the parking lot and across the street. Several of the men from the AA group followed.

When Ruth saw Preacher Nate, Jacob and a half dozen more men crossing the street she said confidently, "Gentlemen, it appears that you are now out-numbered. Our friends from across the street have also joined us. I suggest you move on."

Juwan spun in anger. "Who the fu..." and was confronted by Nathan's stare.

"Don't I know you, son?" Nathan asked quietly.

"That was a long time ago, Preacher," said Juwan, then he saw Jacob. "You!" Accusingly he held up his wrist with the cast. "You!"

"Good evening," said Jacob calmly. "I'm glad you had that tended to, sorry about that."

"Juwan, you know better than to make a move on the Club." It was a deep booming voice and Juwan spun again, this time to face Dennis who had moved to Ruth's side. Dennis was an imposing figure at six-foot-four and two-hundred-and-fifty pounds. Dennis wore a suit and a tie loosened at the neck. He looked more like a preacher than Nathan did.

The tables, not just in sheer numbers, had turned on Juwan and the gang members. But, street code demanded a little bravado.

"This is a public facility, Dennis. Me and the fellas are all just eighteen. You have to let us join the Club."

Dennis laughed. "Give me a break, Juwan. You know better than that."

"You ain't suppose to give up on kids, Dennis," said Juwan sarcastically. "We want to change our ways, man. You supposed to help us."

"Oh, I haven't given up on you, Juwan. Next month, or the month after, soon, Preacher Nate and I will come visit you on our monthly trip down to the penitentiary."

Juwan's face turned hard. He cursed and gave Dennis the finger. Then he turned to the other gang members and said, "Let's go."

"Juwan," Dennis called and held up a clear plastic bag. "Look what I got."

"What, Dennis, what you got?"

"Four pagers I took off of some scared little wannabees," Dennis teased. "Like I said, you know better than to make a move on the Club, Juwan." Dennis' voice had turned hard and threatening. "Tell your new Top Rank, whoever he is, the Club's off limits."

"Dennis, you can't just be snatching private property off of kids. They got a right to carry their beepers...."

"Oh, but I can, Juwan. You see because the gangs use pagers, we require all children to check their pagers at the door. Then we call their parents. If the parents say they gave the pagers to their children, no problem. Juwan, in a few minutes two very angry parents will be here." Dennis seemed to enjoy taunting Juwan. "We're going to talk to them about how to rescue their children—from you. Officer Diaz, you know Officer Diaz, from the gang task force? He'll be here soon, too. You might just want to move along."

"Dennis, you can't just *take* people's property," Juwan said, exasperated.

Dennis laughed, "That's funny, Juwan. Like you and your friends have any respect for private property? Why don't you go file a complaint with the police? Tell them I stole your pagers. Fill out a report, you know, give them your name, address, phone numbers and all. Give them the name of the person who's on the lease for all those pagers. I'm sure, son, they would love to gather that...."

Juwan exploded in an outburst of cursing and threats. He promised to be back. He promised to make them all pay—Jacob, Nathan, Dennis, Ruth and the Club. They turned to leave, but there was one less gang member. While the exchange had gone on between Dennis and Juwan, Nathan made eye contact with each gang member. In one he sensed fear and guilt. Nathan quietly moved to his side, whispered something in his ear and walked away. A few seconds later the young gang member slipped away and followed Nathan into the shadows.

As the tires on Juwan's Buick squealed their exit, Dennis turned to the crowd that had gathered. With a confident smile he called out, "Okay, guys, the show's over. Let's move back into the Club. All you guys and gals who are waiting for the bus or for rides, why don't you step back into the Club and wait, just in case our friends decide to drive around the block."

Jacob fell in with Dennis at the rear of the crowd that moved back into the Club. As they approached the front door, Nathan, his arm around the gang member who had followed him out of the crowd, approached from the side of the building. "Dennis, you remember Roland Ortega?"

"I sure do. I remember when Roland and Juwan came to the Club every day. Roland was one of our best members. But, I warned you even then about hanging out with Juwan, didn't I?" Dennis smiled at the boy who looked sheepishly up at him. "Where you been, Roland? We miss you."

With his arm still around the boy, Nathan said, "Roland's scared, Dennis. He wants out of the gang. Never wanted in, but now he wants out and he needs help."

Dennis' expression changed, "We can help, Roland, but you have to be serious. You have to want out."

The boy looked up. "I do, Dennis, but they'll kill me, man. Juwan, he crazy and all. I mean, he won't think twice about killing me. You hear what I'm saying? We all working for some new guy. He made Juwan and Anthony his lieutenants—they all crazy, Dennis. I'm serious. It's too late, anyway, man. They find out I'm here..."

Dennis moved to put his arm around the boy as Nathan backed

up, completing the transfer. "We can help, son. We even have places around the country we can send you if we have to, until the heat's off. Come on in. Your mother's going to be proud of you. We'll get started on it." Dennis looked back at Nathan. "You got time for a late night snack? You and I need to compare notes."

Nathan nodded. "I'll wait here for you. Take your time. Jacob and I will keep an eye out here."

After Dennis moved through the front door with Roland, Jacob asked, "You thinking the same thing I am?"

"Yeah, last thing the Club ever needs is a drive-by."

"Please, Lord," said Jacob.

"Jacob, Preacher Nate," Mark came busting through the front door. "You seen Hotchie?"

McKEY'S

6

It was after ten before Nathan and Dennis pulled into the parking lot of the trendy new restaurant in the Old Market called McKey's. As they passed the parking spaces which were reserved for the restaurant staff near the back door, Dennis stopped and pointed at the license plate on a new silver-gray Lexus. It was a Washington D.C. vanity plate that read simply "J.J."

McKey's specialized in Rhythm, Blues and Ribs. The old warehouse had been tastefully remodeled. Its cavernous dining area was sparsely occupied by the after show crowd having sandwiches and desserts and enjoying lively conversation. In the crowded bar that was almost as big as the dining area, the singles crowd and those desperately trying to postpone middle age, drank and smoked and swayed and tried to talk over the blues singer and her ensemble. Some still wore the corporate uniform and looked and acted as if they had been drinking since leaving the office.

"Good evening, gentlemen. Welcome to McKey's. My name is Nadine," said the young blond who greeted them. Nadine had a lovely face, but an emaciated body she only slightly covered with a silky, clinging short dress. Her put-on sultry voice made Dennis and Nathan want to laugh and cry at the same time. "Would you like a table, or are you going to join the action in the bar this evening?"

"How about that table right over there?" said Dennis, but it wasn't a question. Without waiting for an answer, he led Nathan and Nadine to a table that offered a good view of the action in the bar.

"Your waitress will be with you in a minute. May I get you something to drink?" she asked not quite as friendly as before.

"Nadine, I hear you have a great honey wheat on draft," said Dennis with a smile. "I'll have that."

"Twelve-ounce or twenty?"

"Twelve is more than enough, thank you," said Dennis.

She said nothing, just looked at Nathan.

Nathan also gave her a genuine smile. "Diet Coke, thank you, Nadine."

Without nodding or saying a word, the sad-faced girl walked away.

"Do you come here often?" asked Nathan.

"First time, hopefully my last. I don't patronize any of Wilson's businesses."

"Second time today I've heard that," said Nathan. "Bob's not so bad, a little arrogant, maybe."

"Shit, Nathan. Wilson's a jackass and from what I hear he hates you. My old friends in the party say he blames you for his loss to Linda Cabinet, says your work on her behalf tilted the scales unfairly."

Nathan shrugged, "It wasn't personal, just politics. He's been civil to me since the elections, and he still tries to find jobs for folks when I call."

"Maybe so, Nathan, but Wilson had plans. Talk is, he planned to run for Senate next time, but his loss to Linda put an end to all those lofty ambitions. I hear his lovely young wife, Cynthia, almost went into a depression when she had to move back here from D.C. It's all your fault my friend."

Nathan shrugged.

Dennis slipped comfortably into his street cadence. "...ass-me, couldn't have wrote that script any better. Conservative *family values* congressman, even though he be divorced and remarried and treats his first wife and daughters like shit, gets his ass whupped by a middle-aged, single mom who just happens to be a respected corporate attorney—and black. No sir, that deserved all the national recognition it received. You could have another career my friend, political consultant."

Nathan just smiled and shook his head.

"Wheat?" asked a young black waitress wearing a genuine smile and a sequined gold skirt that was even shorter than the blond's.

"Here," said Dennis.

They placed sandwich orders and, before the waitress could get away, Dennis read her name tag and said, "Lisa, tell J.J. I need to talk to him."

The smile left her face. "I don't think he's here, sir."

"He's here. Tell J.J. he *needs* to talk to us," said Dennis.

A different waitress delivered their sandwiches and Dennis gave her the same message. They had long finished their sandwiches when the first waitress named Lisa uneasily returned with their check.

"I'll take that up for you whenever you're ready."

"Young lady," said Dennis, "you forgot something."

"Oh, I'm sorry, what...."

"Lisa, we need to talk to J.J." Dennis smiled and opened his hands, palms up.

"He said... uh, he's not here."

Dennis reached for the inside pocket of his suit coat and pulled out a notepad. "Tell you what," he said as he took his pen and began to write. "A guy like J.J. always has a person who knows where he is."

"Sir, I don't know...."

"Or, somebody around here knows his cell phone or pager number." Dennis finished writing and folded the paper. "Whoever that person is, give them this note and have them call J.J.—wherever he is, okay?" Dennis gave her the note and his credit card and a five-dollar bill. He smiled and said, "That's in addition to the tip. Okay?" She smiled shakily and walked away.

"What did you write?" asked Nathan.

"That a concerned social worker and a preacher had some information about Andre and Angela. We could either share it with him or with the police—it's his choice. We'll wait five more minutes, then call Detective Diaz and ask him to join us here."

"Must not have been too far away," said Nathan as he nodded toward the bar.

A nice-looking black man in his mid-twenties, stylishly dressed in tan slacks, attractive sweater and Italian shoes walked toward their table. He smiled broadly and stuck out his hand, "Hi, I'm J.J. Which one's the preacher and which one's the social worker?"

Nathan reached up to shake hands, "Nathan Frye, I'm the preacher."

It was a friendly, firm handshake. "Nice to meet you, Reverend Frye."

"Preacher Nate, will do. Drop the Reverend, please."

"Sure." The young man extended his hand toward Dennis.

Dennis stared into his eyes for a couple of seconds before extending his hand. Then he introduced himself slowly, deliberately pronouncing each word, as if issuing a challenge. "I'm Dennis Livingston, Executive Director of the Parkland Avenue Boys & Girls Club."

"Nice to meet you, Dennis. May I?"

Nathan motioned toward the empty chair at the end of the small table.

"I hear you guys have some information about Angela and Hotchie? They in trouble? I hope not, my mom and I have been worried sick."

Ignoring the question, Dennis asked his own. "So, do we call you Josef, spelled J-O-S-E-F?"

The young man laughed. "So, you've been talking to my mom. She always makes a point to spell..."

"Or, do we call you J.J.?" interrupted Nathan.

"Or... *Juice*?" challenged Dennis.

Anger flashed on the young man's face, but he quickly recovered and found his smile. "J.J. will do."

"Excuse me, Mr. Johnson." It was Nadine, the little blond in the short dress again. In her sultry voice she asked, "My shift is over. Will you or Mr. Wilson be needing anything else this evening?"

"No, Nadine, thank you," J.J. said politely, almost kindly. He noticed the look that passed between his two table guests. "You can go on home."

"You sure?" she said with a little pout.

He smiled. "I'm sure."

"So, J.J., seems you're a busy man. What do you do here at McKey's?"

"I'm the assistant manager in charge of hiring and training waiters and waitresses and bus boys and girls. In fact, I've been meaning to get down to see you, Dennis. I might be able to put some of your older kids to work from time to time. The labor market being what it is, our manager is even willing to take a chance with at-risk kids."

Dennis looked at Nathan with a mocking nod, "At-risk?"

Nathan nodded and looked at J.J. "At-risk, would that be like Andre and Angela?"

J.J. didn't like the way the conversation was going. These two old guys were starting to get on his nerves. With the smile gone, he said, "I'm afraid so. Now, like you said, I'm a busy man. What can I do for you?"

"Well," said Dennis slowly, "we have this dilemma."

"That's right," said Nathan. "You see, J.J., yesterday, after two gangbangers almost killed your little brother...."

"What? Is Hotchie hurt? Who..."

"Cut the dramatics, J.J. Let the Preacher tell you our dilemma."

"I'm getting a little tired of this game, fellas," said J.J. "You said you had information about my brother and sister. Why don't you quit trying to mess with my mind and get it out?"

"Fair enough," said Dennis as he gestured for Nathan to continue.

"As I was saying, yesterday, after Andre was accosted by a couple of young hoodlums, he told Dennis a very interesting story."

"That's right." Dennis nodded.

Nathan continued, "Then this afternoon I visited with your mother and she told me a different story."

"That's our dilemma," said Dennis. "We don't know which story to believe."

J.J. smiled. "Well, I'm afraid both my mom and my little brother are pretty messed up, right now. But, I'd say you can count on Mom more than Hotchie."

"I had a feeling he was going to say that," Dennis said to Nathan, who nodded.

"So, what are these two stories you heard?" asked J.J., showing more impatience with each snide comment that Dennis made.

Nathan continued, "Well, according to your mom, J.J., you're a good son who cares for your younger siblings. She thinks you're too hard on them some times, but you gave Angela a job here at McKey's and now the ungrateful child has run away right before her own graduation. You've tried to keep Andre out of the gangs, but he won't listen to you and doesn't come home half the time, anymore."

J.J. nodded his affirmation, but said nothing.

"But," Dennis strung out the word. "Andre, you see, the Preacher and I, we decided to call your brother *Andre* instead of his street name, Hotchie." Dennis paused for a response. J.J. shrugged as if it made no difference to him.

"As I was saying, Andre, on the other hand...he claims this job here at McKey's is just a front, that you're the new Top Rank in town. He says you're here for a couple of hours every night, but when the bar closes you go collect your crack money brought in by your growing street organization. Andre even claims you're a pathological killer, J.J.—that you almost killed him the other night." Dennis raised an eyebrow and smiled. "Andre didn't use that word, *pathological*. That's my interpretation of what he said, you understand. It means one who *thinks* he's bad but with no conscience. Someone who will do anything that serves his purpose and never feel guilty."

"I've been to college. I know what the word means. My little brother is the delinquent here—and the liar, Mr. Livingston," J.J. said sincerely, but with obvious irritation.

Dennis nodded sympathetically. "We thought that might be the case. I mean Andre claims you're known as Juice on the street. That you're one bad dude who doesn't even love your brother and sister anymore. He claims you want him to sell drugs on the corner and that you tried to force Angela to sell her body to old rich dudes. He claims he hasn't run away from home, but he's scared to go home because you or your goons might be waiting for him there."

J.J. shook his head as if in disbelief at what was being said.

Dennis continued. "Like I said, we don't quite know what to think, but according to Andre, you supply your mother with drugs and you probably kidnapped, maybe even killed your own sister because she tried to quit her job here and wouldn't do what you demanded." Dennis sat back and shrugged. "Andre was pretty convincing. He's pretty worried about his sister. He hates you, though, I'm afraid."

"So, you gonna believe a little gangbanger or me and my mom?" asked J.J. sincerely. He looked around as if his job at McKey's granted him credibility.

"Well, that's why we wanted to talk to you, J.J.," said Nathan. "We really need to pass this information on to the police, but we needed to determine, for our own sense of fairness, which story was correct, whether they should be looking for an incorrigible teenager or a pathological gang leader."

Dennis leaned forward. "We weren't sure when we came in, but I think we understand, now."

"Good, well, thanks for coming in. I appreciate the heads-up. If I can find Andre I'll..."

"We believe Andre," said Nathan casually.

"No doubt," added Dennis.

Juice sat back down, exasperated. "Gentlemen, please.... How can you possibly..."

"The brand new Lexus," said Nathan.

Dennis reached over and yanked hard on J.J.'s expensive gold bracelet, but said calmly, "This bracelet."

Juice twisted away in angry shock and then Nathan jerked at the other wrist. "The Rolex. The rent on your mom's house and your nice apartment. I understand you live just around the corner in the high-rent district?"

Dennis stomped on Juice's foot, causing him to yelp. "The five hundred dollar shoes."

Juice's eyes glazed over. He struggled for control and started to rise slowly. Nathan grabbed one wrist, then Dennis grabbed the other. They were both big men, with huge hands and strong grips. They pulled Juice back to his chair and held onto his wrists and both leaned in.

Nathan said in a low even voice. "You see, Juice, we know Mr. Wilson. Mr. Wilson is a friend of mine. Mr. Wilson pays no assistant manager in any of his businesses the kind of money that you throw around. I'm going to check that out personally with Bob, but I know he doesn't pay anybody that well. Your mom, Juice, is chemically dependent and in denial. Andre's fear is real. We believe Andre."

Juice attempted to rise once more, but the two men pulled him back and leaned in even closer. Their voices were so low and their moves so subtle, that they had not yet even attracted the attention of the handful of diners still left on the restaurant side.

"We're almost done, Juice, sit still," Dennis said menacingly. "You can create a scene, I guess, get your security guard in here from the bar. But you don't want to do that. After all, the preacher and I are both respectable, prominent, long-standing citizens of our community. You're from D.C. and you have a shady history, Juice. Mr. Wilson gave you a chance at respectability, but...."

The expression on Juice's face was full of hate now as he looked back and forth between his two tormentors. He locked in on Dennis.

"Parkland ain't worth your time, Juice. Stay out! You'll just go down sooner in Parkland. And, you mess with the Club again..." He squeezed Juice's wrist even harder. "The preacher and I will create more trouble for you than you can imagine. Something happens to that boy, Andre, or your sister, Angela, if it's not too late for her— we'll make sure that you're the prime suspect. Ain't worth it, Juice. As it is the police are going to be on you so tight you won't be able to move. You're done, Juice, might as well split town now while you can. Got it?"

"I don't know what the fuck..."

Nathan squeezed the forearm he held and Juice shifted his gaze. "Last thing, I'm a preacher and..."

"You the god-damnedest preacher I..."

Nathan squeezed harder and gave a quick jerk. In a hushed, but ominous tone he said, "That may be, but as a preacher I'll tell you this. Until you do right by your sister and your brother, your life will be a mess—nothing will work right. Your filthy drug business..." Nathan looked around, "whatever you got going on here. You're gonna be physically sick half the time. You're gonna have money problems. You're gonna have women troubles. You hear me, Juice? It's all going to hell faster than you are, till you do right by those children. Leave them alone. That's it!"

Both men dropped Juice's arms at the same time. Juice bounded up, knocking over his chair. Finally people were staring, even a few in the bar area. He seemed to be on the verge of hyperventilating. Spittle dribbled from one side of his mouth. Without parting his lips, he worked his jaw as if he was trying to say something, but the words were trapped in his mouth. He spun and stomped away, not stopping as he moved through the bar and disappeared through a door near the restroom.

Dennis and Nathan both leaned back in their chairs and looked at each other. Slowly a smile came to each man's face.

"You'd think we had that scripted," said Dennis. "Think maybe that was the Holy Spirit, Preacher?"

"I thought you didn't believe in God, my friend."

"I'll tell you what, that's the closest I ever felt to feeling *something*. I'll tell you that."

"All these years and I finally make a little progress." Nathan looked up. "Shed a little light, Lord. Shed a little light on this wonderful, stubborn man." They shared a tension-relieving laugh.

"Was that a curse I heard you put on that sorry creature?"

"More the power of suggestion than anything," said Nathan. "But if the good Lord wants to answer it as a prayer, that's okay. And, Dennis, that sorry creature is still a child of God, still redeemable."

"Oh, Preacher," Dennis shook his head in disbelief, and in unison they rose from the table where they had sat for nearly two hours.

"Keep praying for me, Nathan, keep praying."

Nathan put his arm around his old friend and said, "Every day, Dennis, every single day."

• • • • •

Juice burst through the door of the office and didn't even turn on the light. The voice that came from in the corner was mature and truly mysterious, not like the little blond who had greeted Nathan and Dennis.

"See why I hate the man so? I warned you."

Juice didn't answer. He angrily punched a number into his cell phone. "Find Hotchie. Then page me and we'll meet at the warehouse. You hear what I'm telling you? Find him!"

AGAINST THE WIND

7

SATURDAY, MAY 18, MIDDLE OF THE NIGHT

The thunder woke her up. It was still dark. How long had she been asleep? Nighttime was the worst. How long had it been? Angela had lost track of time. Four, maybe five days? A week or more since she'd walked away from McKey's? Had they forgotten about her? It had been at least three days since she'd seen anybody. *They just going to let me starve?*

It was too good to be true when Juice hired her as a hostess at McKey's. She thought maybe he cared for her again, like a big brother should. The job was easy and fun. She got a real paycheck. She didn't even have to keep track of where to seat people—the other girl did that. It wasn't hard to be nice to people, escort them to their seats and make them feel welcome. Angela liked people and people liked Angela, not just the men, either, but the pretty, classy ladies who came to the restaurant. She received as many compliments about her good looks and pretty dresses from the ladies as she did from the men.

She should have known, with Juice there was a hook in the job. It *was* too good to be true. The job kept her up too late and her grades had slipped, but she was still on track to graduate. All of her hard-earned credits from the D.C. high school had finally transferred, and in another week or so she would have been a high school graduate. A month after that and she would be eighteen. She could have left and found a job, a new city, a new place to live—as far away from Juice as possible. She was smart and got along well with her teachers and most adults. She could have done it. Maybe then she could have rescued Andre. All of her hard work, staying out of trouble, trying to keep Andre straight, not using drugs—for what?

What good had it done her? All the hours she spent in church. *No! That was not wasted.* That's what brought her strength now. If Jesus had not been with her, she couldn't have made it this far. She was having trouble praying though. At first, she'd prayed hard, long prayers, like talking to, pleading with, arguing with a best friend, but now it was getting to be too hard to concentrate.

"Oh, Jesus, are you here? You with me, Jesus? Please be with me."

She wanted to hate her mom, but she couldn't. Even though she'd been more of a mother to her little brother than Mom had. Mom was sick, but how could Andre love her so much? How could Mom let Juice...? A sudden noise made her scream. *What was that?*

Angela pulled the blanket around her and scooted back tightly against the wall. Maybe they were coming for her. Maybe it would all be over soon. She hadn't seen Juice since she left his office that night, but, she'd told them to tell Juice that she'd die first. That was days ago.

"Oh, Jesus. Jesus, please help me."

They had blindfolded her when they snatched her off the street on her way home that night. They had been rough, but they hadn't actually hurt her. She'd be no good to Juice if she was all beat up. The big goofy kid, the one they called YoYo, because he nodded his head up and down when he talked, seemed to feel sorry for her. YoYo is the one who brought her the blanket on the first night. He brought the junk food, pop and water. Juwan and YoYo came every day at first, just to see if she'd changed her mind. She could tell Juwan wanted to hurt her, bad. Only his fear of Juice kept him from really hurting her—and from raping her. Juwan had thought about that. She saw it in his eyes.

Angela jumped and screamed aloud at the thunder. She could hear the rain pelting the roof. She wasn't sure where she was, maybe in an old warehouse. They had dragged her up some stairs before removing the blindfold, she remembered that much. The room must have been an office or a storeroom at one time. There were no windows and no electricity. At night it was pitch black. She stayed on the table at night and prayed and sang songs, praise and worship songs that she'd learned at the church in D.C. She should have found a new church right after she moved here. Maybe if she had found a church... If she sang, she couldn't hear the rats and the noises that old buildings make. But since the water ran out yesterday it was hard to sing. But if she didn't sing or pray out loud, her mind wandered and she couldn't stay focused. Angela kept telling herself that the grime covering her entire body was only on the outside. The smell and the filth had nothing to do with what was in her heart.

There it was again! The wind was blowing harder and the thunder was clapping right on top of the building. *Maybe... No! The stairs— somebody's coming!*

"Jesus, please, Jesus."

Angela pulled her knees even tighter to her chest. She began to tremble and cry. Another clap of thunder made her scream again. *It's only thunder!* She was ready to die. She had seen more death than children were supposed to see. She had hoped that moving away from D.C. would have changed things. She should have taken Andre to church. The North Side was better than D.C. The job at McKey's. Things would be better, but now…. She remembered how her friends had looked so peaceful laying in their coffins. Their funerals seemed almost a relief. She wasn't afraid to die, but she was afraid of the pain of dying, of whatever it took to get to the other side. *Footsteps!* She knew that's what she heard. Then she saw a flash of light. Someone was right outside the door with a flashlight. Whoever it was had his hand on the padlock.

"Help me, Jesus. Please, help me."

• • • • •

Jacob turned the corner and was pleasantly surprised to see Ruth out in front of her house. She was running in place as she waited for him. She waved and her smile brightened his mood even more as she fell into step with him. She looked at her watch.

"Seven-fifteen—right on time."

"I'm impressed," he said. "After a long week at the Club, I thought you might sleep in. Especially with this…" he gestured to the skies.

"You didn't think a little rain would discourage me, did you? This is invigorating."

Their pace was strong but comfortable, as was the conversation between them. They crossed the boulevard to the park and ran on the jogging path that overlooked the river.

"That was quite a storm last night. Did it wake you?" he asked.

"Only for a minute around four this morning. I was so bushed that I went right back to sleep. Did you hear the weather forecast before you left the station?"

"The storm cell has moved on. This drizzle is supposed to clear up before noon. Supposed to be," Jacob turned, held out his hands as he ran and broke into song, "a bright, bright sun-shiny day."

She laughed. "Great, we've got some outdoor activities planned for the little kids this afternoon. Guess what?"

Her eyes were wide and her face bright. The rain that beaded on her cheeks gave her a fresh look. Jacob realized how much he was enjoying her company. "What?"

"Someone stole my car last night!"

"Your new car?"

"No, thank God. My old one, but still... Mom got up to make coffee this morning and noticed that the garage door was open and there was no car inside. Mom's convertible was there, but they stole my old beat-up car."

"No one heard or saw anything?"

Ruth shook her head. "And when we went out there we found the light bulb from the garage door opener on the bench. They unscrewed it so they could pull out of there with no lights on."

"That's strange," said Jacob. "Leave your mom's new convertible and take the old one. Were the keys...?"

"The keys were in both of them!" Ruth laughed. "We won't do that any more. Plus, Mom is calling an electrician this morning. She wants those motion sensor lights installed. She wants lights to come on all over the place if somebody even gets close to the house or the garage."

"Good idea."

"I don't know, Mom's already pretty paranoid, and this certainly won't help." Ruth shook her head, then said, "Quiet night at the station?"

"That's one thing I like about it, it's always quiet," Jacob laughed.

"So, what all do you do there?"

"A little bit of everything, whatever's needed. We have a skeleton crew at night. From midnight to four we play a nationally syndicated all night talk show, so there's not much to do. We play some music until the early news show comes on at six."

"Christian music?" she asked.

"A little—some of the better stuff, especially on the days when I do the jockeying for that two hours."

"You're a disc jockey?" she said, impressed.

He laughed. "For two hours in the middle of the night. Not many people tune in at that hour."

"And you get off at seven, so this works for you?"

"This is great, Ruth. It's wonderful to have someone to run with. How 'bout you?"

"This works until the second week in June. That's when the summer hours kick in at the Club. We have that Early Bird program that opens at six-thirty in the morning so parents can drop kids off on their way to work. But I should be able break away about eight every morning. Will that work?"

"That will work. I'll just go back to visiting with Mom at the home before we run. No problem. If something comes up, just call me at the station before seven."

"Any change with Grandma Becky? I was by to see her last Wednesday."

It always pleased Jacob to hear Ruth refer to his mom as Grandma Becky. Their shared love for Becky Riddler was the first common bond, their initial comfort zone, when he returned to Parkland three years ago. Now maybe Maryann was becoming comfortable with him, too.

"No, no change."

They exited the Park and ran in place at the light to check the traffic before continuing. They were now running the stretch that bordered the North Side, the stretch that most concerned Maryann. Jacob found himself relieved that Ruth was not running this stretch alone. It scared him to think she sometimes ran it at night.

"Did Mark ever find Hotchie last night?" he asked.

"No, he never did. When the Club closed, Andre was nowhere around."

"Andre? I thought he liked…"

"Dennis thinks it's good that we all call him Andre, sometimes it kind of helps break the street's hold on kids when you call them by their real names. Look," Ruth pointed. "Something's going on."

Across the street, two blocks ahead, three squad cars were blocking off an alley. The ambulance and the Medical Examiner's car pulled away as Ruth and Jacob crossed the street and walked to the edge of the small Saturday morning crowd of curious onlookers. On the inside of the yellow crime scene tape a plain clothes and two patrol officers talked.

"I'm afraid it's another kid, Ruth," came a thick voice from behind them.

Ruth and Jacob turned.

"Oh, Tod, hi," said Ruth. Her tone had taken on a sense of dread. "A kid? Who?"

The detective didn't answer. Instead, he stared at Jacob. A keen gaze that disquieted Ruth passed between the two men.

Tomas Otero Diaz was a good cop. He didn't look almost sixty. He was short, only about five-nine and a little on the heavy side, but everything about him exuded a clear warning that he was not to be toyed with. He combed his full head of thick, black hair straight back. He used his beady black eyes like lasers. From the time he was eight years old when his parents first came up from Mexico, all Diaz ever wanted was to be a good cop. That kept him in trouble most of the time, not only with the department brass, but also with some of his fellow officers. In his early days on the force he found himself frequently snared in the political fray between the police union and the Brotherhood of Guardians, the black officers' association. By the time there were enough Hispanics on the force to form their own association, Diaz refused to join them. He was so good, they had no choice but to eventually give him the detective shield he had earned, but that only intensified the tension that surrounded him. A few years ago, they assigned Diaz to the Gang Task Force and told him his focus would be Parkland, not the South Side where the Hispanic gangs were growing. The brass had hoped to isolate him in a meaningless job. Maybe he would view it as a demotion and take early retirement. Instead, Diaz tackled the job with such fervor that he made life miserable for any gang that tried to move in on the proud old neighborhood. In the process he endeared himself to the community. The citizens and leaders of Parkland protected him politically which gave him more freedom to do his job. He became a fixture, jokingly but affectionately referred to as the Sheriff of Parkland. Long divorced and kids raised, he seemed to be somewhere on the streets twenty-four hours a day. Because he signed all departmental reports and documents with his initials, T.O.D., many years ago his colleagues began to call him Tod. The best thing about Tod, the thing that made Ruth love the crusty old cop, was that he loved her kids, even the bad ones. Tod cared about kids and that made him protective of the Club and of Ruth.

"Who is it, Tod?" Ruth asked again, interrupting the unsettling stare down between two men she loved and respected. "Was it a drive-by?"

"No, not a drive-by," he replied, still staring at Jacob. Then he finally turned to face Ruth, giving her a symphathetic gaze, knowing the news he had would hurt her. "Someone slit his throat."

Ruth and Jacob both looked to where the body had been laid and saw the awful puddle of blood that the rain had not been able to wash away.

"And, they cut off his little finger."

"Oh, dear God," she said, and looked back into the old cop's eyes, ready for the news. "Who is it, Tod?"

"YoYo."

"Oh, no. Stephon, they killed Stephon."

"Yes, Stephon Taylor." Diaz looked at the new learner's permit in his hand. "He just turned sixteen last week."

"I should go with you to tell his mother," she said.

"Okay, my car's over there."

As they turned to walk away, Ruth looked back at Jacob. He nodded his understanding and then watched Diaz pull his trench coat from the back seat of his car and place it around Ruth's shoulders. The old detective held the door for her while she got in.

With the tail end of the stormfront came a strong cold wind. Jacob walked home, against the wind. He took a shower and went to the nursing home to see his mom.

•••••

Andre woke up confused, wet, stiff and sore. Then he remembered he had fallen asleep on the floor of the abandoned house across the street from his mom's. He had arrived home during the storm to find both Juwan's Buick and Juice's Lexus parked out front. They were looking for him. Later, in the lightning flashes he'd seen the crazed look on Juwan's face as he and two others got in his car and drove off. Andre cautiously rose and looked through the window. The Lexus was gone. He looked at his watch. Mom wouldn't wake up for several hours. He could sneak in, get out of his wet clothes, take a hot shower and maybe get in a nap before twelve-thirty. The Club was open from twelve-thirty to six on Saturdays. Maybe he could spend the night at Mark's again. Mark had already invited him to church tomorrow.

The young boy stood in the hot shower for longer than usual, allowing the hot water to wash his aches away. He wrapped the towel around his waist and quietly made his way down the hallway, past his mother's room to his own. He shut the door, threw the towel on his bed and walked to the old dresser. When he saw the image over his shoulder in the mirror he tried to stifle the scream.

"Good morning, Little Bro." Juice smiled as if he meant the cheerful greeting, but Andre's heart was racing. He desperately looked around the room. He was trapped. He moved a few steps to put the bed between them, but it was all he could do. There was no escape. Panic rose and lodged in his chest. Then from somewhere Andre found his courage, straightened his back, stood and looked his older brother straight in the eye.

Juice bent down and with forefinger and thumb raised the wet pants from the floor where Andre had discarded them a few minutes earlier. "Hotchie, out all night? In the rain? You know better than that."

"Why you change since we move here, Juice?" said Andre. He felt no fear now.

Juice dropped the soggy jeans, took a fresh handkerchief from the hip pocket of his expensive slacks and deliberately wiped his finger and thumb. "What do you mean, Little Bro?"

"Back in D.C., you say you don't want me and Angela messin' with gangs and using drugs. You say, only reason you doing it is so you can take care of us. You were bad on the streets, but you were nice to us." Juice did not try to interrupt him like he usually did. For once he was quiet. Like a dam breaking, the pent-up words spilled out of Hotchie's mouth on a wave of emotion. "You told us you would whip us if you catch us running with the gangs. I wanted to run with you, but you wouldn't let me, man. You tell me and Angela to go to school, get good grades, to mind Momma. You said we were moving here because you had a real job lined up. It was supposed to be different. Then we get here and you change. You make me work a corner selling crack. Okay, but why you so mean all the sudden?"

The silence hung in the room while Juice found his smile again. "Opportunity, Little Brother, opportunity is what makes America great. Lot of opportunity here. And, everybody got to play his part. But," Juice raised a forefinger and waved it slightly, "I've been thinking. And you're right. Time enough for you and Angela to pull your own weight. That's why I've been trying to find you. I've been thinking about our situation."

This seemed more like the old Juice. Something had happened, something was different.

"I've got a business to run, Hotchie. And I have a proposition for you." Juice moved to sit on the edge of the bed and crossed his legs. Andre continued to stand on the other side. "It helps my cover if you and Angela are not involved in my business right now. So, Little Bro, it's okay. You don't have anything to be scared of anymore. You don't have to work a corner anymore. Just mind Momma; stay in school and out of trouble. Okay? And that Club is a good place for you right now."

"Momma's drinking too much, Juice."

"Just beer and whiskey. I told her to never touch the powder or the other stuff. She knows better. Momma's okay. You just do what she say."

Andre nodded, but knew better.

Juice raised his finger again, his look suddenly ominous. "But, Hotchie you keep talking to people, telling them I'm the Top Rank, blowing my cover." Juice was calm and speaking matter-of-factly, "I'm going to have to kill you, do you understand?"

Andre's heart skipped. Things were different. Juice was even colder now, and more menacing.

"You and me got to have a truce. I leave you alone, call off Juwan and the fellas. But, you start telling people I'm a good big brother, who works a good job and takes care of his mother and little brother and sister. You hear me? You say anymore to Livingston, that damned preacher, anybody else... I'll kill you. They ask you anything? You tell 'em you lied on me because I was getting after you about staying out all night gangbanging. You understand?"

Andre nodded. He could live with the truce being offered.

"Good." Juice smiled again and stood. He reached into a pocket of the tailored leather coat he wore and pulled out a pair of gloves.

Andre's voice was on the verge of trembling when he asked, "You got Angela?"

The smile became more sinister as Juice deliberately put on the gloves. "What do you think, Little Brother?" he mocked. "Of course I got her. You ever want to see her again, you keep our truce." He reached into the pocket again and pulled out a switchblade and tossed it on the bed.

"Recognize that? Pick it up, look it over."

Hotchie picked up the knife and shook his head as he turned the knife over in his hands.

"That knife belonged to your good friend YoYo. You want it?"

Andre dropped the knife and stepped back as if he'd received an electrical shock. He stared at the knife on his bed.

Juice laughed. "YoYo won't be needing it anymore. You want it, Hotchie?"

Andre looked up, eyes wide and shook his head.

Juice reached into the other pocket, pulled out a plastic bag and held it up.

"Know what this is?"

Andre nodded.

"Say it, boy!"

"That's YoYo's little finger," he said in a shaky voice.

"That's right." Juice opened the bloody bag, picked up the knife and held it over the bag. "Still got some blood on the blade, it looks like." He pointed the knife at Andre. "You keep pointing the finger at me, Hotchie? Someday they going to come search my pad. But, I'm too smart for that. They won't find anything there that will hurt me, Little Bro. I've built a deep cover. But you know what they'll find at the gang's pad? In the freezer, they're going to find YoYo's finger and his knife." Juice dropped the knife in the bag and carefully closed the seam. "And guess whose fingerprints will be all over the knife?"

Andre impulsively raised his hands and looked at them, then at Juice.

"That's right," sang Juice as he placed the bag in his pocket. He removed the gloves and began to laugh. His laughter grew louder in the hallway. Juice stopped at his mother's room and opened her door. "Good morning, Momma. Your baby boy's home, better get up and fix him some breakfast." Juice laughed louder and continuously as he left the house and walked to his car.

In the bedroom, Andre stood and continued to stare at his hands, tears rolling down his face for his friend, YoYo, for himself, and for Angela, wherever she was.

CELEBRATION AT ANTIOCH

8

SUNDAY, MAY 19, MORNING

Nathan stood at the front of the sanctuary, in front of the stage with its huge pulpit behind him, not really needing a microphone. "Are there any other announcements to be made? As our visitors can tell, we are a busy family. We hope you feel welcome here. Are there any more announcements?"

Mark looked down the pew. Andre seemed eager to experience whatever came next. Every Sunday morning, Jacob sat toward the front of the church with a group of young teenagers he had grown close to through his volunteer work at the Club. Except for Mark Bethel, who sat proudly with Maryann and Ruth toward the back. But, this morning the three Bethels had shown up with Andre in tow and Mark brought his friend forward where they sat together in Jacob's pew. Andre scooted in and sat next to Jacob.

Looking over the congregation and seeing no raised hands, Nathan declared, "If there are no further announcements, then let us prepare our hearts for worship."

Sunday morning worship at Antioch is a grand experience. The simple sanctuary is typical of churches built in the 1920s. Stained glass windows on each side reflect beautiful shades of light across the old bench-style pews. The center aisle rises, slightly inclined from down front where a beautifully crafted wooden pulpit takes center stage. Five large fans hang from the ceilings thirty feet above the center aisle. Behind the pulpit is a rich burgundy curtain that opens to reveal a small, empty baptismal pool. When the pool began to leak twenty years earlier, it was decided not to spend money on repairs. Rather, on those Sundays when the need arose, the entire church marched across the street and baptized converts in the shallow end of the Club's swimming pool. On each side of the burgundy curtain sit big wooden chairs, crafted to match the pulpit, where the pastors and lay worship leaders take turns sitting. The sanctuary is immaculately maintained. Pews, pulpit, and pastoral chairs glisten each Sunday. The rich deep crimson carpet is always vacuumed and clean. Beautiful banners, lovingly handmade by talented church members, hang on each side of and behind the stage, and between each of the tall stained-glass windows.

It is the people that make Antioch a warm and friendly place to be each week. The diverse congregation consists of an equal portion of Black, Caucasian, Hispanic and Asian families.

For Andre's first worship service, Antioch Church, as it does every Sunday morning, jolted to life with a rich mixture of contemporary, traditional, and black worship. Andre was surprised when, following the announcements, Jacob and three kids from their pew joined a diverse group of worshippers who rose from their seats and quietly moved to the front. Jacob and two of the kids were among a group of five guitarists. The other picked up a tambourine and joined a group of six vocalists who stood behind four microphones. A young electric keyboard player who looked to be in a 1960s time warp, nodded to the young Hispanic girl at the drums and the group and the congregation burst into a set of hand clappin', toe-tappin' songs of praise and worship.

Newcomers are sometimes taken aback by the infectious hand clapping, but not Andre—he jumped right in. Visitors and long-time members alike are frequently struck by the sincerity on the faces of young and old around them. After ten or fifteen minutes, the tone changes as the song leaders switch to more melodious worship songs. It's not unusual to see people slowly swaying in almost a trance-like state, or for tears to freely roll down their uplifted cheeks as they proclaim in song what are to them simple truths like 'God is so Good,' 'We Would See Jesus,' and 'Come, Holy Spirit.'

Uninhibited, but orderly, both the reserved and the demonstrative feel at home in the worship at Antioch. Sr. Pastor Nathan Wesley

Frye, his beautiful robe and stole flowing to the music, was most unconstrained. His twenty-eight year old associate, the Reverend Jill Thomas, although radiating love and enthusiasm, and quite striking in her own pastoral robe, was the epitome of quiet reserve. Jill, who stood tall, with her rich deep complexion, and classically beautiful African features, exuded dignity and grace.

As Andre watched her moving slightly to the music, he leaned over to his friend Mark and declared in a loud whisper, "Man, that's the most beautiful woman, white or black, I ever seen, *man.*"

As the singing came to a close and the singers and musicians returned to their seats, quiet exhortations like "Amen," "Thank you, Jesus," and "Praise the Lord" were heard throughout the crowded sanctuary. Andre was surprised again when Jacob remained up front and sat on a stool with his guitar on his lap.

"This song is based on Psalm 107," said Jacob quietly. "It's about how the Lord listens when his people cry out in their distress and trouble. It's called *The Redeemed.*"

The sanctuary full of people sat reverently in silent expectation as Jacob finely tuned his acoustic guitar. Jacob only rarely sang a solo, but, when he did, everyone was richly blessed.

After a slight pause, Jacob looked down at his fingers and began to move them rapidly, but lightly across the strings, filling the sanctuary with the melodious introduction to his song. He continued to play as he looked up from the guitar, closed his eyes, and lifted his voice in an offering of talent pulled from the depth of his heart.

> *Let those he has redeemed,*
> *Proclaim it.*
> *Give thanks to the Lord,*
> *For he is good.*
> *His love endures forever.*

In simple words and verses pulled straight from scripture, Jacob sang of those who had wandered in the desert, of the ones who sat in the darkness and deep gloom, oppressed by their foes, and of others who had become fools. But then he sang of how in their distress they had cried out to the Lord —and the Lord had saved them, redeemed them, restored them to health and wholeness. Between verses the chorus reminded the redeemed to proclaim it.

Sometimes following a solo performance the congregation would break into applause. This morning they sat in reverent silence because the performance was so profoundly worshipful that applause seemed inappropriate.

As Jacob returned to his seat next to Andre, Nathan rose and moved behind the pulpit. He took a deep breath and looked over at Jacob with a smile that reflected his love and appreciation.

"Thank you, Jacob, that was beautiful." Nathan then turned to the pulpit as if he were going to proceed with the worship. Then he paused and looked back at Jacob.

"You know, Jacob. I think it is time to share some of your good news with these kind folks. These folks who have loved and nurtured and supported you since your return. Okay?"

Jacob smiled at his mentor, his AA sponsor, in many ways, his lifeline. If Nathan thought it was time, it was time. He nodded his assent.

Nathan turned to the congregation. "A few years ago our brother Jacob found himself with a lot of time on his hands." The congregation laughed. "So, he took up the guitar. Jacob learned to play the guitar. To watch him today, it's hard to believe he only learned to play seven or eight years ago. He plays as if he were born to play, and has been playing all his life. *Anyway*, when he returned to Parkland three years ago he moved into the apartment above Mrs. Carlson's carriage house." Nathan smiled and made eye contact with Mrs. Carlson who sat in a front pew on the other side of the sanctuary from where Jacob and his young friends sat. Mrs. Carlson, the paragon of aging grace, who for many years was the congregation's pianist and still substitutes occasionally, smiled and nodded. "Mrs. Carlson heard him playing one day and took him into her house where she began to instruct him in how to play the piano and in basic music theory."

Andre looked across the aisle at Mrs. Carlson and then whispered to Jacob, "That old lady taught you to play the piano?"

Jacob just smiled and nodded.

Nathan continued over Andre's whispers. "That was all the instruction Jacob needed to begin writing songs. The last couple of years, with Mrs. Carlson giving me the heads up—'He has another one,' she'd tell me—then I'd twist Jacob's arm to play for us. And do we ever enjoy your songs and your singing, Jacob!"

The congregation spontaneously burst into applause and even from the back where she sat, Maryann could see Jacob blush all over like he had in her garage the other day.

"Well, you should know a couple of other things about Jacob's music," said Nathan. Nathan made eye contact with Ruth. "Some of you know that two evenings a week, across the street at the Club, Jacob teaches children to play the guitar. There is a waiting list to get into his classes. In fact, both Ben and Rachel, two members of our praise band," Nathan gestured to Jacob's pew, "were taught to play the guitar by Jacob."

Andre jerked his eyes back to Jacob and whispered loudly, causing some giggles to emit from the surrounding pews, "You taught these dudes to play the guitar?"

Jacob nodded.

"Can you teach me?" he whispered even more loudly which caused even more giggles and gained Nathan's attention.

Again, Jacob smiled and nodded.

"And that's not all." Nathan smiled broadly at Andre and then looked out over the congregation. "Last year, Mrs. Carlson sent some of Jacob's songs off to one of her old friends in the Christian music business. Two of Jacob's songs have been recorded by a couple of today's top Christian recording artists. Both songs are doing quite well. Mrs. Carlson tells me that very soon both tunes should break into the top ten on the Christian music charts. I hear one is even being played on some secular stations."

"Where did you learn to play the guitar?" whispered Andre.

"Two more songs, including *The Redeemed* that we heard this morning, have been recorded by top artists and will be released soon. They seem to have discovered our man, Jacob."

The audience again began to applaud, but Nathan interrupted, "I'm sure that Jacob would rather you give praise to the Lord who saved him."

"Where did you learn to play?" asked Andre again. Jacob tried to ignore him.

"In fact," said Nathan. "The thing I like about Jacob's songs is that they are not fluff, like so much of Christian music today. They have depth and are always based on scripture. So, thank you, Jacob. But, most of all thank the one Jacob praises in his songs, the one who has redeemed us all."

Andre would not be deterred. "Where did you learn to play the guitar, Jacob?"

Jacob looked down and smiled at his young friend. He whispered, "In prison, Andre. I learned to play the guitar in prison."

9 AFTER CHURCH ROUTINES

"**W**hose cabin?" Juice called. "Very nice. Old furniture and all, it's still nice."

From the patio, she responded coolly, "It's my husband's secret place, and has been in his family for years. I didn't know about it for a long time. The fool tried to keep it from me. I find it comes in handy now and then. A very convenient hideaway." The woman reclined in an old lounge chair and looked out over the lake at the back of the large acreage. The hillsides were coming to life in the fullness of the fertile spring. It was an unseasonably warm afternoon. She sat and basked in the sun, wearing only a pair of sunglasses.

"Come—join me for a drink. You're not shy, are you? There are no neighbors that can see you... not without high powered binoculars anyway."

Juice rose from the bed. He picked up his pants and searched their pockets until he found his antacid tablets. He threw a handful into his mouth, tossed his pants onto the bed and walked out on the patio. What they had just done wasn't lovemaking. It was more of a contest, a power struggle, an ebb and flow of dominance. They had been derisive and cruelly mocking, calling each other vile names. Somehow he knew better than to hit her. There had been nothing pleasurable about it. And now, he was feeling sick to his stomach again.

He walked out onto the patio that was two stories high on the backside of the cabin that was nestled into the tree-covered hill. He ignored both the beautiful view and her gesture offering him the other lounge chair. Instead, he stood over her assessing her nakedness. This was one

75

strange white woman. She was older than he was, maybe by ten years, he couldn't tell because she looked good, *real good*. She had a full head of wavy blond hair, light blue eyes, long slender legs, a tiny waist and the perfect size breasts.

"I don't drink," he said.

"Ha," she ridiculed. "So that's soda water in your glass as you work the bar every evening, talking to the ladies?"

"That's right." He continued to look her over, pointed to his temple and said, "A clear head gives a guy the advantage in the hunt."

She shook her head derisively. "And, I suppose you don't use any of the wonderful white stuff you peddle, either?"

"Definitely not, one must also keep the head clear for business."

"Well, Saint Paul said a little wine will help your stomach feel better," she said with an insidious grin and motioned toward the bottle of dark red wine and the glass that sat on the small round table between the two chairs.

"Saint Paul?"

"The great Apostle, the one who wrote most of the New Testament, in the Bible, you know?"

"Okay." He reached down for the bottle and the glass and wondered if she sensed he was feeling queasy again. "But, Jez," he mocked as he poured the wine slowly into the glass, "You don't seem the type to be quoting the Bible."

"I was in church this morning, lover," she laughed and swept her long blond hair to one side. "In fact, my nickname—most people don't know this—is based on my favorite Bible character." She raised her glass, as if toasting herself. "Must keep up appearances. I go to church every Sunday, even when my darling husband is out of town."

Juice turned his back to the hills, leaned against the deck railing and continued to assess her nude body. She didn't seem the least bit self-conscious.

"So, Jez, you go to church at Antioch? Where the preacher…"

"No," she interrupted. A depraved expression seized her face. She quickly recovered and took another sip of her wine. "I go to the big church downtown, Community Church. We offer three services every Sunday." She lifted her glass again and said contemptuously, "The Lord is really blessing us."

"So, your husband know how you use his little hideaway for Sunday after church romps?"

She smiled. "Don't know, don't care. Like I've been telling you, people only count as long as they're useful. My loving husband may have blown his usefulness to me. Time will tell." She looked up at him and removed her sunglasses. "Does the good Congressman, Mr. Wilson, know about the side businesses you're running out of his restaurant?"

"Don't know. Don't care." He raised the wineglass and returned the toast. "My guess is as long as I give him what he wants, don't let him get pulled into anything, he don't care."

"That's what this is all about, J.J.—everybody getting what they want."

"I got a lot more getting to do before I'm through, Jez."

She said, "That's why you and me, we can help each other. We both know what we want."

"Maybe so, Jez, maybe so. It has worked pretty good so far."

She held onto the wineglass with both hands and coyly looked at him as she sipped the wine. "You owe me, J.J."

"So, what do you want, Jez? Piece of my action? You probably deserve a piece for helping me get set up. Any idea how much I pull in each week?"

She laughed again, this time he was the object of her contempt and it made him uncomfortable. "I don't need your dirty money, J.J."

"You so rich, you don't need no more? Or, you just too good to take drug money?"

"Money is overrated, lover."

"So, what you want, woman? How do I pay you back?"

She put down her glass, sat up cross-legged on the lounge and leaned forward. Her lips were red from the wine. Her eyes narrowed and even seemed to change from blue to a kind of greenish hue. The earlier ominous expression seized her face again. Even the sound and tone of her voice seemed somehow altered as she said, "I want you to help me destroy the preacher, Nathan Wesley Frye, and his sidekick, Dennis Livingston."

It was his turn to laugh contemptuously. He set his glass back on the table and stepped back to look at her again. Her expression remained unchanged.

"You're serious, aren't you?"

She didn't answer.

"Jez, I told you about the other night, how those two dis'd me right there in the restaurant. I hate their guts, but by now they've told everything they think they know to the police. I dodged some old Mexican detective there last night. Livingston and the preacher end up dead, guess who the prime suspect is? You think I'm crazy? Don't owe you that much, Jez. No way."

She said steely, "I didn't say kill them. Killing them makes them bigger than life. I can't have that. I said destroy them, J.J. *Destroy* them. Revenge is sweet, but it's more than getting even. Destroy them and life gets better, for both of us."

"How?"

"I have some ideas, lots of ideas, lover."

He had not seen this smile before, anywhere, on anyone's face. He tried to cover the flash of fear he felt with a laugh. "I bet you do, Jez. I bet you do."

"It's called knowing your enemy, lover. You destroy these men by destroying the things and the people they love."

"Destroying them is better than killing them." Juice smiled as he contemplated what that might mean.

"Yes!" Her excitement grew as he began to understand. "You destroy these men by destroying the reputations they took a lifetime to build. Even better, bring down some of the people they love. Create some chaos around them."

"Create some chaos," he reflected on the words she had used.

She scooted to the edge of the lounge chair, a wicked grin spreading across her lovely face. "You want to get even with them for disrespecting you in your own restaurant? Destroy the confidence that people place in them. Use pain and embarrassment, lover—indirect attacks."

"Indirect attacks." He laughed. "What are you talking about?"

"Go after the people they both love. I know where to start. Jacob Riddler, the guy who keeps interfering with your family? He's like a son to the preacher. And, Ruth Bethel, the cute little piece of ass that works at the Club? She's like a daughter to Dennis Livingston."

"Let me think about that, Jez. Getting Riddler would be sweet, sweet indeed."

She reached out and stroked the inside of his thigh, "Patience, lover, patience. Take your time. Like you said, lay low. Let them think they scared you off. Let things cool off a bit, while we do our homework and make plans. You got a whole army of stupid little punks who'll do anything you say because they're scared of you, and they know you'll put some cash in their pockets."

"And Juwan... I know I can count on Juwan. He runs the street operation for me. I'm staying away from that almost completely now."

"Can you trust him?"

Juice smiled. "He's scared to death of me. Knows better than to cross me. He also knows I'm the brains. He's making some serious money and I'm his connection. He'll do exactly what I say. He's good. Crazy, but good."

"Then, I'll be your intelligence officer. You and I, J.J. Let the dumb little shits in your gang do the dirty work, and they will do it, lover." She pointed to her temple. "We have the brains." Then she grabbed his hand and placed it on her bare chest, above her rapidly beating heart. "You hate them as much as I do—Livingston— especially that goddamned preacher. I know you do."

He began to laugh. She held out her hands. He grabbed them and roughly jerked her to her feet.

She wrapped her arms around his neck and looked deeply into his eyes. The ominous smile finally left her lips as she asked, "You man enough, J.J.?" She kissed him roughly, almost violently. His hands were all over her. He began to lose himself in her again, when she brusquely pushed him away enough to look again into his eyes. "Trust me, J.J. Your reward will be great. Are you man enough?"

Later that afternoon, still nude, she stood in the front door of the cabin in full view of the distant country road and waved good-bye as he turned his Lexus around and drove down the long gravel driveway. She shut the door and leaned against it. The evil green eyes had returned. She began to laugh—a crazed laughter that echoed through the empty cabin. She slowly slid down, her back against the door, all the way to the floor, her haunting laughter out of control.

· · · · ·

Jacob gently brushed the gray hair away from his comatose mother's eyes. He picked up the old family Bible from the nightstand by the bed. He searched through it until he found the verse he wanted. He read out loud, *"Everything is uncovered and laid bare before the eyes of Him to whom we must give account."*

"That was the main text of Preacher Nate's sermon this morning, Mom. It's from Hebrews the fifth chapter, the thirteenth verse. Preacher Nate reminded us of the scandals that have been reported on the evening news over the last few years. He didn't mention names, of course. But, you know all of the politicians, even presidents, the television evangelists, the business people who've been caught doing something unethical. He asked us to think about the responses we've heard from people trying to proclaim their innocence with that 'yes, I got caught with my hand in the cookie jar, but my hand wasn't really in the cookie jar' attitude. They even proclaim their innocence all the way to the jailhouse door. You know Preacher Nate. He had us all laughing. He even asked us what we would do if the worst things we had ever done ended up as the lead story on the Sunday night news. Everybody got pretty quiet."

Jacob looked up from his notes and studied her face like he had done hundreds of times before, hoping for some kind of reaction. Every Sunday after church and every morning after work, either just before, or just after his five mile run, Jacob came to see his mom in the nursing home. He never missed a day. The somewhat jaded nursing home staff had grown to love him, deeply admiring his obvious devotion. On Sundays he shared with his mom the notes he'd taken during the sermon.

Consulting his notes again, he continued, "Preacher Nate said that as bad as that prospect might be, having our worst moment broadcast on television, the thing we need to be most concerned about is God. He said we may be able to hide from other people, but God sees everything. He said that we all *know* that, but we don't always understand exactly what it means. He said that God hates hypocrisy, that putting on airs and pretending to be somebody that we're not is never a good idea. Let's see," Jacob turned his notebook page. "Oh, this is good—it made me think. Preacher Nate said the most terrible lie we ever tell, just might be our life. With God it's impossible to put on airs. Then he went on to talk about what it means to confess our sins, not only to God, but also to each other. It was a good sermon, Mom. It made me think about a lot of things."

Jacob paused. Much had run through his mind as he talked to his comatose mother. For weeks he had told himself that she looked better somehow, but recently the stark reality of her condition had begun to sink in. She was thinner, much thinner, and paler than he had ever seen her.

"Nathan said that it's helpful to have someone we can be honest with, and confess our sins to, but that our confessor didn't have to be a priest or preacher. Mom, I hope you can hear this. Thanks for listening to my confessions these past three months. I hope it hasn't hurt you, and that you're pleased with the direction my life has taken. I am so sorry for all of those years that I brought you such pain."

Jacob looked back to his notes. "It was a good sermon, Mom. Nathan concluded by saying it's important that we clearly identify our sin because God can help us wipe the slate clean when we do. Nate said that it is only when we can humble ourselves and stand spiritually naked before God that we truly receive his full measure of grace."

Jacob closed the Bible and sat in silence for a few moments. Then he rose, kissed her forehead and left the room.

As he walked down the hallway toward the lobby, Jacob was quickly reminded how much he hated the nursing home and that he still felt lousy that his mother had to be there. It was clean and well kept, but it was sterile, bland and gray, not unlike some of the nicer jails where he'd spent time. Becky Riddler was in the Medicaid wing with ten other welfare patients. The staff did their best, but it seemed to Jacob that the home's administrators spent the bulk of their resources on the full-pay patients, and he was sure that they paid closer attention to the concerns of those patients' children and family members. The cost for the full-pay section was nearly four thousand dollars per month. At first Jacob was willing to pay this amount, but he would have used up his entire savings just to have his mother in the nicer part of the home for two to three months. Preacher Nate had advised him against it—there was no guarantee that one of the eleven Medicaid beds would still be open when his savings were depleted. There was also the possibility that his mom might be moved to another home, one not so convenient as the Parkland Nursing Home.

At least he had Shirley, the LPN who was head nurse on the day shift. Shirley was a big, friendly woman who masked her loneliness by smiling at the world. Jacob liked her. She enjoyed and loved her patients—all of them. Shirley was always in a hurry. Her dark curls were always plastered to her damp forehead, and her chubby red cheeks made the rest of her face look very pale. Still, she had a pretty face and a ready and lovely smile.

Jacob heard Andre's shrill voice and Shirley's healthy laugh as he entered the almost empty waiting room off the front lobby. Two patients in wheelchairs, one quite elderly, but another who seemed much younger, were watching the Sunday afternoon matinee on television; at least they were staring at the screen.

"I like your new friend," said Shirley as Jacob approached. Andre sat smiling broadly. "He said his friends used to call him Hotchie, but maybe he would start using his real name again." She smiled at the boy and deliberately pronounced his name, "Andre was telling me all about his morning. Jacob Riddler, you never told me you play the guitar and sing. Andre tells me you've even sold some of your songs. Congratulations."

"Thank you," said Jacob.

"Andre invited me to church."

Jacob looked at his young friend and smiled. "Great idea, Andre."

"It sure sounds different than any church I've ever been to. How come *you* never invited me?" she asked Jacob with a sly smile.

"I don't know, Shirley, I really don't. I should have. Will you come?"

"Yep," said Andre. "She's coming next week."

"No," Shirley corrected. "Week after next, if I can. I only get one Sunday in three off. God and I have never seen eye to eye on a lot of things. I'm even less sure about his son. Between them they seem to have, ah… messed up a lot of things. But, Andre definitely has my curiosity up."

"Like I said, I should've thought of it before. Hey, partner," Jacob playfully punched Andre in the shoulder, "we'd better go if we're going to catch that movie."

"And I have to get back to my buddies over there," said Shirley. "You guys have fun."

Jacob and Andre headed out the door. Shirley watched them leave and mumbled to herself, "I wish I was beautiful or you were damn near blind, fella." She turned and announced to the two patients staring blankly at the television, "I'd follow Jacob Riddler anywhere, even to church."

ANNIVERSARY:

10

DEATH AND NEW LIFE

Early that same evening, just as the sun was going down, Jacob looked across Old Blue's front seat at Andre who was being very quiet. He'd been talking a mile a minute following the movie and through their dinner at the Taco Bell, which was now his favorite place to eat.

Andre is a survivor, thought Jacob. *He'll do what he needs to do to survive, but this kid really* wants *to do the right thing.* As they got closer to his house, Andre subconsciously rubbed his swollen and sore jaw. He had not wanted to talk about it, changing the subject whenever Jacob brought it up. The only time he said anything about it was when they went by Maryann's house to retrieve his bike from her garage. Andre claimed Juwan and Anthony would have never caught him if he'd had his bike that day.

"Stop. Pull over here, right here." The urgency in Andre's voice compelled Jacob to comply without question. He looked over at his young friend for an explanation and was immediately quieted by the intense expression on the young boy's face. Andre was leaning forward and intently staring at something. Jacob followed his gaze. On the left, all the houses were neatly maintained with an abundance of flowers in the front yards and on the porches. Tall trees planted decades ago had created a fresh green canopy over the street. Someone was cutting the grass at one house that appeared to be abandoned. No one sat on the well-kept porches as they had during the first warm Sunday evenings of spring. All the doors had multiple locks and most of the windows had bars of some kind. On the right side of the block, where Andre fixed his gaze, only three houses were left standing. The rest of the lots had been cleared.

Some trees and shrubs remained, but the view across the lots and into the garages, the cluttered backyards and back porches of the homes across the alley were unobstructed.

Andre and Jacob watched what appeared to be an argument going on between a man and a woman at the far end of the block. The man was halfway down the porch steps when he turned and aimed a finger at the woman on the porch. The onlookers could not possibly hear what was being said, but the angry young man was obviously administering his parting shots. The woman's shoulders slumped and she placed her hands over her face. It was obvious that the man's verbal darts were hitting home.

"That's my house, and that's my big brother, " Andre said scornfully, resignation filling his young voice. "Look like God's takin' awhile to answer my prayers. Juice is still on the street creating trouble for everybody. Let's just stay here till he leaves."

Jacob was lost for words. Behind the big house was a large two-story, concrete block garage. A tall chain-link fence framed a nice, roomy back yard. The property showed signs of proud homeownership and care. In the center of the yard was a well-maintained swing set and sandbox.

"You have a nice house, Andre."

"I hate it," the boy blurted out angrily. He turned to face Jacob, then pointed back to the house. "A little ten-year-old girl was killed on that front porch. Mom, Angela and I…we're supposed to be happy that Juice got us that house. That little girl's blood is still on the front porch. No matter how hard I scrub, I can't get it out of the carpet. Man, I hate that house."

Jacob remembered hearing and reading the news stories about the little girl who had been caught in the crossfire of rival North Side gangs. Seeing the house and Andre's repulsion made it more real. It grabbed at his gut.

"So, Juice lives with you and your mom?"

Andre laughed and shook his head. "Angela and I…we tell Mom we'd rather live in the jets, but no, we got to stay here…with that little girl's ghost. Juice got his grip into Momma good. She likes nice things too much." Andre concluded with a sigh, "I hate it, and I hate my brother."

"I'm sorry, Andre. Do you want to stay with me tonight? I have an extra bedroom. Anytime you need a place…."

"Naw, thanks. I better stay with Momma. She needs me tonight. Angela is gone, and we don't know where. No tellin' what Juice has just told her. Look at her."

"Wait here, Andre." Jacob suddenly turned off the ignition and opened his door. "I'm going to have a little talk with your mom and your brother."

Andre jerked toward him and Jacob again saw the fear in his eyes. "No! Don't be messing with him, Jacob. He's..."

"Wait here," Jacob said with authority as he got out of the truck.

LaTisha was sitting on the top step, wearing shorts and a tank top. Her knees were pulled up under her chin, and her arms were wrapped tightly around her long legs. Her running shoes were untied and her socks hung loosely around her ankles. Her cheeks were tear-stained, but she had stopped crying. As he neared the porch it was easy for Jacob to recognize the tell-tale haze she was in. LaTisha greeted Jacob with a warm smile.

LaTisha jumped to her feet, "Hotchie!" she yelled over Jacob's shoulder. "It's all right, baby. You can come home."

Jacob turned in time to see Andre pedaling his bike as fast as he could in the other direction. Jacob and LaTisha both called after him. When Jacob turned back around, LaTisha looked at him pleadingly and then took her seat again on the top step and began to weep. Juice, still smiling, did not move an inch.

• • • • •

A few minutes later Jacob pulled into Maryann's driveway and turned off the ignition. He sat for a minute, mustering the courage to ring the front doorbell. The pleasant surprise on Maryann's face when she opened the door eased his anxiety—a little.

"Jacob! What a nice surprise." She unlatched the screen door and held it open. "Please come in."

"I hate to bother you, Maryann, but has Andre shown up here in the last few minutes?"

"No, no he hasn't. Please sit down." She motioned to the long couch that sat in the middle of the well-furnished living room and then took a seat. "What's wrong?"

Jacob told her of his earlier encounter with Juice and LaTisha.

Maryann leaned back and crossed her long legs, listening intently. Even as he related the story, Jacob was distracted by her beauty. She wore a pair of well-fitting faded jeans and an old Boys & Girls Club T-shirt. Her bare feet rested on the couch directly in front of him. She looked wonderful.

"So, Andre's older brother…is it Juice or J.J.?" she asked.

"He introduced himself as J.J., has J.J. on his license plate, but Andre always refers to him as Juice."

"He was actually nice to you?"

"He was downright charming, Maryann. It almost makes me wonder if Andre is telling the whole truth about him. I tried to talk it over with Andre today, a couple of times, but he kept changing the subject. I believe his fear is very real."

"You know who they rent from, don't you?" asked Maryann.

Jacob shook is head. "No, I don't."

"Cecil and Margaret Andrews."

Jacob looked at her blankly and shook his head again.

"Don't you remember Charles Andrews?" she asked.

"Charles Andrews? Sure, he graduated from Central the year after I did. Black man, very smart. If I remember right."

"Charles' father, Cecil, used to be the finest cabinet maker in this city. Some of the nicest homes in Parkland have kitchen and bathroom cabinets which were custom built by Cecil, including mine. He built that big garage himself. It used to be his shop."

"When I read stories about the shooting, I didn't make the connection that she was their granddaughter," said Jacob.

"Cecil and Margaret loved that place."

"That's obvious, it's beautifully maintained," said Jacob.

"They could have moved from the North Side years ago. Cecil had the money, but was stubborn. He always said that gangbangers and drug dealers weren't going to drive him out of his home or his neighborhood. He was president of the North Side Neighborhood Association." She paused, then added sadly, "But, they moved out right after the shooting. Cecil and Margaret seemed to age overnight—they were absolutely devastated."

"Their granddaughter wasn't Charles' child, was she? It seems to me that she had a different last name." said Jacob.

"Oh no," said Maryann shaking her head. "Charles is an attorney. He's done all of my legal work for years. When he finished law school, Charles had his pick of several prestigious firms that offered him jobs," said Maryann. Jacob sensed a degree of pride in her voice. "Young, good-looking black attorneys were in high demand back then—especially with high-powered firms. Now he's a senior partner with Barrett Helms, one of the largest firms in the state."

"Wow," said Jacob. "That's great. I always liked Charles, and I'm not surprised to hear about his success."

"Remember their youngest daughter? She must be over thirty now. She's working on her Ph.D. somewhere back east, near D.C., I think."

"So, what happened? I mean the shooting and all?" asked Jacob.

"Cecil and Evelyn had a lot of trouble with their middle daughter. She got into drugs, married twice, both of her husbands were losers. She just up and disappeared one day. Cecil and Evelyn took in the three kids, a boy and two girls."

"So they raised their own three and then had to raise three more?"

"They never complained, not once that I ever heard. The oldest child was a handful when they got him because he was already running with the gangs. Charles told me that Cecil thought he and Margaret could save the little girls from the gang lifestyle, and they tried with the boy, but after two or three years, Cecil had to kick him out of the house. He was about sixteen or seventeen years old. They hadn't seen their grandson for weeks when one day he showed up at the house. He rang the doorbell, and the little one, about ten years old, answered the door. She was so happy to see her big brother." Maryann shrugged her shoulders and said with resignation, "It was a drive-by, except that they killed the little girl by mistake. It ripped the heart right out of Cecil and Evelyn." Maryann paused, looked up and was touched by the tears that were welling in Jacob's eyes.

"Oh, God," said Jacob. "What happened to the boy and the other daughter?"

"Charles has the other little girl. She's about thirteen or fourteen now. She's beautiful—looks just like her mother. No one has seen or heard from the big brother since the shooting. Either he is too ashamed to face his family or too afraid of the gangs…or maybe he's dead. Charles is worried about his parents."

Jacob shook his head dejectedly. "Makes me wonder what kind of chance a kid like Andre has."

Maryann got up from the couch, a thought suddenly occurring to her. "Excuse me, Jacob. Mark is upstairs in his room. I'm going to go up and ask him to call Andre's house and see if he has made it home yet."

She returned in a few moments and took her seat in the middle of the couch. There was still distance between them, but Jacob could not help but think how nice it was to just be sitting in her living room so close to her.

As she settled in to the plush couch and crossed her leg toward him, she smiled and said, "Mark called Andre's house. His mother answered. She promised to have Andre call if he shows up and we're supposed to call her if he shows up here."

Jacob nodded then looked around. "Maryann, I'm just amazed at your house. You've done a beautiful job decorating. How long have you lived here?"

"Thank you, Jacob. I love my house. We moved in about fourteen years ago. I didn't have much money the first couple of years, but then my insurance agency took off. Most of the major remodeling was done during the three years that Joe was fighting cancer. Toward the end, it was like he needed to be sure it was all done, before...I...ah, well, I haven't done much since." Maryann sat back, raised her crossed leg, locked both hands around her knee and shook her head, a gentle smile appearing on her face. Jacob was sure she was smiling at her memories, not at him.

"I think the worst arguments Joe and I ever had were about living in Parkland. When my folks died, I wanted to take the little inheritance I received and use it as a down payment on a new house northwest of town." She shook her head. "Joe wouldn't hear of it. He said he'd not only been called to his work at the Club, but to the neighborhood as well."

"Joe loved Parkland, and the Club," Jacob said. "Even when we were in high school. I couldn't believe—still can't—that he turned down several full athletic scholarships at big universities, to take a partial one from the Club so he could work there for little more than minimum wage while he went to school."

Maryann nodded and added, "He took on a full work load at school, got mostly A's and worked forty-plus hours a week at the Club. He was dedicated, driven like no one I've ever known."

"So, obviously, Joe won the argument...about the house and where you would live?"

"Not really. Mark settled the argument for us," she chuckled.

"Mark? I don't understand." Jacob reveled in her smile and the content look on her face.

"We were able to adopt Mark. We'd been trying for years to have another child, but...then our good friend, Mary Dale, the Executive Director of Child Saving Institute, asked us one day if we would like to adopt a racially-mixed baby boy. Two days later, Mark Andrew was ours. He was less than a week old, and that was the end of the argument. The first time I held that baby in my arms, I don't know, there was such a special closeness. I don't believe we could have bonded better if he'd been my own. Parkland is the perfect place to raise a racially-mixed child, and I wouldn't change a thing." She looked around the room and smiled. "I really love this place."

"I'm glad for you, Maryann. You and Joe deserved each other. I remember…the night I split. Joe tried to talk me out of it. He called me a coward, and that hurt—but that's exactly what I was."

• • • • •

Jacob desperately knocked on the apartment door. When he got no response, he knocked harder. He nervously ran his fingers through his shoulder-length hair. He heard movement in the apartment behind him, but nothing in Joe's. Joe had to be home, he never partied. He started to knock again when the door opened.

Joe Bethel stood in the doorway wearing only his gym shorts. He was tall, over six-foot-four and had a lean build. Joe had excelled in all high school athletics and although he and Jacob had graduated three years ago, Joe was still in perfect shape. His collar-length brown hair was sticking out in all directions. There was confusion on his handsome, angular face. His athletic prowess had helped him overcome the adolescent self-conscious shyness brought on in part by the slight hair-lip he now covered with a full mustache. Experience, academic success and his rewarding work at the Club had matured him, and had given him confidence. Not yet twenty-one, Joe was a young man with clear life goals.

"Jacob, what are you…"

Jacob pushed past his friend into the tiny apartment and began to pace between the kitchen table and the rumpled hide-away bed. Joe shut the door and rubbed the sleep out of one eye. He looked over his shoulder at the clock on the wall. "It's five-thirty in the morning, Jacob. What's going on?"

Jacob continued pacing while he mumbled incoherent phrases. Finally, he stopped and looked at the only true friend he'd ever had. "I've got to leave town, Joe. Last night, something terrible happened…I didn't mean it. I was drinking. I don't even remember it, but…."

Joe sat down at the small kitchen table. "What, Jacob? What happened?"

Jacob finally stopped pacing. He tried to form the words, but they wouldn't come. He was too ashamed.

"What?" repeated Joe.

"It doesn't matter." He started pacing again. "You'll find out. I guess. Everybody will. It'll kill my Mom...and Maryann." Jacob reached into his back pocket and pulled out a crumpled envelope. "I need you to give this to Maryann for me." He held out the envelope. "Tell her...I'm sorry. Tell her she's better off without me."

"Wait, wait." Joe waved his hands and refused the envelope. Jacob dropped it on the table. "You're leaving town? Jacob, whatever you did, we can work it out."

"No! I could go to jail, Joe. I'm not going to go to jail, man. Do you hear me? Just give Maryann the note. Okay?"

"No, you owe it to her to look her in the eye and tell her yourself," he said angrily. He picked up the envelope and tossed it toward Jacob's side of the table.

"Listen to me!" Jacob slammed both palms on the table. "I don't love her. We were just kids when we started dating. I make her cry all the time, anyway. Nothing's going right for me and I just lost my scholarship." He tossed the envelope back at Joe.

"What?" said Joe. "You lost your scholarship?"

"Right after the season. I...haven't told anybody, yet."

"Why?"

"I don't know. Coach just doesn't like me, man. I flunked all my spring semester classes and I lost my job. I'm no good for Maryann. She's just eighteen and she deserves to go to college, man, but she wants to get married right away! I'm not ready to settle down, okay? Just give her the note, please."

Joe picked up the note and looked at it. He shook his head. "Jacob, this is the coward's way out and you're not a coward. You need to stay here and face whatever it is. Maryann loves you and I'm sure that she'll stick by you."

Jacob shook his head. "No, no I can't. She deserves someone better...someone more like you. I just can't...."

"Stay, Jacob. I'll help you. The Lord..."

"Don't give me that 'Lord' shit, okay? Not now. I'm in serious trouble, Joe." He headed toward the door. "I gotta go." Jacob moved past Joe who continued to sit and stare at the envelope with Maryann's name scrawled on the front.

"Jacob?"

Jacob paused in the open door, his hand on the knob, their backs to each other. "Yeah?"

"What about your mom?"

"I don't know." He said as he shut the door. "I just don't know."

• • • • •

"Again, Maryann, I'm twenty-two years too late, but I am so sorry."

Maryann smiled and nodded. There was no bitterness in her voice when she said, "You hurt me very badly, Jacob Riddler. You really did and I married Joe Bethel on the rebound."

"Maryann, I don't..."

"It's okay, Jacob. Joe was wonderful, he really was. He was loving and patient. When Ruth was born, he was a wonderful Daddy to her. Talk about a special bond.... It was fabulous. About a year-a-half into my marriage, it hit me—I loved Joseph Bethel with every ounce of my being. I fell on my knees and thanked the good Lord for my husband. I was the luckiest... the..."

She suddenly burst into tears, dropping both elbows to her knees holding her head in her hands. Maryann's entire body wracked with her deep sobs.

Jacob was dumbfounded. *Oh, God. Oh, God, please, help me. What should I do?* He wanted desperately to reach out and take her into his arms, to hold her and comfort her, but he couldn't. Across the room he saw a box of tissue on an end table. He quickly retrieved it and pulled several out as he returned to the couch. He sat down next to her on the couch, their knees almost touching.

"Here," he said meekly, not quite knowing what to do.

She nodded slightly as she took the tissues he offered. Regaining her composure, she slowly sat up, wiping her eyes and blowing her nose. She even laughed a little, a laugh that hinted at her embarrassment for having lost control. Her attention was diverted slightly by the sound of the telephone ringing.

Maryann reached out and took the fresh tissue from Jacob's hand, smiled and nodded. It was a signal to him to just give her a moment to regain her composure.

"Mom?" Mark called from his room, oblivious to his mother's emotional state.

She laughed a little more and called back in a brave but shaky voice, "Yes?"

"Andre just called. He's home, and he says everything's cool."

"Okay, Honey, thank you."

"Maryann, I'm so sorry. I hope I didn't say anything wrong."

She shook her head vigorously, still wiping her eyes. "No, Jacob." She reached out and grabbed his forearm. Her touch felt warm and made him feel good and ashamed at the same time. She held on to him briefly and then let go as she began to talk.

"Jacob, it was nothing you said. I grieved deeply when Joe died, but I'm through it now—so are the kids. We're all getting on with our lives. It's just that I'll never forget him, and I'll be forever grateful for the time we had together." She reached out again and grabbed his arm, as if seeking support from him. "Today is the anniversary…seven years ago today Joe was diagnosed with cancer. He fought a brave fight. Several times we thought he had beat it. But, three years later, exactly to the day, he died. Today is the fourth anniversary of his death."

Jacob's jaw dropped. The blood drained from his face. He stared at her and she shook his arm.

"Jacob? Jacob, what is it? What's wrong?"

As if coming out from under a spell, coming back from somewhere, some dark place, Jacob blinked and looked into her dark eyes. "Seven years ago today, this very day…I was sentenced to prison as a habitual criminal. I thought my life was over. I was wrong. One night in a cold jail cell I discovered that my life—my real life—was just beginning."

SUSPICION

11

On his way home Jacob stopped by Andre's house. LaTisha did not invite him in, saying that Andre was asleep. She acted as if nothing were wrong. Jacob could smell alcohol on her breath and understood her denial. As he drove on home he became increasingly uncomfortable with the growing anger he felt about Andre's situation.

He pulled into the alley and parked behind the garage of Mrs. Carlson's house at the other end of Parkland Boulevard from Maryann's. He lived in an apartment above a large garage that was at one time a carriage house. In fact, when he first returned to Parkland three years ago, Jacob lived with Preacher Nate for several months while he built the apartment above Mrs. Carlson's garage. The deal was that she would provide the materials and one year of free rent if he would provide the labor. At the end of the year, she told Jacob to take the rent money and donate it to Antioch or to the Club instead.

Jacob opened the driver's door, but just sat in Old Blue for a while. He said out loud, "Why do kids have to...kids like Andre...the deck is stacked against him." Suddenly, he banged the steering wheel with his fist. "It's not fair, Lord!" Jacob immediately recoiled at the angry tone he'd just used with God. "At least tell me what to do about it."

Jacob got out and slammed the door. With his head down, he started up the stairs leading to the apartment, subconsciously making a mental note to fix the loose step. He wondered if Mrs. Carlson was still awake, and looking at his watch he discovered that it was only ten o'clock.

Mrs. Carlson and her husband had been a part of the original Parkland Baptist group that had merged with Memorial Baptist nearly twenty years ago. It seemed no pastor was willing to consider a call to Parkland Baptist, a small, mostly white congregation whose membership was declining as more and more folks moved to the western suburbs. Memorial Baptist was a small but vibrant black congregation on the North Side with a zealous and dedicated minister named Dr. Matthew Millard. Dr. Millard was a formidable orator with a powerful voice in the local civil rights movement. Memorial Baptist was burned to the ground, and the late Mr. Carlson headed up a delegation from Parkland Baptist. Their message was simple, but revolutionary. "You good folks have a wonderful pastor and no building. We have a nice building and no pastor. Let's merge into one congregation."

They named the new church Antioch Baptist, but everybody in Parkland simply refers to it as Antioch. It began to grow and to this day is one of the few successfully integrated and diverse congregations in America. When the congregation felt they needed an associate pastor, they asked one of their most faithful members to accept the job—a fiery young Christian who like Jacob had found the Lord late at night in a lonely jail cell, named Nathan Wesley Frye.

Dr. Millard, the refined black scholar, took Nathan, the Kentucky boy, ex-con and alcoholic, and mentored and discipled him for ten years and made a preacher out of him. When Dr. Millard died, the congregation asked Nathan to become its Senior Pastor. In the ten years since, Nathan has been discipling and mentoring young black pastors until they are called to churches of their own. Reverend Jill Thomas was his fourth disciple and the first woman pastor that he trained. Over the years, even before Dr. Millard died, and with his help and encouragement, Nathan had also mentored men just out of prison. Nathan had told several close associates, including Dennis Livingston, that Jacob was the most thoroughly changed individual he had ever known.

Jacob paused halfway up the stairs, turned around and decided to go check on his landlady, music teacher and special friend.

"Ah, don't make me wait any longer."

Startled, Jacob almost tripped again over the loose step. Gathering himself, he looked up at the dark landing and saw Officer

Diaz sitting on the top stair.

"Looks like you've had a bad day, son. Want to tell me about it?"

"As soon as I catch my breath. You scared me to death. Do you make a habit of doing that to people?"

"Well, I don't always mean to, but I do seem to shake people up now and then."

Jacob invited Diaz in. Although he'd seen Diaz around, most recently at yesterday's homicide scene, they had not talked since he'd returned to Parkland. This was another conversation he'd been avoiding.

Officer Diaz looked around the spacious, skimpily furnished apartment. There was one large room with a small, but modern and quite functional kitchen in one corner and two bedrooms and a large bath on the opposite side. Except for a piano that stood in the middle of the big room, a couple of stools, an old desk against one wall and the small kitchen table surrounded by four mismatched chairs, there was no other furniture. A few matted posters and pieces of art hung on the walls. Two guitar cases lay on the hardwood floor next to the piano bench and a couple of music stands stood nearby. There were songbooks and sheet music everywhere.

"This is a huge apartment," said Diaz. "But don't you think a little furniture would be nice?"

"It's only me. I don't get many visitors," said Jacob while pointing to one of the kitchen chairs.

As they each took a seat, Jacob said, "It's been a long time, Officer Diaz. Can I get you something cold to drink?" Jacob leaned back in his chair and opened the refrigerator.

"How 'bout a beer?"

"Sorry, I don't drink anymore. I haven't had a beer in seven years, but I've got Diet Coke and ah...Diet Coke. Sorry, not much choice." Jacob wondered why he was so nervous and why he felt the need to defend himself.

"How 'bout some coffee?" said Diaz with a wry smile. "I mean if you have time, and if it's not too much trouble."

"Sure." Jacob closed the refrigerator, stood up and began to prepare a pot. "Any leads on YoYo's murder?"

"No, nothing." said Diaz. The silence was becoming uncomfortably thick as Jacob finished preparing the coffee. He pushed the button on the coffee pot and took a seat at the table.

"You looked deep in thought out there, maybe even a little perturbed." Diaz had began his probe.

For the second time that evening, Jacob told the story of taking Andre home. After he filled their coffee cups, Jacob told the officer about his follow-up visit and the uneasy conversation he had with LaTisha.

Diaz took a sip of the hot coffee and leaned back in the chair. "So, Riddler, what do you think about this character, Juice?"

Jacob was confused, not by the question but by the look on Diaz' face and the accusatory tone of his voice.

"You and he have words, a falling out?" Diaz added.

"No. Not at all. The guy smiled, stuck his hand out and thanked me for looking out for Andre. He said his mom was worried sick, and that the boy is very troubled right now. He stays out all night, running with the wrong crowd. Juice even thanked me over and over and then gave me his card and a certificate for a free meal for two at his restaurant."

"At McKey's?" asked Diaz.

"Yeah," Jacob dug into his pocket and passed a business card across the table. "He claims to be the assistant manager of McKey's."

"That's what I hear." Diaz stared at the card. "May I keep this?"

"Sure, do you know the place?"

Diaz nodded as he placed the card in his shirt pocket. "Four, five years old. Real trendy. Right on the edge of the Old Market, downtown. They did a nice job of converting it from an old warehouse. The bar is almost as big as the entire restaurant. They mostly cater to the young professional scene. It's a hopping place, especially on Friday and Saturday nights." Diaz raised an eyebrow. "Never been there? It's run by your buddy, Bob Wilson."

Jacob shook his head.

"So, answer my question. What do you think of Juice?"

"He's a smooth-talking slime, a real con-artist. I don't know what they pay him at McKey's, but it's not enough to drive a Lexus SC 300, rent a nice house for his mother...expensive clothes, gold jewelry..." Jacob shook his head then looked up and again, confused by the smirk on Diaz face.

"So, how come you came to see me, Officer Diaz?"

"Came to check you out for myself."

"Check me out?"

"Yep, maybe you're the smooth-talking slime, Riddler."

Diaz looked Jacob in the eye and Jacob realized just what a cocoon his AA meetings, Preacher Nate, Antioch, his job at the radio station, his renovation projects, Mrs. Carlson and his music had provided him. In three years, this was the first time a policeman had been around to see if he was connected to any illegal activity. All of these things had not only filled his time and helped him to stay focused, but they had also kept the police away.

Jacob waited for Diaz to continue. During the long pause, Jacob held Diaz' gaze and half smile with his own serious expression.

"You're not offended?" pried Diaz.

"Offended?"

"That I would suspect that your work at the Club was not as...altruistic as it might appear?"

"My work at the Club?" Jacob considered Diaz' implication, then said, "No. I understand. You have a job to do, and I have a history. I'm not proud of my history, but it makes sense that you'd come to see me. It took you a long time, though. I've been back for three years."

"Well, I got to thinking, maybe you and this Juice are running some kind of a game on us. Maybe you and him have made some kind of deal."

"I don't run schemes and deals anymore."

"Except...," Diaz raised his finger and said with derision, "except with Jesus of course. Did you learn all about Jesus in prison?"

Jacob smiled and leaned over the table. "I learned that I was a bastard—a no-good bastard who always blamed other people for my problems. I learned that we're all bastards, Officer Diaz, but God loves us anyway. You're right, I made a deal—with Jesus. I turned everything in my life over to him and when I got out of prison I came straight home to help my mom, hoping to make up for some of the pain I had caused her. But, I also made a deal with Preacher Nate. I let him oversee my re-entry into society. I'll never be able to repay him for all he's done for me since then."

"I understand you've been spending a lot of time down at the Club?"

"For the past year I've volunteered two evenings a week and some-

times Saturday afternoons. I teach kids to sing and to play the guitar."
"Why?"
"At first, because Preacher Nate told me to. Now I do it because
I enjoy it. Dennis and Ruth tell me I'm good at it. To tell you the
truth, I *need* to do it. It's a small way I can make up for some of the
bad things I've done. But, it's more than that. It's therapeutic. I know
I get more from the kids than they get from me."

"So, is Nathan still running your personal rehab program?"
"He could if he wanted to." Jacob shrugged. "But not so much
anymore."

"Riddler, do you remember me? Do you remember the first time
we met?" Diaz' tone had changed—it was menacing, and his stare
was icy.

"Yes," Jacob replied, but he was caught off guard.

"You must've been about twelve or thirteen?"

"I was ten," Jacob interrupted. His own tone now icy.

Diaz paused, then started in again. "You and your mom got away
with a big one that time, boy. Ten years later, the big phony star
athlete," he taunted. "You got out of town just in time, didn't you?"

Jacob couldn't help it. For the second time this evening, his eyes
welled up and a lonely tear slowly trickled down his cheek. His tone
was now full of sorrow and regret, he asked, "How is Jeannie?"

Now Diaz was thrown off—not only by the tears, but by the
question about his younger sister. He pushed back from the table.
"Riddler, either you're the one in a thousand that has been *re-ha-bil-
i-tated*," the word dripped with derision as it rolled off the old cop's
tongue, "or, you're the smoothest con man I ever met in my life. But,
I want you to know something. As long as you were wrapping your
sorry life in Preacher Nate's religious shit, going to AA meetings and
stuff, I could have cared less. But, now that you're down at the Club
where you could do some serious damage, I'll be watching. I can't
believe Dennis would let you near the place." Diaz shook his head.
"But, *I'll* be watching. Are you really a new man? That's great. But
if you do anything to hurt the Club," Diaz pointed his finger, "or Ruth
Bethel, you won't make it out of town this time."

Again Jacob asked, "So, how is Jeannie?"

Diaz took a deep sigh. "She's dead. She died six years ago."

Jacob was shocked. "How?"

"Heart attack."

"Heart attack? How old was she?"

"Thirty-three," answered Diaz. "She had a rough time. She was wild from the time she turned thirteen, and was too pretty for her own good. From about age seventeen she went downhill, and got heavily into drugs. She supported her habit by prostituting herself."

"I'm sorry...I didn't...."

Diaz shrugged, "One day she decided enough was enough. Preacher Nate..." Diaz smiled and shook his head. "Don't get me wrong, Riddler, I love the man, but sometimes," Diaz pointed to his head, "he gets a little mushy, and thinks he can save everybody." He sighed again. "But he did help Jeannie. She was ready, I guess. Somehow Nathan got her into a treatment program. The last five or six years of her life she was a sober woman. She even worked at the Club as Joe Bethel's secretary. That's why I care about what happens to Ruth. I owe that much to Joe."

"I didn't know all that." Jacob struggled for words. "I...I'm glad...I mean that she found peace...before...."

Diaz nodded and continued, "Jeannie and I became close. For the first time since she was a little kid, I enjoyed my little sister again. Except, she was always trying to drag me to Preacher Nate's church." Diaz smiled at the memory. "I miss her, but I'm grateful for those last six years."

"I'm sorry. I truly am."

"Yeah, me too." Diaz couldn't believe that he'd told Jacob, of all people, about Jeannie. He pointed across the table. "Nathan's had some failures, too, Riddler. You, I'm not so sure about. Like I said—I'll be watching."

JACOB'S TRUST

FRIDAY, MAY 31
AFTER MIDNIGHT

The Friday noon basketball game had been over for a while. Jacob and Nathan were the last ones left in the locker room. They were sitting across from each other talking when Dennis walked in.

"Hey, where were you?" asked Nathan. "We only had nine guys and Jacob's team got the sub. Full court, four-on-four, with no subs is hard on an old guy like me."

"Believe me, fellas, I'd rather have been here," said Dennis as he loosened his tie and took a seat at the end of the bench where Jacob sat. His face lit up as he continued, "But, I was at a meeting where I wrapped up the final funding for our summer program. It looks like the Club will be open from six-thirty in the morning for the Early Bird Program until eleven at night for the teenagers."

"Great," said Jacob.

Nathan reached over slapped his old friend on the shoulder, "That's wonderful, Dennis, congratulations."

"Thanks. Now Ruth and I have to find about three more evening staff by next week." Turning to Jacob, Dennis asked, "How are you doing, Jacob? I hear you have an eager new student."

Jacob laughed. "I've never seen a kid so eager to learn."

"Who?" asked Nathan.

"Andre Fitzgerald. Since he heard me play in church two weeks ago, he's pestered me to death."

"Really? That's great," said Nathan.

As he finished packing his gym bag, Jacob said, "You're not going to believe this. The next day, two weeks ago Monday, he gets out of school, rings Mrs. Carlson's doorbell and asks her if she can teach him to play the piano like she taught me."

Both men's hearty laughter boomed through the locker room.

"Did she say yes?" asked Dennis.

"I'm sure she did," said Nathan.

Jacob smiled and nodded. "Every day he goes there straight from school for an hour before he comes here. Mrs. Carlson says he's picking it up as quick as any student she's ever had. Then he pestered me until I had to let him participate in both of my guitar classes."

"Isn't she wonderful?" Nathan said.

Jacob turned serious. "It's good I've got both of you together. I need to run a couple of things by you, just to be sure it's okay."

Both men turned their attention to Jacob, sensing his concern.

"In the last two weeks, Andre has spent the night at my place about half the time. He's also spent the night at Maryann's with Mark several times. Is that okay? I mean, he comes to my apartment when the Club closes, he practices on my piano for a hour or so, then I have to leave him and go to work. He's unsupervised, you know?"

"It's probably safer than walking home through the North Side. The streets aren't safe for any kid, especially an ex-gang member," said Nathan.

Dennis asked, "Do you let his mother know?"

"When she answers the phone." Jacob's annoyance was obvious as he continued. "I always leave a message, but I think the kid could be gone for two weeks and LaTisha wouldn't even notice."

"She hasn't shown any interest in your program, Nathan?" asked Dennis.

Nathan said sadly, "No, Reverend Thomas has made several attempts, but Juice makes it too easy for her. He pays her rent, buys her food, and keeps her in nice clothes. She hasn't hit bottom yet."

"Some strange psychology, isn't it?" said Dennis. "Here's this guy running gangs and drugs, maybe killing people and still providing for his mother. But, his little brother is not safe in his own mother's house."

Nathan asked, "Has he talked about his situation with either of you?"

"Clams up whenever I try to raise it," said Jacob.

"Me, too. He doesn't have anything good to say, but he's afraid, Nathan. I'm sure Juice has threatened him. Ever since we confronted Juice at McKey's, Andre has quit talking about him and his sister Angela."

"And no one's heard anything from Angela?"

"Not a thing. I talked to Tod yesterday. There's nothing—no sign of her at all," said Dennis.

"Should we do something?" asked Jacob. "Should we tell someone that the kid is living in an unsafe environment?" Jacob looked at both men, who had already begun to shake their heads no.

"There's no one to tell," said Dennis.

"There *should* be someone to tell, but not in this county. It would only make Andre's life worse," said Nathan.

Jacob shrugged, not quite understanding.

"If we alert Child Protective Services, they're likely to do nothing or they might take him out of the home," Dennis began to explain. "If they do that, he'll end up at the county's Youth Development Center. Jail is jail no matter what you call it. He'll be housed there as a status offender, which means he's a 'non-criminal.' Yet, because of his age, he'll be housed with little hoodlums and wannabees, and maybe even with some serious gangbangers. It'll take months to find a group home or a foster placement. More than likely, an overworked case manager will finally get around to visiting LaTisha's nice home and determine that the best place for Andre is at home, and he'll just go back home, ending up a lot worse off just by being in the system."

Jacob felt the anger beginning to rise again. He sensed these good men were also incensed by the frustratingly unfair situation.

Nathan picked up where Dennis had left off. "This country's juvenile justice system is anything *but* just. And the county we live in is one of the worst. At one end of the spectrum, cocky kids get warnings and lectures from tired out judges. It's not necessarily the judges' fault. They have very few options and in this tax-cutting era, even fewer resources."

The preacher was on a roll about something he passionately cared and obviously knew something about. "One kid might get seven warnings, another kid, for the same offense but from a worse family situation, maybe only gets three warnings before being sent to the 'Big' house—the State Reform School in Geneva. At the other end of this dysfunctional spectrum, we are killing flies with sledgehammers by trying more and more kids charged with serious crimes as adults. Supposedly, they receive all of the rights of an adult, including the presumption of innocence."

Dennis interjected, "There's little likelihood that he would be tried by a jury of his peers. Usually these trials are more to satisfy an angry public."

Nathan nodded, "At least, thanks to the Club, sometimes first-time, non-violent criminal offenders are offered an alternative to imprisonment. They can work here doing community service."

"But," said Dennis. "Andre hasn't committed any criminal acts."

"Dennis is right. In this case, he's best not to call anybody. Kids Andre's age just fall through the cracks. They're too old and too big to be cute—they're often angry and unappealing. People find it hard to believe they've been abused, and most of the time, they'll be treated as criminals even if they've done nothing wrong."

"Yeah, but what do we do? It's just not fair." Jacob was exasperated.

Nathan said, "There's not much we can do about the fairness of the situation, Jacob. Andre isn't the only one. There are millions of kids in similar, even worse situations all around this country."

"That's why we're here, Jacob…to fill the gaps in the lives of kids like Andre," said Dennis. "He's pretty resourceful. In addition to you, he's found a friend in Mark Bethel, and Maryann lets him stay with her a few nights a week. It sounds as though Mrs. Carlson has taken him under her wing. That's pretty typical of good street kids like Andre. Sometimes, with kids his age, we're better off letting the community help rather than getting them tangled up in the system."

"Believe me, Jacob," said Nathan, "between Mark, you, Maryann and the Club, Andre has a much better chance of surviving his situation than he would getting sucked up into this county's bureaucratic mess. Either way, the next three to four years will be precarious for him. If we can get him through them without serious damage, he'll be okay. On the surface, the odds are stacked against him. That's where the Club, and it looks like you, come in. He's latched on to you like a lifeline."

Jacob said thoughtfully, "I hope you're right. I'll certainly try. Nathan, do you think it's okay for him stay at my house, with me being an ex-con and all?"

"I think so," said Nathan. "You might mention it to your parole officer. Tell Sam you've talked to me about it. He can give me a call if he's concerned, but I doubt he will be."

"Who's going to complain?—Juice?" said Dennis in disgust.

"But, when I'm at work at the station, Andre's all alone in my apartment."

"He feels secure there, Jacob. It's probably the soundest sleep he gets all week. He gets himself up and gets to school on time?"

"Yeah, he gets up in time to go home, shower and change before school, and he's usually gone by the time I get home. He always leaves me a thank-you note, too."

"That way he can check on his sleeping mom without having to be there the night before to watch her drink herself to sleep," said Nathan.

Dennis moved to the locker room door and before leaving said, "Jacob, you're doing the right thing. And, I want you to know your guitar and singing classes are just great. I appreciate all the time you're volunteering."

Nathan and Jacob finished gathering their towels, zipped up their gym bags and left the locker room together. In the lobby of the Club they found Ruth and Detective Diaz engaged in small talk. Ruth beamed when she saw them, a contrast to Diaz' serious demeanor.

"Jacob, guess what? They found my old car," said Ruth.

"Really, where?"

"In Lebanon, Missouri. Wherever that is."

"It's a little town just northeast of Springfield," said Nathan. "On Interstate 44."

Diaz said, "How the hell did you know that, Nathan?'"

Ignoring the question, Nathan asked, "Did you catch the thief?"

"Nope. I figure whoever it was just drove it till it ran out of gas," said Diaz. "According to the locals no damage was done to it." Diaz switched his gaze to Jacob. "Riddler, Ruth told me that you had a box of new tools stolen from your truck?"

"That's right."

"The kid that was killed a couple of weeks ago, a kid called YoYo? He had a pawn ticket in his pocket. It was for a box of tools." Ignoring the questions and the shock on Jacob's face, Diaz said matter-of-factly, "Call me at the station later this afternoon and I'll arrange for a time when you can go down to see if they're yours."

"Thanks, I appreciate it."

"Nathan," said Diaz. "I need to talk with you and Dennis for a minute." Without waiting for an answer he turned on his heel and walked toward Dennis' office.

Before following the crusty old detective, Nathan smiled and shrugged at Jacob and Ruth. "See you tonight Jacob. Have a great day, Ruth." Dennis was waiting for them and offered chairs across form his desk.

"Tod, what have you learned about Juice Johnson? Did you talk to Bob

Wilson?" asked Dennis.

"You guys may be right about him, but I haven't been able to find out anything. I even tailed him a couple of times after he got off work. He went straight home and stayed there. If the guy is running a street gang, he's discreet about it."

"What did Bob say?" asked Nathan.

"He admitted the guy came from a tough background, but Wilson claims J.J. is one of the ones who 'overcame his environment.' They met in D.C. when Wilson was in Congress taking part in an investigation into drugs and street violence. He says J.J. is smart and has worked hard to build a better life for himself and his family. He was working in a similar job at a D.C. restaurant when Wilson offered him the opportunity to come here."

"Did you ask him if he pays the guy enough to live the way he does?"

Diaz shrugged, "Wilson says a couple of years ago, while they were still in D.C., he taught J.J. how to invest and play the market. He even lent him money for a couple of hot stocks that paid off. I don't like Wilson, but he told me that he frequently gives people like J.J. a chance to work and turn their lives around. He said J.J. has even hired a couple of ex-gang members to work at McKey's. Wilson appears to be proud of the guy."

"Have you talked to Juice?" asked Nathan.

"Sure, he's pretty smooth. He said he was concerned about his little brother running with the gangs, and that he's glad that the kid spends time down here at the Club. He asked if I could help him locate his sister. Can't believe she ran away just a few weeks before graduation." Diaz continued with a crooked grin. "J.J. says he probably came down on Hotchie too hard." Diaz said with mock concern, "But it was only 'because he was so worried about him.'"

"And you believe that?" asked Nathan.

"Andre told me the same thing—that since he found the Club and the guitar class, there was nothing to worry about—everything was cool. He also asked if I knew anything about his sister, Angela."

"You're right, Dennis," said Nathan. "Juice has gotten to the boy. He's really scared."

"Keep an eye on J.J. or Juice, or whoever he is, Tod," said Dennis. "I'm telling you, he's into some bad stuff. He's smooth, but..."

"I told Wilson the two of you were concerned about his choice of managers."

"What did he say?" asked Nathan.

The old cop's eyes glinted with mischief. "Wilson laughed and said to tell you that J.J. has worked out better than some of the people you've sent him over the years. He said his two most promising workers right now were Juice Johnson and Jacob Riddler."

Nathan shook his head in disbelief. "Well, Bob's right about Jacob, but *we're* right about Juice. Keep an eye on him, Tod. He's bad, real bad."

"Okay, but are you two sure you know what you're doing letting Jacob Riddler spend so much time here at the Club? It's one thing to take a chance on somebody at a restaurant or the graveyard shift at a small time radio station, but here? With all these kids around?"

Nathan and Dennis looked at each other, then Dennis said, "Ruth tells me he's one of our best volunteers. I've heard the kids he's working with perform, and they're good. Plus, some of our toughest kids are in his groups. He is reaching them with his guitars and music. It's good for both Jacob and the kids."

"I agree," said Nathan. "He's been home for three years now. There's been nothing...."

"This Club is more important than your rescue efforts, Nathan," Diaz shot back.

Nathan was stunned by the angry jab and was unsure how to respond. Dennis said, "Tod, there's no need to use that tone with Nathan. He knows how important this Club is to the community, maybe more than anyone."

"I know that," said the old detective in a slightly conciliatory tone, "but surely you don't need volunteers badly enough to use an ex-con like Riddler."

"Jacob's not the only volunteer from Antioch, Tod. There must be a half dozen or more people from Antioch volunteering here—as tutors, PC instructors, group leaders, coaches, mentors, all kinds of things."

"I know that, but...."

"Tod, you're right about one thing. Jacob Riddler might need these kids more than they need him."

"No, no," Dennis interrupted Nathan, shaking his head. "That was true in the beginning, but not now. Riddler is good, especially with the tough kids who have had some gang association. Listen, I'm confident that Jacob's okay. He's fine."

"Me too, Tod. I'd bet my life on it," said Nathan.

"Would you bet the life of one or two of these kids?"

"What are you getting at?" asked Dennis. "Do you know something I ought to know?"

"I know a lot. He wasn't the All-American athlete everybody thought he was growing up around here." Diaz paused, then continued, "Look, I hope you guys are right. Riddler seems clean since he has come home. I stopped by to see him a week or so ago, and he seemed sincere, but he was into some bad stuff before. I made some calls to Miami PD. He was suspected of a lot more than he was convicted of."

"Most criminals are," said Nathan. "Listen, Tod, over the years we've had seven or eight people come to us from prison. Some struggle for awhile, and some just don't make it. Jacob, for whatever reason, is the most thoroughly changed man I've ever worked with. I'm convinced that his conversion was real. The guy who went to prison, the guy you knew twenty years ago, he's as good as dead and buried. Jacob Riddler is a new man."

"Are you sure?"

"As sure as there's a God in heaven," said Nathan.

Dennis laughed. "I'm probably less sure that there's a God or even a place called heaven." Looking at the old cop he said, "Tod, I'm in the business of turning lives around. I think Jacob has done that. He's more than okay, he's become a good role model for the kids. My staff thinks he's okay. But, I'll keep an eye on it, and I'll pay close attention."

"Speaking of God in heaven," Nathan said with a sly smile. The other men rolled their eyes and both looked at him. "If you ever heard him sing some of his worship songs, you'd know he's for real. This Sunday in church Jacob will be singing a new song he wrote. Mrs. Carlson says it's his best ever and the boy has written some good ones." Nathan paused and made eye contact with both men. His eyes extended the invitation before he said anything.

"Why don't you come hear it for yourself?"

• • • • •

Juice loved late Friday evening crowds. The peripheral players, those who took their responsibilities too seriously, had gone home by now. A hipper set had joined those who remained from the after-work crowd. McKey's bar was hopping with those intent on having a good time. The single folks and the almost single again crowd, mingled and mixed and slyly assessed each other. The alcohol flowed freely, but the powder could also be had and Juice was always vigilant. This crowd was full of opportunity and the police paid less attention to this phase of trafficking.

Juice's cell phone buzzed against his hip. He quickly stepped into his office so that he could hear, not bothering to switch on the light.

"This is J.J., can I help you?"

"Good evening, J.J. How's business?"

"Hi, Mr. Wilson, business is great. Both the bar and the restaurant are hopping. You coming over later? I'll make sure things are set up for you if you are."

"I'm afraid not, J.J. I'm at the airport catching the last flight out to D.C. By the way, what happened to that little blond girl? Nadine I think is her name."

"She disappeared on us, Mr. Wilson. Probably went back to Dallas, not sure. We tried to help her, but the lure of the street was pretty strong. Thanks for taking a chance on her."

"No problem. Too bad, she was a nice, sweet girl. I liked her, a lot."

"I've already found a replacement for her, Mr. Wilson. You'll like her, too. She's working tonight."

"Really? You work fast, J.J., and I like that. Does the new girl understand our expectations, J.J.?"

"Absolutely, Mr. Wilson, Absolutely."

"Wonderful, I'll be home Monday or Tuesday. See you when I get back, J.J."

Juice flipped his tiny phone closed and returned it to the holder on his belt. He went back to the bar in a light-hearted mood. He spied the woman sitting on a stool at the other end of the bar and quickly navigated his way through the crowd. There was not an empty stool to be had as he wedged his way in to stand next to her. He said nothing, waiting for her to sense his presence. He subtly leaned against her shoulder. Even through the smoke and the jockeying mass of warm bodies he was aroused by her smell.

She looked straight ahead and addressed him. "Mr. Johnson, business is good on all fronts, I assume?"

"Very good. Will your husband be joining you, Jez?"

Unfazed by his sarcasm, she responded coolly, "Depends, probably not."

"So, Jez, alone on a Friday night, again?"

She turned and looked at him for the first time. "Only if I choose to be."

Juice backed off slightly, creating just enough room for him to slowly undress her with his gaze. Her curled lip told him she didn't mind. Her green eyes were harder to read. He was suddenly uncomfortable.

"What's it been, two weeks?" he said. "Too bad I have to take care of business tonight,"

"Of course, it's the weekend and you're only halfway through your business day when this place closes. I understand, Juice darling." She continued to stare, unflinching in her utter coldness.

Juice smiled with satisfaction and looked over the pulsating crowd. He whispered in her ear, "When we close here, even a few of these folks will get in their nice cars and drive to one of my corners on the North Side."

He looked to her for response and saw her smirk deepen. She seemed to enjoy the uneasy silence between them. Finally, she let him off the hook. Without bothering to whisper, she said, "My sources tell me it was one of your kids that got his throat slit a couple of weeks ago."

Juice jerked his head around, hoping no one heard the comment, and gave her a warning look.

She was unfazed. Still smirking she said, "I also hear that Preacher Nate and Dennis Livingston have stolen another member of your little family— snatched him right out from under your nose and slapped him on a bus to recovery land."

His stomach churned and he felt his pants pockets for the package of antacids. He'd left them on his desk. "Plenty of kids, there are always plenty of kids available," he said with more confidence than he felt and looked over the crowd again.

"I have some very interesting intelligence—if you're man enough to do something with it," she taunted.

"What's that, Jez?"

"Guess who's been jogging around Parkland every morning the last two weeks, from eight to about nine, every day but Sunday?"

"Who, Jez?"

"Nathan Wesley Frye's disciple and Hotchie's adopted big brother, Jacob Riddler and Dennis Livingston's cute little protégé, Miss Ruth Bethel. Together, running, every morning."

"Saturdays, too?" he asked.

"That's right," she cooed.

WHEN
13 SPARROWS FALL

SUNDAY MORNING, JUNE 2ND

The worship service was just winding down when Maryann entered the double doors at the back of the sanctuary. In the last year she had finally been able to enjoy attending church again. At first, she only came because the children wanted her to join them. Ruth and Mark seemed to understand both her anger toward God and her need to be in church. She found Nathan Frye's preaching to be a wonderful balance between comfort and challenge. Even though Maryann was fifteen years older, she and Reverend Jill Thomas had developed a comfortable friendship. Today was the first Sunday of the month, Communion Sunday, which she especially enjoyed at Antioch.

She found Ruth near the back of the sanctuary where she usually sat. Mark was up front with Andre again. As she worked her way down the aisle to sit next to Ruth, the younger woman smiled and whispered, "Just in time. Jacob is singing again this morning."

As the rest of the praise band set down their instruments and returned to their seats, Jacob, as he had two weeks ago, pulled a stool to the front and adjusted the microphones. He looked out over the congregation till he found and made eye contact with Ruth. She smiled in expectation.

"A couple of weeks ago, early on a Saturday morning, Ruth and I were out jogging and we came across a crime scene just as the ambulance was pulling away. A sixteen-year-old gang member named Stephon Taylor had been brutally murdered. I haven't been able to get it out of my mind. I find myself angry and asking God why these chil-

111

dren have to die."

Jacob looked over the row of kids from the neighborhood who sat with him every week. Andre squirmed nervously in his seat. "I'm also bothered by all of the children I know who live in dangerous, unhealthy situations. In another lifetime, I used to be one of the people who helped to make life unhealthy and dangerous for children. Anyway, I came across something Jesus said. It's found in the tenth chapter of the book of Matthew. I like Matthew, because like me, he was a person who preyed on innocent people, but Jesus called him and gave him a purpose in life. Matthew found forgiveness and then tried to pay back for the wrongs he had done. As I read this passage and began to put some of the words to music, I'm not sure why, exactly, but I found that it helped. I was less afraid. I was more at peace about the children."

Jacob looked down at the guitar and quickly re-tuned it. He looked up again. "I wasn't sure what to call this, maybe, *Be Not Afraid*; or, *More than Many Sparrows*. I thought about, *What You Hear in the Dark*, but I decided to call it *When Sparrows Fall*. Anyway, here it is."

Jacob played a lively introduction on his guitar. It was an upbeat tune with a touch of rhythm and blues. And then he began to sing, his words clear, crisp and full of feeling.

What I tell you in the Dark
You must speak of in the daylight.
What is whispered in your ear,
Proclaim from the rooftop.

Be not afraid.
There is nothing concealed,
That will not be disclosed.
All things that are hidden,
Will be made known.

Be not afraid,
Of those who kill the body,
But cannot take the soul.
Not one sparrow falls
That I do not know.

Be not afraid.
You are my beloved children,
I am your Heavenly Father.
You are worth more to me
Than many sparrows.

What I tell you in the Dark
You must speak of in the daylight.
What is whispered in your ear,
Proclaim from the rooftop.

The congregation broke into applause. Jacob enjoyed the applause, but it also made him uncomfortable. He self-consciously nodded, set his guitar down and returned to the pew where his proud young friends waited. Andre whispered loudly, "Awesome, man, awesome."

The Reverend Jill Thomas walked to the front of the church as she applauded. She said nothing, but the way she smiled at Jacob demonstrated her appreciation for his song and its meaning. As the congregation's applause subsided, Andre leaned toward his friend Mark and whispered for the third Sunday in a row, "That's the prettiest woman, black or white, I ever seen, man." Mark simply smiled and nodded. "I'm serious, man," added Andre.

"It is now time for the family of God to share its joys, its sorrows, its praise, and its requests with the loving Father of us all," she began. During the short pause that followed, Jill seemed to make eye contact with each one gathered there. Her smile was genuine and reassuring. "Let us bow our heads and as is our custom, speak directly to God, as you would to your best friend. In the presence of these, your family, tell him what is on your heart." As the prayers began, Nathan knelt in front of his chair on the stage.

A heavyset black woman, with two young teenagers and a toddler next to her on the bench stood and began, "Lord, yesterday I spent all my food stamps. I planned real good too, Lord. This mornin' the fridge broke. Lord, if it don't start workin' before the end of the day all that meat's gonna spoil, Lord. Please, help that old refrigerator kick in again."

Jill began the response, "Lord, in your mercy," and the entire congregation joined in with, "Hear our prayer."

A well-dressed man sitting toward the back with his wife, both in their mid-sixties, stood next. "Dear Heavenly Father, my wife and I are grateful that in our basement is a perfectly good refrigerator that we're happy to give to our sister in danger of losing her food," he said.

Jill said, "Lord, with thanksgiving," the people said, "Hear our prayer." And a few more added, "Thank you, Jesus."

Next a shy white man stood, his long hair pulled into a neat ponytail. He wore clean, but tattered work clothes. Two small children accompanied him. With difficulty he stammered, "Lord, ah, this my first time speaking to you, but…I don't even know for sure what made me come this morning—the children, I guess. But, Lord. I got my truck outside. I was thinking, if I can get some help right after we get done here, we can get that refrigerator moved so this lady and her children don't lose any of that food, Lord."

"I'll help you, brother," shouted one, followed by half a dozen others. Their offers to help were mixed with more praises.

With rising enthusiasm, Jill began, "Lord, O Lord!" She got everyone's attention and paused. The continued praises fell to a beautiful chorus of whispers, "With great praise and much thanksgiving for the love of your people."

"Lord, hear our prayer," the people shouted while the woman with the thawing freezer wept.

For the next ten minutes, people rose with more routine requests and praises, for sickness and healing, for lost and new jobs, for safe travel, for those graduating from high school and college, for a lost family member and for a variety of lost, damaged, or blooming relationships. Just as it seemed the prayer time was coming to an end, a high-pitched voice trying to sound grown up arose from between Jacob and Mark.

"Lord!" If anyone had fallen asleep, Andre Fitzgerald's nervous, almost screamed greeting to the heavenly throne surely woke them up. A little softer he continued, "It's me, Andre. I want to pray against my brother, Juice. He's bad, Lord, real bad. He sells drugs to kids and all. He kills people. He threatened to kill me if I talk, Lord. But, like Jacob's song said, I'm not going to be afraid anymore. Plus these people, my friends, they won't say nothing. And, Lord, be with my sister, Angela, wherever she is, if Juice don't have her. Why you let Juice hang around, Lord? Plus, Lord, and this is real bad, he got my momma in some kind a spell, Lord. We all be better off if he was dead, Lord. But, at least get his sorry ass thrown in jail. That's all I guess. Oh, thank you for letting my friend Mark bring me to this place, Lord. I like it here. That's all, Lord…for sure. Bye."

"O, Lord, in your mercy."

"Hear our prayer."

• • • • •

It was a beautiful afternoon that first Sunday in June. After church, Antioch's congregates stood around in the front yard as cars passed on the avenue between the church and the Club. They talked, laughed, shook hands, and hugged each other longer than they usually did. Planned and impromptu gatherings were underway, restaurants were decided upon. Finally, the yard, brilliant green with the fresh grass of summer, began to clear of people.

It took Diaz a while to make his way back to Nathan. While Diaz waited his turn, the pastor spent time with all who stopped, several people he knew made their way over to offer a genuine welcome and exchange small talk. Complete strangers went out of their way to introduce themselves and make him feel welcome. Diaz was impressed with the congregation's racial diversity and what seemed to be their genuine love for one another. He had heard about Antioch for years. Nathan's challenge to come and hear Jacob's song had given him the excuse, the rationale he needed to attend the worship service. When he finally made it to the back of the church, Diaz sincerely shared his positive impressions with his old friend. Nathan asked him to wait a minute, he wanted to personally introduce Diaz to the young Reverend Jill Thomas. That took some time because she also drew a crowd following every service. Diaz now made his way out the double doors. From the top of the steps he saw that Jacob was one of the dwindling flock still on the front lawn talking. He was surrounded by a group of young teenagers and a heavyset, but pretty woman in a nurse's uniform.

Jacob felt like he'd shaken hands with every person in attendance that morning. He was overwhelmed with love and acceptance, and was genuinely humbled that his song had touched so many. He was surprised when he saw Diaz making his way over to him just as he was introducing Shirley to Maryann.

"Nice to meet you, Maryann," said Shirley, sticking out her hand. "I know your daughter, Ruth. She comes frequently to visit Becky, Jacob's mom. Ruth is a wonderful young woman."

"Thank you," Maryann replied warmly. "I agree, Ruth is very special and she says you do a wonderful job, that you really care about your patients. It's a pleasure meeting you, Shirley."

Turning back to Jacob, Maryann said as she dug in her purse for keys, "I've got to run. Mark and Andre went with Ruth. We'll throw the hot dogs and hamburgers on as soon as you get there." Her smile broadened and she turned back to the nurse. "Shirley? Would you like to join us?"

Surprised, but pleased, Shirley stammered, "Oh, no. No," she pointed to her uniform and looked at her watch. "I have to work today and I have just enough time to grab a hamburger and get to work. But, thanks."

"Okay, another time." Maryann turned a different smile on Jacob. "See you soon." They nodded and she turned to leave. "It was a pleasure meeting you, Shirley."

Shirley liked her. What was not to like about Maryann Bethel? She was a strong, self-assured woman. She'd done a great job with Ruth. She was more beautiful than a woman had a right to be. Shirley also knew that something was brewing between Jacob and Maryann. Even as she continued to chat with Jacob, Shirley knew that any chance she harbored for him was not possible. Their chitchat was interrupted by Diaz, who Shirley thought was a shorter, older version of one of her favorite actors, Edward James Olmos. *Even his voice is similar,* she thought as Diaz stuck out his hand to Jacob.

"Nice song, Jacob."

"Officer Diaz, you were here? I didn't see you."

After a pause, and without letting go, Diaz said, "I think maybe you are for real, son." The tough old cop squeezed Jacob's hand even harder.

A stunned Jacob said, "Thank you, sir. That means a lot. I can't tell you how much it means to me for you to say that. Thank you."

Still not letting go, Diaz looked Jacob in the eye and squeezed his hand harder yet. A few seconds of intense eye contact quickly became an awkward pause. Diaz said, not in a menacing, but in a matter of fact way, "If this is the greatest con of your life, though, I'll personally kick your ass all the way back to Miami or straight into any penitentiary between here and there."

"I understand, sir, but I meant every word I sang in there. I may screw up again someday, but...I *want* to live the rest of my life serving God. I mean that."

"I think you do mean it. I think you are for real this time. I hope so. I need a good success story right now," said Diaz with a crooked, but friendly grin, as he finally let go of Jacob's hand.

Jacob thanked Diaz again and said good-bye to Shirley.

Shirley, who had heard the whole exchange, said to Diaz, "Hi, my name is Shirley Mason. You sound like a cynical old cop." She smiled and stuck out her hand.

"Oh, but that I am, Miss, I am indeed." To Shirley it sounded like a line out of a classy movie.

"Well, don't worry, officer. Jacob's for real."

"What makes you say that? I want to believe him. I think he believes it himself. I've just seen too many men like him."

"Come on," said Shirley. As she crooked her arm, "You can buy me a burger, fries, and milkshake and I'll tell you all I know about Jacob Riddler."

"You're on. I love fast food."

He took Shirley by the elbow and directed her toward his unmarked, beat-up old police car. Only Diaz observed what no one else had, a silver gray Lexus SC 300 sitting in the shade of a tree on a side street, its lone occupant slumped behind the wheel.

Juice had viewed the churchyard goodbyes and was unaware he'd been made. Even as he fought the nausea that continued to haunt him, he chuckled as he watched the old brown cop and the chubby white nurse walk away arm-in-arm.

Juice's head bounced a little with the Sunday morning Jazz show that played on his radio, *My, my, the preacher do have a big family. We just gonna have to plan a big weekend for the family.*

PICKED UP

14

FRIDAY, JUNE 14

Now when the attendant of the man of God had risen early and gone out, behold an army with horses and chariots was circling the city. And his servant said to him, "Alas, my master! What shall we do?" So he answered, "Do not fear, for those who are with us are more than those who are with them." Then Elisha prayed and said, "O Lord, I pray, open his eyes that he may see." And the Lord opened the servant's eyes, and he saw, and behold, the mountain was full of horses and chariots of fire all around Elisha.

—II KINGS 6:15-17

"Quite a story, Mom," said Jacob as he closed the big tattered old Bible he read from every morning. "I wish I could see something like that. You think God still protects his people like that? With an army we can't see?"

It had been an exhilarating two weeks, beginning with the overwhelming support he had received from the people at Antioch to his song, *When Sparrows Fall.* The cookout afterwards at Maryann's had been the first of four meals he'd had at her house over the last two weeks. He loved running every morning with Ruth. A week ago the summer program at the Club had begun. They were still short of trained staff so Jacob had volunteered every night. Every evening the place had been packed with teenagers until the eleven o'clock closing, just in time for Jacob to get down to the radio station. Ruth did a marvelous job of

119

planning and coordinating. The Club was buzzing with activity and excitement in every area. Jacob loved it. Every morning Jacob shared every exhilarating detail with his mom.

He laughed. "To tell you the truth, Mom, I'm bushed. I'm so glad this is Friday. Ruth and I don't run on Fridays since I play basketball at noon, so, I'll get a little nap this morning. But, as soon as our game is over, I'm going to go home and sleep until time for my AA meeting tonight. I'll get caught up on some sleep over the weekend. But, what a great week. I'm so proud of Ruth and the staff at the Club."

• • • • •

On nice mornings, Nathan rode his bike the six blocks from his little home in Parkland to his office at Antioch. As he dismounted from his bike he saw officer Diaz making his way across Parkland Avenue from the Club.

"You're up and about awfully early," Nathan greeted the old cop as he held the back door to the church open. "Come on in and I'll put on a pot of coffee."

Diaz motioned back toward the Club. "We both beat Dennis. He's not in yet, but Ruth is there and the place is already full of kids."

"They've had a great first week of summer," said Nathan. "It's been a wonderful week."

Nathan turned on the lights and the two men made their way down the hallway to the church kitchen where they made small talk as he prepared the coffee. As they took seats around a folding table Diaz said, "I've been trying to find out more about this Juice character."

"What have you found out?"

"Not much, really. I suspect somebody's selling a lot of cocaine through the bar at McKey's while unsuspecting good citizens are having dinner in the restaurant, but it's out of my jurisdiction. I did pass it on. Something else going on there, but I can't put my finger on it."

"What do you mean?"

"Not sure," said Diaz gently. "Juice is the assistant manager. The manager is a guy named Gerald Hampton. I get the feeling Hampton only tolerates Juice, that Juice is not pulling his weight."

"I'm not surprised by that," said Nathan. "Why doesn't he fire him?"

"He wouldn't say much, I just got the feeling he didn't have the authority to make Juice do anything, much less fire him. Remember that kid, YoYo?"

"Sure, Stephon Taylor, he was killed about a month ago. I went to his funeral. His aunt attends church here."

Diaz nodded. "I was finally able to find a cop in D.C. that remembered Juice."

"Does he have a record there?"

Diaz shrugged again. "Not much, but they suspected he was part of one of the gangs. Couldn't prove anything. Just like here, Juice seemed to be legitimate. He used his charm as a waiter at an upscale restaurant frequented by Washington power brokers."

"That's probably where he met Bob Wilson."

Diaz nodded, "Wilson is pretty up front about that. That's where they met. J.J. was a likable kid who was trying to overcome life on the streets, Wilson wanted to give him a break, that kind of story." Diaz raised an eyebrow. "But, it seems this gang Juice was suspected to be a part of had an interesting signature."

"A signature?" asked Nathan.

Diaz nodded. "When they really wanted to make their point, they didn't resort to a typical drive-by shooting to kill someone."

"Let me guess," said Nathan. "They slit people's throats, instead."

"That's not all. They also cut off a little finger."

• • • • •

Following the Friday noon basketball game, Jacob stopped by the grocery store on his way home. He parked Old Blue next to the old carriage house and was looking forward to the long nap he had promised himself.

"Jacob!"

Mrs. Carlson waved as she came out the door of the screened-in-porch on the back of her house. Jacob gathered up the grocery bags from the front seat, slamming the door with his foot. Concern lined Mrs. Carlson's face.

"Maryann has called you twice. I guess she just missed you at the Club. She is frantic to talk to you."

"Really? Why? What's wrong?"

"I'm not sure. Something about Mark and Andre being in trouble. Come in. Come in. Use my phone," she said opening the screen door.

"Here." He sat his bags on a table. "Let me leave these here and I'll just run over there. If you would, call her and tell her that I'm on my way."

He turned and trotted back to Old Blue. When Jacob pulled around to the back of Maryann's house, he found her sitting in her Sebring, engine running, top down and door opened, waiting for him. He slid in the passenger seat and shut the door. Maryann was on her cell phone and without acknowledging him began to back out of the driveway.

"Look," she said into the phone with authority, "Just tell Officer Diaz that Mrs. Bethel and Mr. Riddler are on their way to the station and Mrs. Bethel would appreciate it if he would meet her there.... Never mind! That's all he needs to know. Will you please? Thank you."

Maryann returned the phone to its cradle and headed for downtown.

"What's up? Where are we going?" asked Jacob.

"To the police station." Maryann said with an exasperation Jacob had never seen before.

"Why? What..."

"Mark and Andre have been picked up by the police."

"Picked up? What for?" asked Jacob.

"For breaking windows and spraying graffiti at Parkland Junior High School."

She was angry and Jacob couldn't help it, but it hit him again how beautiful she was. She was wearing a gray business skirt. It rose more than halfway up her thighs as she frantically alternated between the accelerator and the brake. After only a couple of weeks of sun she needed no stockings. Her tan, smooth legs blended well with the leather seats. She had left the matching suit jacket at home and her ivory silk blouse beautifully accented her flushed cheeks. Perspiration pasted a little curl of her dark hair to her forehead.

"Do you believe it?" she said, banging her clinched fist on top of the steering wheel. "Wait until I get my hands on those kids." She turned to Jacob.

"Thanks, Jacob. Dennis is out of the office. Ruth is a hundred miles away on a field trip. I can't reach Diaz and I don't trust myself to do this by myself. I can't believe those kids would..."

"Maryann..."

"I mean, what were they doing over there anyway? Mark is supposed to be at the Club. What would possess...?"

"Maryann," Jacob said a little louder.

She stopped and glanced at him.

"I think," he said carefully, "it would be wise not to jump to any kind of conclusions. I think you need to hear them out first. It doesn't sound like something that Mark…"

"I know!" She was agitated. "Ruth has told him how important it is that he be a good influence on Andre. Now, it looks like just the opposite has happened, that Andre…"

"Maryann," Jacob interrupted again. "It doesn't sounds like Andre, either. Don't jump on them until we hear them out."

"Well, why would the police…"

"The police make mistakes, too. Let's just hear them out. What did they say?"

"I didn't get to talk to them. I just got a call," she checked her watch, "a little less than an hour ago. They said that my son was at the station. They said Mark and Andre and, I guess, three or four other kids were involved. They said I would have to come down and get him. I tried to call…what's her name? LaTisha Johnson, but as usual, no answer."

"Okay. Calm down. This isn't the beginning of a life of crime. Believe me, I ought to know." He playfully mock-punched her on the arm. She looked at him. He smiled and she smiled back.

"Thanks again, Jacob. I know myself well enough to know that I do not handle this kind of thing well. Thanks."

● ● ● ● ●

As they walked up the long slanting sidewalk in front of the Police Station at 15th and Leavenworth, two women were walking out with two young teenagers whom Jacob recognized from the Club. Each boy wore a sports T-shirt and baggy, khaki shorts that were so big on them that the crotch hung nearly to their knees. Their pants were cinched up with silver-tipped belts that were also too big, the overlap hanging down their legs. Each boy had two or three gold chains around his neck, wore expensive jogging shoes and had key chains that swung from their belt loops to their pockets to complete the uniforms that indicated their gang status or, at least, that they were wannabees.

One boy walked defiantly in front of the two women and the other boy. He moved with the familiar street gait by rocking up on the right toe with each step while slightly swaying his shoulders. He wore his base-ball cap backwards. His mother looked as though she had given up. The other woman was in the midst of a verbal assault on the other boy, who was not nearly so cocky as his partner was. As they got closer it was obvious from her lecture that these two kids were also involved in the window breaking and graffiti incident.

When they were almost even with Jacob and Maryann, the boy began to put his hat on, like his friend, bill backwards.

"Give me that goddamned hat," the older woman said, snatching it and hitting the boy upside his head at the same time. As they took two more steps she vainly tried to rip the hat apart, then angrily threw it into a public waste container. She slapped the now defeated boy on the side of the head again. "And when we get home young man, we gonna burn those pants and your black jacket with that ugly pirate and bones on the back. And you gonna wear those new jeans I bought you. You hear me? Do you?"

"Yes," he said, his defiance growing even dimmer.

She hit him again and demanded, "Yes, what?"

"Yes, Grandma," said the boy, respectfully this time.

The first boy turned the corner and the other mother walked on, in a daze, as if she hadn't heard any of the exchange.

• • • • •

A few minutes later a police officer delivered Mark, dressed in gym shorts, a sweaty T-shirt and running shoes, to the waiting room.

"Mark, are you okay?" said Maryann. Jacob, sensing the exasperation returning to her voice, took over.

Jacob walked up and put his arm around Mark, who warily answered his mother. "Yeah, I'm okay. This is so bogus...I can't believe...."

Jacob pulled together three metal chairs into a corner of the room where others in the room could not easily overhear them.

"Here. Sit down and tell us what happened," invited Jacob just as a thunderstorm erupted outside. As the lightning and thunder pounded on the plate glass windows of the modern jailhouse, Mark told his story.

• • • • •

It did not take Mark long and, just as he was completing his story, Officer Diaz came through the revolving door, shook the rain from his umbrella and pulled a chair into the group. With his crooked grin he said, "Well, what have we here? An Antioch prayer meeting?"

"I wish that was it, Officer Diaz," smiled Jacob, relieved to see the old cop. "Mark, Andre and four other kids were picked up this afternoon. Mark has just finished telling us an interesting story," reported Jacob.

"Yes, *very* interesting," said Maryann in a steely tone. "Son, I want you to know that I believe you." She reached over and put her hand on his forearm. Jacob sighed with relief as Maryann continued. "Just to make sure I understand, let me tell Officer Diaz what you told us. You correct me if I get it wrong. Okay?"

"Okay."

"Maryann looked from Mark to Diaz. "Mark and Andre had just finished at the Club. Andre headed home. Mark decided to take a run. He wants to be in top shape for football practice in August." She looked at Mark and he nodded affirmatively.

"As he came around the back side of Parkland Junior High, he heard Andre yelling at these four kids, telling them how stupid they were. It seems Andre came up on them just as they had finished their graffiti work and were now throwing rocks at the windows. Andre was angry and yelling at the boys. Andre told them how stupid they were to be mixed up in gangs, especially Juice's gang." She looked back at Mark. "They were about to jump on Andre when you ran up. It looked like you and Andre were going to have to defend yourselves, right, Mark?"

Again, Mark nodded.

"Then the police cars pulled up, one at each end of the street. You were glad to see them. The other boys started running and the four police officers took out after each of them. You and Andre did not run. Correct?"

Mark emphatically nodded his head.

"But, they arrested all six of you. They either wouldn't listen or didn't believe you. The other boys said it was you and Andre who had done the graffiti. You tried to tell them that the staff at the Club would vouch for you, that your clothes were still there. You both showed them clean hands, with no paint on your fingers, right? One policeman tried to get the others to listen, but they, especially one officer, shouted him down. So, they took you all in, threw you in a room together, where you almost had to defend yourselves again and still no one has heard you out."

"Very interesting," said Diaz. "Very interesting. Mark, did you notice the name tags of any of the officers?"

"Just the one who was so mean. The fat guy, the one doing all of the shouting. He's a real jerk. His name was Struve, S-T-R-U-V-E. Plus, he'd seen Andre before or something. So, Struve just knew Andre was mixed up with the gang. And it's not so. Andre hates his brother. He doesn't wear the baggies or the colors or anything anymore. But, Officer Struve," Mark dragged out the name derisively, "he wouldn't even listen and got into a shouting match with his partner."

Then with an angry glare Mark said to Diaz, "When he got angry at his partner, Struve called us niggers and half-breeds."

All three adults shifted uncomfortably in their seats. Diaz sighed and said, "Struve is a real piece of work. Rumor has it he is into some strange right-wing stuff. Funny thing is he goes to church every Sunday—go figure," Diaz shrugged with open palms.

Jacob could sense Maryann's anger kicking into gear. They were sitting side by side, so close their knees were touching. He could almost smell the anger over her musk perfume.

"Let me see what I can find out," said Diaz. "Are any of the other guys still back there?"

"We saw two of them leaving with their mothers, or grandmother, I guess," said Jacob. "I recognized them from the Club. The one kid is not too bad, really."

"Yeah, the other two, plus Andre, they're still there," said Mark.

"Tod," started Maryann, "I tried to call Andre's mother, but I didn't get an answer."

"He talked to her," said Mark.

"Andre got through to her?" asked Jacob. Then to Maryann said, "Maybe that's why you couldn't get through. Is she on her way here?"

"No."

Mark had all of the four adults' attention. They sensed his concern.

"He hung up on his mom," said Mark.

"Hung up on her?" said Maryann. "Why?"

"She told him she would get in touch with Juice. That Juice would be up to get him." Mark looked, helplessly, in turn, at each of them.

"Let me go see what I can find out," said Diaz.

• • • • •

"Whoa, was I glad to see my man, Tod, here," said Andre smiling from ear to ear. "I almost had to mess up those two little, stupid wannabees."

"Hey," said Diaz, "those two finally did the right thing."

Andre shrugged and smiled, "They better."

"I talked with the other two kids. They basically backed up what Mark told us. One boy is spending the summer with his aunt. Their parents, or rather an aunt and another grandmother, are on their way to get them. They had to find transportation. I'm sorry, Maryann, but I couldn't find Struve. So I can't get the charges dropped tonight. I'll work on it. The worst is that you'll have to come back to juvenile court in a month or so. It should be routine and I might be able to talk some sense into Struve between now and then."

"Let's get out of here, man. I'm starved," said Andre.

"Tell you what, Andre," said Diaz. "Give me a few minutes to check some messages, then why don't you come with me? We'll stop and get something to eat on the way to your house. I want to ask you some questions about Juice. Then I need to talk to your mom. Okay?"

"Can we stop at Taco Bell?"

• • • • •

The thunderstorm was subsiding when Juice parked his Lexus down the street from the police station. He sat behind the wheel waiting for the rain to let up a little more before heading up the walk. He was looking forward to his encounter with his little brother who had done a good job of avoiding him lately. Then he saw Andre and the old Mexican cop sharing an umbrella as they left the station. They were joking and laughing like old buddies as they climbed into the unmarked police car. Juice slammed both fists on the steering wheel as he squinted through the rain-covered windshield.

"You're dead, Hotchie. You're dead."

• • • • •

Maryann and Jacob took Mark back to the Club to get his clothes from the locker, and they headed home. It was 5:45.

"Let me fix us all something to eat. *I'm* starved," she said, doing a pretty good impersonation of Andre's high-pitched, energetic voice.

Jacob and Mark laughed at the memory, relieving the tension.

"Okay, but while you do that, Mom," said Mark. "I'm going up to take a shower."

"Great, honey. I'll have something ready for you when you come down," said Maryann affectionately.

Mark took two stairs in one step, stopped and turned. "Mom?" He came back down the stairs to face her.

"Yes?"

"It means a lot to me that you believed me. Thanks." Mark gave his mother a hug.

Maryann just smiled and nodded her head as Mark bounded up the stairs three at a time. Maryann turned and walked to where Jacob stood by the door. She slipped her arms around his waist, buried her head in his chest and began to sob. Surprised by the gesture, Jacob put his arms around her, hesitantly at first, then sensing her need, held her close. She continued to cry and hold him tight. She felt so good in his arms. Jacob was aware of every place they touched—his hands on her back and hers on his. Her cheek against his chest, his chin in her hair that smelled so clean, so fresh, even at the end of a long, hot day. The warmth of her breasts and her thighs that pressed tightly against him went straight to the center of his being. He could have stayed there forever. She began to talk, without pulling away, her face still buried in his chest.

"Oh, Jacob. I feel so guilty. I was so willing to believe he did something wrong. I was ready to jump on him without hearing him out. I heard that grandmother and watched her whip that kid. I wanted to do the same thing. If you hadn't been there. If you hadn't made me calm down, made me hear him out, there's no telling what I might have said."

She raised her head and looked up at him. Jacob resisted the temptation to kiss the tears from her cheeks. All he could do was smile and meet her gaze. She lowered her head again, squeezed him harder and said, "Thank you. Thank you, Jacob."

"You're welcome, Maryann." He wanted to stroke her hair. Instead, he tentatively rubbed her back lightly through the silk blouse as he talked. "Mark is a wonderful kid. You've done a great job with him and Ruth. You should be so proud."

"I am proud. But, it's been hard with Mark. He needs a father. He thinks the world of you, Jacob. Thanks for being our friend." She spoke softly into his chest.

"You're welcome. Thank you for being my friend and including me in your family. The last two weeks have been..." The frog in Jacob's throat made the words hard to deliver.

Maryann raised her head again. This time she looked him in the eye, rose on her toes and kissed him, not long, but long enough, not passionately, but full on the mouth and with enough emotion and affection that Jacob's heart skipped a beat and his knees nearly buckled.

"Well," she said, still looking him in the eye as she began to loosen her hug and slowly pull away. She moved both hands to rest on his chest and said, "I'd better get us something to eat." She patted his pounding chest once and turned away.

"Maryann...I'd better go."

"Don't you want something to eat? It won't take long," disappointment obvious in her tone.

"Oh, I'm starved," he said, attempting his own Andre imitation. They both laughed. "But, I have an AA meeting tonight and I'm supposed to pick this guy up that I work with. It's his first meeting. We usually go to the Diner afterward."

"Oh, then yes, you'd better go. Here." She grabbed an apple from a basket on the countertop. "This should hold you over."

They shared an awkward, nervous laugh. He took a half step toward the door.

"Great. Thanks, Maryann...for..." He held up the apple. "For everything." He bent down and gave her a kiss just like the one she'd given him.

They smiled, then broke again into self-conscious laughs. She reached out and squeezed his hand as he backed out of the door with a smile on his face.

RUN OVER

15

It was still raining early the next morning when Jacob ran around the corner and was pleasantly surprised to see Ruth out in front of her house. She was running in place in the rain waiting for him. She waved when she saw him and her smile brightened his mood even more as she fell into step with him.

"I'm impressed," he said. "After a busy first week at the Club, I thought you might sleep in."

"No way!" She turned her face to the falling rain. "You know I love to run in the rain. This is invigorating."

"Congratulations on a great start to the summer program," said Jacob.

"It was a great week, but I'm glad the Club is closed on Saturdays during the summer." She picked up the pace a little. "Thanks for helping Mom yesterday. She said you helped her stay calm and kept her from jumping all over Mark."

• • • • •

The wipers throbbed a steady beat on the windshield of the stolen Ford Expedition XLT. The kid behind the wheel was fidgeting and nervous.

"You think they gonna to be runnin' on a day like this? You think they comin', man?"

"Don't know," said his older partner who reclined in the passenger's seat. "Just have to wait."

"Suppose they don't come? I mean even some white people are too smart to run in the rain. Why people do all this runnin' anyway? How we gonna know they the right ones? Man, this is one big car. Where'd you get it?"

131

The older youth in the passenger seat ignored the questions and lit another cigarette. Suddenly, he sat up. A couple came running around the long bend on the tree-lined boulevard. "There! Here they come. That's them. You know what to do. Ease out, build speed slowly and when you have a path, at the last minute gun it!"

"Oh wow, oh wow. This be it. Here we go," said the driver as he awkwardly pulled the gearshift into drive.

"Easy, start picking up speed." The older youth was sitting on the edge of his seat. "Pick up speed, I said."

The kid was wide-eyed and seemed not to hear.

"Pick it up!"

The vehicle came to a stop.

"What the…"

"That's Ruth, man. I can't run over Ruth." The kid looked straight ahead in a daze. "I didn't know we were supposed to kill Ruth."

"Listen to me, you dumb little shit. You want to be in the gang, you got to go through the initiation. You know that. Run that bitch over and her friend, too. Now!"

The kid looked back and forth between the running couple and his seedy mentor.

"But," he pleaded. "That's Ruth. She works at the Club. She's okay. She never hurt nobody, man. She's good to everybody. My momma loves Ruth."

His partner pulled a gun from his team sport jacket. "Ruth is the one we are *supposed* to take care of, you hear me? Now take your foot off that brake and run them over and if they ain't dead you back this big-assed car over 'em again. Then we split on foot. Go! Or, I'll shoot you dead, here. Right now. You hear what I say? Drive!"

The kid floored the over-sized vehicle and pointed it at the running couple. By the time Ruth and Jacob noticed the vehicle that sped toward them, it was too late. From inside the vehicle the wide-eyed couple seemed to fill the windshield. Ruth looked right into the soul of the boy behind the wheel. At the last split second the kid screamed and jerked the wheel. The gun went off. At the same instant Jacob snatched Ruth off her feet and dove with her in the other direction. The vehicle slid violently into the curb and flipped upside down. As the Expedition skidded on its top, the unearthly sound of metal scraping against pavement pierced the early morning air. A huge cottonwood tree halted its slide. It was a terrible crash.

Ruth screamed and began to fight against Jacob, attempting to rise.

"Ruth, oh God. Ruth, are you okay?"

"Yes, yes! Get off of me, Jacob. We have to help those boys."

Jacob wanted to continue to cover her, protect her from harm, make sure she was safe, but he got up. Ruth immediately took charge. She ran to the older youth. He was a broken, bloody mess. She prayed desperately as she worked, but she threw herself into what needed to be done while Jacob stood, frozen in shock. Tears streamed down her face as she searched for a pulse in the youth's throat.

"Oh God, Jacob. I think this one is dead." She looked at him, then called over his shoulder, "Call 911! Hurry!"

Jacob turned in time to see a lady in her robe turn and rush back into her house. Jacob suddenly came alive and ran to the overturned Expedition. Ruth was right behind him. The boy lay on his back, half in, half out of the mangled driver's door. He was covered with blood. He was alive, conscious and writhing in pain.

"It's okay, son," said Jacob as he fell to one knee by the boy. "Help is on the way. It's okay."

Jacob heard a gasp and looked up to see Ruth with her hands over her mouth, eyes wide. She fell to both knees on the other side of the boy. The boy looked into her eyes and reached out with a bloody hand to grab hers.

"It hurts, Ruth. It hurts so bad."

"I know, Amman, I know. I'm here. Help is on the way." With her free hand, she gently touched his cheek.

"I'm sorry, Ruth. I didn't want to hurt you, but they…"

"It's okay, Amman. It was an accident. Listen!" Ruth looked down the block. "Here comes the rescue squad. They're almost here."

When the squad arrived, Jacob moved away to let them work, joining the small early morning crowd of spectators, some in bed clothes and robes standing under umbrellas. Ruth stayed with the boy, talking to him and comforting him. She disappeared with him into the back of the ambulance.

"What happened, son?"

Jacob turned. "Nathan! I don't know…it all happened so fast. We were taking our morning jog and these two kids…they almost ran us over."

"Ran you over?"

Jacob nodded, still in shock. "Then, at the last minute the driver swerved and barely missed us."

"Are you okay?" Nathan nodded toward Jacob's badly scraped and bleeding knees.

Jacob looked down, becoming aware of them for the first time. "Yeah, sure, I'm fine. So is Ruth, but Nathan, the one boy is dead and I don't think things look too good for the other one."

"Do you know them?" asked Nathan.

"Not the older one, the...dead one, but the driver is Amman White."

"Oh, God. He's a member of our church, at least his mom and younger brothers are. His mother has been worried sick that the gangs had their grip on him."

At that moment, a shell-shocked Ruth appeared in the open door of the ambulance. Nathan began to move toward her. Jacob followed.

"Nathan," Jacob said quietly and Nathan slowed his walk a little and leaned toward Jacob. "Ruth wants to believe it was an accident, but it wasn't. They were trying to run us over. At the last minute, the kid lost his nerve, otherwise, we would have both been killed. They found a hand gun in the front seat."

Nathan nodded gravely. "Let's keep that between us. We'll tell Tod, but no need to let the press get hold of that. Let them think it was an accident."

Jacob nodded and they turned their full attention on Ruth.

"Oh, Preacher Nate," called Ruth mournfully. She jumped from the back of the ambulance and fell, sobbing into the big man's arms. "We lost him," she sobbed into his chest. "Oh God, we lost him. He's dead, Preacher Nate. Amman's dead. They're both dead."

BRIGHT GLOOMY SUNDAY

16

SUNDAY, JUNE 16

$\mathbf{M}$aryann and Jacob sat on her deck enjoying the warm summer after-noon. They were content to enjoy each other's presence on this beautiful but sad day. It had been a somber service at Antioch that morning. The usual sense of joy and celebration was muted by the community's grief. Mrs. White, Amman's mother, and her children were there. Friends and church family did their best to offer her comfort.

For the third straight week, Maryann invited Jacob and Andre over to her house following church. Today there was no cookout. Instead, they half-heartedly nibbled on cold-cut sandwiches and chips. Andre was especially quiet. After eating, Jacob agreed to drive Mark and Andre to the Crossroads Mall where they planned to catch two movies with dinner in between at the food court.

The boys had waited on the deck while Jacob returned to the kitchen to say goodbye to Maryann. She was bent over returning food to the open refrigerator when he approached and said, "Thanks for lunch, Maryann. I'm leaving to take the boys to the movie."

"Oh," she spun quickly to find herself only a foot away and staring into his eyes. "You're welcome." She rose on her toes and kissed him lightly on the cheek. "Do you have plans for this afternoon?"

"No, not really."

She reached out and grabbed his hand. "Come back after dropping the boys off. We can sit and talk. I need the company."

When he returned, he found her sitting on the deck. She had changed into comfortable shorts, a colorful top and sandals—and wore a smile that

135

seemed to welcome him home. He wanted to tell her how pretty she looked, but he could find neither the courage nor the words.

Maryann had no problem finding the courage or the words to compliment him. "You're still a good-looking man, Jacob. How do you do it?"

"Thank you. Do what?"

She smiled and he remembered how she used to flirt with him when they were teenagers. "I think you're in better shape at forty than you were at twenty. What's your secret?"

He shrugged, "My last stint in the penitentiary—all I did was take college classes and workout."

"Didn't you have to work?"

"Sure, the last two years I was a special assistant to the Chaplain."

She nodded and then asked, "What happened, Jacob? You were always a little wild and drank too much, but I never thought…"

"I'd end up in prison? Yeah, me either. I don't know, Maryann, a combination of things. Alcoholism really took over my life. I couldn't hold a job and then I got heavily into drugs. I had to support my habit, so…I think I was so guilt-ridden, about leaving Mom…and you. And some of the things I did…I was a really stupid criminal. It was like, easier in prison—life was easier. I felt like I deserved to be there."

"Well, what turned you around?"

"A letter from my mom, and God."

"Mom and God?" she asked.

"I had written her a letter, thanking her for still loving me. I asked her how she could still find it in her heart to love me. She wrote back that the love she had for me had been planted in her heart by God and that he loved me even more than she did. I guess I was ready. I got down on my knees in that jail cell and gave my life to God. I asked Jesus to come into my heart and he did."

"That easy? No flashing lights."

"Not really. I felt my body fill up with a warmth—it was a real physical sensation. A couple of guys said something had 'lit me up.' The chaplain, a great guy, turned out to be an old friend of Nathan's, anyway, he said it was the warmth and glow of grace, the filling of the Holy Spirit. All I know is that it was real and the experience completely changed my life."

She nodded, satisfied with his answer. "I'd like to feel something like that someday."

The conversation that followed came easy, but there were also comfortable periods of silence. Just being with each other was more than enough for both of them that afternoon.

The warm afternoon stillness was interrupted by the sound of Ruth's Mustang pulling into the driveway. Maryann and Jacob exchanged relieved glances knowing that Ruth was home.

"Thanks, Mom," said Ruth as she climbed the stairs to the deck and flopped into one of the comfortable patio chairs around the table where her mother and Jacob sat. "I love my new car."

"You okay, Honey?" asked Maryann. "How'd it go?"

"It was tough." Ruth sighed deeply. "Understandably, Mrs. White is having a very difficult time, and she's a mess right now. Jill was wonderful with her. We've finished with the funeral arrangements, thank God. This is just so sad. Amman was really a good kid. Do you have any coffee, Mom?"

Maryann jumped up. "I'll put some on. Good idea."

As the sliding door to the kitchen closed behind her mother, Ruth surprised Jacob when she said, "I know that was not an accident yesterday. You saved my life, Jacob. Thank you."

"Amman turned at the last second. If he hadn't, we…."

"I know." She glanced toward the kitchen. "Mom doesn't need the anxiety of knowing and Amman's mom doesn't need the pain. She has enough grief right now. Okay?"

Jacob nodded agreement.

"Andre was sure quiet," she said. "What's your take on that?"

"He suspects the same thing Nathan and I do."

"That his brother, Juice, was behind this?"

"Something's going on. What do you think? Why would someone want try to run us down?"

Ruth nodded toward the patio door and they said no more.

Maryann came through the sliding door. "Coffee will be done in a minute. Did you learn any more about the accident?"

"Tod says the car was stolen and that both boys were high on crack cocaine," said Jacob.

Ruth added, "With the wet streets, an oversized vehicle…."

"Who was the other boy, Ruth? Was he a Club member?"

"A long time ago. I didn't even remember his name, but he has a long record of gang involvement. Our records show that he was a member for a couple of years when he was eight or nine." Ruth shook her head. "Another one that fell through the cracks."

"You and your father. He thought he could save them all, too. You can't, you know," said Maryann.

Ruth nodded and said, "I'm so tired of burying children. That's three dead kids in what—three or four weeks?"

Jacob sighed deeply. "The odds some of these kids are up against— they have so much to overcome, and so many things against them. But you do a great job at the Club, Ruth—you're making a tremendous difference in the lives of so many kids." To Maryann he said, "You should see how she organizes and runs things at the Club. They've put together a great summer program."

Maryann smiled in acknowledgment. "You are making a difference, Ruth."

"I know." She sighed. "I know." She looked up at Jacob. "Speaking of odds to overcome, Jacob. You've said some things over the last year that lead me to believe that you're too hard on yourself."

"What do you mean?" Jacob was caught off guard. The shift of attention to him was without warning. He suddenly felt anxious.

"The odds were working against you, too. You had a lot of obstacles, a lot of things to overcome. It's no wonder you had problems."

"No, I brought my trials on myself. I had a good mother, good friends at the Club and at church. I have no one to blame but myself."

"Maybe so, Jacob, but your daddy died before you were born and your mom married a man she didn't love. Grandma Becky told me that from the time you were ten years old, she was in a fog, barely functioning sometimes. You practically raised yourself."

"And, I left her when she needed me," Jacob countered in a self-accusatory tone. He felt almost panicky, and his heart was racing. "I don't really need to rehash my history, Ruth. It's behind me."

Ruth was undeterred. She said gently, but firmly. "I don't think it is. I have a sense that you still need to deal with some things as the final piece of your healing process."

Jacob looked to Maryann for help, but she just smiled and shrugged. "She is her daddy's girl. I think you're about to deal with some things." Jacob just wanted to get up and leave, except he loved Maryann too much, and was growing quite attached to Ruth also.

"Grandma Becky told me that before you were ten you had to endure horrible abuse from your stepfather—you *and* Grandma Becky."

Maryann gasped. "Jacob, I didn't know that!"

He briefly met her eyes, then turned back to Ruth. "Mom told you about all that," he said sadly.

Ruth nodded. "Right after you started volunteering at the Club. It was like she needed me to know. She wanted me to understand what you had gone through. She wanted so much for me to love her son." She smiled at her mother and then at Jacob. "And, I do."

Jacob was stunned. He felt himself blushing again. "I…" He paused trying to make a decision about what to say next. Finally he leaned closer to the table and said, "Listen, what I'm about to say is important." He paused and both women met his eyes. "Yes, I had it tough. But, you need to understand—a lot of kids, like Andre, like Amman, yes, like me, they have it tough growing up—but, they're still responsible. A lot of kids do okay in spite of the odds. Andre can overcome what he's up against if he wants to. If he lets us help him.

"Growing up, Mom was good to me, even in her depression, or whatever it was. I never lacked for food, clothes, or a bed. I also had the Club, the folks at church, people like your parents, Maryann, my teachers and coaches at school, and I had a four-year scholarship at the university. These were all gifts of grace straight from God that I chose to reject. Some of the kids we work with at the Club have parents with drug problems, some have lost brothers and sisters to drugs and drive-by shootings. As a kid, I never had to fear for my life walking to and from the Club."

Jacob raised an index finger to make the next point. "Don't forget, my skin is white. Make me black or brown and you multiply my problems growing up. And, some of the guys I knew in prison, guys from New York, D.C., or L.A.—I've seen Miami…the homes and neighborhoods they described sounded more like third-world countries. These kids have grown up in war zones. Parkland has always been a good community, and even the North Side doesn't compare to Miami or Watts."

He paused again and neither woman interrupted the silence. They knew he had more to say.

"The root cause of most of my problems is that I kept making the wrong decisions—one right after another from the time I was ten years old."

Maryann and Ruth were both touched by the conviction with which Jacob was speaking.

He turned and looked at Ruth, "If you say I'm a victim, somehow the mess that I made out of my life was Ralph Riddler's fault, not my own. Then you sell people short. You won't be able to help them like you want to. You sell God short because you discount the crowning achievement of his creation, the mind, the soul, the free will of each and every person born into the world. Into each one God places the Light and each one is responsible and accountable. The greatest day of my life was the day I simply acknowledged that I was a sinner and asked God to forgive me. And, Ruth, all of the kids you love so much?"

She smiled and nodded.

"You must love them enough to make them choose between right and wrong. Teach them how to make good decisions—moral, ethical decisions, no matter what messes they encounter. That's the greatest gift your mom and dad have given to you and Mark."

Maryann now understood why Ruth and Mark were so impressed with Jacob's work with the kids at the Club. He'd been there. No one understood better than he did. He loved them. The kids at the Club, especially those in his guitar classes, had to know that, but he also expected the best from them and demanded that they do the right things. *Joe must be pleased,* she thought, *that his old teammate is back where he belongs sharing Joe's passion for the kids.*

"Jacob?" Maryann searched his eyes. "I've known you since primary school. I didn't know Mr. Riddler abused you. He was so…such a…"

"Fine 'Christian' gentleman?" Jacob said with a bitterness Maryann had never heard. "I heard old Brother Stanley say that at his funeral. When Brother Stanley said Ralph Riddler had gone to meet his Lord, I remember thinking if Ralph's in heaven then heaven is a place I never want to go."

"Oh my, was it that bad?" asked Maryann.

Ruth asked, "Did you know that one of the worst beatings he ever gave your mom was after she had been to Stanley for *counseling?*"

The look on Jacob's face told Ruth he had not known. "She told me that one time, in desperation she went to Brother Stanley and tried to tell him what was going on."

"Tried to?" asked Maryann.

"Stanley didn't want to hear it. Instead, he said crap like, 'Ralph's a fine man, he works hard, you're lucky to have such a good provider for you and your son.' Stanley quoted scripture and told her that Ralph was the head of her house, that she should go home, obey her husband, and try harder to be a 'good' wife."

Maryann's anger seethed. "That pompous old...you know Parkland Baptist Church in those years functioned in spite of that self-righteous, old fart."

Jacob said sadly, "He was pretty useless, wasn't he?"

"That night," Ruth continued the story. "The same day that she'd been to Stanley for help was when Ralph gave her the worst beating ever."

"Stanley told him?" asked Maryann.

Ruth nodded. "Every detail. He called Ralph at work and told him everything Grandma Becky had said to him in confidence."

"I remember that night, but I never understood it until now."

Jacob was lost in the vivid memories. After a few seconds, Maryann broke the silence. "The best thing that ever happened to Parkland Baptist was the merger with Memorial. Antioch has been a special place from day one. Old Dr. Matthew Millard *was* a fine Christian gentleman, Jacob."

"That's what everybody says. I wish I could have known him. I remember him as a kid. It seemed like every time there was a civil rights issue, he was on television. Ralph called him a black agitator."

"It's interesting, Dr. Millard and Nathan were so different, yet so effective in their own ways. They were a wonderful team. During those ten years, you could watch Nathan's development under Dr. Millard's tutelage," reflected Maryann.

Ruth looked at Jacob. "Dr. Millard was the best thing that ever happened to your mom, Jacob."

"She sure loved him, I know that."

"He really saved her life," Ruth said. "You know, Dr. Millard had two doctorate degrees, one in theology and one in psychology. He was exceedingly patient with your mom and eventually brought her out of her depression."

"I'm so grateful, too. When I got out of prison, Mom was a completely different person. The couple of years before her stroke, I felt like I really came to know my mom for the first time. We grew so close."

"What happened, Jacob?" asked Ruth.

"What do you mean?"

"When you were a child?"

Jacob looked at Ruth, his anxiety running high again and shook his head, pretending he didn't understand.

"You're not facing something. Your songs are full of so much meaning and passion. They're beautiful. They're also somehow...I don't know, so tortured, and full of regret. Jacob, it means a lot to the kids—maybe even more to the folks at Antioch—to know that you've made it all the way back. But something's still unresolved in your heart. I'm sure of it, you're just too hard on yourself sometimes. Something happened about the time you were ten, something very traumatic. It might help to talk about it and bring final and lasting healing to your life."

"Of course," said Maryann, as if understanding a mystery for the first time. "Everyone thought your mom had gone into that deep depression as the result of losing her second husband in a tragic accident. That's what my mom and dad always thought. But we never knew about the abuse. She wasn't grieving *him*, was she?"

Jacob shook his head.

"Jacob?" Ruth reached across the table and held his forearm the way her mother had a few weeks before. Her touch felt reassuring, but different, somehow. He looked into her deep blue eyes. "You can trust us, Jacob, if it would help to talk about it. You know that we both love you."

Jacob looked from Ruth to Maryann. Maryann affirmed Ruth's declaration of love with a simple nod.

"I've...I...haven't told...not even Preacher Nate. I..." He looked again from one lovely face to the other. "I don't know what purpose..." He looked from one to the other again and knew he really had no choice. He was now compelled to tell them. He sighed, "You better bring out the whole pot, Maryann. This may take awhile."

After Maryann returned and poured each of them a cup of coffee, Jacob took a deep breath and peered into the steaming cup as if in that dark liquid he might find the words. After a few seconds he began.

"It was a warm day. Much like this one. I'd just turned ten. I was coming home from the Club after baseball practice. So, it would've been about five-thirty in the afternoon...."

17
AT LONG LAST, CONFESSION

*J*acob turned the corner and saw Ralph's car in front of the house. He almost turned around and went back to the Club, without eating dinner, like he often did whenever Ralph was home for dinner from his job as manager of the Blackstone Hotel downtown. But today he was really hungry. The Boys Club in those days closed for an hour each evening so the boys could go home for dinner. Maybe it would be okay.

Jacob didn't mind his stepfather's foul mouth, the cuss words he preferred to use when talking to Momma or him, nearly as much as he hated the way Ralph lectured him all the time, especially when he quoted scripture. Even at ten years old, he knew something was very wrong with that. Ralph never cussed when he was around the church people. He even stood up in front of Parkland Baptist Church and talked sometimes. He didn't preach, but he read the Bible and prayed at times. He used a deep, well-practiced, phony voice. Jacob thought he was trying to sound like Reverend Stanley. He wondered why people didn't burst out laughing when they heard it.

Sometimes at home, Ralph mixed Bible verses and cussing together, using that same tone of voice. He used words Jacob would definitely have gotten in trouble for using at the Club or around Momma. Sometimes Ralph screamed Bible verses while beating up on Momma, calling her an evil slut and a Jezebel. Jacob was smart and learned how to stay out of the brutal man's way. He spent every hour he possibly could at the Club. Momma wasn't as lucky. He hated Ralph.

143

A year earlier he had learned how to use the dictionary. In spite of what Ralph always said to him, he knew he was pretty smart. Learning was easy for Jacob. One day he looked up the word "bastard." Deep inside, Jacob knew it was really Ralph who was the evil one, not Momma. Momma didn't even ask her son to call Ralph "Dad." Even though she never said it, Jacob was sure that Momma must have known Ralph was evil.

Sometimes, when she was able to, she gave Jacob extra money and told him to hang on to it, in case he needed to, he could eat a hamburger at the Parkland Diner instead of coming home. Without really spelling it out for him, Jacob knew that on the rare occasions Ralph came home for dinner, she wanted her son to stay away until Ralph went back to his job at the Hotel. But tonight he didn't have any money. He thought that maybe he could slip in and hide until Ralph left, then Momma could fix him something to eat. If Ralph left soon, maybe Jacob could eat and still get back to the Club in time for woodworking shop. When he was old enough he was going to join the auto-mechanics class—that would be cool. He was already reading some books about cars that he had gotten from the library.

*Jacob cautiously entered the small house through the front door. He heard Ralph's angry shouting and foul language coming from the kitchen. He started to turn around and leave, but then he heard a loud slap followed by his mother's sharp cry. Ralph's hideous laughter filled the house. Jacob slowly walked down the dark hallway until he could see into the kitchen. Ralph had Momma—what was he doing! He had her bent over the kitchen table. Her dress had been pulled up and he was standing behind her. With one hand he held her by the hair, with the other...*was he spanking her? *Ralph's eyes were wild.*

He was hurting Momma! Jacob could see her tortured face. Her eyes were closed, but the tears flowed freely down her cheeks. She cried and whimpered like the puppy Ralph had forced him to take back to the pet store.

Then she opened her eyes and saw Jacob in the hallway. She gasped. "Oh, God, no. Please." Momma tried to warn him with her eyes. With her head she motioned for Jacob to leave, but Ralph was jerking on her hair like a madman. In the years that followed, Jacob would see many things, but never anything that compared to the look of utter humiliation and inconsolable despair that he saw in his mother's face that day.

When Ralph saw Jacob standing frozen in the hallway, petrified and unable to move, the madman roared with laughter. A sick look of euphoric pleasure flooded his contorted face. That horrifying laugh haunted Jacob mercilessly for years, and the scene he witnessed was the seed of many torturous nightmares.

"Come here, boy." Ralph's eyes were bulging. "Let me show you what an Ozark Mountain slut is good for."

"Oh, God, please, no" she whimpered desperately. She looked at her small son and shook her head. "Go, Son, go—ahhhh!"

The sound of his mother's voice jolted Jacob's paralyzed limbs into action. He turned and ran down the hallway and out the front door. The wicked laughter seared through his entire being. He stopped in the middle of the front yard feeling strangely detached, like he was walking in a dream. He stood for a moment numb and then opened his shattered heart to the seething, silent rage that nestled its way into his soul and stayed with him for too many years.

Jacob ran to the backyard. There he found a pile of old boards from the basement stairs that were being replaced. Years later, as he told the story for the first time ever to Maryann and Ruth, Jacob couldn't remember planning what he was about to do. He was moving as if he were on automatic pilot. Finding a two-by-four with rusty nails sticking out of one end, Jacob crept onto the back porch, and peered into the kitchen.

Ralph was sitting at the end of the kitchen table with his back to the door. Momma was standing at the stove, straightening her dress, and sobbing while she finished cooking the meal that she'd prepared to feed Ralph's other appetite.

Jacob quietly opened the door. The old fool was barking orders and blathering vile opinions about Momma and her bastard son. He didn't even hear Jacob come through the kitchen door and plant himself behind the chair. Jacob held the two-by-four just like Coach George at the Club had taught him to hold a baseball bat. He took aim for the back of the wretched man's head. Jacob held his breath and swung as hard as could, hitting Ralph in the back of the neck. The rusty nails penetrated deeply. When Jacob let go, the two-by-four dangled from

Ralph's neck and blood started running in ugly rivers down his back.

Ralph squealed like a stuck pig and shot straight up out of the chair. Momma screamed. Ralph grappled with the two-by-four. He yanked on the board wildly until he was finally able to pull it out of his neck.

Ralph stared in shock at the two-by-four in his hands. Ralph and Momma seemed to comprehend what had happened in the same instant. Momma's hands flew to her mouth. Jacob could see the terror in her eyes and face. Ralph's eyes glazed over and turned an ugly, menacing green. It was those wild green eyes he would see in his nightmares for years to come. Ralph was in a rage. He began to shake violently and broke into a foul tirade. Madly, he swung at the boy's head with the two-by-four. Jacob ducked and the two-by-four splintered as it hit the doorframe directly behind him.

Jacob took a couple of tentative steps toward his mother. He wasn't sure whether he was seeking safety or if he should try to protect her. Ralph reached for him, then grabbed the butcher knife from the kitchen counter. He raised it over his head and Jacob flashed for a moment, remembering the picture in the old family Bible of Abraham with his knife raised and poised to kill his son Isaac.

"Nooo!" With two hands Momma grabbed the iron skillet that still had steak sizzling in it and hit Ralph, hard, on the side of the head.

Jacob ran to her. Momma grabbed him and pulled him to her, placing her own body between Jacob and her husband. Jacob buried his head in her belly and felt safe, but only for an instant, until he heard his mother groan. Ralph had been stunned. His knees were wobbly, but he was moving toward them. Momma let go of Jacob, moved toward Ralph, and began pushing him. Then Jacob realized what she was attempting to do. Ralph was dazed and off balance, but Momma still could not move him. Jacob ran three steps and, like a free safety, buried his head in Ralph's rib cage. Jacob bounced off, but was quickly on his feet to help his mother make the final push. Ralph screamed as he fell backwards into the empty stairwell.

Mother and son grabbed each other and fell to the kitchen floor. They heard Ralph hit the cement floor. On hands and knees they crawled to the edge of the hole and peered into the gloomy basement. There he lay, face up; his eyes, which had lost their scary green hue, were staring blankly up at them.

"Stay here," she said, pulling him away from the opening. "Stay right here." Momma ran out to the back yard and through the cellar door. When Jacob heard her enter the basement, he crawled on his belly back across the kitchen floor and peered through the hole. Momma cautiously moved, slightly bent, toward the body. Just as she was about to kneel next to him, Ralph moved his head and looked at her. She screamed and stood up. Ralph groaned, so did Momma. "Noooo! Let him be dead, Lord."

Momma jumped to her feet and ran back through the cellar doors. She didn't stop in the kitchen. Jacob could hear her vomiting in the bathroom. In between the horrible retching, he heard her crying, praying, "Please, God. Please. Let him die. Let him die."

Jacob stopped crying and stood up. He went out into the yard and down through the cellar door. The winter clothes were hung on one side of the basement. He took one of Ralph's suits out of the dry cleaner's bag and carefully re-hung the suit. Jacob quietly walked over to Ralph and without hesitation, held the bag over his face. He may have already been dying, but he wasn't dead yet. Jacob saw the plastic bag being sucked into his open mouth, and Jacob could see the fear in the man's eyes. Jacob held the bag over Ralph's face until there was no longer any movement. Then Jacob turned and went to find Momma. She was in the living room, crying and trying to explain to the people on the party line that she need to use the phone.

"It's okay, Momma. He's dead." He pulled on her arm. "Momma, he's dead."

She stopped talking into the phone and with a pitiful look said, "No, no, I have to...to call an ambulance." She looked away and began to talk into the phone.

Jacob grabbed her arm again, harder until she looked at him again. He shook his head.

"What?" Momma saw something in her son's face. " What? Oh, my God. What?"

"He's dead. I killed him."

Jacob saw terror in her eyes for the second time that afternoon. She hung up the phone and screamed at him, "Oh, God, no. What did you do? God, no, please."

• • • • •

Jacob paused in his story. Ruth and Maryann were speechless. The setting sun cast a long comforting shadow across the lush, green backyard. Finally Ruth said, "Oh, Jacob, and you've carried this for all these years?"

He nodded.

"You've never told anybody what happened till now?"

Again, he nodded.

"You were just a child. He was so evil...." said Ruth.

"I know, but it still haunted me. As a kid, even in high school I was always afraid someone would find out. I tried so hard to... 'be a good kid,' even after I started drinking, so that no one would ever suspect."

Maryann said, "No one ever did. I never remember anyone thinking it was anything but an accident."

"Officer Diaz did."

"Tod did?" asked Ruth.

Jacob nodded. "I think he had just made detective about that time. He didn't believe our story."

"What happened, after your mom hung up the phone?" asked Maryann.

"Mom ran back downstairs. She screamed again when she saw the bag over Ralph's face. She screamed at me again. I thought she was going to lose it. I was really scared then. It was strange. I wasn't scared doing it, putting the bag over his face and all. But, Mom, the way she reacted really scared me. I remember thinking she was going mad.

"But then, all of a sudden, she became very calm. She hugged me, told me it was okay, and that it wasn't my fault. She took charge. She removed the bag from Ralph's face and calmly looked for a pulse. There was a little blood on the bag. She calmly tore it into small pieces and flushed it down the toilet.

"She went back upstairs to the kitchen and quickly washed up the blood from Ralph's neck that had spilled on the floor and the chair. There wasn't very much—the nails hadn't hit a vein or anything. She took that broken two-by-four back downstairs and laid it next to Ralph's head to make it look like he'd fallen on it. While she did all of this, she went over with me what our story would be.

"She said we had to lie for our own good. She said it was okay because Ralph was a bad person. She was afraid that no one would believe us and that they might take me away from her if we told the truth. She went over the story with me several times while she cleaned up and then she called the police. The whole thing, including the clean-up, took less than half-an-hour.

"When Detective Diaz arrived, I could tell that he was suspicious, but Mom and I stuck to our story. We told him we were just getting ready to sit down for dinner like we did every night. It's funny, I remember that part of the lie was the hardest for me to tell...that Ralph was *helping out*—that was another big lie. He grabbed the hot skillet handle. It burned him and he dropped it. He slipped in the grease and fell backwards into the empty stairwell, landing on his back. Mom ran out into the backyard and through the cellar door to him. He'd fallen on the two-by-four with the nails sticking out. Mom pulled the two-by-four out and Ralph died in her arms. She was pretty convincing; she cried hard and everything.

"I could tell Officer Diaz didn't buy it completely. He grilled me pretty hard, too. He asked me if my mom and Ralph argued much. He asked if I ever saw my mother crying.

"It's funny. I remember wanting to tell him everything. I wanted to tell him how that bastard hurt my mom all of the time—how he hurt me—that she was *always* crying. I wanted to tell him that I'd done it, and that I was glad Ralph was dead. But I honestly thought I would go to jail for the rest of my life. Ralph was the only father I remember and all I ever remember him telling me was that I was just like the Jacob in the Bible. I was a no-good, sleazy con man. Even while I was trying to keep my story straight with Officer Diaz, I was remembering all of the negative predictions Ralph had made about my life. At ten years old I thought they were coming true. Ralph used to tell me all the time that I would grow up to be a murdering, no-good thief."

"How could anyone say such things to a child?" asked Ruth indignantly.

Jacob shook his head at the memory. "He turned out to be right. I never killed anybody else. But I sure turned out to be a no-good con artist."

"You're being too hard on yourself, again, Jacob," said Ruth.

Jacob smiled at her innocence and continued. "I have often wondered what might have happened if I'd told the truth back then.

Maybe things would've been different. Maybe not. They may have taken me away from Mom. Things could've been a lot worse."

"You're a different man now, Jacob," said Ruth.

"That's true. It's like all those years...that was a different person altogether. I don't even understand that other guy...how I...."

"Maybe so," said Maryann thoughtfully. "But, I really liked the guy I knew back then. Conversion is a mysterious thing, it's true. We become new people. But, it's also true that if we allow him to, God lets our true self be born. You're still the same person, Jacob, but different. You were always kind and sweet." She smiled. "You still are."

"And you and your mom never talked about what happened after that?" asked Ruth.

"No, we acted as if the story was true. At church, we let them all believe that Ralph was a wonderful man and that Mom was truly grieving. My worry for Mom probably made me look like I was grieving." Jacob looked out over the yard. The birds were singing their relaxing evening melody. "That was the last time I ever saw Mom take charge of anything. For the next ten years she barely functioned. She was so fragile, and always on the verge of losing it. Right after the funeral, she was hired on as a waitress at the Parkland Diner. I ate all my meals there. I don't remember her ever fixing another big meal."

"The only home-cooked meals you got back then were at my house, while we were dating," said Maryann as more of her memories began to make sense.

Jacob nodded, then continued, "You know Mom, she never drank, but she was on a 'friendly' drunk for ten years. She smiled all the time but she was really numb and completely out of touch with reality. She would tell me how wonderful I was, but there were times that I was more the adult than she was. I became the parent. I took care of her more than she did of me. I was also able to come and go at will, to do anything I wanted and she never challenged me. Her most common line was, 'That's nice, sweetie. You're such a good boy.' Even when I started drinking heavily, she never said a word. She was at her best on Sundays, at church.

"I didn't even contact her for several years after I left. I felt so guilty for abandoning her when I knew she badly needed me. When I did finally call her, she began to grow stronger, and started to write to me. Over the years her letters got better and better. Until I got some help from the prison chaplain, I honestly thought she'd gotten better because her 'no-good' son had been totally out of her life. When I came home I heard how much people loved Dr. Millard, and then I began to understand. He's a legend around here. I'm so grateful for the way he patiently brought her back to herself.

"I have come to respect and admire Mom since I've been home. And, she learned to cook again. It was so wonderful to go to church together." Jacob paused to soak in the memory. "Dr. Matthew Millard was her lifeline. His disciple, Nathan Wesley Frye, is mine. Every Sunday after church, until she went into the nursing home, I'd spend all day at her house. She fixed me some wonderful home-cooked meals. Those were special afternoons."

Ruth interjected, "Shirley tells me you still share the notes from Nathan's sermons with her every Sunday."

Jacob nodded. "On Sunday afternoons, we have talked about a lot of things, but you know, we never talked about the day Ralph died. Not once, since the day he died. That's why I'm not sure if she even remembers; maybe she's suppressed it, although it really doesn't matter anymore.

"Ruth, you never know what some of those kids at the Club are coping with every day. From the time I was ten years old until I was fifteen, I spent all my time at the Club. I was there every hour it was opened. Mom worked every day and night at the diner. I would only leave the Club long enough to go eat dinner with her there. George and the staff at the Club literally raised me. They didn't know it, but they were more of a parent to me than Mom was. She couldn't help it. I didn't go to the Club as much when I started playing basketball at Central. That's also when I started drinking heavily. I never went by there after I'd been drinking. I knew they'd climb all over me, but I still dropped by, even after I turned eighteen. I even worked there a couple of summers. Then George left. He took a job with a new Club that was just starting up back east somewhere. The rest of the staff turned over. The last time I dropped by the Club was a couple of weeks before I split. I think I was looking for help, but all of the people who'd been so good to me as a kid were gone. But, growing up I don't know what my life would've been like without the Club. I thank God for it every day. I'm grateful that now I have a chance to give back.

"Ruth, it's a wonderful work that God has called you to. You're so gifted and you're doing a great job. I know everyone tells you this, but your Heavenly Father and your earthly father in heaven are both proud of you. You don't know it, but you're helping to raise a lot of kids at the Club."

Jacob looked at the bottom of his empty cup. "I hope you both can still love me after knowing all of this."

• • • • •

It was early evening and the bar traffic was light, even for a Sunday. Juice was in his office washing down his second package of antacid tablets with soda water when his cell phone rang.

"Hello," he answered irritably.

"That fiasco yesterday was pretty stupid, J.J."

"How'd you get this number, Jez?"

"Trying to run them over with a kid not big enough to look over the steering wheel?" She laughed and mocked him.

"How'd you get this number?" he demanded.

"That's the best you can do, J.J.?"

"No problem," he tried to keep the irritation from his voice. "Like you said, patience, lover, patience. And, always have a backup—a plan B."

She said nothing and just laughed into the phone.

"Stay tuned, Jez, stay tuned. The night is young and the weekend ain't over yet."

"Oh, really?" He had her interest. "Something's happening yet this evening? What?"

"Tell you what, Jez. With Mr. Wilson gone off to D.C. again, his apartment can be ours tonight. Meet me here and you can be there when Juwan calls."

18 THROUGH THE EYES OF A FOOL

"Andre, my man, it's been a sad, long day." Jacob thought back on the worship at Antioch and then his grueling session on the deck with Ruth and Maryann. "A tough day, but a good day, too. Are you as tired as I am?"

Jacob drove Old Blue into the driveway beneath his apartment and turned off the ignition. He saw Mrs. Carlson's light go off and smiled, knowing that she was waiting up for him. He could hear the hum of the air conditioner in his apartment, which meant she had been over to turn it on for him during the heat of the day.

"I'm not ready for bed," the boy said defensively as they stepped out of the cab of the truck. "You said we could play a little guitar and sing and all, because you didn't have to work tonight."

Jacob met his young friend at the foot of the steps and put his arm around his shoulder. "That's what I do when I'm tired—play my guitar and sing a little. I said I was tired, not sleepy." Jacob dropped his arm and led the way up the narrow stairs.

"Jacob. Wait…." Andre began in a low tone that Jacob could not quite hear over the hum of the air conditioner.

From the darkness at the top of the stairs came a deep voice, "Hot enough for you gentlemen?"

Jacob jumped back and uttered a startled grunt. "You did it again, Officer Diaz. Why do you have to scare people like that? I 'bout fell down the steps."

Jacob was half-mad at the old cop, but Andre's laughter, now full-blown and always infectious, started Jacob laughing. Jacob patted his own chest as if he was trying to calm his heart.

"That was a good one," Andre laughed, holding his side and sitting down on the step. "I tried to warn you, man." Andre laughed and pointed to Jacob.

"Looks like you two have gotten pretty chummy," said Diaz, and Jacob got the uneasy feeling he used to get when cops were laying the groundwork for the interrogation that would surely follow. Jacob didn't answer. Andre was still laughing.

To the boy, Diaz said, "You sleep over with Jacob often, do you, son?" Jacob was now confident of the suspicion he heard. He instantly recognized in himself the hurt and disappointment that whatever it was he was still not above suspicion for the old cop.

"Uh-oh. Sounds like you have some questions to ask. You want to wait here while I drive Andre home?" Jacob asked.

"No! I can't, I don't want…" Andre, too, now sensed that this was not a social call. He hadn't done anything—lately anyway.

"No, I'd like to talk to both of you—for just a minute, anyway."

"Officer Diaz, I'll answer whatever questions you have, but not in front of…."

Diaz nodded. "Afraid so. It involves him, too. This won't take long. Maybe we better move to the kitchen," he said as he wiped his brow both ways with his open palm and pulled himself from the top step where he'd been sitting.

Jacob could not imagine what Diaz wanted and did not offer to put on coffee this time. He wanted to get this over with.

"So, Andre," began Diaz as he wiped his brow again and settled into the same kitchen chair where he'd sat on his first visit to Jacob's apartment a month ago. "Mr. Riddler here, he's pretty nice to you, isn't he?"

"Yeah. He be real nice—all the time."

Neither Andre nor Jacob took a seat. Jacob leaned against the kitchen sink on one side of the table. Andre moved to the other side and half sat, half leaned against the windowsill, staring down into the alley. He wondered how much Diaz knew.

From the head of the table, Diaz focused first on Andre. His tone was friendly, but all business as if he expected "the truth and nothing but the truth so help you God."

"How old are you, son?" asked Diaz.

"Fourteen. I'll be fifteen in November, right after Thanksgiving," answered Andre, a little defensively. Jacob smiled, remembering some of the kids teasing him about being only twelve.

"A nice guy like Jacob here, he probably doesn't wait for your birthday. Buys you things now and then, does he?"

"Yeah."

"Like what? Those Air Jordans you're wearing?" said Diaz pointing to Andre's expensive shoes.

"No," the boy said curtly. "My Momma buys my clothes. Jacob buys me food and tickets to the movie, things like that."

"Why does he do these things for you?"

"Because he a Christian," said Andre matter-of-factly and as if Diaz should have known. Diaz was a little taken aback. Jacob smiled again, but could not figure out where Diaz was going. Was Andre in trouble? Did he suspect Andre of shoplifting? Jacob didn't think Diaz would be going to all this trouble for something like that.

"What do *you* do for Mr. Riddler? In return for him being so nice to you and all?"

Andre paused, could not think of much and felt guilty, shrugged his shoulder and said, "I'm his friend."

"Special friends?"

"Yeah, I guess so."

"Mr. Riddler doesn't ask you to do special things for him?"

"No, not really."

"I mean in return for all of the special things he does for you?"

"No."

"Do you guys ever watch movies, you know, videos, when you come over?"

"No."

"No movies?"

"No, this dude don't even own a television. I tell him he ought to get one," said Andre, looking at Jacob. But, when he saw the pain in Jacob's face he realized this was no time for joking and looked back at Diaz. "All I do is sleep over sometimes. After the Club closes."

"Mr. Riddler lets you sleep over? He works all night, don't he?"

"Yeah, except Saturdays and Sundays. Like tonight. He's off work."

"So, he lets you kind of come and go when you want to?"

"Yeah. He gave me a key. Lot of times he wakes me up when he gets home from work, then he goes and jogs with Ruth. I let myself out. I do clean up a little and take out the garbage," said Andre proudly, remembering something he does for his friend. "Then I lock up and head over to the Club."

"So, it's your job to take out the trash and pick up the beer cans and stuff?"

"Jacob don't drink—you know that," said a shocked Andre. "He belong to AA, man." Andre's irritation was growing.

"Where do you sleep when you come over? In his bed?"

"Got my own bed," said Andre pointing to the open door across the room.

"Hold it, Officer. Sit down, Andre," said Jacob firmly as he too moved to the table, now understanding clearly what this was all about. Jacob sat down across the table from Diaz. Andre sat between them. He pushed back away from the table and glanced back and forth between the two men, aware of the growing tension.

"Let's cut to the chase." Jacob folded his hands on the table as he leaned forward and looked Diaz in the eye.

Diaz smiled a crooked grin and leaned back a little from the table.

"Andre," said Jacob, but still glaring at the older man. "Officer Diaz is beating around the bush, trying to get some information. That's his job. But, let's save him some time. What he wants to know is do you and I have sex together? He wants to know if I expect you, in exchange for all of the things I do for you, to do sexual things to me or let me do sexual things to you. He wants to know if I buy you beer or drugs in exchange for sex. That's what he's getting at."

The shock and horror on Andre's face turned to anger as he turned his gaze from Jacob to Diaz and back again. He jumped to his feet and struggled to find the words that were not necessary for Diaz to hear anymore. The reaction was enough to answer his questions.

"You…you crazy, man! Jacob…he ain't like that. He probably don't even know about stuff like that, man…Jacob…Jacob a…he a Christian, man. You may have been to our church a couple of times, but you don't know nothing, Diaz! God oughta come down and smack you on the head. Shit, man! Don't matter if you a cop—you need your head examined."

"Andre!" said Jacob. He had to say it again, a little louder to get his attention and interrupt the flow of words from the boy's mouth. "Andre! It's okay. Officer Diaz is just doing his job. It's okay." Jacob was stifling a laugh and was relieved to see that Diaz was also smiling. "Sit down, Andre." Jacob pointed to the chair. "It's okay. Sit down."

Andre quit talking and returned to his chair, but he was so agitated, he was having trouble sitting still.

Diaz looked at the boy and smiled. "Listen, son. Jacob's right. I'm just doing my job. Sometimes it's a shitty job, too. Part of my job is being suspicious, and part of it is looking into tips and following up on complaints."

"Well, I ain't complaining about nothing," said Andre, still mad. "Jacob is like a brother to me. He way more a brother than my real brother. When you gonna talk to Juice? When you gonna lock him up, man?"

"I have been, Andre. Remember I talked to you about him? But you didn't give me much. I talked to your mom. She says he's a hard working, caring big brother, and she says you're the one who's running around with the gangs. She says Juice is just trying to help you."

Andre got agitated again, but didn't say anything, remembering the truce Juice had forced upon him.

"Andre," said Jacob, "has Juice threatened you about telling anybody about what you know?"

Andre nodded his head and the two men let the silence hang there, hoping the dam would break. "And, he might still have Angela. I don't know."

They waited, but that was all Andre said.

"Andre, I need to talk to Officer Diaz alone. Would you step outside on the steps and wait for a minute?"

Andre nodded and got up.

"Don't go anywhere, okay? This won't take long."

Andre nodded again as he left the apartment. The two men looked at each other across the kitchen table.

"Complaint? Tip?" asked Jacob. "What led to this, Officer?"

"The boy's mother called the station earlier today. She told a couple of different people that you were sexually abusing her son. But she insisted on talking to me. I stopped by there earlier this evening. She told me—quite sincerely—that she was concerned about all the time that Andre was spending with you. She said you had the boy watch pornographic movies, allowed him to drink beer, and that she was worried about you sexually abusing him."

Jacob shook his head sadly. "That was earlier this evening?"

Diaz nodded, revealing no remorse for his suspicion or any other emotion.

"We were just by there ten minutes before we got home. She and I had a pleasant conversation, as pleasant as one can for as high as she was, but…LaTisha thanked me for caring so much for Andre, for teaching him to play the guitar, for the Club, for taking him to church. She went on and on. She even thanked me for letting him spend the night—I don't get it."

"Had she been drinking?"

"I don't think so, she was too wired, too energetic. I'd say crank."

Diaz nodded in agreement. "That's what I thought, too. We've seen an increase in it lately and we've closed a few meth labs in the last month. It's quickly becoming the drug of choice. It's cheaper and the high lasts longer than cocaine."

"But it has terrible long term effects: paranoia, memory loss, hallucinations," said Jacob. "She's really in trouble."

"The woman tells lies on you and you're concerned about her?"

Jacob shrugged. "I think Juice is behind this. I think he's probably threatened her as well. Tod," Jacob paused, realizing he'd used the old cop's name for the first time. There was no visible reaction from Diaz. "I think he was behind that attempt to run Ruth and me over yesterday. I think Andre thinks so, too, just by the way he can't talk about it. Don't you have anything on him?"

Diaz shook his head. "I've even tailed him, personally. Half dozen times or more after McKey's closes. He goes right home to his apartment and doesn't come out again. I haven't seen anybody going or coming either. I think there's cocaine being sold in the bar at McKey's, but that's true of most yuppie bars. I've turned that information over to Narcotics. McKey's is out of my jurisdiction. So far, nothing. If he's connected to street gang activity, he's built a pretty deep cover for himself. But, he'll slip up, sooner or later."

"If he doesn't kill somebody first." There was a pause in the conversation, then Jacob asked, "Tod, you still suspect that I would..."

"I'll be honest with you. I don't want to believe it. But, when you think about it, it fits. Pedophiles build the trust of the parents, they let the kids stay over, they buy them things. Some have elaborate fronts, like attending church or regularly volunteering at places like the Club, just so they can be around kids, teaching guitar.... When what they really want is..." Diaz shrugged. The look on his face said, "Make me believe you, give me a reason."

Jacob sighed and said, "It fits...and you especially, given my history you would have reason to suspect, but, Tod, I swear to you..." Without flinching, he looked Diaz in the eye and continued. "I'd die. I swear it. I'd die, before I intentionally hurt one of these kids. Andre's home life is so bad. He's trying to leave the gang. That's the only reason I let him come and go here."

"You're not afraid to die?"

"I'm more afraid I'll screw up the living part, but I wouldn't hurt one of these kids. I swear it."

Again, the room fell into an eerie silence, Diaz wanting to believe and Jacob even more desperate that he would.

• • • • •

They had played a little game. When she entered the room he had tried to grab her, but without uttering a word, she pushed him into the big recliner in Wilson's apartment above McKey's. She moved to the middle of the floor and as he told her of the plan, with each detail she liked, she slowly removed a piece of clothing. She stood now wearing only a necklace, garter belt, stockings and high heels. She reached up and released her long blond hair. As she slowly shook her head, it fell over her shoulders. Her pasty white cheeks flushed with excitement.

She spoke for the first time. "Wonderful, my love, wonderful." Her voice was not a whisper, it was too loud. It had a gravelly yet still mysterious feminine quality. "If the old cop is killed, the papers will report the reason for his visit because you made sure LaTisha talked to several cops throughout the day. If the cop makes Hotchie leave with him, they'll both be killed and the story will be even better. The press will not be able to resist! I can see the headlines now." Her eyes took on their familiar, fiendish green hue as she raised both hands above her head spreading them slowly as if unfolding a banner. "Detective killed after investigating sexual abuse of a child. Grieving mother and older brother still in shock." She unfurled one imaginary headline after another. "Or, Detective and boy killed leaving home of suspected child abuser. Suspected child abuser, an ex-con, active at the Club and Antioch church. Livingston and Frye under fire." She began to laugh and took her first steps toward him.

• • • • •

The door slowly opened as Andre snuck back into the apartment. He shut the door behind him, turned to the two men. With his brown eyes wide, he said in a loud, excited whisper, "Anthony! He hidin' outside in the alley. He got a gun!"

"Anthony? Who's…"

"Isn't he one of the guys that was beating on you in the alley that day?" asked Jacob.

Andre nodded vigorously. "He's bad, too, real bad. He's crazy man, he'll do anything Juwan tell him. He brags about the people he killed. He waiting to kill somebody, maybe me. Juice said he'd kill me if I talked to anyone. He probably thinks…"

"Okay, Andre, tell us what you saw. Are you sure?"

"I was sitting on the top step. I thought I saw something, then I heard some rustling noise behind those big bushes. Then I saw him when he lit a cigarette. He hidin' behind the big bush right next to the neighbor's garage."

Andre's adrenaline was flowing, but he spoke clearly. He was sure of what he had seen.

"He has a gun?" asked Diaz. "How do you…"

"After he lit his cigarette, he held it up like this and cocked it." Andre demonstrated the pumping action. "I heard it click. I saw it, man. He got a gun. He here to kill someone. Juice or Juwan sent him. That's the way he is."

"I'd better get some backup. Where's your phone?"

"Dude don't have one of those either," Andre said with frustration. "I tell him everybody gotta have a phone." Andre looked at Jacob as if to say, "See, I told you so." He looked at Diaz. "Don't you have a flip, man? What kind of detective don't carry a cell phone?"

Diaz couldn't help but smile and shrugged. "Recharging. Plugged into the cigarette lighter in my car. You guys stay here," said Diaz as he pulled his police-issued .357 Magnum from under his coat. Jacob knew Diaz would probably be going up against greater firepower from Anthony, and for the first time in seven years he wished he owned a gun again.

"Be careful," was all Jacob could say.

Diaz moved slowly out the door with his back leaning flat against the outside wall of the house and disappeared down the steps. After what seemed like ten minutes, but was in reality closer to ten seconds, Jacob and Andre heard commotion and cursing as Diaz fell down the last half of the steps. He hit hard and with a deep grunt.

"Damn that step! Stay here, Andre." Jacob jumped up and quickly headed out the door. Andre was afraid, but he quietly followed his older friend into the darkness.

Jacob made it to the bottom of the stairs just as Anthony stepped out from behind the bush. Multiple gold chains around the young gangster's neck reflected the streetlight and competed for space on his sweaty chest and his black silk shirt. He was holding his pistol sideways, horizontal to the ground, like street punks do in the movies, but it was pointed at Diaz. It was difficult to see in the low light of the dark alley, but Jacob immediately recognized the silhouette of a semi-automatic weapon.

Anthony was jumpy; he chewed hard and fast on a toothpick sticking out of the corner of his mouth. His feet shuffled with the excitement of the moment. He looked all around and then turned the gun from Diaz to Jacob and back again. As Jacob took the last step down, a big grin came over Anthony's face; his gold tooth now competing with the necklaces for the street light's reflection.

Jacob saw a light come on in Mrs. Carlson's bedroom and hoped she was able to see enough to know she should call the police, but he prayed, *Please God, keep her and Andre inside.* But Andre was already behind him silently standing halfway down the steps.

Diaz, dazed at first, now understood he'd lost his gun in the fall down the steps. It felt like his ankle and his left arm were broken. He saw the street punk moving toward him, smiling. He was pointing the gun at the old cop's heart. For the first time in months, Diaz thought about his kids, and for the first time in many years he prayed. He asked God to be with his kids, to bless them, and to keep them from harm.

Andre quickly assessed the situation and was ready to jump over the side of the steps and run down the alley for help, maybe drawing fire, giving Jacob a chance. Then he saw Jacob's foolish move. A warning scream stuck in Andre's throat when he saw Jacob take two steps.

"Okay. Okay, you dumb piece of shit. I kill you first—then the pig. That the way you want it? I been wanting to waste your sorry ass, too!" Anthony spit the chewed-up toothpick from his mouth defiantly.

Jacob raised his hands over his head. He looked up out of the dark alley to the star lit sky and screamed as loud as he could, "Open this fool's eyes so that he can see why I'm not afraid to die, Lord."

Anthony was so shocked he uttered a stifled scream and took a step backward, right into a shallow sinkhole in the tattered alley pavement. He grunted as he turned his ankle. A burst of gun shots filled the air and splinters rained down harmlessly on Jacob as the bullets pelted the wall of the carriage house garage over his head.

Jacob launched himself from where he stood, tackling Anthony before he had a chance to recover. Crashing into a pile of garbage cans, they began wrestling over the gun that Anthony clutched in his hands. Anthony was no match for the well-conditioned Jacob and the struggle did not last long.

"Here!" said Diaz holding up a pair of handcuffs as Andre bounded to the foot of the stairs. Andre grabbed the cuffs and took them to Jacob. Beams from Mrs. Carlson's yard lights suddenly filled the alley. All over the neighborhood porch lights were coming on, and sirens could be heard in the distance. At the far end of the alley, on the side street, headlights off, Juwan pulled away, not wanting to attract any attention.

Jacob handcuffed Anthony's hands behind his back and left him lying face down in the alley dirt and the spewed garbage. Jacob picked up the gun and carried it as if it was something foul and putrid. "Here," he said and handed it to Diaz who had pulled himself up to a sitting position on the bottom step. "Andre, see if you can find Tod's gun." To Diaz he said, "You okay?"

Diaz looked up and into Jacob's eyes. "You're *not* afraid to die, are you?"

"Not really, but I'm glad it wasn't my time."

"Well, I am afraid to die and you saved my life, Jacob. That was about the stupidest…"

"Jacob! You all right?"

Jacob could see Mrs. Carlson on her porch and hear the fear in her voice. It filled him with deep anger that someone so sweet, so innocent, would have to fear anything happening in her own backyard. He tried to sound reassuring. "Everything's okay, Mrs. Carlson. Nobody's hurt. I'll be up in a few minutes. Really—it's okay."

"Here's your gun, Tod," said Andre.

"Now are you ready to tell me what you know, son?" asked Diaz.

Andre looked over to where Anthony laid, expecting to see a menacing stare, but Anthony was still dazed, and in shock. Andre looked back at Diaz and slowly nodded his head, tears beginning to pool in his big beautiful brown eyes—eyes that had seen too many things that children should never have to see.

•••••

Jez lay with her head on Juice's chest, looking up at him with excited anticipation, her green eyes glinting with evil mischief. Juice held the phone to his ear, saying nothing. He didn't need to; she read the news through the growing tension in his body as they lay entwined on the bed. Her haunting, baneful laugh began to rise from her chest as she pushed away and was fully unleashed by the time Juice let loose with a hideous scream. He jerked himself up and threw the cell phone across the bedroom, shattering the gilded mirror on the wall.

19 FORGIVE IN ORDER TO BE FORGIVEN

THURSDAY EVENING, JUNE 18

Ruth stood at the back of the music room enjoying the sounds coming from the seven guitars, eight counting Jacob's. This was the new beginners' class. By popular demand Jacob was now teaching two classes on Tuesday and Thursday evenings, and loving every minute of it. This class was mostly made up of teens, but the ten-year-old boy was the fastest learner, and the oldest, a chubby girl of eighteen, worked as if her life depended on it. They all worked hard for Jacob. Their faces were masks of concentration as they struggled to move their uncooperative fingers of one hand up and down the necks of their guitars, while strumming across the strings with the thumb of the other.

Jacob sat at the front of the room on a tall stool. He strummed his guitar and sang a phrase from an old Harry Chapin song over and over again as he demonstrated, slowly leading the way from one chord to another. With encouragement in his voice, he patiently sang, "Hold that D chord, on the old guitar till you find…the G. Bring it down to…old E minor, till the…A chord brings us home again to…D."

Jacob's most accomplished student, a tall, gangly boy of about fifteen, with stringy dishwater-blond hair that fell across his forehead, was moving about the room helping struggling students place their fingers on the correct frets. He seemed oblivious to the adoration of a couple of the young teenage girls in the class.

Finally, at nearly nine-thirty, Jacob stopped. He cradled his guitar on his lap like a child and beamed broadly at the class. "You guys are great! I mean it, you're picking this up so fast." He looked to his helper for confirmation. "Aren't they, Tony? Aren't they picking this up fast?"

The teenager smiled and nodded enthusiastically. Jacob continued, "I can't believe how fast you're learning. Keep practicing that song until you can do it without looking down at the chords. Those of you without your own guitars be sure to sign up for practice time before you leave. Tony will sign you up, okay? You have to practice, practice, practice. Okay?"

Ruth pitched in and helped Jacob and Tony return the guitars and music stands to their storage areas and tidy up the room. When they finished, Tony took a crumbled piece of paper out of the back pocket of his jeans, unfolded it and handed it to Jacob for him to sign.

Jacob took the sheet and signed it, but looked it over closely before handing it back. "Tony, if I read this time log correctly, you've more than completed the community service hours assigned by the court. Did you know that?"

"Really?" Tony took the sheet and looked it over. "Wow, that's great. But, can I still help you teach the class?"

"Sure, you bet. You're a big help."

Ruth added, "Tony, we're all very proud of you. I talked to your mom just now. She says you're doing great. I understand that your grades are even coming back up to where they were before you got in trouble. Good work."

Tony nodded sheepishly, but the satisfaction on his face was obvious. "Thanks. See you Thursday, Jacob."

When they were alone Ruth asked him, "Stories like Tony's make it all worthwhile, don't they?"

"He's a good kid. Andre usually helps me with this class, too, but I haven't seen him tonight."

"He and Jill are across the street. She wants to know if we can come over to talk."

"Oh yeah," Jacob smiled. "He has a big time crush on Jill, you know. 'Reverend Thomas the prettiest woman, black or white, I ever seen.'"

Ruth laughed. "You do a better Andre imitation than Mom. That was good."

"I must have heard him say it a couple of dozen times. Every Sunday after church, every time someone mentions church, 'You know, that Reverend Thomas is the prettiest woman, black or white, I ever seen.' He must be in seventh heaven, finally spending some time with her."

"Maybe," said Ruth. "But, Jill sounded pretty somber to me."

"Do you know what's up?"

"I'm not sure. She said that Andre needs to talk to both of us at the same time."

The Club was winding down, the kids were beginning to leave and parents were standing out front by their cars talking as they waited for the children. Ruth and Jacob had to stop and talk to several as they made their way out the front doors, down the steps and across the street to the church.

They found Jill and Andre waiting for them in her office at Antioch. She welcomed them with her usual warm smile. Andre had trouble making eye contact. A couple of years ago, when the church hired Jill as the associate pastor, she had no office. A couple of the men in the church got together and custom-made one for her in the far corner of the basement fellowship hall. The walls were covered with bookshelves bursting with all kinds of books. At first, Jill preached only occasionally, when Nathan was out of town. But, recently he was sharing the preaching duties with her almost equally. The books were further evidence of the scholarship and preparation she put into her preaching. Nathan's and Jill's preaching styles were very different but they really complemented one another.

The rest of the office furnishings were simple, but nice. There were only two side chairs so Jacob brought a folding chair in from the fellowship hall. Tuesdays was one of the few evenings when there were no church or community meetings being held in the basement hall. They were alone in the church, so he left the door open.

Jill looked at Andre who sat closest to her and smiled. Then she began. "Andre and I have had an interesting afternoon and evening. He needs to say something to both of you, but let me give you a little background first." She looked at Andre again and he nodded.

"Andre spent several hours with Officer Diaz this afternoon. Andre bravely told him everything he could about his old gang, even though he had agreed to a truce with his older brother not to talk. Then they came by here looking for Nathan. Diaz thought that Andre could benefit from a little counseling. You see, Andre really feels bad about some of the things he has done in the past and about some of the terrible things members of his old gang have done. But, Nathan is out of town tonight. So, Andre and I spent several hours together. We went over to his house and spent some time talking with Mrs. Johnson. I promised Andre that I would try to help his mother out. He's really worried about her. LaTisha and I had a good talk. We're going to try to get her some help, but Andre understands that it's totally up to her—she has to want it bad enough to work hard for it."

Andre, who had been staring at his hands in his lap throughout her explanation, looked up and nodded seriously. He understood that his mom had to want to get help with her problems.

Jill smiled and continued, "I was going to drop him off at the Club, Jacob, to help you teach your beginners' class, but during dinner at Andre's favorite place to eat..."

"Taco Bell?" interjected Jacob.

Jill smiled and nodded. "At dinner our talk turned to spiritual things. We talked about forgiveness and starting over and getting and staying clean. So, we came back here to continue our talk. I showed him some verses from the Bible that seemed to help."

"I like that one from the old book, you know the one about snow, and the blood being washed away. We don't need no more blood," said Andre. "Been enough blood."

"Yes," said Jill. "The one from the book of Isaiah in the Old Testament, '...though your sins be as scarlet, your heart shall be white as snow.'"

Andre nodded.

"I explained how God sent his son, Jesus, to wash away our sins. That when we accept Jesus, we just have to ask God to forgive us and no matter what, our hearts are washed clean, just like fresh-fallen snow. I explained that although we will still have to deal with the consequences of our actions, we don't need to feel guilty anymore. Plus, God sends his spirit to be with us, to help us through whatever life may send. And, that someday, we'll all be with Jesus and reunited with each other." She paused, then continued quietly, "That was really important to Andre, because...he's afraid his older sister Angela may be dead."

"Angela was really religious. If anybody's gonna get to heaven, it's Angela," Andre said. "Back in D.C. she tried to get all of us, even Juice, to go to church with her. None of us did. Juice says we don't need that religious shit—excuse me. She tried to tell me all about Jesus and all, but I wouldn't listen. Jill," he looked up into her smiling face. "She made it all…you know, simple and easy to understand."

The three adults smiled at Andre and nodded. Jacob looked around the book-filled room and was profoundly struck by the simple, but not so simple paradox.

"So," Jill continued when she was sure Andre had finished his point, "Andre and I prayed together. He asked Jesus into his heart and he asked God to forgive him of all of his sins."

Ruth leaned over and gave the boy a hug. "That's wonderful, Andre, just wonderful."

"Now he needs to ask the two of you to forgive him for something. When he gets this off his chest, he'll feel even better."

Jacob was surprised. He said, "Andre, you haven't done anything to me, I don't have anything…"

"Let him tell you," Jill gently interrupted. "Go ahead, Andre."

Andre looked up at Jacob, then back down to his lap. He mumbled, "I stole your tools."

Jacob wasn't sure he heard correctly. "You what? I didn't…"

Andre looked up and said louder, clearly. "I'm the one that took your tool box out the back of your truck. After you been so nice to me. I mean, you keep Juwan and Anthony from beating me up and then I steal your tool box." He looked up at Ruth. "And I'm the one who stole your car, Ruth."

Neither Ruth nor Jacob knew what to say at first. They were surprised and shocked. Jill said nothing. She had confidence in them to say the right thing. Andre sat, shoulders slumped staring at his fidgeting fingers. He couldn't look up.

Jacob and Ruth smiled knowingly at each other. Jacob scooted his chair closer to Andre, reached out and placed his hand on one of the boy's knees. "Andre," he said gently. "Andre, look at me." The boy looked up and met his eyes. "Andre, I forgive you. It's okay."

Ruth put an arm around the boy's shoulder and said, "Me, too, Andre. I forgive you, too."

He looked back and forth, from Jacob to Ruth and back to Jacob. "No kidding? I mean, after you been so nice to me. I mean, all those nights you let me spend at your house, taking me to Taco Bell and stuff—I felt so bad, man, you know?"

Jacob said, "Andre, I went to prison for something a lot worse than stealing a tool box, or even a car. Even worse, I ran out on people who had been good to me. Just like you, I had a mom who needed help, but, *I* ran out on her. I've asked everyone who loved me to forgive me. Most importantly, I asked God to forgive me, and he has helped me to forgive myself. So, how can I not forgive you, Andre? You're forgiven. I forgive you. God forgives you."

Andre turned to Ruth. "But, you never done anything bad, Ruth. I mean you been good to everybody. I stole that car right out of your garage. Then, a week later, I'm eating hot dogs and hamburgers at your momma's house with all those church folks. I felt so guilty. Mark, he's my best friend now and I stole his own sister's car."

Ruth laughed. "Well, Jill and I neither one ever did anything to go to prison for, but I've screwed up in my life, we all have. We all need forgiveness, Andre. And if we want forgiveness, we have to be willing to forgive. I forgive you, too, Andre."

"Stealing a car is worse than a tool box. I could go to jail for a long time."

"I won't press charges, Andre." Ruth laughed. "I got my car back, and I sold it. It's over. You'll never do anything like that again, right?"

"Never. I promise."

"Good," said Ruth and Jacob in unison as if the matter were closed and forgotten.

Andre looked at Jill with relief on his face. Jill opened her hands, palms up and said, "See, I told you so." Then she looked at Andre and said, "You want to tell them why you stole the tool box and the car?"

Andre looked back down again and she asked, "Do you want me to tell them?"

He nodded.

"Okay, I'll bet you're tired of telling this story. I'll tell them, but you jump in anytime, okay?" She looked at Ruth and Jacob, then began. "He stole those things because he was trying to help his sister Angela get out of town."

"Ah," said Ruth.

"I see," said Jacob, both beginning to understand.

"Juice was punishing Angela because she wouldn't have sex with some rich dude. She said 'no way' so Juice had Juwan and Anthony snatch her. The gang was keeping Angela hidden in an old warehouse near the Old Market. She had been there for days with little food or water, but she still told Juice she would not have sex with the man. Right so far, Andre?"

Andre looked up and nodded.

"So, Andre finds out where they're keeping Angela. He steals your toolbox, Jacob, and has a friend hock it for the money. Andre breaks Angela out of the warehouse, gives her the money…" Jill looked at Ruth, "and, your car, Ruth, so that she could drive away, as far away as she can. Angela wanted Andre to come with her, but he said somebody had to stay and take care of their mother."

"So, Angela got away?" asked Ruth.

Andre shrugged. "I think so, but we were arguing so loud about me going with her, somebody might have seen us, you know and followed her. Juice may have got to her."

"But, he's not sure. Juice led him to believe that he has her. So maybe he found her before she made it out of town. He might be bluffing, but…" Jill sighed, "Andre's not sure."

"Who told you?" began Ruth, then it hit her and she gasped. She covered her mouth with both hands and looked at Jacob. He also understood.

"Stephon Taylor," said Jacob. "YoYo lost his life trying to help you spring Angela, didn't he?"

Andre didn't look up. He nodded and a tear dropped from his cheek into his lap. "Is YoYo in heaven?" he asked, his voice breaking.

The three adults looked at each other. Jacob scanned the bookshelves again and then he said, "I think so, Andre."

"Me, too," said Ruth.

"But, he didn't know Jesus," the boy protested.

Jacob leaned down close to Andre again. "Sometimes, Andre, I think people are following Jesus whether they realize it or not. I think it took a lot of courage for Stephon to stand up against the gang and try to help Angela. I think Jesus knew Stephon and I think whether Stephon realized it or not, he was following Jesus. I don't know a lot about a lot of these things, but I know God loves Stephon—I *know* that. We can trust God."

Andre looked up at Jacob. "Can you take me home? I want to stay with my mom tonight."

"Sure, I'll take you home. Let's go."

After saying good-bye and receiving hugs from both Jill and Ruth, Jacob and Andre left for home. When Ruth heard the fellowship hall door shut behind them and she and Jill were alone her pent-up rage exploded.

"Jill, how can anybody be so cruel, so evil? That poor kid, how much more will he have to go through? I can't believe this."

"I know."

"How long will this jerk Juice get away with this? What did Tod say?"

"He called just before you got here. I think he's pretty frustrated, too. He hasn't gotten anything out of the guy that tried to shoot them the other night."

"So, Anthony's not giving up anything on Juice or the gang?"

"More than that, he's mute—not talking to anybody."

"I don't understand," said Ruth.

"Tod says that Anthony seems to be in a daze. He's not talking or responding to anybody. They have transferred him to the psychiatric ward. It's like he saw something, or was traumatized somehow by the incident in the alley."

"A street thug traumatized by a shooting?"

Jill shrugged. "This afternoon, Tod dragged Juice downtown for questioning. He wasn't getting anywhere, then a hot-shot lawyer shows up. Both Juice and the lawyer put on a pleasant front. Pretty smooth-talkers, I guess. Based on what Andre told him, Tod got a search warrant for Juice's apartment."

"Anything?" Ruth asked.

"We didn't get much chance to talk." She pointed toward the empty chair. "Andre was here. But, I don't think he found anything at the apartment. There's no question that Juice has a real job of some kind at McKey's. Andre says it's just a front, but so far, it's just Andre's word against Juice's."

Ruth shook her head in frustration. "There has to be something linking him to this gang activity. Andre is not just making all this up."

"Tod said they could get a search warrant for LaTisha's house, but they would probably just turn up her drugs and that would leave Andre all alone."

"I can't believe such a low-life would pay his mother's bills."

"Pretty strange," agreed Jill. "Andre said his big brother used to be nice to all of them. He even warned them never to get involved with the gangs. He said that since they moved here, something came over him, something evil has gotten into him. Andre says he gets *meaner and badder all the time.*"

Ruth stood and began to pace. "Did Tod talk to Wilson? He's a sleaze himself, but I can't believe he would knowingly let someone like Juice use one of his businesses as a cover."

"I think he's out of town again. Nathan says Tod has talked to him before, but Mr. Wilson says Juice is doing a good job. Mr. Wilson seems to be proud of him for turning his life into something good."

"How's he know? He's always back in D.C. Word is that he's contemplating a run for the Senate. Can you believe that? Lose to Linda Cabinet after just two house terms and two years later he's thinking of a run for the Senate?"

"He could win, too," said Jill. "It would be a great political comeback."

"God, I hope not."

• • • • •

"You want me to come in with you, Andre?" asked Jacob as he pulled Old Blue to a stop in front of the house.

"No, I'll be all right." Andre opened the door and paused. He looked back at Jacob. "We brothers now? I mean since I asked Jesus into my heart?"

Jacob smiled and held out his hand for Andre to give him five. "We brothers, partner. You and I—forever."

Jacob did not leave until he was sure Andre was safely in the front door. Even then, he whispered a prayer before he drove away begging for the boy's protection.

Andre walked into his mother's bedroom. She lay fully clothed on her back. A smoldering cigarette was in the ashtray next to the almost empty bottle of vodka.

Juice been here, he thought. Juice's idea of supporting Momma was to bring her vodka so she wouldn't use drugs. "Momma? Momma, you okay?"

Her heavy breathing was the only response he got so he put out her cigarette, covered her with a clean sheet that he pulled from a dresser drawer and turned out the light. As he left the room he said, "Night, Momma."

After going to the bathroom and brushing his teeth, he stripped to his jockey shorts and crawled into bed. He pulled the sheet up and rolled over on his side. His bare foot hit something cold and wet. Startled, he jumped from the bed and turned on the overhead light. He returned to the bed and slowly pulled back the sheet to see what was in his bed. When he saw it he stifled the scream that caught in his throat and whispered a desperate prayer instead, "Oh, God. Oh, Jesus. You got to hang with me now, Jesus. Please, Jesus, please."

Outside, a half-block away, Diaz sat in the unmarked car. When neither the search of Juice's freezer nor the gang's hide-out had turned up Stephon's finger in the baggie, Diaz knew that Juice had set them up. Diaz knew that now Juice must know that Andre had told them everything. Diaz was determined not to let anything happen to Andre. He'd stay here every night for a year if he had to, until they put this guy away. Nothing would happen to this kid. *Not this one, Lord. Dammit, not this kid.*

NATHAN'S
STORY
20
LATE FRIDAY NIGHT, JULY 12

They sat in Nathan's beat up old Ford down the street from Andre's house. It had been a hot sultry day. A thick haze clung to the streetlights. Nathan's window was open and Jacob had wedged a magazine under the hinge of the open passenger door so that the dome light would not shine. Even so, no breeze could be felt. Even the limbs of the trees that lined the street seemed to sigh and sag in the late night heat and humidity. They weren't necessarily hiding, but neither did they want to draw attention to themselves. They parked down the street so that Andre wouldn't notice their car.

"Thanks for helping me organize these late night watches, Nathan. Tod would've never gone along with this if you and Dennis hadn't pushed it."

Nathan took a drink of iced tea from his mug and nodded. "You've done all the organizing. That old cop would've sat out here for a year, all by himself, without ever asking for help if you hadn't spotted him. He's a stubborn old buzzard."

They laughed, then Jacob replied, "But, he's a good man. He's got that crusty exterior, but he loves these kids, he really does."

"He'll be here in an hour. You can head out if you need to get to work."

Jacob looked at his watch. "I've got a few minutes. I don't have to be at work until eleven."

It had been late June when Jacob had finally learned of Diaz's nightly vigil. One night after the Club closed Jacob drove Andre home and spotted the old cop down the street sitting in his unmarked police

173

car. Diaz told him about the finger in the baggie that they had *not* found. Andre was in danger, Diaz felt responsible for having put him there, and they still had nothing concrete on Juice. Anthony was still unresponsive at the psyche ward. There had been very little serious gang activity in the last month.

Jacob, Nathan and Dennis then ganged up on Diaz, insisting that they would help protect Andre. Jacob recruited help from the Friday evening AA group. Nathan quietly secured the help of a few men at Antioch and, reluctantly, Diaz even recruited a couple of cops from the gang task force to work one or two nights a week when they were off duty. Jacob kept them all scheduled and organized. No one had to work more than one or two nights each week and they were usually able to work in pairs. Even when it wasn't his turn, Diaz often showed up just to check on things.

The volunteers quietly went about their surveillance. At an organizational meeting held at the Club, they decided on not letting anyone, except for Ruth and Maryann—not Andre, or the Club staff, or even the police brass know of their vigil. The group called themselves *The Watchmen*. They communicated by cell phone and Diaz had provided them with a portable police radio to be used only if they saw something. Jacob even broke down and finally bought a cell phone and a pager so that he could stay in touch with the volunteers. If Andre decided to spend the night at Jacob's or at Maryann's a call was made and the watch shifted location.

But as LaTisha's depression deepened, Andre spent fewer nights at Jacob's or at Maryann's with Mark. Jacob was impressed by his young friend's devotion. Reverend Thomas and Ruth made several more attempts to get LaTisha the help that she needed. After each visit, she seemed to pull herself together for awhile, as if to prove to herself that she didn't need any help.

"It's been a quiet month," said Nathan.

"I know, but Tod says we can't relax until Juice and Juwan are in jail. He says sooner or later they'll flub-up."

"Isn't Juwan the one whose arm you broke?" asked Nathan.

"Yeah, seems like a long time ago, but it was only last spring. Tod says he seems to have disappeared. No one has seen him in weeks."

"The heat's on," said Nathan. "They've really put a dent in the drug and gang activity this summer. He's probably moved on till it dies down again. He'll be back."

"You think it's okay for me to take a couple of days?" asked Jacob.

Nathan looked across the seat and even in the dim light could see the conflicting emotion in Jacob's face. "Sounds like you need the break, Jacob. I don't remember you taking any time away in the three years you've been back." Nathan picked up some papers from the front seat. "You've given me the schedule and all the names of The Watchmen. I'll take care of things."

Jacob stared ahead and nodded. "I'll be back in time for my Tuesday night guitar class."

"The Club's having a wonderful summer, isn't it?" asked Nathan.

"It really is. It's packed with kids, from the early bird program starting at six-thirty in the morning to the teen program that shuts down at eleven every night. It's such a well-rounded, broad-based program. I'm so impressed with Ruth. She has wisdom and maturity well beyond her years. She's the most dedicated person I've ever known and she's tough, too, Nathan. She handles the personalities on that staff pretty well. They all know who's boss and she's only twenty-one years old. Dennis has done a good job of bringing her along and training her."

"Dennis and her father," said Nathan. "Joe Bethel was the best."

Jacob nodded, then added, "I've got to go by her house in the morning to let her know I'll be back in time for my regular class."

Nathan said, "A couple of days in a canoe, on the Niobrara River, just you, the river, a campfire and the sky at night. Sounds great."

"Yeah, I'm all packed. I'm leaving as soon as I get off work tomorrow morning. But, I'll be back on Tuesday. I just need to get away, to think…and to pray."

Neither man said anything for awhile. Then Jacob turned to face his mentor. He smiled and asked, "No questions? No suggestions about how to pray?"

"Need some?"

"Yeah, maybe." Jacob paused, then continued, "Nathan, you said you'd tell me your story someday. You said three years ago that it wasn't important, that all I needed to know then was that you had traveled the same road and would be able to help me along."

Nathan drained the cup and screwed it back onto the thermos before commenting. "So, you think it might help to hear my story?"

"Maybe. What do you think?"

Nathan turned and faced the man who felt like a son to him. "Someday, my friend, we'll take a week and go fishing, maybe to Canada. We'll sit around the campfire at night and I'll tell you the whole story."

"Okay," said Jacob, a little disappointed. "What I'm most interested in is how, after you got out of prison, how did you...did you plan all along to be a pastor?"

"God knows I didn't," said Nathan as he shifted his weight in the driver's seat. "Okay, here it is in a nutshell. Someday, the whole thing, but for now, Nathan's story in brief. It might help."

"Great." Jacob shifted so he could see the preacher's face. The dim beams from the street light accented his craggy features.

"I used to tell my story a lot. At first, it seemed to help people, but dramatic conversion stories tend to make celebrities out of people. That's why I've encouraged you, Jacob, to only tell your story in AA meetings, with people who have gone before you, people you can't con and will not put you on a slippery pedestal."

"That was good advice, too. It's taken a lot of the pressure off."

Nathan nodded and continued. "It's been over twenty years now for me. I think I've mellowed with time. There are some things I only began to understand in recent years."

"Sounds like the making of a good book to me," joked Jacob.

Nathan didn't laugh, but responded seriously, "I've been thinking about that, writing a book. Maybe we can take that trip sometime and I can test it on you."

"I'd love to hear it, honestly," said Jacob.

"Tonight you get the five-minute version. I was born in Louisville, Kentucky in 1950. My mom was a professor at the University of Louisville, and my dad was a World War II hero, a student attending school on the GI Bill. Neither of their parents approved of their marriage."

"Really? How come?"

"My mother was a brilliant woman who taught sociology. She was from a well-to-do family, the stereotypical East Coast liberals. My Dad was a from a lower middle-class working family. He grew up in Louisville, in an old neighborhood called Portland which was a lot like Parkland but more rundown, I'm afraid. Their marriage was doomed from the start."

"The cultural differences?"

"No, my dad's alcoholism. Plus, he must have seen some horrible things in the war. He was one of the few who made it from D-day through the end to V-E Day. He had three Purple Hearts and won the Congressional Medal of Honor. The local war hero status just added to the pressure. They split up not long after I was born. He died when I was four. He was in a coma for three weeks following a barroom fight."

"Do you remember him?"

"Only vaguely. When I was ten, my mother took a prestigious post as head of the Sociology Department at Berea College in Kentucky."

"I've never heard of it," said Jacob.

"Very unique school. It was founded in the 1850s by Abolitionists as a model of integrated education. It is one of the most heavily endowed schools in the country. Most students are from the Appalachian states, twelve...I don't know, maybe fourteen states total. The students cannot attend Berea if their parents make too much money. And, every student is required to hold a job."

"Wow, that's different."

"It is. My mother loved it. So did I. She soon married another professor at the college. Mom was a true believer in the goodness of humankind. She was very socially involved and when the civil rights movement began in earnest, she was there on the front lines, marching and protesting throughout the South. My stepdad and I didn't really get to know each other very well. He was pretty aloof."

"Did your mother ever meet Dr. Martin Luther King?"

"She did, in fact. She credited him with her conversion to Christianity."

"Really?"

"She said one evening at a campsite somewhere down South, she had this overwhelming sense of a presence about her, almost an aura, but with a personality. At first, she thought it was just being in the presence of Dr. King. She had such admiration for him. She approached him and asked him about what she was feeling. He told her that he was not at all sure, but perhaps Christ was making his approach to her."

"Fascinating."

Nathan nodded. "She studied, she read, she talked to other professors at Berea and finally decided to make a profession of faith. She gave her whole life to new faith. It made her even more committed to social justice. Her conversion was the final blow with her family, however. It also created problems in her marriage. Agnosticism was the preferred religious preference, I guess. My grandparents were encouraged when Mom had remarried someone of her own social standing, but when Mom announced that she had converted to Christianity...I never saw or had contact with my grandparents again...until Mother's funeral, and I've had only one contact since."

"How sad," empathized Jacob.

"It really was," said Nathan. "My mother was one of the Civil Rights workers who was killed in Alabama during the early sixties. My stepfather was a brilliant man, but he was also a very cold man. He really had trouble handling an angry teenager, and he gave up on me pretty quickly. I bounced from one institution and foster home to another from the time I was thirteen until I ended up in jail for the first time at age nineteen. I was so angry. I hated God because I blamed him for the fact that I had no family. Strangely enough, I didn't blame the hate-mongers who had killed my mom, rather I blamed the black folks for whom she had fought so bravely."

Nathan paused and Jacob waited for him to continue.

"I did some terrible things, Jacob. I was full of rage. That's why after my conversion and after I was released, I think God brought me here, to Parkland, to Dr. Matthew Millard. I needed to be nurtured, guided and loved by a caring black man. God knew what I needed and brought me here."

"So, now," said Jacob thoughtfully, "you mentor ex-cons and young black pastors."

Nathan nodded. "That's certainly part of it, my need to pay back. Just like your need to work with the Club."

"But, when you came here, you weren't planning on being a pastor?"

"Oh, no, not at all. I was one fired-up Christian, though. I'll tell you that. As I think about it, I was pretty obnoxious. I had it all figured out, three years of Bible study in prison and I had all the answers. Dr. Millard had his hands full with me...and my big mouth."

"Another reason why you encouraged me to..."

"Keep your mouth shut for awhile," Nathan interrupted, pointing his finger at Jacob and laughing.

"So, how did you become a pastor?"

"Simple answer? I was called by God and his people. Longer answer, it was just after the merger between the all-white Parkland Baptist and the all-black Memorial Baptist. The new church, Antioch, took off, and it touched a nerve. It was something people longed for—a functioning, fully-integrated church. We grew like crazy. Dr. Millard was overworked and growing older. I was already doing a lot at the church. Every free hour that I had I was there."

"And at the Club?" asked Jacob.

"Yes, and at the Club. Dr. Millard really pushed us all to volunteer at the Club. He had to get after me, though, and remind me that it was a secular institution, that it would be unChristian to overtly proselytize at the Club. He taught us that it was Christ-like to serve—to minister without any expectation of return and to love others unconditionally. He was a great man. I wish you could have known him."

"Me, too. From what Maryann tells me, Dr. Millard, more than anybody else, helped bring my mom back."

"That's true. He was a wonderful counselor as well as a powerful orator."

"So, was it Dr. Millard who got you into the ministry?"

Nathan shook his head. "Not really. I was completing my undergraduate degree in journalism at the time and working odd jobs, going to class and working at church. Anyway, at a business meeting one night, the issue of hiring an associate pastor came up. There was overwhelming support for the idea. Your landlady's husband, Mr. Carlson, stood up and said, 'I think God has called Nathan to be our associate pastor.' Shocked the hell out of me, I'll tell you that. There was very little discussion, a vote was taken and only one vote was cast against the idea."

"Whose?"

"Mine!"

"That simple? That's all it took?"

"That's all it took. I started as a part-time pastor while finishing up my degree. The church was good enough to send me for more education over the years. But, yes, it was just that simple. God and his people called and I said, yes—eventually. Then they set about training and educating me."

"But, you don't want people to call you doctor or reverend. How come? You have a Ph.D. in theology, from Notre Dame, right?"

Nathan shrugged. "I prefer pastor, or preacher."

Jacob nodded as he looked down the dark street.

"Is that what this canoe trip's about? Trying to figure out if God is calling you?"

Jacob nodded.

"Seems to me that it's pretty obvious, Jacob." They made eye contact and Nathan continued. "You have two gifts—music and kids. Your music touches people in deep and powerful ways and you have a way with children, especially, according to Dennis, with the little hard nuts, the tough guys."

"You know what, Nathan?" Jacob asked with a level of excitement that surprised Nathan. "This month, the royalty checks on two of my songs amounted to more than three months' salary at the radio station."

Nathan put his head back and roared approval. He slapped his protégé on the leg and said, "Congratulations, son, that's wonderful."

"So, do I do it full-time? Write music? I mean, I know it may not be steady income, but my agent is sure that *When Sparrows Fall* will do even better. He says I'm going to get an advance on that one. It's hard to believe, I might be able to make a living doing something that I love so much. Maryann says she can sell me an individual health insurance policy that will cover everything but an alcohol relapse, and I don't plan on that happening."

"Why not go for it? Then you'll have more time to teach kids at the Club. You can always pick up another job if you have trouble selling songs in the future."

Jacob looked back up the street and nodded.

"That's not all, is it?"

Jacob shook his head.

Nathan said, "You're trying to figure out this blossoming relationship with Maryann and her children."

Jacob turned to look at his mentor again. He smiled. "You're good, fella, real good."

"Not so hard to figure out. At least, Maryann's not hard to figure out. She seems very taken with you. You, on the other hand, seem to have grown a little aloof over the last month or so."

This time it was Jacob who pointed his finger. "Now, you're scaring me. *She* scares me. I'm scared, Nathan. I have all these…mixed emotions. I love her, but…I'm not sure if it's…that kind of love. You know? I mean,

I have these...sexual desires, but...I don't know."

"Jacob," Nathan interrupted. "Those are natural feelings. You're a man. She is one beautiful woman. There's nothing wrong with that."

"I know. I know that, but...I mean, I never thought I would marry. Especially after what I'd...my history. After coming here and...you know."

"Working with me, the Protestant celibate?"

"Yeah," Jacob laughed. "I mean, I never took a vow of chastity...." He laughed a little and shook his head. "But, I just assumed I'd forfeited my right to be married. I know God's forgiven me, and I've forgiven myself. Like you say, forgiven yes, but there are consequences to be paid. I mean, I have all of these emotions. I thought Maryann and I...we would just be friends, that I could be her friend, you know...I mean, I love her. And, Ruth and Mark, what great kids, I love them, too. If I could be a big brother, a father-like figure...Maryann seems to be encouraging that, too. But..."

"You don't think you deserve her, do you?"

Jacob recoiled. The always-pleasant smile left him. "I don't, Nathan. I hurt her terribly once, but it's much more than that. After some of the things I've done, I'm not sure if I'm healthy enough, emotionally. God, Nathan, I don't want to hurt anyone, ever again, especially not Maryann or her kids."

Nathan wanted to tell him to go for it, that Maryann was wonderful and well worth the risk. An ache from deep in his memory sliced through Nathan's heart. He wanted to grab his young friend and shake him. He wanted to move closer, get in his face and tell him, *Don't blow this! If she's interested in you again, you'd be a damned fool to let it pass you by.* But, he didn't. Instead Nathan said, "Jacob, none of us deserves the gifts of grace that God sends us."

"I know, but..." Jacob looked up, a tear slowly snaking down one cheek. "I've never told you why I left town so suddenly, twenty years ago."

• • • • •

Jacob needed a drink, badly. When the graduation party for Maryann finally ended, he took her to the apartment he shared with his mom. It was where they always went when they wanted to make love. His mom worked the late shift at the Diner and never got home before two in the morning. It didn't matter, though, because Jacob always had Maryann home by eleven-thirty. He told Maryann it kept her parents happy and on his side, which was true—Maryann's parents loved him. He had them fooled, too. The real reason was that he had plenty of time to drink afterward—if he got her home early enough.

Tonight, they'd had a terrible argument. She wanted to set a wedding day for early September, around Labor Day weekend. He tried to tell her—that with her mind and intellect—she had just graduated third in a class of six hundred—she deserved to go to college. They could wait to get married, he'd argued. She said her father had agreed she should go to college, and had promised to help them if she did. He only had two years left, she'd said. They'd be college students together. She didn't know that after two years of college he had barely one year's worth of credits. He'd flunked every class this past semester because he quit going after the coach told him at the end of basketball season that his scholarship would not be renewed next year. She was in tears when he dropped her off at her house and refused to come in. He needed a drink.

Bob Wilson and his other friends were throwing the real graduation party tonight at the new motel on the western edge of town. The place had a dome with swimming pools, hot tubs and all. Tom had rented twenty rooms and bribed the manager to look the other way. The place was hopping when Jacob arrived. He quickly found the two-bedroom suite where Tom had set up the bar. It wasn't long before Jacob was feeling good again. As guys and girls paired off, some with strangers, some with sequential partners, Jacob continued to sit on the couch in the suite and drink and watch the ebb and flow of activity.

About one-thirty in the morning, Jeannie Diaz, only seventeen, but already very much a woman, entered the suite by herself. Jeannie was tall and athletic. As a junior last year she'd been a star on the Central High School basketball team until she'd been suspended for her temper. There was only one week of softball season left and she was still on the team, its all-conference shortstop. Jeannie wore a short, tight white skirt that accented her long, brown, muscular legs. The top buttons of her silk blouse were left undone. The bottom of her blouse was pulled tight and tied in a knot that lay just above the navel on her flat stomach.

Jeannie finished the beer in her hand while she talked and laughed with two other girls, but she kept smiling at Jacob on the couch. Soon the suite cleared out and the other girls tried to get Jeannie to go with them, but she stayed. She smiled and kept her eyes fixed on Jacob as she leaned over the cooler, then reached through the ice with both hands and retrieved two bottles of beer. She cooled her ample cleavage with one as she walked across the suite to join Jacob on the couch.

Jacob couldn't remember what happened after that. He had vague memories of Tom and others returning to the suite—of their jeers and teasing as he tried to get up from the couch, of everyone laughing when Jeannie pulled him back into her lap. He excused himself and went to the bedroom. A few minutes later, from the other room he heard Jeannie say something. Was she mad? Then he heard the guys laugh. Jeannie came into the bedroom and shut the door behind her. As she crossed the room, she removed her blouse.

"Jeannie," he tried to mumble. "Don't...I can't."

She dropped her skirt and with a pout said, "What's the matter? Don't you like brown-skinned girls?"

"No...I mean, yes. Jeannie...."

"Then let's just take a nap together, Jacob. Maybe in the morning...."

"No! I..."

Her head was on his bare chest when he woke up. It wasn't morning. At least the room was still dark. He tried to focus on the alarm clock. Four-thirty? His arm was asleep under the weight of her body. He tried to move her. Maryann? No...No! Jeannie, get off me. Get up..." Then he felt it, maybe smelled it. It wasn't sweat on her head. "Oh, God...no. Jeannie?"

With difficulty he was able to pull his arm out from under her. Jeannie's head flopped to the pillow. "Jeannie?" She didn't answer. He found the lamp's switch and its rays sent a searing pain through his pupils to the back of his head and down his neck. But, what he saw sobered him up. Her face was a bloody mess. Her panties were gone. She was nude and..."Oh, God," he moaned. "Jeannie! Jeannie, I'm sorry. Wake up! Wake up, Jeannie, please."

She didn't wake up, but she was breathing. He was nude and covered with her blood. He quickly devised a plan. He showered and dressed. There was no blood on his clothes. Another couple had collapsed on the couch in the living room. Three others were passed out in the other bedroom.

Jacob called the rescue squad from a pay-phone, then went home and packed his belongings. By six-thirty he had written a goodbye note to

Maryann, awakened Joe Bethel and given him the note, called the hospital to check on Jeannie and was crossing the Parkland Bridge. He did not return for nearly twenty years.

• • • • •

Jacob was exhausted and tears were streaming down both cheeks. He looked at his mentor and friend, his spiritual father. "That's why I don't deserve Maryann or any other woman. Any man who's capable of such...he's better off, just being alone."

"Jacob," said Nathan firmly. "You're wrong."

"I know, Nathan. I'm forgiven. God forgives me. Maybe I've forgiven myself. For God's sake, even Tod seems to have forgiven me, but still...."

"Jacob, you don't understand. I happen to know that Tod believes..."

Jacob suddenly sat straight up and snatched the police radio from below his feet where it lay on the floorboard. A car was slowly coming down the street toward them with its lights off.

"Tod, Tod, this is Watchman One."

Through the radio static came Diaz's voice, "I'm on him."

Another car, headlights on high beam, turned onto the block and fell in behind the car that crept past Andre's house. As it came up to where Nathan and Jacob sat, the car stopped briefly and the driver's window came down. A hand came out of the window and pulled the trigger on an imaginary gun. "Bang! Bang!" the driver taunted, then stepped on the gas. As the car turned the corner the squeal of its tires cut through the urban night.

Diaz didn't bother with a chase. He pulled to a stop next to Nathan's car, rolled down the window and said, "Looks like Juwan has returned."

From a block away, they could hear the tires squeal again.

• • • • •

Just before seven the following morning, Jacob was getting ready to leave the radio station. He was depressed, and depression was an emotion he hadn't felt in over seven years. Throughout the night, as he went about his duties at the station, he tried to pray, but it hadn't helped. He sat at an old desk and jotted some notes to the station manager and the tech who would take his place on Monday night.

He heard the door shut behind him and turned to face Officer Diaz. "You and I need to talk," said the old cop. "This okay?"

Jacob stood to face this man he'd come to believe was his friend, the man who had somehow forgiven him, but his heart sank lower and the pit in his stomach became unbearably heavier. With a growing sense of foreboding he nodded his head. He pointed back at his chair and mumbled, "Sure, but there's only this one chair."

Tod shook his head. "It's okay. This won't take long."

Jacob didn't know what to say, so he said nothing, waiting for Diaz to speak.

"After you left for work last night, Nathan and I talked."

Jacob nodded. Maybe until his talk with Jacob, Diaz hadn't realized it was actually him who had hurt his sister.

"You didn't rape and beat my sister, kid."

Jacob was stunned. "What?"

"It wasn't you. You didn't do it. If I'd realized you thought you had, I would have told you a long time ago."

"But, when I woke up…Jeannie was…"

"I know. Everything pointed to you for awhile, especially the way you split town and all. Jeannie was in a coma for two days and Wilson and his rich friends tried to pin it on you. Several witnesses said they saw the two of you go into the bedroom."

"But, what…who?"

"Jeannie. When she came to she remembered everything. She said she had followed you into the room. She even admitted trying to…seduce you. She was pretty wild, we all knew that."

"I remember…."

"You were drunk, kid. She said all you could do was murmur something about Maryann, about how you didn't deserve her and all. Jeannie said she just laid down next to you and fell asleep."

"But, when I woke up, the blood…her poor face." Jacob looked down at his hands like he always did when the memory came over him, always making him question how he could have done such a thing.

Tod shook his head. "You didn't do it. Wilson and three other guys came into the room. Everyone was drunk. It was a wild party. They pulled her out of the room kicking and screaming and you didn't even wake up. When she fought them, someone, I don't know who, maybe all of them started hitting her. They took turns on her and then threw her back in bed with you."

"But...you mean...I didn't do that to her?"

"You didn't do it, kid. Maybe if you'd hung around...."

"But, then...no one was arrested or punished?"

"Are you kidding? They all backed each other up. Jeannie was way this side of being a virgin. They had several witnesses...then Bob Wilson's dad and some of the other fathers used their influence. Jeannie didn't want to pursue it. The only thing that hit the paper was that the manager of the hotel was fired for allowing the party."

"I didn't do it."

"You didn't do it."

Detective Tod Diaz had seen and heard a lot in his long career, but he never had a grown man collapse in great relief and sob in his arms before. But he'd never exorcised a demon before, either. He stood there, awkward at first, as Jacob wept on his shoulder. He looked around, glad there were no windows in the tiny office, but it was okay. It felt good—even cleansing.

THE
DISCOVERY

21

SATURDAY, JULY 13TH

"You've already been to the grocery store and back and it's only nine o'clock, Mother. You ever hear of sleeping in on a Saturday?" Ruth reached out to take one of the bags from her mother. Maryann flashed her smile and a rolling eyebrow at her daughter's good-natured teasing. Ruth thought how pretty her mother looked in her T-shirt, shorts and running shoes. It was a beautiful morning and Ruth thought her mother had a special glow.

"I thought you'd be out running with Jacob." said Maryann.

"He's not running this morning. I came by to see if you wanted to run with me. You're already dressed for it."

"I was planning to go to the health club as soon as I unpack these groceries."

"Run with me this morning," said Ruth. "I need some time with my mom."

"It's a beautiful day," said Maryann. "I'll run with you, if you'll take it slow for the first three miles. Then you can drop me off back here and go run as hard and long as you like."

"You're on." Ruth started to unpack the bag of groceries. "By the way, you just missed Jacob."

Ruth's growing suspicions were confirmed when her mother stopped putting away groceries and seemed to smile even broader as she tried to ask nonchalantly, "Jacob was here?"

"Yes, he wanted to ask if you and Mark could pick up Andre for church tomorrow since he won't be around. He was sure in an upbeat mood, too."

Maryann returned to putting away groceries and tried to make her question sound like small talk. "Really? How come?"

"I don't know, he just seemed happy."

"How come he won't be around tomorrow?"

"Oh," said Ruth with a glint in her eye, "he decided on the spur of the moment to take a canoe trip down the Niobrara River. He stopped by on his way out of town. He was going to stop by the nursing home to see Grandma Becky and then head out."

Ruth heard the disappointment in Maryann's voice when she asked, "Oh, is he taking some kids from the Club canoeing?"

"Nope. He's going all alone."

"Really? All by himself? Why?" said Maryann, thinking a canoe trip sounded delightful. She was half-mad that she hadn't been invited. Scenes of a canoe, water, swim suits and starlit nights flashed through her mind. She turned and, with what Ruth thought was a little agitation, began to put groceries away.

"Well?" said Maryann when Ruth didn't answer. She stopped again and found Ruth smiling at her.

"Well, what?" Ruth teased.

Embarrassed to be so transparent to her too-smart-for-her-own-good daughter, Maryann tried valiantly to return to her nonchalance.

"Well, why is he taking a canoe trip down the Niobrara all by himself?" she asked.

"He said he had some things to sort out. He said he wanted to be alone with the Lord for awhile, by himself."

Maryann thought, *Oh no. Why does the Lord always let me fall in love with such religious men? That sounds just like something Joe would've said. It's not something Jay Riddler would've said in the old days. Jacob is* a different person. That's when it dawned on Maryann. She had just admitted to herself for the first time that, in fact, she was in love with Jacob Riddler—again.

"Mom? Hello-o? Earth to Mom?" Ruth teased, breaking her mom's spell.

"What?" Maryann feigned irritability.

"Jacob said to tell you he would be back Tuesday afternoon. Can you make it till then?"

Maryann grabbed a dishrag and flung it across the kitchen as her daughter laughed and retreated out the back door. "Hurry up, old lady," she teased.

"I'm going to run you into the ground, little girl," yelled Maryann and then she said out loud as she stored the last can of soup, "Thank you, Lord, for the joy that girl brings me—from day one."

● ● ● ● ●

Monday Afternoon, July 15th

Jacob came out of the shower when he heard the knocking on his door. *Andre must have found out I got back early*, he thought. Naked and dripping wet, he pulled on a pair of cut-off jeans and, barefoot, with his towel in his hand, started for the door of his apartment. He opened the door and was once again bowled over by the beauty of Maryann's smile.

Maryann stood on the landing smiling, allowing her eyes to move over Jacob's wet, lean, just-right body. *Just something about a freshly scrubbed man*, she thought, and said, "Aren't you going to invite me in?"

"Maryann?" Jacob said as if he didn't recognize her. "Sure. Sure. Come on in. I'm sorry. I got up at dawn and drove all morning. I just got out of the shower. Here, sit down. Let me..." He moved to the kitchen counter and reached for the coffeepot. "I just put this on." He let go of it and said, "It's still perking. I...ah...I'll be right back."

Maryann sat at the little kitchen table, amused at his discomfort. She enjoyed watching him quickly cross the spacious room of the large apartment to his bedroom. When he returned a Club T-shirt covered his lean abs and hard chest.

"Yes, this coffee's done. Would you like a cup?" he said as he moved back into the kitchen and reached into the tiny cupboard for a mug. "What...How come you..."

"Mark said you dropped by while I was on an appointment. Glad you're back. I tried to call you, but...."

"Oh," He looked at the cell phone that lay on the kitchen table. "I didn't have it turned on." Then he seemed to drift off somewhere.

"So?" inquired Maryann.

Jacob came back from wherever he'd gone, and just looked at her.

"Did you have a nice trip—all by yourself?" she asked.

"Maryann," he began tentatively. "I needed to get away. I needed to think, to pray. I've been confused about what the Lord wants from me. So I went canoeing. I was asking for a sign from the Lord."

He paused and they made an uncomfortable connection with their eyes, unable to look away, the words were coming hard for Jacob. Maryann raised an eyebrow giving him permission to continue.

"Well, I got my sign—big time. I just don't know how to tell you about it...I don't know what to say. I would never assume...I can't expect...."

"Oh boy, why don't I like the sound of this? Why do I feel like a high school kid again?" Maryann looked away, rolling her gaze around the suddenly chilly apartment. She looked back at the confused face of Jacob. "Let me make this easier for you. Okay?"

Jacob was dumfounded, almost scared. All he could do was nod.

"We've had a good summer. It was nice renewing our friendship. I'm the one who asked if we could be friends again. Right? But now, after a couple of kisses, weeks ago." She waved her hand. "You think I want more. But, the Lord," her anger beginning to rise, "has shown you the light. You're going to go off somewhere like a Lone Ranger for the Lord and do wonderful things and write your songs. Well, I wish the Lord would speak more clearly to me for once."

She teared up, just a little, then continued in a calmer, more resigned tone, "I thought he *was* speaking to me for a change. That's just like something Joe would've said, 'The Lord showed me, the Lord told me. The Lord this, the Lord that.' So, Jacob Riddler, just go off with the Lord, wherever he takes you. I'm going to ask the Lord to let me fall in love with a guy not so fired up for him for a change. I just can't compete."

Maryann paused, took a breath, calmed herself and continued, "I'm sorry, Jacob. That was terribly unfair."

"Maryann, that's not it. That's not what I was going to say...While I was out there...it...came to me."

Maryann was confused. Suddenly, at once, it became clear. She understood.

"Oh, my God. You know, don't you? You figured it out."

Jacob met her gaze, "Yes. It hit me like a ton of bricks. I woke up in the middle of the night and I knew."

"How did you figure it out? I thought you might someday. When you first came home, I was afraid you would, but...how, when?" asked Maryann.

"You were right. I was having all of those feelings and doubts. I sensed you were...I couldn't figure out my feelings about...for you, and the kids. I couldn't figure out what God wanted...what you want from me. I don't know, but as I canoed down the river, God helped me to understand that my resistance toward going further in our relationship, yours and mine, Maryann, was that when everything was said and done, even after all that's happened, I hadn't forgiven myself...Did I hear you right? Did I hear you say you'd fallen in love with me again?"

"God help me yes, yes, Jacob, I have," said Maryann. "What?" She laughed at the look on his face. "What?"

"I thought, maybe, but to hear you actually say it. It's just so amazing. So...incredible. I'm so happy."

Jacob reached across the table and took both her hands. They looked deeply into each other's eyes.

"Me too, Jacob. Me too. Go on, how did you figure it out?"

"I was just floating down the river, thinking and praying. It was late in the day, the sun was setting and as I came around a bend, there was an old abandoned farmhouse sitting on a small rise above the river. It seemed to glow orange in the setting sun. And...there was something familiar about it."

"An abandoned old house?" she asked.

"There was just something so familiar. The scene reminded me of one of the few pictures I ever saw of my mom and dad. It was taken right after the war, just before they moved to town, in front of some relative's farmhouse down in the Ozarks. Something about that abandoned farmhouse reminded me of the picture. Then, later that night—bang! I wake up. In the middle of the night, I knew it instantly."

Jacob turned, reached back over his shoulder to the kitchen counter, picked up an old brown photograph and slid it across the table for Maryann to view.

"This was in a box of Mom's belongings that Shirley gave to me after Mom slipped into the coma."

"Oh, my. Oh, my goodness," she said. "I always thought there was a close resemblance, but oh my, this...let's see, when this picture was taken Grandma Becky would've been..."

"About twenty, no more than twenty-two. This was after my dad had come home from World War II and before they moved to town. She was only sixteen when they married, just before he left."

"It is more than a resemblance. Ruth Ann is the spitting image of her Grandma Becky." Maryann looked up from the picture into the eyes of their wonderful daughter's father.

"Jacob, this summer, after getting to know you again, I prayed about whether to tell you this or not. For some reason, God doesn't seem to give me signs. I'm sorry, I..."

"Maryann, you have nothing to be sorry about."

"Jacob, what are we going to do? Should we tell Ruth? Does she have a right to know?" asked Maryann, afraid of answers to her questions.

"Maryann," Jacob reached for both hands again and looked into her eyes. "I had a lot of questions racing through my mind all the way home this morning. But, for me, the answer to the question about should we tell Ruth is easy."

Maryann said nothing, knowing he would continue.

"I don't think we should tell her. Ruth's memories of her dad are more than memories; they're her inspiration and life force. I see no reason to...I'm so grateful to Joe. He was a wonderful man."

Maryann nodded. "I had no idea that I was pregnant when you left. In fact, I figured Ruth must have been conceived the last night we were together, following my graduation party. For weeks I was a basket case, a broken-hearted teenager and Joe knew it. He was over every day. He got me out of the house, took me places and tried to cheer me up. He was a wonderful friend."

Jacob said, "When I told him I was leaving and asked him to give you that note, he tried to talk me out of it. He told me I was taking the coward's way out. He said I should look you in the eye and give you a reason. I remember telling Joe that you deserved someone like him. You still do, Maryann."

"I don't know what I would have done without him. I was devastated all over again when I found out I was pregnant. Joe was the only one I told. To Joe, the answer was simple. We'd just get married and everybody would think the baby was his. So, we eloped over the 4th of July holiday. July 5th was our twenty-second anniversary." Jacob saw in her gentle smile that she had absolutely no regrets.

"And no one ever suspected?" asked Jacob.

"No, from the day you left, Joe was at my side every minute. Everyone just assumed I was on the rebound. I think there were even some who thought the reason you left was because I'd dumped you for Joe."

"Even your parents?" asked Jacob.

"If they did, they never said anything, even after Ruth was born so early. She was a tiny baby anyway, not quite six pounds, so that helped. And, they were so happy. It hadn't taken them long to fall in love with Joe. They already liked him and they appreciated the way he was there for me when you left. And they just adored Ruth Ann."

"I always respected him, all through high school and all, but the more I hear about Joe Bethel—what a special person," said Jacob.

"That afternoon you told us about your childhood, I kept thinking about how your mother and I had both done the same thing. We were both desperate women who married men we didn't love because they were there for us. We both thought these men were good Christians. Neither one of us had any idea. About two years after Joe and I were married, I woke up one morning and realized that I loved this good man with every fiber of my being. I fell on my knees and thanked God for his wonderful goodness to me. But, it was just the opposite for your poor mom. I'll never understand such things."

"When did Ruth and Mom become so close?" asked Jacob.

"Not until five or six years later. Your mom was in worse shape than I was when you left. We were all worried about her, but Dr. Millard began to work with her from the moment the two churches merged. It wasn't long before she started to get better. When my parents died, it was like Becky realized that Ruth needed a grandma and she adopted her. They became real buddies."

"And my mom never...?"

"Joe thought she knew. I wasn't sure. But she never said anything. But, Becky babysat Ruth a lot, especially after I started up my insurance agency. She never took a dime."

"And Joe never had a problem with that?" asked Jacob.

"No, he thought it was wonderful that they had each other. Joe said Becky and Ruth needed each other. He said when we all get to heaven, God will help us sort everything out. Joe said Ruth and Becky both knew on an unconscious, spiritual plane and that's what made their relationship so special."

They sat silent for a moment, studying their clasped hands.

"Jacob," said Maryann softly. He met her eyes. "It's the same, between you and Ruth. You know that, don't you?"

"I was thinking that, but it seems almost sacreligious for me to say it. From the day I first met her at the Club, watching her with those kids, I have felt a strong bond—something special."

"It is the same for her, Jacob. She thought you were pretty special from day one. Mark, too, but especially Ruth.

"Do you think she would approve of you and me...?"

"Ha! Are you kidding? She's already encouraging it. She's even enlisted Evelyn in the effort," laughed Maryann as she lifted their hands slightly and squeezed. "Evelyn said, *sit the boy down and tell him you love him!*"

"Maryann, what would Joe...? How could you ever love me, or anybody, but especially me after being so happily married to Joe?"

"Jacob, I grieved hard, but good. Life goes on. And Joe made it clear that I should remarry someday. I didn't want to hear it then, but Joe insisted that we talk about it. It was like, after he knew God wouldn't heal him *on this side*, as he used to say, he said he knew that I was meant to be married. Joe said any woman who enjoyed screw..." she blushed and smiled, then continued only slightly censored, "sex like I do couldn't hold out for too long. I'm ready to start over with someone. Joe would approve."

"But, it's so sudden. We really don't know each..."

"We were childhood sweethearts." She held up one hand to prevent his interrupting her. "You are a different person. But the person I thought I loved twenty years ago and the person I'm growing to love today, they're the same. And I came to know you again at church and especially through my children and through Andre, even before we started up again. There's nothing sudden about this. Joe's been gone four years now."

Jacob was smiling from ear to ear now. "I can't believe it. It's too good, too good. I thought all of these things on the way home from the Niobrara, but I kept telling myself not to get my hopes up—that it would be too good to be true."

"Anything else you were thinking about on that long ride home?" she said suggestively and was shocked when he didn't pick up her clue.

"Yes, yes. I was thinking how grateful I am to Joe for being such a good father to Ruth. And if you and I getting together was God's will, and if you felt the same way, maybe I could return the favor by being a father to Mark. I mean I can't be a dad at this point to Ruth, more of a friend and advisor. But maybe…a boy Mark's age needs a father, you know?"

Maryann held onto his hands and pulled him to his feet with her. Looking deep into his eyes, she wrapped his hands around her back and slowly ran hers up his chest and around his neck. He smelled fresh, clean. She moved against him and rose to kiss him. The kiss began as it had the couple of times before, then she pushed her tongue into his mouth and the pent-up passion of both their years rose quickly to the surface. He turned her slightly, pressing her between him and the counter. They kissed and held each other, not able to get enough of each other.

Maryann broke their embrace, took his hand and looking him in the eye, took a step toward the bedroom. Jacob stopped her, pulled her back into his arms.

"Maryann, my sweet, sweet Maryann," he whispered as he gently pushed a wisp of hair to the side of her lovely face, now flush with desire. "I want to do this right this time. I want to…"

"Wait until we are married?" she said out of breath and incredulously.

He smiled and nodded.

"Jacob, we have done this before, many times. Neither one of us are virgins. I love you. We are forty years old…."

He kissed her, first on the mouth, then the nose, the eyelids, each cheek, her mouth again, and her forehead. He held her tightly and spoke softly, his cheek laying against her soft black hair.

"I know. I know. But, this is important to me. I want to court you. I want to date you, and buy you flowers. I want people to know we are dating. I want to give the kids a chance to get used to this. I want to set a good example for them. I want to do it right this time. I know it's crazy, but I feel like a virgin again and I want to make it holy. I can't tell you how tempted I've been to reach down and hold your hand in church."

Maryann burst out laughing in his arms. "Lord! Oh Lord, deliver me from temptation and from these holy men." With a smile, she looked up at him.

"Okay, Jacob Riddler, but I want to warn you. This better not be a long courtship and, you will soon learn what Joe Bethel did—I'm not easy to resist."

"I can't wait. You'd better get out of here. Mrs. Carlson is probably suspicious already. Are you free this evening for dinner? We have a lot to talk about."

"Mrs. Carlson is probably happy for me—for what she thinks I'm getting up here that I'm not." She pouted and reached up to kiss him again. "Okay, lover boy, we'll do it your way. It's really quite sweet and it makes me love you even more. Pick me up at seven, and wear your Sunday best. I'll be wearing something very provocative."

Arm in arm they moved to the door.

"Maryann, I love you. I still find it hard to believe this."

She kissed him again, "Never, never doubt it again. I love you, too, Jacob."

After one more gentle kiss on the landing, Maryann started down the steps. As the door shut behind her, Maryann laughed when she heard his muffled voice, "Yes! Yes! Thank you, thank you, thank you, Jesus!"

22 FALSE WITNESS

Jacob's spirits soared as he floated around his apartment. Maryann was in love with him again! This time he would not squander the greatest gift of his life. He had a wonderful daughter. She would never know he was her real father, but he was confident that she loved him. And soon, he would have a son, a wonderful son. He could see his life clearly for the first time. Maryann and a family, a real family. He and Maryann, together. Yes, they would make it something wonderful, something...holy. He sat down at the piano. His heart was full. He would write a song, a song to Maryann.

The knock on the door was so tentative at first that Jacob didn't hear it. When he finally heard it he reluctantly rose from the piano bench. Then he moved quickly—maybe she had come back—maybe she remembered something else, something wonderful she just had to say. Jacob expectantly threw open the door.

The look on Diaz's face was strained. The joy that radiated from Jacob did not help.

"Tod, come in. How you doing?" Jacob motioned toward the dirty cast that immobilized the wrist that had been broken the last time the old cop was at his apartment, six weeks ago. "When does the cast come off?"

"Not soon enough."

Jacob smiled and asked, "Did you see Maryann? She just left."

The weary old cop stepped into the apartment and Jacob closed the door behind him. He attempted a smile. "Yeah, she was beaming from ear-to-ear."

Jacob could not contain himself. "Tod, keep this quiet. I mean...I've got tell someone. She loves me, she does. She told me so. Do you believe it? After all these years, she loves me, again."

"Everybody else figured that out weeks ago, kid." Diaz's smile faded and he looked away.

Jacob sensed his mood and asked quizzically, "What's wrong?"

Diaz looked up. "Kid, this time, it's not me...I got to ask you to come downtown with me. I'm sorry."

"Downtown? What for?"

"Young fellow, about fourteen got beat pretty bad with a crescent wrench. He's in a coma at University Hospital." The two men made eye contact again. "Your crescent wrench. It has your nameplate glued to the handle"

"My wrench?"

"Supposedly there are three eyewitnesses. They say you beat the boy."

"Witnesses?"

"LaTisha Johnson and her son...Andre Fitzgerald."

"Andre! Andre said he saw me beat a boy with a wrench?"

Diaz nodded. "And, Juwan and his mother claim that back in May you broke his wrist...Andre says he saw that, too."

"He did! Juwan and Anthony, the kid that tried to kill us in the alley. They were beating up on Andre. In fact, it's probably the same wrench. It was the only one that wasn't in my toolbox when Andre stole it. That day when Andre and I got back to the truck, I just threw it on the floor. I guess it's been there ever since...Juice! Juice is behind this. He orchestrated all this, and probably threatened to kill LaTisha if Andre...and kill Andre if she...he turned their love for each other on me."

Diaz sighed and nodded in agreement, "I hope you got a great alibi for the last couple of days."

"Oh, that's just great. Last night I was in the middle of nowhere sleeping under the stars, next to a canoe, by the Niobrara all by myself. Didn't see or talk to a soul. Oh, no."

"Did you buy any supplies out there, any gas receipts, anything like that?"

"Yeah, but I paid cash. I didn't even keep any...maybe there's something in the garbage bag in the front cab of my truck. I don't think so, but maybe."

"I'll go and check it out as soon as I drop you off downtown. But, it's worse, Jacob."

"Worse, how could it be worse?"

"Juwan cleaned himself up. He must have borrowed clothes from his buddy, Juice. He was wearing a nice knit shirt with long sleeves to cover the tattoos. Took off his gold chains and got a haircut and he and his mother went to the newspapers. By the time I left the department to come here, the television and radio stations had showed up. I talked to Dennis on my way here. He's already getting calls from reporters questioning his judgment about letting you volunteer at the Club. Someone even gave the press information...somehow they already have your criminal records."

Jacob sat down, stunned. "I can hear it now, 'known felon, convicted drug trafficker works with little children at Club.' Tod...? Oh, my God."

"I know, kid. Let's go see what we can do. I already called Preacher Nate. He said he'd get Charles Andrews and meet us at the station. Sometimes I hate my job. Let's go."

Jacob stood, "Tod?"

"Yeah."

"Aren't you going to read me my rights?" Jacob said with trepidation.

"I hope not. We're officially in the investigative stage now." He reached for the door. "I'm going to turn you over to another detective for questioning so I can see if I can turn up anything."

• • • • •

Shortly after five, Juice's cell rang.

"My, my, my! Nice work, Josef."

"Jez! You like that? I got em all—Riddler, the Preacher, the Club—they're all embarrassed and falling all over themselves. You watching the news? It's the lead story."

Jez laughed and broke into an anchorwoman imitation. "Several prominent community and business leaders who serve on the Board of Directors of the Boy & Girls Clubs asked that their names not be used. Each of them expressed concern that a person like Jacob Riddler with his criminal, violent past could be volunteering at the Club. One person was heard to say, 'I just find it hard to believe that

Dennis Livingston would know all about Riddler's background and still let him work at the Club. It just seems, at a minimum, very poor judgment.' Nice, very nice."

"I owe it all to you, Jez. Like you said, be patient, close down the street operation, go legit for a few weeks, live off my investments and bide my time, just bide my time. Good advice, Jez. Hey, what're you doing tonight?"

"I've got us a room at the Downtown Suites. Knock three times on suite 1225. Get there well before the evening news comes on."

"My reward?" he asked. "It's been awhile, Jez."

"You've earned it, love. It will be the best ever."

• • • • •

Nathan reached across the gray tabletop and grabbed Jacob's forearm. "We'll get through this, Jacob. We'll get through it."

"Not now, Nathan, this can't be happening now. I was going to focus on my music, on working with the kids. Maryann...she loves me, Nathan. Look, look at this." Jacob reached into his back pocket and pulled out a sealed envelope and tossed it on the table. "That's my letter of resignation to Bob Wilson, thanking him for giving me a break when I needed it, telling him I was going to devote myself full-time to my music. I wrote that this morning, as soon as I got back to my apartment. I called his office to get an appointment with him, to deliver it personally and to thank him. He's out of town until Friday. I even thought about telling him that I forgive him for...for what happened...for framing me, but that was so long ago. I don't know who did what so I decided to let it drop. But, I can't work for him anymore, plus I don't have to. Now..."

Nathan picked up the envelope and looked at it. Jacob read something in his face and asked, "What, what is it?"

"It was on the news, Jacob. Bob was at a political caucus in D.C., but they found him and told him the story. He fired you on the spot and he took the opportunity to take pot shots at Dennis. He said, unlike Dennis, he had let you work at his station at night, behind the scenes, away from children. So you could prove that you were reha-bilitated. He said he'd given you a chance to turn your life around and that he was disappointed in you, deeply disappointed."

"What? He doesn't want to believe what you and Dennis and Tod have been telling him about Juice, but I'm automatically guilty. I can't believe it. Why? Why is this happening, Nathan? Maryann and I, we love...Have you seen her? Is she okay?"

"She's livid, fighting mad. It's a good thing she can't get her hands on Juice or LaTisha right now. She called Charles before I did. Charles is good, Jacob—the best, and I hate to say it, but it doesn't hurt in this case that he's black."

Jacob looked into the eyes of his friend. "Nathan?"

Nathan nodded and Jacob continued.

"You...Tod—neither of you asked me if I did it."

"Don't have to, Son, we know better."

"Even if I somehow get by this, I'll never be able to work at the Club again, not after all this publicity."

"Let's just take it one step at a time, son," said Nathan. The door to the little room opened. "Here's Charles, now."

Charles Andrews, even at the end of a long day, still looked fresh. His white shirt was crisp and his blue suit and silk tie looked as if they had just been pulled from the closet. He looked confident as he somberly pulled up a chair and sat down. It had been a long afternoon. "Jacob, the DA agrees there may be something fishy here, but he feels he has no choice, given the eyewitness accounts."

"Juice! Juice is behind this."

"With the collaborating testimony, I'm sorry, they're going to place you under arrest."

Jacob sat back in his chair and stared at the ceiling. Nathan placed his big hand on Jacob's forearm.

"But, I was able to get your bail hearing set for this evening at 7:00. With any luck you won't have to spend the night in jail."

"Where's Tod? I guess he's going to have to read me my rights after all."

"He and Dennis are over at LaTisha Johnson's," said Charles. "They're talking to her and Andre. Juice has retained a lawyer for them, so he's there, too. I don't know what good it will do, but they're trying to talk to them, now."

"It's ironic, too," said Nathan. "Dennis said he had some good news for them at the same time."

"What?" said Jacob and Charles in unison.

Nathan shrugged. "He said he'd tell me later, he didn't have time then."

Jacob looked at his friend and mentor. "Nathan, until today, I could have accepted this. I could have gone back to prison even for something I didn't do, trusting that God had a reason, but now, after today...oh, God, this is serious. My parole could be yanked."

Nathan placed both hands, palms up on the table and looked first at Jacob and then Charles.

The three big men joined hands, bowed their heads and began to pray. Nathan went first, then Charles, then Jacob.

• • • • •

"So, LaTisha? Andre? You're both sticking with this story, that you, Andre, saw Jacob Riddler, in a fit of rage, take his crescent wrench from under the seat of his truck and beat this boy into a coma. Then he made you help him put the boy in the back of his truck, cover him with a tarp and dump him in the alley for dead. And, then, Miss Johnson, a couple of hours later, Andre tells you about it and you call the police and tell them where they can find the body. That right?" Diaz was digging hard, trying to get to the bottom of the story.

LaTisha and Andre both sat on the couch in the living room of LaTisha's North Side home, the same one where Charles Andrew had grown up. The home where his parents had lived until the tragic drive-by that killed Charles' niece. Diaz and Livingston both sat in dining room chairs they had pulled up to the couch so that they could make as much eye contact with LaTisha and Andre as possible during the interview. The attorney retained by Juice had been referred by Bob Wilson and stood a little off to one side as Diaz asked his questions. The attorney's name was Amos Haddad, a small man who was at least sixty years of age.

Andre's eyes were red-rimmed from crying. He barely nodded his head in answer to Diaz's questions. LaTisha defiantly did the same as she took a drag on her cigarette.

"Gentlemen, you've asked us the same questions at least five or six times, and you keep getting the same answers. I think my clients have been more than cooperative."

Tod didn't even turn to look up at the little man behind the couch, but Dennis glared at him for the interruption—to no avail. The little man had been through many such scenes as a defense attorney. He was not easy to intimidate and anyone who underestimated him, or was fooled by his small stature or his wispy gray hair and wrinkled brow, paid the price.

Amos Haddad looked Dennis in the eye and said, "And, since you, sir, are not an attorney, or a police official, we have been more than accommodating, I'd say. Anything else, Detective?"

Tod didn't answer.

Dennis addressed LaTisha. "Miss Johnson, I have another matter to discuss with you, not related to this, but I will not speak of it in front of this man."

"Wait a minute," Haddad began warily.

Diaz stood up and began to move toward the door. "Then you won't need me, either, will you?"

"No, this is not police business. At least not yet," replied Dennis. Diaz was out on the front porch before the sentence was concluded.

"My client will not allow you to trick her, Mr. Livingston."

"It's about the welfare of your daughter, Angela. Miss Johnson, would you like to know where she is and how she's doing?"

Andre and his mother looked at each other. They both nodded eagerly.

"Then you'll have to ask this man to leave because none of us should trust him to keep her location a secret. He will be bound to tell his client if he hears our discussion."

"Mrs. Johnson, do not let this man trick you into saying anything."

"Out!" shouted LaTisha.

"Get out!" screamed Andre as he jumped to his feet. He pointed to the door where Diaz stood on the porch, his back toward them. "Get out so we can talk to Dennis."

Haddad regained his composure and smiled. "Very well," he said and turned to join Diaz on the front porch. Andre followed and shut the door behind him, then turned to face Dennis.

"Angela is alive? Juice don't have her?"

"Come back and sit down on the couch with your mother, Andre. I have some good news for you."

With shaking hands, LaTisha lit another cigarette. Andre took his seat next to her and Dennis continued. "I received a call this afternoon from a man by the name of Larry Stonehedge. Larry's an old friend of mine. He's the Executive Director of the Boys & Girls Clubs in another city several hundred miles away from here. This afternoon, Angela showed up there."

LaTisha gasped and some spark of life began to return to her dull eyes.

"She walked into the Club where my friend works. He called me. I talked to her on the phone just before Tod and I came here. Angela told me she was driving her car down the street and saw the Club. She remembered how the Club seemed to be helping you, Andre. So she walked in, asked to see whoever was in charge. She asked Mr. Stonehedge to call me and get a message to you that she's okay."

"My baby girl is okay?"

Andre smiled and seemed to come alive. "She made it. She got away. All right, Angela!"

"Yes, Miss Johnson, Angela is okay. More than okay. My friend says she has a good job and a little apartment. She looks healthy, and she's made some good friends. I understand she's doing very well."

LaTisha put her cigarette out in an overflowing ashtray and wiped her eyes and cheeks with a crumpled tissue. "Oh, thank God. Where? Where is she? Can I call her? I want to talk to my baby girl."

"I'm sorry, I can't tell you that. She made my friend and I promise not to tell you where she is. She doesn't want anyone else to know. She's afraid Juice might find out and come after her. So, I can't tell you where."

Andre looked at his mother and then at Dennis. Dennis detected a plea for help in his big brown eyes. Andre said, "Angela's right, Dennis. It's better we don't know." He glared at his mother. "Now you got to know what kind of man your son, Juice, has become, don't you? Don't you, Momma? Especially after what he's making us do." He raised his voice. It was a frantic mix of anger and anxiety. "Momma! You understand now? Now do you believe what I been telling you?"

"But, it's not Juice, Baby, it's that Juwan."

"Momma!" LaTisha retreated and her eyes seem to glaze over again. Andre was losing her and he looked desperately at Dennis, then leaned closer to LaTisha. "Momma," he toned down his voice a little and said firmly, but gently, "Juwan take his orders from Juice, Momma, you know that. Juice is the one making us lie. And Juice will have Juwan kill us, too, if we don't go along. At least we know now he don't have Angela, like Juwan claimed. Momma, don't you dare."

"I won't, Baby."

"Don't even tell Juice we know she's okay. You hear me, Momma?"

"I promise, Baby. I won't tell nobody." She slowly rose from the couch and gathered up her cigarettes and lighter. "I got to go lay down, Baby. I'm so tired."

Dennis and Andre watched her walk, zombie-like, from the room.

"Andre," Dennis said gently. "Angela wants you to know, she has a nice apartment. She's working. She says you can come live with her. The Club there is really nice."

"I can't," said Andre. His eyes followed the path his mom had just taken from the room. He looked back at Dennis. "I can't."

Dennis nodded and said, "Let's talk about this lie Juwan is making you tell on Jacob."

"What am I gonna do? Juice don't have Angela, but..." Again his eyes looked after his mother. "Juwan's crazy. He'll kill me and Momma."

•••••

A few hours later, Diaz found Nathan and Charles Andrews sitting with Jacob in the courtroom. They sat at the defense table waiting for the bail hearing to begin.

"How are you doing, Jacob?"

"Better, much better, I guess."

Diaz nodded, but didn't smile. "There's probably fifty people out in front of the court house. There's another twenty or so right outside the door."

"Really? Who?" asked Jacob.

"People from church, some of the parents of kids from the Club. They're all supporting you, Jacob. I even saw a few signs. There will at least be another point of view on the evening news. They're talking to reporters. A lady from Channel Six is interviewing Reverend Thomas right outside the door."

Nathan put his arm around Jacob's shoulder and gave him a reassuring hug.

"Plus, I did find a couple of receipts in the cab of your truck. You may have an alibi after all, especially if someone remembers you. I'll drive out there next week, if I have to, even if they do take me off the case. But, you may have trouble with this hearing, Charles."

"What do you mean?" asked the unflappable attorney.

"They're taking you off the case?" asked Nathan.

"The stakes just went up. I just got a call from the hospital." Diaz looked at Jacob. "The boy died. He was making progress, but suddenly went into cardiac arrest and died. Jacob will soon be charged with murder."

Jacob moaned and Nathan said, "Oh, dear God."

Charles asked, "How did it go with Andre and Miss Johnson?"

Diaz shrugged. "I had to leave. Dennis was still talking to them when I left."

At that moment, Andre swaggered into the courtroom, smiling from ear to ear. He waved to them as if he were arriving at a social gathering and then made his way to the front just as the judge entered the room.

• • • • •

"You're getting better, Juice darling," she purred, "much better."

"That's because I feel good, better than I've felt in a long time."

"Here it is!" Jez jumped out of the hotel bed to retrieve the television remote from the top of the console. "The evening news."

A junior high school class picture of the murdered boy was on the screen. Jez pushed the volume button in time to hear the lead-in to the program.

"There are startling new developments in the beating death of young Kimani Grove." As a mug shot of Jacob is shown the lead-in continued. "Is this man, a volunteer staff member at the Parkland Boys & Girls Club, a model of rehabilitation, of someone who has pulled his life together? Or, is he a cold-blooded killer? More on this unfolding story when the ten o'clock news continues on Channel Six. Stay tuned."

Juice motioned for the clicker as he continued to recline in the bed. Jez pushed the mute button then tossed it over. She moved toward the clothes she had piled on the chair.

"Where you going? The night is young and I feel like celebrating."

She picked up her black lace panties and began to step into them. "Shouldn't you get back to McKey's?" she teased. "Mr. Wilson might finally let Mr. Hampton fire you for being gone so much."

Juice laughed, his mood buoyant. "Yeah, right."

She snapped the bikini into place around her firm waist and reached for the matching bra. "Sorry, love. Hubby is out of town again. He'll be calling soon and I can't wait to tell him the breaking news."

"He mess around on you when he's out of town?" Juice taunted.

She shrugged. "Don't know, kind of doubt it. He can't afford any more indiscretions." She let her silk sleeveless dress fall over her, slipped into her expensive sandals, sat down in the chair and crossed her long legs. A slit in the long dress revealed her beautiful, tan thighs. "Hubby and I have an understanding—don't ask—don't tell."

Juice looked like a kid ready to open a birthday present as he pressed the mute button, bringing the sound back up. A serious young anchorwoman began the broadcast.

"There are startling new developments in the Kimani Grove case. Chief investigative reporter John Marian is at the courthouse, reporting live."

The scene shifted to the front steps of the county building. An older, obviously seasoned reporter holding a microphone began his report.

"Startling developments indeed, Carol. As we reported at five, Jacob Riddler, a convicted felon still on parole, but also an active volunteer at the Parkland Avenue Boys & Girls Club, was accused in last night's brutal beating of Kimani Grove, a fourteen-year-old who just moved to town last week. Allegedly, there were eyewitnesses and Riddler was arrested this afternoon.

"But, this evening just prior to the bail hearing, there were some surprises in this late-breaking story. First, Kimani Grove died this afternoon at Saint Joe's Hospital. It was expected that Riddler would be charged with second-degree murder. The hallway outside the courtroom was swelling with people who showed up in support of Riddler. Many of them were parents of the kids he works with at the Club. Some of Riddler's music students sat in a circle and played their guitars and sang songs that he had taught them. Some people were members of Antioch church, and of well-known community activist, Nathan Frye, commonly known as 'Preacher Nate.' The church is located just across Parkland Avenue from the Club. I spoke with a few of these people before the hearing and they reported to me that their confidence in Jacob Riddler remains unshaken."

Juice laughed derisively at the reporter on the screen.

"Very interesting, John," said the young anchorwoman, "Anything else?"

"Well, it turns out, Carol, that those parents' faith in Riddler was right." The television screen displayed footage of a stunned Jacob, a proud and smiling Maryann on his arm, being escorted out of the courtroom by Nathan and Charles Andrews. "All charges against Riddler have been dropped."

"What!" Juice leaped from the bed and moved as if he were going to attack the television, which now showed a split screen for dialogue between the young anchor and the reporter.

"John, as you mentioned earlier, there seemed to be a strong case against Riddler. What happened?"

"Two things, Carol. At first, it seemed that Riddler had no alibi. It was his wrench that was used in the beating of young Grove. Riddler claimed that he'd gone on a solo canoe trip to the Niobrara River. As I said, it appeared Riddler had no alibi. But, Carol, this afternoon evidence was developed, including gas and food receipts and telephone interviews with several people in the western part of the state who remember him being at the river. In fact, our investigative reporters helped to further develop some of these leads after people from Antioch Church made the initial phone calls. I spoke with a woman who works at the campsite where Riddler spent Saturday night. She recognized Riddler from the photo that I faxed to her. She said he was one of the nicest people she's ever met. Riddler rented a shower and slept in her campground the night that Grove was beaten. She had his signature on a time-punched sign-in card. Although the boy was beaten with Riddler's wrench, Riddler couldn't have done it."

Juice moaned and Jez began to laugh, a deeply evil chortle.

"But, John, what about the eyewitnesses who claimed they saw Riddler beat young Kimani Grove? And, supposedly he had broken another boy's arm with his wrench back in May?"

"Carol, this case is one of the most fascinating that I have ever covered. Just before what was supposed to be the bail hearing on the assault charge, one of the eyewitnesses—a young boy—walked into the courtroom. Just as the judge walked in he jumped up on a front-row seat and began to shout that the whole thing was a setup."

On the television was footage of Andre, with his face made indistinguishable by small squares, standing in the courtroom, gesturing dramatically.

"We're not going to show his face or give you his name because according to the young witness..."

Juice sat down hard on the bed when he saw Juwan's picture on the screen. Jez's laughter grew louder as she picked up her purse and car keys.

"Juwan Walcott, a purported gang leader on the North Side was apparently out to frame Jacob Riddler and embarrass the Boys & Girls Club because it has been so successful in rescuing young people from his gang this summer. This young witness said that Walcott threatened to kill him and his mother and his sister if they did not go along with the scheme."

The serious young anchorwoman asked, "John, what made this young man come forward now and tell the truth?"

"Another strange twist, Carol. The witness said that with the help of Riddler and the Club, he had left the gang and that his life has been threatened several times since. He said that by coming forward now, in this very public way, if something happened to him or his mother, the police would know to look for Walcott and other members of his gang. In other words, by being so public with his accusation and creating this commotion in court today, telling everyone about Walcott's threat, he has created a screen of protection for him and his mother. And Carol, the other young man whose arm was broken by Riddler several months ago?"

"Yes, what about that?"

"It was Juwan Walcott. Riddler broke Walcott's arm, using this same wrench, when he came upon Walcott and his gang beating up on this same young witness back in May, the day after he had left Walcott's gang."

"Then, John, who did kill young Kimani Grove?"

"Carol, the police have arrested Juwan Walcott. He is being interrogated at police headquarters as we speak."

The picture switched back to the station where the young anchorwoman said, "What a story! At the end of our broadcast we will have a special half-hour show on issues related to this fascinating, twisting story. Sandy Davis is standing by for an exclusive interview with Reverend Nathan Frye of Antioch Church and with Dennis Livingston, the Executive Director of the Parkland Avenue Boys & Girls Club. You won't want to miss it. We'll be right back with the rest of the news."

Juice clicked off the set, unaware that Jez had left. He heard her laughter fade as she made her way down the hallway. He put his head in his hands. "You're dead, Hotchie. Sooner or later, you're dead. It don't matter that you didn't tell him about me, Hotchie. You broke the truce. You destroyed my street action. You dead!"

23 RELUCTANT HEROES

THURSDAY EVENING, JULY 18TH

The sun was setting as they walked hand-in-hand along the recreational path that ran through Riverside Park along the river. They walked slowly like people in love do, trying to squeeze every second out of the day. They nodded politely to the occasional cyclist or jogger or skater, but they were truly in a world of their own. When they came to the big Cottonwood tree that grew on the gently sloping hill above the bend in the river, like they had done on both Tuesday and Wednesday evening before, they left the path, climbed to the base of the tree and sat down on the lush grass. She passed her arm through his and they sat in silence for a time. The swift currents of the river below had an almost hypnotic effect. They seemed to find peace and calmness of soul as they watched and listened to the river's flow.

Maryann finally spoke. "Three different restaurants and three romantic dinners in a row." She squeezed his arm. "Thank you, Jacob."

He answered only by patting her hand. After a few minutes of just sitting and enjoying each other's presence, he glanced at his watch.

"Are you on again tonight?" she asked.

He smiled at her and said, "No, all the volunteers are still committed. But, I want to call Tod a little before eleven, just to touch base."

"You think The Watchmen are still necessary?"

"Maybe more so. Until they finally put Juice in jail."

After a few more minutes of silence she said, "Tomorrow night I'll fix you dinner before your AA meeting. I don't know what their schedules are, but maybe the kids can join us."

211

Jacob nodded as he watched a whirlpool form in the fast current and then disappear as the river carried it around the bend.

"You're quiet all of a sudden. All talked out?"

He laughed a little and again placed his hand gently on the one that held his arm. He looked into her dark eyes. "We've done a lot of talking, every afternoon and every evening the last three days. It's been wonderful."

"So what are you thinking now?"

He looked back toward the river and gathered his thoughts. She waited patiently. The hum of the city in the distance and the constant surge of the river's current joined with the crescendo of night sounds from the park behind them to create background music for the moment. "That it all seems too good to be true," he said. "I was so scared on Monday. I thought I might lose it all, at the very moment I had found it, found you again...and now, three days later, it seems that more than I've ever dreamed could be possible is laid out before me. It's like I can see my life clearly for the first time. I never dreamed I could make money writing music, it was a hobby...no, it was therapy...but I am." He looked at her. "Making money, that is. It's amazing, but I am."

She squeezed his arm and smiled.

"In my wildest dreams," he continued, still looking at her, "I never imagined you could love me again."

She kissed him gently on the cheek, then lightly on the lips, but said nothing. Her eyes invited him to continue.

"And, grace on grace, I have a wonderful daughter that I can be close to. Monday night, after we all got back to your house, she pulled me aside and gave me a hug. She told me she was proud of me and that she'd never doubted my innocence. The last three mornings as we ran," he looked at the path they had just left, the same one he ran every morning with Ruth, "she's so...she runs and talks a-mile-a-minute." They shared a laugh at the thought of their daughter. "She's so...good, so...full of life. She makes me feel good when I'm around her. She makes everyone feel good."

She just smiled and nodded. Even though they had decided not to tell Ruth that Jacob was her real father, it pleased Maryann to share her pride in their daughter with Jacob.

Jacob continued, "And, and I'll be a father to a great boy who needs a father. I keep thinking I'll wake up from this wonderful dream, Maryann. You know how you're having a dream, a good dream, and you start to wake up, but you keep your eyes closed because you don't really want to wake up." He looked into her eyes again, seeing her love and desire. He sensed her hunger for him and it made him ache, it both thrilled and frightened him. He was barely able to speak. "That's how I feel, Maryann. I don't want to wake up."

She closed her eyes and leaned into him. It was a long kiss. The passion grew and for an instant they almost forgot they were in a public place. Their lips were still lightly touching when she whispered, "It's real, Jacob. I love you with all my heart and I want to spend the rest of my life with you." When he softly touched her cheek with trembling fingers, she opened her eyes and they looked into each other's soul, becoming one.

• • • • •

The next morning, after his run with Ruth and following his visit with his mom at the nursing home, Jacob took the stairs in front of the Club two at a time. His spirit matched the bright summer morning—there was not a cloud to be seen. This morning the conversation with his daughter had been even more exhilarating than the fast pace they had run.

If there was a cloud in Jacob's life, it was his mother's deteriorating condition. This morning, Shirley's demeanor and tone of voice seemed to be gently preparing Jacob for the end. His mother could not last much longer. He read to her from the family Bible and told her of Monday's ordeal, and of the wonderful developments in his life. Somehow he sensed that his mom understood, and was pleased. He even felt that she was not surprised. He'd never felt closer to her.

This was Jacob's first visit back to the Club following the false accusations and the bizarre courtroom scene on Monday evening. The staff and kids warmly greeted him as he entered the Club. He popped his head into Dennis' office and pointed to the clock behind the Club director's chair. It read 8:55. "I'm five minutes early. Do you want me to come back?"

Dennis looked up and smiled. "Good morning, Jacob. Please, sit down. Just give me a second to sign these award certificates for the Chess Club members."

While Dennis signed his name over and over again, taking time to read each name on each certificate until he reached the bottom of the stack, Jacob took the few minutes to study the office. It was full of books, binders, training manuals and papers. But it was neat and not at all cluttered. Jacob knew that over the years, Dennis had received a lot of recognition and many awards for his work. But the only thing other than photographs and paintings, most of them done by Club kids over the years, were two college diplomas that were professionally matted and framed and hung on the back wall over the credenza. The top of the credenza, the desk, the bookshelves and the walls were covered with photos of Dennis, his wife, Eileen, and their two daughters.

Finally, Dennis signed the last certificate, put down his pen and gave Jacob his full attention. "Thanks for your patience."

Jacob nodded and then looked around the office. "Dennis, you have a beautiful family. How old are your girls?"

Dennis picked up one of the older pictures, one of his girls in early adolescence and smiled as if reliving the moment. "Twenty-one and nineteen. They're both away at school and neither one of them came home for the summer," he said with a twinge of regret. "Heather is on a study tour in Europe, and Jacque is on a summer church mission in South Africa."

"They're beautiful. You must be very proud."

"I am. And I miss them like crazy. They're so close in age, it seemed like overnight and they were gone." Dennis continued to smile at his girls for a few seconds and then returned the picture to its spot on his desk. He turned a different, but genuine smile on Jacob. "If Ruth's instincts are right, and they usually are, you may be a family man yourself soon."

"Isn't it amazing! I can't believe it. I can't believe how good God has been to me."

Dennis continued to smile, but shook his head. "You guys just all flow with the God-talk, don't you?"

"Oh." Jacob laughed. "I guess we do. Just comes naturally after awhile. But," Jacob paused. "I believe the God-stuff, Dennis, but I didn't mean to offend you."

Dennis lifted his palms from the desk. "Oh, no, I'm not offended. I respect it, in a way. I know you believe it, Jacob. I know."

"Ruth tells me you don't...believe in God?" It was not an accusation, just a question.

Dennis leaned back in his large executive chair. The sounds of children's laughter and excitement wafted in from the hallway and the adjacent game room. The affection he held for Ruth was apparent in his tone when he asked, "Did she tell you that she's praying for me, too? Along with Eileen and my daughters and Nathan, and maybe even Tod now, of all people."

Jacob smiled and nodded. "She says you really do believe, you just don't know it, or…you're too stubborn to admit it. How come?"

"How come I don't believe in God?"

Jacob nodded.

"Sometimes I do believe. Maybe most of the time, but then I find myself angry with him."

Jacob shook his head, confused.

"How can you not believe in God, when the evil in the world is so real?" Dennis said.

When Jacob shook his head, Dennis leaned forward, his elbows on the desk, his big hands making gestures as he spoke. "I mean, with all the evil in the world." He pointed at Jacob as he made his point. "I believe in evil, maybe even in the devil. So," he leaned back, "there has to be an opposite, a counter-balance. But why doesn't God *do* something? Why does he allow such horrible things to happen…especially to the children, the most innocent ones?"

"I don't know. I wish I did," said Jacob.

"But, you still believe—you're not angry?"

"I still believe, but I *am* angry. I think God is angry, too. I think Ruth's right. Whether you believe it or not, God is in you, Dennis. I think your sense of justice, your anger, in fact, come from God. It's what drives you, it's the source of your passion."

Dennis smiled a crooked grin at Jacob's analysis, then subtly changed the subject. "Are you angry with your old buddy, Bob Wilson?"

Jacob nodded, "A little, but I'll get over it."

"Have you heard from him?"

"Just through the manager down at the station. He called to tell me that Tom had called from D.C. to say he was glad that I'd been cleared and that I still had a job."

"And you said?"

"No, thanks. I'd already decided to quit. The manager asked me about giving him two weeks' notice, but I told him I didn't think I owed it to Bob."

Dennis picked up the morning edition of *The Herald*. "He's quoted this morning about how the justice system worked this time. He said he's sorry he was so quick to judge you and that it's a good lesson in innocent until proven guilty."

Jacob nodded. "He also said that he still wonders about the wisdom of someone like me volunteering at the Club."

Dennis waved off the comment and asked, with a note of skepticism in his voice, "So, Ruth tells me you're going to try to make a living writing music for contemporary Christian singers?"

Jacob moved to the edge of his chair with enthusiasm. "Dennis, I got another royalty check in the mail yesterday. This month's was the biggest yet. I think I can do this full-time, at least for awhile. *The Redeemed* is now in the top ten on the Christian charts and it's even getting some play on secular stations. I received an advance on a new song called *When Sparrows Fall.*"

"Fantastic, Jacob. Congratulations."

"Thanks. God has blessed me...Oh, I'm sorry."

They both laughed then Dennis said, "So, are you ready to start back to work here? I'll double your salary," he joked.

"Sure, if you think it's okay. I've only missed two classes. Seems like I've been gone a long time. Are you still catching flack? I thought we were going to give things a while to settle down?

"Just the opposite. Every parent or board member who's called the last couple of days has expressed their support. Even some," he raised his index finger, "not all, but some who gave me a hard time last Monday, before the truth was learned, have called to apologize. And the staff is unanimous, not to mention the kids. I think if you didn't continue as a volunteer I'd really hear about it."

"Okay," said Jacob. "I'll be back Tuesday night."

Dennis looked at his watch. "How 'bout you coming back in... thirty minutes?"

"What?"

"Right before you got here, Ruth stepped in. She has a field trip with a busload of the younger kids to that big program going on at the Children's Museum. A couple of hundred kids from schools and agencies around the city are supposed to be there. Ruth said one of the entertainers can't make it. She wondered if you could fill in with some of those crazy kid sing-a-long songs you do."

Jacob stood up and said enthusiastically, "Sure, let me run up to the music room and grab a guitar and I'll head down there. It'll be fun."

"I think I'll go, too," said Dennis. "I need to get out of this office. Can you drive? My car's in the shop."

Jacob answered in a deep Southern drawl, "Sure, Old Blue'll be real proud to have the executive director of the Club in his passenger seat."

"Where'd you learn to talk like *that?*" asked Dennis as he stood up.

Jacob shrugged, "Same place I learned to play the guitar. Same place I found God. Same place I asked Jesus..."

"Go get your guitar and I'll meet you at your truck," snapped Dennis in mock indignation.

A few minutes later they turned off of Parkland Avenue and made their way to the south side of downtown. The Children's Museum was on a narrow street in a refurbished warehouse not far from the Old Market and McKey's. They turned onto Eighteenth Street and found themselves in bumper-to-bumper traffic. They were ten or twelve car lengths behind the Club bus that was waiting in line behind other buses to turn into the parking area on the side of the museum.

Dennis looked at his watch. "How long will it take you to set up?"

"I just need a stool and a microphone. I can even stand up if I have to."

"We're okay then," said Dennis. "These kind of things never start on time, anyway."

Just then two rough-looking white guys who appeared to be in their twenties walked between Old Blue and the car in front of them. They walked with purpose, but their eyes were darting in every direction. Jacob sensed the tension and the combustible adrenaline in their movements. "What are those two up to?" he asked.

"Are those what you call skinheads?" asked Dennis.

Jacob nodded. "Based on the bald heads, the ragged jean vests, the tattoos and..."

When the two reached the sidewalk they turned and began to walk toward the buses. On the back of the vests were matching insignias that crudely combined an iron cross that was surrounded by a version of the confederate flag placed above a swastika. Below the insignias was written *The Pure Brethren.*

"Definitely!" said Dennis with disgust.

As the skinheads approached the back of the Club bus, Jacob saw what each young man carried in his right hand.

"Dennis! Look!" Jacob tried to turn Old Blue out of the line. Frustrated, he hit the accelerator and plowed Old Blue into the bumper of the car in front of him.

Dennis screamed, "What the hell you doing, Jacob?"

Jacob threw the truck into reverse and as he laid on the horn, he crashed into the car in back of them. It worked. He had enough room to turn Old Blue onto the sidewalk.

Angry now and confused, Dennis screamed, "Are you crazy?" as Jacob hit the curb and bounced up onto the sidewalk. Jacob alternately worked the accelerator and the brake and laid on the horn. Pedestrians on the sidewalk screamed, some cursed and barely got out of the way as Old Blue streaked by.

"Jacob!" Dennis tried one more time. Then he saw the rifles, too. "Oh, God."

The skinheads were even with the Club bus and had turned their automatic rifles on it, ready to fire when they heard the crashes and the horn and the people behind them screaming. It took only a second for them to readjust their aim to the old blue pick-up truck that was barreling down on them.

"Duck!" screamed Jacob. The windshield shattered under the automatic fire of both rifles. Jacob felt a sickening thud and slammed on the brakes. The firing stopped immediately. Quickly he opened the door and rolled onto the ground almost on top of the skinhead whose chest was crushed and bleeding under Old Blue's left front wheel. The skinhead's eyes were open but they had a distant blank look. Blood gurgled from his gaping mouth.

Jacob started to become sick at his stomach. Since Ralph's death, Jacob had never killed another human being. Even in his years as a criminal, it was the one thing he'd never done. It was a promise he'd made, not to God, but to himself. After the trauma of watching Ralph die, he swore he'd never kill another person.

Over the screaming cries of panic that came from terrified children and pedestrians, Jacob heard vile curses mixed with desperate cries for help. He jumped to his feet and ran around the back of the truck.

The second shooter had barely avoided Old Blue but not the passenger door as Dennis threw it open and jumped from the cab. The momentum of the door and the truck had knocked the skinhead flat on his back and sent his automatic rifle sliding across the sidewalk. Before the skinhead could get up or gain any sense of bearing, Dennis was on him. As Jacob came around the truck he saw Dennis' terrible fury being unleashed. Dennis was pummeling the screaming kid with his fists and then with both hands he grabbed his victim by the tattered vest and jerked him upward. "Who are you? Who sent you here?"

The skinhead unleashed a screaming string of vicious insults and racial slurs. Dennis slammed him back to the sidewalk and the shaved head made a sickening thud against the concrete. The screaming stopped. Dennis was able to slam him one more time before Jacob tackled him and pulled him off the now unconscious man.

Dennis twisted away from Jacob and spun to look at him. Instantly, all rage was gone. Both men looked at each other and then down at the unconscious skinhead. He looked young, maybe not quite twenty and Jacob prayed silently, *Don't let him die, Lord. For Dennis, don't let him die.*

"Jacob! Dennis!" Ruth screamed as she exited the bus. "Oh, God, are you all right?" When she saw the skinhead pinned under Old Blue's front tire, she froze and groaned. Jacob and Dennis both ran to her, each putting an arm around her, turning her away. The first police cars arrived on the scene.

"We're okay," said Jacob.

"The children?" asked Dennis. "Are the children okay?"

Ruth nodded and fought the tears and the panic still in her throat. "I saw them just as they raised their guns. Oh, God," she looked back and forth between them, then over her shoulder at the dead man under Old Blue. "I was at the front of the bus, leading some songs. He pointed...he aimed his gun...right at me. He was smiling. The other one was ready to fire at the children. Oh, God, it would have been...who are they?"

"Skinheads, neo-Nazis," said Jacob with disgust and anger. "Hate-mongers." Whatever remorse he'd felt was gone in the realization of what could have happened.

Ruth looked back and forth between the two men who each still had an arm around her. "First the gangs, now these guys show up?" She looked up at Jacob. "We seem to be under some kind of attack...a siege or something. I don't understand...." She began to cry, not hard, but the tears freely flowed down her tortured face.

"What happened here?" yelled a cop who ran toward them with his gun drawn. Three more were right behind him. One of them saw the skinheads and said, "I'll call an ambulance." Another asked, "Anybody else hurt?" Several others arrived from the other direction and immediately began to try to calm and control the growing crowd.

Ruth quickly pulled herself together. "I've got to get back to the bus, to the children. Thank God. Thank you, thank you both." She turned to the officer who had arrived first. "Officer, I saw the whole thing...it seemed to happen in slow motion. I'll tell you everything, but first I have to check on the children in that bus. Come with me. Help me to reassure them that everything..." she paused and looked again at Jacob and Dennis, "thanks to these brave men, everything is okay."

• • • • •

Mindy Martinez worked in her hometown because she wanted to; she chose to. She also chose to live among her people on the South Side. She was a distant cousin of Officer Tod Diaz, but her ancestors had come to town over a century ago to work on the railroad, long before Diaz's parents. Mindy wasn't bad looking, but she could have been more attractive, even pretty, if she cared more. She was devoted to her large extended family and was the favorite aunt of a slew of nieces and nephews, but her passion was her job. At thirty-five, she was already somewhat of an icon in the community, and not just on the South Side. She wasn't necessarily liked everywhere, but she was respected.

After graduating with honors from Kansas State's prestigious School of Journalism, she had received several offers to work for big papers in cities on each coast and in Florida. It wasn't just that she was bilingual—she was good, and had great instincts. When she covered the murder of Stephon 'YoYo' Taylor back in May, her instincts told her there was more to this than gangs and drugs—it was more than just kids killing more kids. She'd been right, and now she was close. One of her best professional attributes was patience. She hadn't even told her editor everything. She didn't have to anymore. She made her conservative superiors nervous, but they had learned to trust her instincts, too. In a few days she would make a trip to Springfield, Missouri to talk to a young woman named Angela. If her instincts were right, she'd be able to put the final pieces on her story.

The people in the waiting area were standing now, waiting for the door to the jet-way ramp to open and the stream of departing passengers to unload. She and Cynthia Wilson had exchanged pleasantries only because their roles required it. Cynthia had been one of the last greeters to arrive, but had used her charm to work her way to the front of the crowd. Cynthia needed to get to her husband first and help him get his bearings. She needed to explain to him why there wasn't a bevy of reporters to greet him. Some said Cynthia Wilson was a better politician than her husband was. Most people credited her with helping him to finally grow up and into his potential, and they had to admit, the second Mrs. Wilson had been good for him. Except Mindy. Mindy did not agree. Mrs. Wilson was more ambitious than her husband and was far more ruthless. She was clearly the one most devastated, much more so than her husband was by his unexpected loss to Linda Cabinet. But to Mindy, such traits by themselves did not a good politician make. When you got to know Bob Wilson, scoundrel or not, you couldn't help but like him. He could tell a bald face lie as well as anybody, but the truth was also obvious: he cared about and liked people. The more one knew about his pretty, young, charming wife the harder it was to find anything to like.

Mindy wondered how Mrs. Wilson would handle the story that would finally break sometime in the next few weeks. How would the first Mrs. Wilson and their teenage children handle it? Neither wife, speculated Mindy, would be surprised. Mindy began to make her move. She wanted to offset Cynthia.

Bob Wilson was the fourth person through the door. He was an impressive man, well over six feet tall with broad shoulders and a full head of black, wavy hair. Although he would have a difficult time running full court with his old high school basketball teammate, Jacob Riddler, Wilson carried his bulk well. He wore fine suits and carefully selected, tasteful ties. His broad, genuine smile accented pearly white teeth. Wilson was a big, likeable guy. The expectation on his face was betrayed by a touch of confusion. His smile seemed to teeter, like it wanted to desert him. As if grabbing a lifeline, he pulled his young wife to his side and bent down to kiss her cheek.

"Only Mindy's here?" he whispered. "Didn't the news release about my role in the caucus go out? Didn't anyone tip them? That's why I took this early flight to make all three newscasts, noon, five...."

"You've been upstaged by another story, Darling," she purred. "It's okay, but watch yourself."

Before the exchange was over Mindy was at his other side. Cynthia, as if to prevent her from getting to him, grabbed onto his left arm. She always grabbed the left arm, so his right would be free to shake the hands of well-wishers and old friends as they walked through the terminal. Tom had a lot of old friends. He considered Mindy to be one of them.

"Mindy," he said warmly as he stuck out his hand. "How's the best reporter west of the Potomac?"

"I'm great, Bob. How are you these days? I understand the party caucus went well? Rumor has it, you're going to run for the Senate."

After greeting several other people, Wilson gave her his attention as they walked. "I haven't decided yet. But, you know, Mindy, the loss to Congresswoman Cabinet was one of the best things that ever happened to me. It gave me a chance to think, to get in touch with what I believe and what our shared vision for this country should be."

"So, a defining moment in a career of public service, Bob?" Mindy asked. She knew he was trying out his well-rehearsed lines on her. She thought, why not give him another one? It worked.

He stopped; they all stopped. Bob looked Mindy in the eye and raised his index finger. "Exactly, a defining moment." All three of them knew the game they were playing well.

As they walked together, the crowd got ahead of them because Wilson was always stopping to greet someone. Cynthia was charming, as well, and also shook hands with folks, but then would quickly reattach herself with both hands to his arm. She looked up at her husband when he talked as if she adored him. Soon they were alone at the top of the escalator. Wilson again brought them to a stop. His curiosity, his need to know why there were no other reporters there had overcome him. Mindy had counted on it.

"When did you start covering the political beat, Mindy? I thought you did the crime stuff."

"Oh, that's right, you were in flight and couldn't possibly have heard the news. All the local folks are wrapping up down at the courthouse."

Cynthia squeezed his arm, as if to warn him, but said sweetly, "It's really good news, Darling. You'll be pleased."

"I'm sure," said Mindy. "Your old teammate from high school, Jacob Riddler, and Dennis Livingston are heroes—big time. This will hit the national news. If they want, they'll be on all the talk shows over this one."

They moved off to a corner of the airport where they would not be interrupted while Mindy and Cynthia took turns relating the details of the story, how the quick action and unselfish bravery of Jacob and Dennis had prevented a terrible hate shooting from occurring.

"In one short week, Bob, your old friend went from being a villain to a national hero. They'll probably make Jacob Riddler the national poster boy for prison rehabilitation programs," she baited him. "And gun control."

"And rightfully so," he said. "Like I said yesterday, innocent until proven guilty. I was wrong to jump to conclusions before I knew the facts. I need to give Jacob a call. I want to apologize as well as congratulate him. Do you have his number, Mindy?"

"Not on me. But, I can get it. I'll call your office later today."

"Good," he said and took a step as if to leave.

"Tom?" Mindy began sincerely with the one question that had brought her to meet Wilson's plane. "What do you think about the rumors that this Juwan character, the one who tried to frame Riddler for the murder of that boy, is an associate of one of your assistant managers?"

"J.J.? J.J. Johnson?" he volunteered.

Mindy detected Mrs. Wilson give her husband a subtle warning squeeze as she continued to hang onto his arm. Mindy said, "Yes, J.J. I've met him. He's very articulate and seems to get along with everybody at McKey's, but there are some who believe that he's using his job there as a front for other activities, that there is some connection between Juwan..." she pretended to check her notebook, "Walcott and J.J. Johnson."

Wilson pondered the question carefully and then said, "Obviously, Mindy, I've heard the rumors. Off the record?"

Mindy nodded.

"Nathan Frye came to see me several months ago. You know he and I still work together on things we care about, like at-risk youth and the rehabilitation of people who've been to prison. It was Nathan who called me three or four years ago while I was still in Washington. Nathan suggested that I should take a chance and hire my old friend, Jacob. I'm so pleased Jacob was cleared today. I really must call him."

Cynthia subtly pulled her husband toward the hallway, but Mindy was too good to be sidestepped. She said quickly, "So, Nathan came to see you several months ago about J.J.?"

Wilson stopped and Mindy detected a flash of annoyance in Cynthia's face. "Yes, he did. Still off the record?" When Mindy nodded, he continued. "Nathan shared similar concerns as those you suggested. I looked into them and I've kept a close watch on things since. I haven't seen any evidence or anything to lead me to believe it's true. In fact, J.J.

has approached me several times and encouraged me to give an at-risk young adult a job. Again, off the record for now, we've even hired a couple of ex-gang members. Not a lot, you know, but we always have a couple of kids on the edge working for us, you know? Sometimes it works, sometime it doesn't."

"So, you think your efforts with J.J. have worked?"

"Oh, yes. Yes, I do. J.J. comes from a very troubled background. He has a single mom whom he provides for. He's worried sick about his younger brother and sister. He thinks his sister is on drugs and a prostitute somewhere—it's so sad. He's been trying to keep his younger brother out of the gangs. The lad seems to have a wild imagination. Maybe that's what was behind the accusations against Jacob to begin with, I don't know. But, Mindy, whenever you get involved in the lives of troubled people, you don't win them all. Sometimes it seems you lose more than you win."

Good response, thought Mindy. Already have your cover-up story, just in case. She said, "Bob, I'm not sure there's even enough here to write about, you understand. But, if something else, something more concrete comes out, I'll come see you, first, on the record. Fair enough?"

"Fair enough."

Bob and Cynthia started walking arm in arm toward the escalator that would take them to the parking area. Mindy stopped him with one last comment. "Bob, that last part, something like…" she placed her pencil on the notebook, ready to write if she received permission. "That part where you said, 'when you get involved in the lives of troubled people, you don't win them all. Sometimes, it seems, you lose more than you win.' On the record?"

"Absolutely," he said as the escalator took him and his pretty young wife, arm and arm, down and away from her.

"See you soon, Bob…and Cynthia," Mindy mumbled to herself.

24 UNFINISHED JUSTICE

TUESDAY AFTERNOON, JULY 23RD

"**A**re you ready?" Jacob said as he came through the office door. "The boys are waiting in the back seat of your car. It's definitely a top-down day."

"Yes, I'm ready." Maryann was disgusted. Evelyn was on the phone. Maryann said to her, "Still getting the answering machine?" Evelyn nodded. Maryann said to Jacob. "We can't get a hold of LaTisha. I talked to her last night and she sounded drugged up or something. I told her to call if she wanted a ride. I'll bet she's not even coming to juvenile court to be with her son. I can't believe it."

Jacob said, "I just hope she doesn't show up with that smooth-talking Juice."

Evelyn pushed the redial button. "Go ahead and leave. Dennis said he'd meet you outside the courtroom. I'll keep trying to reach Miss Johnson. If I get through and she needs a ride, I'll go get her. Maybe she's caught a cab already." Evelyn made a shushing motion with her free hand. "Go ahead, you guys."

Jacob smiled at Evelyn and said, "Thanks, Evelyn." To Maryann he said gently, "We'd better go."

"It's ridiculous that we even have to go at all. It's been over a month, and I thought the matter had been dropped. Tod says all but one of those other boys now back Mark's story, but we still have to go to court? Don't good kids have any rights? I just don't understand," Maryann said before she disappeared into the hallway.

Jacob smiled and exchanged a knowing glance with Evelyn. Jacob

225

said, loud enough for her to hear him out in the hall, "Juvenile court is not like adult court. Ruth told me kids have very few *rights*, that the judge isn't charged to determine innocence or guilt, but to do the right thing for the children involved. Tod says it should go quickly—it's pretty routine."

"I hope so," she said as she opened the hall closet door. "Juice is still conning everybody into believing he's an upstanding businessman and Mark and Andre have to go to court." Her high heels clacked as she stomped down the hall and back into the office. Her suit coat was neatly folded over her arm. "That's whose trial I wish we were going to this afternoon."

As she came close to Jacob, Maryann's agitated demeanor changed. She stopped and looked at him. "I'm sorry, Dear, ranting and raving like an old momma bear. Thanks for taking a break from your music to come with me."

"No problem," said Jacob, as he was finally able to open the door for her. "But, we better go. I don't think it's ever a good idea to be late for court, especially juvenile court. Andre's all excited. It's like an adventure to him. He can't wait to 'testify against those sorry little wannabees.'"

"Hey, your Andre imitation's getting better," said Maryann. She stopped halfway through the opened door and gave Jacob a kiss. "I love you."

"I love you, too." Over her shoulder, Jacob saw Andre first and then Mark, too, give him the thumbs-up sign from the back seat of the Sebring.

"Good luck," Evelyn called after them and returned to her work, happy her friend and partner had the support of a good man. She was warmed by their affection for each other.

• • • • •

LaTisha looked in the mirror again. She had started getting ready several times. She was supposed to be somewhere, she knew she was, but where? Her hand shook as she raised the dark red lipstick to her lips.

The phone! She dropped the lipstick into the sink. She just stared at it. Before her eyes it turned into an ugly red bug. She screamed and then the phone rang again. The bug turned back to lipstick. *Why does the phone just keep ringing like that? Why doesn't Andre answer it? Where is that boy?* "Angela! Where's Andre?" *But Angela's not here. She ran away. When was that? Long time ago. Maybe she dead...no, she's okay.*

That nice man say so. Who was that man? He was good-looking. That man promised to be there today with Andre. Andre! *She was supposed to go somewhere with Andre and the nice...no, Mark's momma was supposed to pick her up...LaTisha a good momma, too. Can't nobody say she ain't. She had to get ready. That was a good-looking man. Nice man, too.*

LaTisha didn't like what she saw in the mirror. It depressed her. Long ago, before the drugs, she was pretty. The boys, then the men, had loved her tall, supple body. Her skin was so fresh and clean all the time. LaTisha loved to get ready then. Sometimes she wore short skirts that showed off her long, firm legs. But sometimes she found the long, silk-like skirts and dresses were even better at attracting men, especially if there were buttons she could leave undone over her perky breasts. LaTisha loved getting ready then.

Today, she didn't like whoever that woman was in the mirror. She was no longer supple, but skinny. She had large dark circles under her dull, tired eyes. Her complexion was dull and spotty. LaTisha couldn't bear to look anymore. She left the lipstick in the sink and walked back into the kitchen.

"Angela, answer the...Andre? You want something to eat this morning?"*Where were the children?* She worried about her children. Angela running off like she did and Juice—he the only good one—Juice say Andre being bad. He don't seem bad. "Andre? You gonna eat some breakfast before you leave, Baby? Andre? Got to eat something...Andre?"

She wished she had some crank. It gave her such energy and helped her mind work, but Juice say meth is bad for her. Juice loved his momma, yes he did. She lit a cigarette and then picked up the bottle of vodka. Juice will know what to do. She needed a nap. She'd take a nap, then get ready. She took the wall phone off the hook in the kitchen and let it drop to the floor.

"Hello...Mrs. Johnson...? Hello? LaTisha? Hello...Anybody there?"

• • • • •

Things had gone well in juvenile court, so far. The defiant boy that Jacob and Maryann had seen in front of the police station a month ago was not there. The clerk explained to the judge that earlier this month she had already sent him to the State Reform School in Geneva for another unrelated incident. The angry grandmother was there and her boy was dressed in a white shirt and tie and looked more afraid of his grandmother than the judge. The other two boys looked hard and were pretending they didn't care. Their mothers sat behind them and looked more tired than Judge Collins.

Judge Carlene Collins was over sixty. Deep down, Judge Collins loved the kids and occasionally she let it show.

She was also tired, very tired and worn down by years of watching kids stream in and out of her chambers. Her reservoir of patience had long ago been depleted. She expertly and expeditiously processed the cases, shuffling kids and their parents in and out of her courtroom as quickly as she could. She had seen a lot over the years and was not easily conned. It didn't take her long to get to the bottom of things. Like most adults, she took an immediate liking to Andre and asked him first what had happened. With his usual flair and energy, Andre told the story.

The courtroom was more like a large conference room. Judge Collins sat at one end of a large, oblong table. The children and their parents sat at the table with the judge. Maryann, Mark and Andre sat on one side of the table. The other three boys and their parents sat on the other. Clerks, probation officers, attorneys, which none of the boys had, and youth advocates like Dennis and Jacob were not allowed to sit at the table, but in chairs along the wall.

Andre soon had everyone laughing. Even Judge Collins could not help but smile as Andre told of trying to stop the other boys from breaking windows and spraying graffiti on the walls of the Parkland Junior High School. When she'd heard enough, she stopped him. She asked Mark if the story Andre had told was true. She reconfirmed that he, too, had nothing to do with the vandalism. She turned and addressed the other side of the table.

"Is what Andre says true?"

None of the boys answered. The two hard cases looked over the judge's shoulder to some spot in the corner of the ceiling that all defiant teenagers seem to find when they refuse to communicate, knowing full well their silence communicates volumes. The other boy looked at his hands that were folded in front of him on the table until his grandmother pushed his shoulder. "Answer Judge Collins. You tell her what you told me."

Without looking up, the boy said, "Andre and Mark didn't do anything. They just tried to stop us."

Judge Collins looked over Mark's shoulder and said to Dennis, "Mr. Livingston, can I assign these three to the Club for community service and probation?"

"Of course, Your Honor."

Judge Collins went on to give a stern warning to the three guilty boys. If they showed up in her court again, they would join their friend in Geneva. Andre seemed to enjoy the lecture being laid on his one-time tormentors. Judge Collins told all three of them to report to the Club that afternoon. Mr. Livingston's well-trained counselors would lay out the rules, negotiate curfews and explain the conditions of probation with each boy and his guardian. Two of the boys would be required to complete two hundred hours of community service under the Club's supervision. The boy—who had cooperated under duress from his grandmother—would be required to do only a hundred and fifty hours of supervised community service. The seasoned judge warned the boys that if Mr. Livingston, at any time, reported back to her any lack of cooperation, they were headed to Geneva. She asked each boy if he understood, and she made each one say, "Yes, ma'am." Then she told them they could leave.

Everyone in the courtroom stood, and the judge added, "Mrs. Bethel, could I ask you and Mark and Andre to stay a bit longer?" She looked to the back chairs. "You, too, Mr. Livingston and Mr. Riddler, if you don't mind. Come and join us at the table." She motioned for her clerk to stay as well.

Judge Collins looked over the reading glasses perched on her nose and asked, "How does it feel to be a hero, Mr. Riddler?"

"I don't feel like a hero, Judge. The man I killed was only twenty years old. He had a lifetime ahead of him."

"But you saved the children." She looked at Dennis. "Both of you evidently saved this community from a terrible disaster. I want to thank you."

Both men nodded.

The judge continued, "Like everybody else, I've read the papers and seen the television reports. Those skinheads were a long way from home. Do you know why they picked our community to plan this attack?"

"Not that I know of, Your Honor. The FBI is on the case. They knew about this group. It was pretty small, but, no, no one really knows why."

The judge shifted her gaze to Jacob. "I've also read the stories about you, Mr. Riddler. Congratulations on turning your life around. I didn't realize you had written *Redeemed*. It's one of my favorites songs."

"You listen to Christian radio?" chimed in Andre.

The judge smiled and looked in his direction. "Don't be so surprised, young man. I've even been to your church a few times. Nathan Frye is one of the best preachers I've ever heard. I've admired his work in this community for years."

"You should hear Reverend Thomas. She's good, too."

Maryann, Jacob and Mark halfway expected Andre to add, 'She the prettiest woman I've ever seen, white or black.' Instead he said sincerely, "Thank you for believing Mark and me."

Judge Collins smiled and removed her glasses. Her facial expression, her hands, her movements, everything communicated her concern. Everyone could sense the change in her mood. "Andre, you're also the brave young man who stood up in court last Monday and defended your friend, Jacob, here. Aren't you?"

"Yes, ma'am."

"I thought so. Andre, where is your mother today?"

Maryann, Jacob and Mark were impressed with the judge's obvious concern. All three were encouraged by the dialogue. Dennis' stomach tightened. He knew the Judge well. They had worked together for years. The Club was one of the juvenile court's only alternatives to incarcerating young offenders. They had great respect for each other, but Dennis was afraid of the direction these proceedings seemed to be taking. He understood better than the rest that court was still in session.

Andre said softly, "She been sick a lot lately. She's not feeling good."

"You're worried about her, aren't you?"

Andre nodded. "Jill and Ruth are trying to help her."

"Jill and Ruth?"

"Jill is Reverend Thomas. Ruth works at the Club."

The judge looked at Maryann and smiled. "Oh, that Ruth. I know Ruth. If Ruth is trying to help, that's good. Ruth is a wonderful young professional."

Maryann smiled at the judge, full of pride at the compliment to her daughter. She then exchanged smiles with Jacob, taking great pleasure in their secret about Ruth.

Judge Collins picked up her glasses and turned them in her hands, as if discovering them for the first time. She looked at Mark, but addressed Andre in a kind voice. "Andre, you seem to have some good friends here."

"I do, Judge. These people and Preacher Nate and Jill, Reverend Thomas, they helped me to change my life. I was a gangbanger, stealing things and selling drugs for Juice's gang."

"Juice—who's he?"

"He's my big brother. Everybody think he's so good and all. I mean, he got a good job, but it ain't a real job, you know. He the top-rank in town. He's my brother, but he's bad—real bad."

"Andre, I want you to do me a favor, okay?"

Andre nodded in expectation.

"I want you in your own words to tell me the story of your life. In your own words. Take your time." She then nodded at her clerk, who got up to go rearrange her schedule. "Will you do that?"

He did, he told her everything. He told her about their lives in D.C. before moving here. He told her how his friend YoYo had died trying to help him free his sister. He told the judge how he and Jacob met the day Jacob broke Juwan's arm. And with a dramatic flair, he told her about the recent confrontation with Anthony in the alley. He told her about the Club, how Mark had taught him to quit stealing and about Antioch, how Jill had helped him become a Christian. The judge patiently listened, asking a few questions along the way to encourage Andre to continue. He told her about spending the night at Jacob's, and how Jacob was teaching him to play the guitar and Mrs. Carlson was teaching him to play the piano. Finally, after nearly forty minutes of telling his story, he cried when he told her about his mother's methamphetamine and alcohol addiction and how his mother had resisted the numerous attempts to help her.

Maryann had to wipe the tears away and the concern of Judge Collins was unmistakable.

"Andre," said the judge. "You are a very brave young man." She looked around the table. "And—you have some wonderful friends." Once again she paused to study her glasses before continuing. "Andre, I'm concerned. It seems to me that you're in danger, *grave danger,* and that your home is not a safe place for you."

"Judge," interjected Dennis. "May I add something here?"

She was obviously irritated by the interruption, but nodded.

"For over a month, Jacob and I and Nathan Frye have organized a group of volunteers. We've worked with Detective Diaz to coordinate a nightly watch outside Andre's house, or Maryann's or Jacob's— wherever he spends the night, there are two men keeping watch."

Andre sat up and looked at Jacob in surprise.

"Let me make sure I understand, Mr. Livingston," said the judge caustically. "For well over a month, you've known this child is in danger and you did not call Child Protective Services?"

"Your honor, as you know, there are very few alternatives for adolescent status offenders. You're right. This is a brave young man who made great strides, living in the community. The youth center..."

"I'm well aware of your opinions about the youth center. We've argued about it before, but at least there he'll be safe."

"No, he won't, Your Honor." Dennis' exasperation was growing and the others began to grow uncomfortable. "The youth center is full of gang members. We're working hard, damn hard to keep this boy safe...."

"Enough! Don't you ever curse in my courtroom, Mr. Livingston."

"I'm sorry, Your Honor, but it's just not fair. You cannot..."

She held up her hand and Dennis knew he'd lost.

"Your Honor?" he pleaded anyway.

She shook her head and looked into the confused eyes of her charge. "Andre, I'm going to assign our best caseworker to you and, for your own good, I'm going to send you to the youth center for awhile."

"For awhile? Your Honor, a kid Andre's age will get stuck there. Please reconsider."

"Mr. Livingston, you say one more word and I'll hold you in contempt of court. You have exhausted my patience. I should charge you with dereliction of duty for not reporting this case to Child Protective Services. Only my respect for the work you do prevents me. Now shut up! Not another word."

When she looked back to a wide-eyed Andre she said, "Son, come with me. We'll complete this in my chambers."

The group sat in shock at the angry exchange between the kind old judge and Dennis who sat in seething silence as the judge ushered

Andre out of the room. He looked back once at his friend, Mark, before going through the door.

When the door shut behind them, Dennis slammed his fist on the table. "That's it! Let's go." He stood up almost knocking the chair over. The others remained seated.

"Go?" said Mark. "We need to wait for Andre."

Dennis spun. "He's not coming back!" The surprise he saw in Mark's face at his angry tone helped Dennis to gain control and refocus. "Mark, I'm sorry. Andre's not coming back in here. She's sending him to the youth center. He'll go straight from here to the youth center."

"The youth center? But...he didn't do anything wrong," protested Mark.

"She thinks he'll be better protected from the gangs at the youth center."

The reality of what had just happened sunk into the group.

"You mean," asked Maryann, "the three guilty kids get released to their parents and Andre gets sent to the youth center?"

"It's called Juvenile *Justice*," scoffed Dennis as he stalked around the room.

"How long will he be there?" asked Jacob.

"Months!" exclaimed Dennis. "Her best caseworker...they go through caseworkers so fast.... They're young, under-trained, underpaid, and carry ridiculously heavy caseloads. It could take weeks before they even finish the write-up and then, there'll be no placement for Andre. Foster homes for ex-gangbangers are hard to find."

"Can I visit him?" asked Mark.

"No, I'm afraid not," said Dennis his anger subsiding into resignation. "Only immediate family. They'll let Nathan and Jill, but..."

"You and Ruth?" asked Jacob.

"Oh, they'll let me in—they better," said Dennis. "But no one else. And visiting hours are from two to five and six to eight on Wednesdays and from one to three on Sundays."

"That's it? That's the only time all week you can visit him?" asked Maryann.

"That's it. Prisoners in the county jail have more privileges than kids at the youth center," said Dennis as he pulled his cell phone from his suit coat pocket and began to dial.

Mark said angrily, "Great, Juice and his addicted mom can go see him, but I can't."

"Hi, this is Dennis. Go get Ruth for me. Get someone to cover for her. This is important." Dennis continued to pace as he held the little phone to his ear. No one said a word. It took over a minute before he said, "Hi, see if you can find Jill Thomas and meet me in exactly one hour at Andre's house. She needs to know what happened to her son today—thanks to her. I'll tell you all about it."

Maryann waved at him and said, "We'll go by and tell her."

"Your mom says she'll come by and fill you in...I'm going to go see Charles Andrews, if he's available. Okay, meet me in one hour at LaTisha's doorstep. It's time we wake her up. Sure, if he's available, bring Nathan too."

VISITORS

25

Jacob stuck his head, still wet from the shower, in the door of Dennis' office. "Got just a minute?"

It had been a month since Jacob and Dennis had thwarted the sinister attack by the two skinheads. They had always gotten along well and respected each other, but without a word being spoken about it, both of them realized the experience had deepened the bond between them. Jacob was profoundly grateful for the courage and even-handedness that Dennis had shown in standing by him during the Kimani Grove ordeal. And Dennis struggled on several occasions to find the words to express his gratitude to Jacob. Not just for the quick thinking that had prevented a catastrophic disaster, but also for preventing him from killing the second skinhead. He wanted to thank Jacob for interrupting his rage just in time, before it took him into a dark place he never wanted to enter. So far, the words hadn't come. The connection between them made words unnecessary—for now.

It had been a month since Andre had been sent away. The youth center on the western edge of downtown was not far away, but the isolation of the place made it seem much further. The day that Andre was ushered out of the courtroom by Judge Collins, reporters from CNN, the Today Show and numerous newspapers and periodicals began to show up. They wanted to do stories about Jacob, the ex-con, who was now a local hero and popular songwriter who thwarted the evil attack on a busload of children. Jacob refused every offer for an interview. Stories were done anyway, but without Jacob's participation.

235

Dennis took every opportunity to highlight the important work being done by the Boys & Girls Clubs around the country. Nathan served as Jacob's spokesperson and did respectful interviews, insisting that Jacob was a very private person who had only done what he had to do, and was not interested in any notoriety. Nathan explained that Jacob only wanted to get back to his music and his volunteer work. Nathan took every opportunity to point out the success of faith-based approaches to rehabilitation.

Each story highlighted the songs that had been recorded by different Christian artists. Kids and staff members at the Club were interviewed. One reporter for a national television news show even did a delightful interview with Mrs. Carlson, the hero's teacher. Every story also told of the false accusations of murder against Jacob. Jacob refused every interview and tried his best to stay away from the cameras and reporters. He only left his apartment to go to the Club, and from there he would sneak out the back door to escape to Maryann's house. Somehow, the mass of reporters had overlooked the love angle. For a week or so, Jacob even had trouble on his morning jogs and his daily visits to his mom in the nursing home. There, a reporter discovered nurse Shirley, who profusely sang Jacob's praises. Still whenever he confronted a reporter Jacob would simply smile and repeat, "No comment," or "I'd rather not discuss it," over and over again. Finally, the reporters seemed to have had their fill and left town.

In a strange twist of fate, the more Jacob avoided the press, the more mysterious and spiritual he was portrayed. As a result, his songs, *The Redeemed* and *When Sparrows Fall*, climbed back into the top five on the Christian music charts. *When Sparrows Fall* touched a nerve with a public grown weary of children dying violent deaths and began to work its way up both the rock and country charts as well. Christian and secular artists from Los Angeles and Nashville were calling Jacob's agent wanting to buy his songs. Dennis and Nathan found the whole thing amusing and worked hard to shield Jacob and to make sure the press honored his wishes.

Dennis took off his glasses and motioned toward the chairs across from his desk. "You bet I have time for you."

Jacob sat down and placed his gym bag in the chair beside him.

"How was the game, today? No heart attacks?" Dennis teased.

"We missed you. A lot of the group is out of town or on vacation. But—we had a good three-on-three game. Where were you?"

"It's the last day of the summer program. I have to get the maintenance and repair work lined up. A couple of local unions are doing some free work for us next week and it was the only time they could meet. Remember," reminded Dennis, "there will be no game next week. The Club will be closed to prepare for fall and they'll be painting in the gym."

"You warned me I'd be ready for a break when the summer was over," laughed Jacob. "I was only here two or three nights a week. I can't imagine how tired Ruth and some of your other folks must be."

Dennis smiled and nodded. "Boys & Girls Club professionals are even more glad than parents when school finally starts again."

"Dennis," Jacob leaned forward in his chair. "I just want to thank you. It's been wonderful volunteering here this summer. Thanks for sticking with me through the rough times."

"You're welcome, Jacob."

"Thanks, too, for handling all the media inquiries after the skinhead incident. I don't know what I would have done during the last month if you and Nathan hadn't taken that on. I couldn't believe the media frenzy."

"It has pretty well died out." Dennis shuddered at the thought of what might have been. "You doing okay?"

"I'm all right, Dennis. At first I was having trouble dealing with the fact that I had killed someone...someone so young who had an entire lifetime before him...but when I think about...one second more and those assault rifles would have.... The skinhead who survived is not very intelligent. Tod says the dead guy must have been calling the shots. No one knows why they came all this way and what made them pick out the Club bus. Except that they wanted maximum media attention."

Dennis shrugged. "At least there was a lot of attention directed to the Club—it might even help raise a few dollars."

"At least the Club deserves the attention, Dennis. You have a great staff. The place was packed every day. It's such a broad program, with so many opportunities for all the kids."

"It was a great summer," Dennis agreed. "We kind of got off to a rough start, but the last month was particularly good. I think we've nearly neutralized the gangs, at least here in Parkland."

"It's too bad that another innocent boy had to lose his life in the process," said Jacob.

"Too many boys and girls are dying in cities all over this country, Jacob. It turns out Kimani Grove wasn't all that innocent, anyway. He was heavy into the street life already. The good news is, Juwan Walcott is going to go away for a long time."

"Juice was behind that whole thing, and all the other stuff—that's what bugs me."

"He'll get his, Jacob."

"I hope so," said Jacob. "Have you been up to see Andre this week? I can't believe he's been there for a month already."

"I saw him Wednesday afternoon. He's pretty depressed, I think. No matter what the politicians try to tell you, the youth center is a jail for kids and it's a dreary place. The cards and letters from all the Antioch folks have helped."

"Do you think your plan might work?"

"It's up to you and Maryann to give it a chance. Are you sure you know what you're doing? Are you still up for it?" asked Dennis with a sly grin.

"I'm as nervous as I can be, but yeah, we're more than up for it."

"I'll be working with Charles this week on the legal documents. He's trying to float some trial balloons and is hoping to find a friendly judge."

"One that might overlook my past?" asked Jacob.

Dennis smiled and nodded.

"Okay then, I'll see you a week from tomorrow, if not before," said Jacob.

"And," teased Dennis, "I'd advise you to never forget that date for the rest of your life."

Jacob laughed and confirmed, "10:00 AM, Saturday, August 31, at the home."

• • • • •

Across the street, Nathan bounded up the back stairs. He was always full of energy after ninety minutes of basketball. He opened his office door and froze. He had visitors.

Sitting in the two chairs in front of his desk were Juice and a young man, evidently a new lieutenant. As always, Juice was well-groomed and wore an expensive suit. He could have passed for a young stockbroker. His companion wore a brand new warm-up suit and high top, black leather tennis shoes. He looked uncomfortable, even a little scared. Nathan thought he couldn't have been any more than sixteen or seventeen. Nathan hadn't seen Juice up close since their late Friday night confrontation at McKey's last May. Juice looked thinner, and despite the gleaming smile, his complexion looked poor and his face was drawn.

Without standing, Juice smiled broadly and said pleasantly, "Good afternoon, Preacher. How are you today?"

Nathan threw his gym bag into the corner and walked to his side of the desk. Ignoring Juice's greeting, he made eye contact with the other young man, "I know you, don't I, Son?"

There was no answer.

"Relax, Preacher. Even though you been messing in my life lately, I just want to talk—see if we can't work something out. Sit down, sit down."

Nathan did not sit down. Instead he crossed his arms and leaned against the windowsill behind his desk.

"You wouldn't happen to know where my mom is, would you?" Juice's tone was not angry, but it contained a definite challenge.

"I do," said Nathan, still looking at Juice's young companion.

"I thought you might. She left everything, so I assume she'll be needing..."

For the first time, Nathan switched his gaze from the teenager to meet Juice's eye. "She won't need the things you bought her anymore."

"I see." Something dark passed over Juice's face, but he quickly found his front. "Well, good, good. She needs to get her life together. I'm glad you're helping her."

Nathan said nothing. He also never flinched in making eye contact.

Juice shifted, crossed his legs and raised both palms in a conciliatory gesture. "Preacher, I'm serious. I want to try to set things right."

"It's not me you have to set things right with."

Juice uncrossed his legs and leaned forward, "Well, maybe you can help with that—help me get right with God and all."

"I could."

"Come on, Preacher, you supposed to love everybody, even me."

"That's right, Jesus said to love even our enemies."

Juice raised his index finger and pointed at Nathan. "That's just it. I don't want to be enemies with you. Listen, I've changed my ways. I'm working hard at McKey's. Jelly, here, he's my head bus boy. He's helping me find kids who need work. I've hired a lot of kids from the 'hood here. And, I want you to know, I plan to give Hotchie a good job when he gets out of the youth center."

Nathan continued to stare at him.

"Last time I talked to Momma, she said Mr. Livingston told her that Angela is doing fine."

Nathan said nothing.

"That right, Preacher? My little sister doing okay?"

Nathan nodded.

"So, Hotchie's in the youth center, Momma's getting the help she needs, and Angela's doing fine. It seems to me that your concerns been answered. You and me—we ought to be able to put our differences behind us, Preacher."

"Juice, I told you back in May that your life would be a mess until you did right by your sister and brother. Your sister barely got out of town when her life was in danger because she wouldn't whore for you—and maybe a kid gets his throat sliced for helping her. Your little brother is sitting in the youth center because a well-intentioned judge thinks that's the best way to keep him safe from the gangs—your gang. And your mother is finally getting help for an addiction that you helped to feed. It seems to me, Juice, that you've dug a deeper hole than ever. I see only one way out for you."

"And what way might that be?" Juice asked with a smile.

"It's just a matter of time, Juice. You're smart. You don't dress like a gang leader. You can turn the street lingo off and on. You move comfortably from the street to McKey's because you've learned to use your natural charm to put them at ease. You don't look threatening...until you *want* to be threatening. You're shrewd. You've built a nice cover for yourself at McKey's. Somehow you've even fooled Bob Wilson."

Juice smiled a little more, as if acknowledging all that Nathan had said.

"Maybe there's more going on with Bob than just fooling him. You seem to almost have a hold on him."

Nathan detected a sense of pride behind the smirk on the gang leader's attractive face.

"Whatever, seems to me, it's too late for you to do *right* by Angela and Andre, even by LaTisha, so there's only one option left for you."

"That right?"

"That's right," replied Nathan.

"And what option might that be, Preacher?"

"You'll either soon be dead," Nathan purposely paused, but saw no change in Juice's expression—no anger—no fear, "or, you'll soon be sent to prison for the rest of your life. That's not all bad, sometimes it's in bondage that we truly find our peace, our true selves—true freedom. I've seen it happen to dudes even more far-gone than you. Except...you seem different to me, Juice. I wonder about you."

"So, what makes me different?"

"You're a good liar, but more than a liar." Nathan's tone was more analytical than confrontational. "All crooks and thieves are skilled liars, but you seem...to live the lie. And you live it well. You're a living, evil lie. You live so comfortably behind a wall of pretense, yet..." Nathan looked back at the teenager who didn't understand much of what was being said, but still sensed the battle that was taking place. While pulling the teenager into his eyes, Nathan continued speaking to Juice. "Yet—you can attract and then hold the loyalty of children. After you have them, you seem to control them by terror and fear. Even when they're in custody, like Juwan and that poor, miserable Anthony...you still seem to be able to control them." Nathan looked away from the wide-eyed teen. Juice's expression had not changed. The slight smile told Nathan that Juice had enjoyed the analysis, even agreed with it. Nathan's tone changed: "Except for Angela and Andre, two brave kids, your own blood, in the end you couldn't control them. They figured you out and broke away. But...I haven't figured you out...yet."

They stared at each other. The teen tensed, sensing the growing friction, but didn't move. Again, something seemed to pass over Juice's face. Nathan saw something almost like a shudder pass through his body. He waited for the explosion, but once more Juice seemed to regain his composure.

Juice sat up and smiled. In a sincere tone, he said, "Preacher Nate, from the beginning, I've tried to tell you and Mr. Livingston that you had me all wrong. My life was on the wrong track in D.C. until Bob Wilson gave me a chance. He's the one that taught me how to relate to people. He taught me how to dress, how to invest my money. He gave me an opportunity to learn the restaurant business. Since moving here, I've tried to be a good son and a good brother. I'm glad you've stepped in to help my mom. Maybe Hotchie will get the help he needs. I want to put our differences behind us. I'm legit now. I really am. I think I could use help in spiritual matters. Will you help me, be my spiritual mentor?"

This time it was Nathan who shook his head in disbelief and smiled slightly. Nathan had lobbed a couple of explosives over Juice's wall of pretense, but the wall itself remained intact.

Juice continued, "I brought a peace offering. Mr. Wilson says when we've done well it's time to pay back. I know that churches always need funds." Juice reached into his coat pocket and pulled out an envelope. "And preachers, I know they don't get paid much." Juice held up the envelope and smiled. "So, use this any way you like. I appreciate what you're doing for my mom and Hotchie. If they need something...if you need something...any way you like." Juice tossed the envelope into the middle of the desk. "I'd like to get to know you better. Maybe I can help you sometime."

"Thank you," said Nathan sincerely. During the whole exchange he had remained perched against the windowsill, his arms crossed over his chest. He lowered his arms, took a step toward the desk and reached for the envelope. He opened it and counted ten new one thousand-dollar bills. Nathan smiled, waved the bills like a fan and said, "Thank you very much...J.J."

Juice smiled and shrugged at his young companion as if to say *I told you*.

Nathan turned with the money and walked toward the back corner of the small office. As he did he turned his eyes on the teen. "Jelly, I do remember you. You're Audrey May's grandson. You came to this church when you were a child, didn't you?"

"Yes, sir," the boy answered and uncomfortably looked to Juice. Juice smiled as if to encourage the dialogue. "Audrey's my gramma. She used to bring me all the time."

Nathan picked up a small garbage can with a black bar across the top and set it on the desk. He smiled at the boy, then bent to plug in the cord that hung from the black bar.

"Jelly, I see your gramma every week at the nursing home. You know, she prays for you all the time, every day."

"Yes, sir. I know that."

"Son, when a gramma like yours is praying for you, you might as well just give in and come back to the Lord."

As he said the word *Lord*—before Juice knew what happened, Nathan had shredded the ten bills.

In horror, Jelly looked at Juice and what he saw there terrified him.

Nathan calmly took the plastic bag out of the garbage can and deliberately tied it off, never breaking eye contact with Jelly. "Don't be so afraid of him, son." Jelly jerked his eyes back to Nathan and experienced a different kind of fear, almost a comforting fear. "Be afraid of the God your gramma prays to." Still looking at Jelly he tossed the bag into Juice's lap. "When that scum bag in his fancy suit leaves." Nathan pointed his finger at Jelly. "You stay put, right there in that seat. Be afraid of God, boy, not him. Stay put."

An evil-laced tirade finally erupted from Juice. He jumped to his feet and made a step toward the desk. Nathan never broke eye contact with the boy. "Stay put, son."

Juice threw the plastic bag and it hit Nathan in the face. Nathan just smiled and pulled the boy further into his eyes.

Juice leaned over and hissed into the boy's ear. "Let's go!"

"Stay right there, son. He's a liar and his lies can't hurt you. I'll help you. Stay there."

Juice launched a vile list of threats against Jelly if he did not follow him out of the office. Nathan just smiled at the boy and shook his head.

Juice made a move toward the door, then came back and snatched the bag of shredded money from the desktop where it had landed. He stormed out.

Jelly stayed.

SURPRISE!

26

SATURDAY, AUGUST 31,
LABOR DAY WEEKEND

Maryann returned from the bathroom next to the master bedroom. Her senses were alive, tingling. She even felt the lush carpet between her toes. Then she noticed the grin on Jacob's face.

"What? What are you smiling about?" she said as she laid down next to him on the oversized bed. She laid her head on his shoulder and pulled one bare leg over his thigh.

"Honestly?" He pulled the fresh sheet over their nakedness.

"Of course, honestly," she purred as she snuggled closer.

"Well, you came out of the bathroom in all of your glory and I was reminded of one of Preacher Nate's sermons."

"One of Nathan's sermons," she pouted as she playfully pounded him once on the chest.

"Well, actually just the title of one of his sermons—'Naked Grace.'"

They burst out laughing, the easy laugh of lovers that sustained itself beyond the humor.

Suddenly, Maryann stiffened. "Oh no! What's that?"

"I heard it, too." said Jacob.

Maryann bounded up and looked out the back window. "It's the children!" she exclaimed. She reached down beside the bed to grab her jeans. She threw them on and grabbed a sweatshirt out of the drawer.

"Hurry up!"

"I'm trying!" He laughed as he reached for a sock. "I have more clothes to put on than you. You only threw on two items, for cryin' out loud."

They tried getting out the bedroom door at the same time.

245

"A fine mess you've gotten us into this time, Ollie," pined Jacob. They continued to giggle as they took the steps two at time down to the living room and laughed harder as Jacob's socked feet slid on the hardwood floors in the dining room. In the family room, Jacob threw his shoes under and his sock feet on top of the coffee table as he fell onto the couch. They heard the kids in the kitchen now. Maryann flopped down next to him on the couch and hit the television remote just as Ruth called out,

"Hello-o, we're home."

"In here," returned Maryann trying hard to get her laughter under control.

"What in the world are you watching—wrestling?" asked Ruth.

Maryann and Jacob started laughing again.

"No," said Maryann, flipping the channel again. "We were just channel surfing as you came in. Not much of anything on."

"Pre-season NFL is on and so is the Pig Skin Classic," said Mark without much enthusiasm as he came into the room.

"Hey, fella," said Jacob as Mark took the remote from his mom and punched in the college game. "You look a little down."

"Coach announced the starting quarterback today. It wasn't me."

Ruth came up behind him and tousled his hair, "Yeah, but he said you would play in every game, probably every half. Not bad for a sophomore."

"I'm starved," said Mark, changing subjects and his mood.

"So, what's new?" joked Maryann. "There's ice cream and some of the frozen pizza you like in there."

"Great, come on," said Ruth to her little brother.

As Mark and Ruth went into the other room, Jacob whispered, "Do you think they suspected anything?"

"Don't think so," said Maryann snuggling into him. "We didn't have any close calls like that when we were teenagers." And the laughter erupted again.

• • • • •

Sunday Morning
September 1st

As was her custom when the time in the service came for prayers for the family of God, Reverend Jill Thomas smiled, rose from the large chair behind the pulpit, stepped off the small stage and moved to the front of the church. Her smile seemed especially beautiful to Mark today and she seemed to make brief eye contact with him as she paused before speaking. Mark smiled at his memory of Andre, declaring in a whisper to him every Sunday morning that Reverend Thomas is 'the most beautiful woman, white or black, in the whole world.' Mark remembered how much Andre enjoyed the singing and praise time. He wondered if Andre even realized what day it was in the youth center. Suddenly his mom and Jacob were trying to make their way past him and Ruth and into the aisle and he understood that while he'd been daydreaming, Reverend Thomas had called his mom and Jacob to the front.

Reverend Thomas embraced both Maryann and Jacob before standing at their side and in her rich voice saying to the congregation, "Pastor Nathan has an exciting announcement that he would like to make."

Pure joy exuded from Nathan's face as he moved to the front to join them. Nathan hugged first Maryann and then Jacob. Then he stood between Maryann and Jacob, his big arms wrapped around both of them as he addressed the congregation.

"You want to know a secret?" he said in a loud mock whisper and paused, heightening everyone's anticipation. Mark looked questioningly at his sister. Ruth just smiled and shrugged. She knew nothing.

"Yesterday morning at ten o'clock a small party of us: Reverend Thomas and I, Tod Diaz and Shirley Mason and Dennis Howard *and* Jacob Riddler and Maryann Bethel, we all went to visit Jacob's mother Becky Riddler who, as most of you know, has been in a coma now for several months at the Parkland Nursing Home. And you know what? As we were leaving, I think I saw a smile on Miss Becky's face." He looked at Jacob and nodded as he continued. "I think she knew we were there. I *really* do.

"And, Miss Becky had reason to smile yesterday, and today. I sense her presence here in spirit. For while we were there, in fact the reason for our visit, was so that in the presence of Miss Becky and these other witnesses, it was my and Reverend Thomas' pleasure to conduct a wedding, right there in Becky's room. Ladies and gentlemen, brothers and sisters, it's my great pleasure to introduce to you…Mr. and Mrs. Jacob Riddler. Son, you may kiss the bride."

As Nathan stepped back he pushed Jacob and Maryann together. When they kissed, the congregation spontaneously rose and applauded. The pianist launched into a soulful wedding recessional. Ruth grabbed Mark's hand and with tears streaming down her face, she dragged him to the front to first embrace her mother and then her new father. "I'm so happy. I'm so happy," she kept saying.

Mark smiled from ear to ear, but not knowing what to say or what all of this meant. The hug he gave his mom was sincere. Mark stuck out his hand to Jacob. Jacob grabbed the hand and pulled Mark into a bear hug. As the congregation continued to applaud, tears streaming down many faces, the new family, arm in arm, went back to their seats in the second pew next to Diaz and Shirley, who was wiping tears from her chubby cheeks.

Maryann and Jacob held hands and turned their eyes toward the front.

Reverend Thomas addressed the congregation, "It is now time for prayer. I have one special prayer request before we begin. For about four weeks now we have been praying for our young brother Andre Fitzgerald, sometimes called Hotchie." Her affection for the boy was obvious in her tone.

"Andre, in a strange twist of justice, is stuck at the Douglas County Youth Detention Center. Keep in mind he is there as a *status offender*, which means had he been an adult, there would've been no grounds to hold him. He is in a frustrating holding pattern, waiting for the courts and the social welfare bureaucracy to work.

"I was up to see him last Wednesday evening and will go again this afternoon. Dennis Livingston from the Club was also there. We both agree. We are very worried about Andre. I think he has gone into kind of a depression. His cheerful demeanor is almost gone and his beautiful face has developed serious acne problems. So, please, please pray for him and continue to send him cards and letters of encouragement.

"There is some good news. We have also been praying for Andre's mother, LaTisha Johnson. LaTisha has just successfully completed thirty days of treatment for her chemical addictions. She seems to be a new person. I'm so encouraged. LaTisha still has a long way to go, however. She is not ready to re-enter the reality of her world, for many reasons. Thanks to intervention by Pastor Nathan and his connections in the treatment community, LaTisha will move to a halfway house for women in the western part of the state. She may be there for as long as six months. We'll be ready to support her when she gets out. But, what that means is that unless we can figure something else out, Andre could be stuck at the youth center, or at least in the juvenile justice system for a long time.

"Mr. Livingston, Pastor Nathan and Charles Andrews," she paused to make eye contact with Andrews who sat at the back of the church with his family. He nodded to her. "They are working on a plan. So, we must pray today for Andre, for LaTisha and for the efforts that are already in process to get Andre out of the youth center. We want to see him placed in a safe and secure environment until he is able to rejoin his mother.

"Let us pray."

• • • • •

"Well, I'm glad we don't have to sneak around like we did last night," Jacob said as he and Maryann dried each other off following their first shower together.

"Oh, I don't know," teased Maryann, "the threat of getting caught kind of added to the excitement. Maybe sometime soon we can make love under a starlit sky on a mountaintop, or on a deserted beach—wouldn't that be fun?"

Jacob sensed she wasn't teasing.

"You're so beautiful." He turned her around to dry her back and was able to observe the front of her in the large mirror. "I will never get tired of just looking at you."

Maryann didn't say a word, but led him by the hand to her bed, as she had wanted to do months ago. They sat on the bed, their feet on the floor, and kissed.

"Do you think the kids…?"

Maryann tilted her head, smiled and said, "What? Know we're making love? Of course. That's the kind of thing old married folks like us do."

"I just feel funny with them downstairs in the family room."

Maryann chuckled.

"Thank you," she said softly, her hand caressing him softly on the cheek as she gazed into his eyes.

"For what?" he said.

"For making this…holy. This is special." She showered his face with light kisses.

"Maryann, I'm scared."

She leaned back to look into his face.

"Of what?"

"I'm not a good lover. Last night was the first time, at least in the last twenty years, that I ever made love sober. Booze and money were always more important to me than sex. I'm not very good at loving a woman. And..."

"And?" she prompted.

"You seem good at it." He laughed. "Very good."

"I am *very* good," she purred and ran her hand up his thigh.

Jacob looked into her beautiful face and saw there her love for him. "Did you enjoy last night?"

"Yes, of course. It was sweet and intimate."

"But, not great?" He was afraid to hear the answer.

"Maybe you've progressed a little bit since the back seat days of our youth," she teased.

"That's what I was afraid..."

She interrupted him with a kiss, one hand on each side of his face. She broke the kiss, smiled at him and kissed him again. She looked deep into his eyes and she saw the doubt and confusion there.

"You're all the man I'll ever need, Jacob Riddler. We have the rest of our lives to explore one another. We'll learn as we go, from each other. In the beginning, I can teach you some things. Soon you'll be teaching me. That's the way it works. You want me to teach you how to please a woman?" she asked.

"Yes, yes, I want to please you more than anything."

"Okay. Good. Well," she said with delight, "this could be fun. Your first lesson will be about touch. Slow and easy."

"Slow and easy?"

"Or slow and light might say it better. Sit right in the middle of the bed with your back against the headboard."

Jacob smiled, his heart pounding, and allowed her to take charge.

"Umm, um, you're a good-looking man," she said, smiling back.

THE
ANNOUNCEMENT

27

TUESDAY, SEPTEMBER 3RD,
MID-MORNING

Dennis walked into the Parkland Diner the day after the Labor Day holiday a little late for his ten o'clock meeting with Nathan. The morning sun was shining through the windows that ran the entire length of the historic building. Dennis had to squint before he saw Nathan waving at him from a booth at the far end. The lunch crowd had not yet begun but there was still a spattering of people throughout the diner. Most were older retired people. The banter was light and laughter came easy. A few business meetings and sales calls were also taking place over iced-tea and coffee. Out on the sidewalk a steady stream of pedestrians passed by the windows on their way to and from the Old Market and downtown offices.

"Good morning," said Dennis, as he slid into the booth and stuck out his hand. "Sorry I'm late."

"No problem, traffic is heavy for this time of day." Nathan looked out the window and down the street. "What's up with the news trucks down at Community Church?"

"You haven't heard? Bob Wilson is announcing his candidacy for the U.S. Senate."

Nathan squinted down the street, trying to see. "From the front steps of the Church?"

"Does that bother you?" asked Dennis.

"It does, I think. Seems to be an implied endorsement by the church," said Nathan.

Dennis shrugged. "You don't think your work on behalf of Wilson's

251

last opponent, now Congresswoman Linda Cabinet, wasn't seen as an endorsement of her by Antioch?" Dennis smiled and jabbed further. "It's okay for poor, small churches with liberal tendencies to make an implied endorsement, but it's somehow wrong for larger, rich churches with conservative bases to do the same?"

"Ouch!" Nathan grimaced. "Good point. But, I was always careful in that campaign to say I was speaking as an individual and Linda didn't hold a press conference on the church steps. She's not even a member of Antioch."

Dennis just smiled and raised an eyebrow in disbelief.

"Okay, I think you got me. You're right," surrendered Nathan with a grin. "That's why you and I are good for each other. We keep each other honest."

"Probably," Dennis agreed with a smile. "I bet it was hard for the pastor at Community Church to say no to Wilson anyway. Don't they have an educational wing dedicated to Wilson's father?"

"Yes, that's true. The Wilson family has been long-time members and supporters of Community Church. They've been very generous over the years, generous to a lot of other causes, too."

"Sometimes I think you admire Bob Wilson," challenged Dennis.

"I admired his father." Then Nathan challenged, "And it appears that you can't stand Bob."

"Exactly," said Dennis. "He's a hypocrite. He's probably over there right now making a speech about family values, implying that God is on his side, his beautiful blond 'trophy' wife smiling and looking up at him adoringly. You're right, I can't stand him."

Nathan took a sip of his coffee. "Bob is...I believe, a man who wants to do right. In his heart of hearts, I don't think he's a bad man. He has made mistakes. Who hasn't?"

Dennis shook his head and smiled. "My friend, you can find the good in anybody."

After the waitress brought Dennis his iced tea and had refilled Nathan's coffee cup, Nathan noticed increased activity outside the diner and strained to look out the window and up the street.

"Looks like the press conference is over," he said.

Dennis looked at his watch. "Just in time to get on the local midday news shows and then hop a plane back to D.C. in time to make the national news. He's probably got a bushel basket of sound bites all ready."

Nathan laughed and said, "Brace yourself."

"Why, what...?"

Suddenly the front door of the diner opened. In walked Wilson, his wife Cynthia and an entourage of handlers and press people. Immediately they began to work the customers. But this was not work to Bob Wilson. He was a natural who enjoyed campaigning and meeting people. As he made his way from table to table, Nathan was impressed again by the number of people Bob Wilson knew by name.

Cynthia Wilson made eye contact with Nathan first, before her husband spotted the preacher. The broad smile on her beautiful face vanished, but just for an instant. In that instant a chill shot up Nathan's spine.

"Preacher Nate!" boomed Wilson when he saw Nathan sitting at the far booth. He hurried past other patrons, his hand outstretched toward Nathan. "Great to see you." Wilson was playing to the cameras, but he was also genuine. Not holding grudges was a political strength. Wilson's facial expression changed to one of discomfort when he drew even with the booth and realized Nathan shared it with Dennis Livingston. He recovered, but not as quickly or as thoroughly as his wife had a few seconds before. Wilson warmly shook Nathan's hand and then extended his hand to Dennis. "Dennis, how are things at the Club?"

Dennis looked at the extended hand and Nathan wondered for an instant if Dennis would in fact return the gesture. Then slowly, Dennis offered his hand and said, "Things are fine at the Club, Bob, just fine." The cool, even tone of his voice and the expression on Dennis' face exacerbated Wilson's discomfort even more. Dennis nearly pushed Wilson to the edge when he stared into his eyes and held onto his hand just a tad longer than expected. Cynthia quietly moved to her husband's side and locked her arms around his left arm.

"Great, that's great. Keep up the good work," said Wilson when he was finally free of Dennis' grip. "That was quick thinking by you and Jacob at the Children's Museum. Thank God you acted so quickly and decisively." He turned back to Nathan and said, "It was also good to know that Jacob was completely exonerated. I'm so relieved. Your faith in him was justified. You've really handled the press well, too, Nathan. Please give Jacob my best."

"I'll do that."

"So, Preacher," purred Cynthia Wilson who clung to her husband's arm. "Can we count on you to support the right candidate this time?"

Nathan again felt a cold chill climb up his back to the nape of his neck. "I have great respect for your husband, Mrs. Wilson."

"Please, call me Cynthia," she cooed.

Nathan nodded. "Cynthia, I will listen closely to Bob's position on the issues."

"That's all we can ask," said Bob as he patted Nathan good naturedly on the shoulder. "And you know, Nathan, the Lord works in mysterious ways. I think it's been good for me to step back these past two or three years. I have a better feel for what this city, this state needs. And, I have to confess, Congresswoman Cabinet and I don't always agree on issues, but she has done a good job of representing this district. I think I will look back on my defeat to a good person like Linda as a defining moment in my career of public service."

"That's very gracious of you, Bob," said Nathan.

The expression on Dennis' face hadn't changed since he had let go of Wilson's hand. His silence and his stare seemed to be keeping Wilson slightly off balance. Cynthia sensed it and continued to hold on to his arm.

"Will you come see me?" Wilson asked Nathan. "I would like to pick your brain about your views on some important issues. Truly, I would." He looked into a camera when he said, "I want to spend the next year, between now and the election, listening to the people of this state."

"Sure, I have some other issues I'd like to visit with you about anyway," said Nathan. "Juvenile justice issues like the inappropriate incarceration of status offenders."

"Good, I want to hear your thoughts. Would you like to walk with me? Maybe you can ride with me to the airport. That way we can..."

Nathan smiled and interrupted. "I'll call you."

"Good, good. Call me. I really want to talk."

This time Cynthia interrupted him. With both hands she grabbed her husband's arm above the elbow and leaned her body against his. "Darling," she said seductively in his ear. "We'd better go, you have a busy schedule today." They said good-bye and turned to find the narrow path between booths blocked by Mindy Martinez.

"Mindy!" said Wilson as he stuck out his hand instinctively. "Thanks for coming."

"Told you, wouldn't miss it. Bob," her voice turning serious. "Any comment on Nadine Flemming?"

Every instinct in Cynthia's body went on full alert and she gave her husband a not-so-subtle squeeze. Wilson shook his head and lifted his eyes to the ceiling, "Nadine...Flemming? No..." He looked back at Mindy. "Help me out, should I know that name?"

Mindy pretended to check her notes. "She worked for you...for about three months earlier this year, from March through the end of May." Mindy thought she saw a flash of recognition in his eyes, but she didn't expect him to acknowledge what he knew about Nadine. Not yet, not until he knew what she already knew. He would try to flush her out, to see where she was going.

"She worked for me? A lot of people work for me." He smiled and motioned with his hand as if asking for more help.

"If my source is right, Bob, she was one of your hostesses at McKey's. Eighteen or so, blond...."

"Oh, yes, Nadine. She only worked for the restaurant a short time. She's one of those kids we took a chance on. Last I heard she went back to Texas. Dallas, I think, where she grew up. Nice girl."

"She's dead." Mindy's eyes moved quickly between Wilson and his wife. She sensed shock in his eyes, something else in hers. Relief? Mindy continued, "Earlier this week they found her badly decomposed body in the woods northeast of town, near the river bank. Identification was made late yesterday."

"Oh, my. How sad, how sad," Wilson began as his wife began her subtle pull. "You know, as Reverend Frye and Mr. Wilson here can attest to, when you take a chance and get involved in the lives of hurting people, like Miss Flemming, you win some and you lose some." He shook his head sadly and looked at Nathan. "Sometimes it seems you lose more than you win. It's so sad."

As the entourage made its way out of the Diner, Mindy stood next to the booth where Nathan and Dennis sat while her pencil flew across several pages of her notebook. Neither said a word, waiting for her to finish. Without looking up she asked, "Either of you have the opportunity to work with young Miss Flemming during her short stay in town?"

"No," said Nathan. "But we met her."

Dennis looked up, confused, searching his memory. Then he, too, remembered. "Was she the young, emaciated little blond who seated us at McKey's the night we jerked on Juice's chain?"

Nathan nodded. "She seemed so lost, trying so hard to look and sound like...a woman, I guess."

Mindy asked, "Anything stand out about your encounter?"

Dennis shook his head, but Nathan said, "Yes, there is. It has kind of haunted me. I don't know why, but...We were talking to Juice."

"Juice, not J.J.?" asked Mindy.

"Juice is his street name with the gang," said Dennis matter-of-factly as Mindy continued to take notes.

Nathan continued, "We were talking to Juice and she came up to our table and said something about her shift being over. But I remember she asked if Juice or Mr. Wilson would be needing her tonight. He told her no, she could go home and she seemed...I don't know, disappointed or something."

Mindy smiled as if she knew something.

"Want to join us, Mindy?" offered Nathan and he scooted over to make room for her. "I'd like to talk to you about juvenile justice issues."

Dennis jumped in, "We even have a great case study of juvenile justice gone wrong—it might make a good story."

She smiled and closed her notebook, glanced toward the retreating entourage and said, "Love to, but not right now. Got to follow the story. Thanks, guys."

After she left, Nathan asked, "You ever going to tell me what's going on between you and Bob Wilson? The disdain hung in the air like a damp fog."

"I just don't like him—he gives me the creeps," Dennis with a smirk. "And he knows I think he's a creep." Dennis continued to smirk at Nathan.

"What?" asked Nathan. "What's that crappy grin all about?"

"I told you that same night last spring, at McKey's. Cynthia Wilson does not like you."

"You noticed it, too? Good, I thought maybe I was imagining things."

The crooked smile on Dennis face became more pronounced. "You're not imagining anything, Preacher. She hates you."

Nathan leaned forward across the table, eyes wide. "I swear, Dennis, when she first laid eyes on me...just for a split second...if looks could kill...whoa!"

"She's one beautiful woman. I have to give her that," said Dennis. "Her friends tell me she's smart, too. And she may have more political ambition than him, if you can believe that."

Nathan shook his head at the thought. "Dennis, the instant she laid eyes on me? Just for an instant?"

"Yeah."

"They turned green."

"What?" said Dennis.

"Her eyes. They turned an eerie, kind of misty, swamp-like shade of green." Nathan shuddered involuntarily.

"Jez is a piece of work," said Dennis.

A quizzical look came over Nathan. "What did you call her?"

"Jez, that's her nickname, Jez."

SOME GOOD
NEWS—MAYBE

28

TUESDAY, SEPTEMBER 3,
LATE AFTERNOON

Andre wasn't feeling good. He ached all over, but his spirits were better. The reports about his mom from Reverend Thomas were good. She had almost completed treatment and was going to a halfway house for women. Andre thought that was good—maybe. He'd had his hopes up that when she completed the treatment program he could go home, he could get out of this place. But he knew she would need more help.

Reverend Thomas had also given him a note from Maryann and Jacob. They were married now. That was good. But, maybe Jacob wouldn't have as much time for him anymore to teach him to play the guitar and all. They said in their note that they hoped by the time they got back from their honeymoon that he would be out of this place. What did they mean about all being together again?

This morning he'd gotten a bunch more cards from the people at Antioch, people he didn't really know, but they all wrote things like they knew him. Many of them had said that they were praying for him. That was good. Mark had written to him again. He got a couple of letters a week from him. And Mrs. Carlson had sent him more cards and letters than Mark. That was good.

And now, he had a visitor. If only his head didn't hurt so badly and if only his throat wasn't so sore. But he was glad that he had a visitor.

"Tod, I knew it was you," he said with a raspy voice as he entered the room. "You the only one that can see me except on Wednesdays

259

and Sundays. I knew it was you."

"Hi, kid," said the old cop as he put his arm around the boy and moved him to a couple of chairs in the corner of the visitors' lounge. "You okay, kid? You don't sound so good." Diaz reached over and put his hand on the boy's forehead. "Feels like you got a fever."

"I'll be okay. Reverend Thomas told me all about Jacob and Maryann. Ain't that cool, Tod?"

"That's why I'm here. I might have some good news for you, kid. Looks like your mom is going to be in the halfway house for at least six months, maybe more."

Andre nodded sadly.

"But, she's doing great, kid. She really is—a star pupil, according to Ruth. When she gets out, Reverend Thomas and Ruth will help her find a job and you and your mom will rent one of Antioch's apartments."

"I know, Reverend Thomas told me all that. It's good news, like you say, but it means I'll be stuck here the whole time."

"Listen, kid, it's not a done deal, yet. But, Charles Andrews, your attorney, found a friendly judge. The judge gave him some things to do, get your mom to sign some papers and stuff. Mr. Andrews is supposed to meet with the judge again on Thursday morning. If that goes well...you'll be able to stay with Jacob and Maryann until your mom gets out."

"Really!" Andre jumped up and made a 360-degree spin and fell back into his chair. The exertion made him dizzy, but he still said, almost yelled, "Awright! Thursday? I'll be out of here on Thursday?"

"Whoa, calm down, probably not Thursday," said Diaz. Even though he, too, hoped it could be Thursday, he didn't want to get Andre's hopes too high. The old cop continued, "Even after the judge approves the order, there are some more legal and Social Service hoops that have to be jumped through. But this time next week, you should be out. So Maryann and Jacob will take a short honeymoon over the weekend. They plan to get back next Sunday and, if all goes well, you'll get out of this place on Monday. Can you wait one week, just six more days?"

"One more week sure beats six months." Andre offered his palm and Diaz responded with the high-five." Andre said, "Sure, I can wait."

"Well, it's not a done deal yet," cautioned Tod. "Charles and I are going to see your mom tomorrow. We'll explain to her that Maryann and Jacob will only have temporary custody until she gets through with treatment. It should be good motivation for her to stick with the program."

"She'll sign. You might want to take Reverend Thomas with you—Momma likes Reverend Thomas."

"That's a good idea. Like I said, kid, this is close to being a done deal. I'd hate for you to be disappointed if it doesn't happen like we hope. I just thought you might need a little good news."

"Oh, man. This is good news. Thanks, Tod."

"You should know this, too. Maryann and Jacob weren't planning on getting married for several more months, but they decided to get married now hoping it will help get you out of here."

"Really?"

"Really. Charles thought it would help with the judge to place you with a married couple and Maryann's history kind of balances out Jacob's."

"Wow...that's great they'd do that for me. 'Course everybody knows they in love, man."

"Pretty obvious at that, wasn't it?" Diaz laughed, then continued, "They love you a lot, too, kid. A lot of people do. You keep your chin up okay? On my way out, I'll tell them to get you to a doctor."

"I'm okay. I'm great now," Andre said. He could hardly sit still he was so excited, fever and all. "Thanks a lot, Tod. Thanks for coming to see me. I can't believe it, I'm going to live with Mark."

"Andre, keeping you here was wrong. It's a damn shame, kid. Punks shooting and stealing don't get stuck in here this long. Sometimes adults and their so-called systems just screw kids pretty good. I'm sorry, kid."

• • • • •

Juice stood naked and sipped a glass of dark, full-bodied red wine. From the window of the suite at the top of the high-rise downtown hotel, he looked out over the city far below. In the distance he could see planes landing and taking off from the airport. She had called him from there after putting her husband on an airplane back to D.C.

"So, J.J.?" she said and waited for him to turn to face her. When he did, he found her sitting up in the bed, back against the headboard. She smiled and raised her hands behind her head and slowly bent one of her long legs. She rocked toward him slightly. "Which view are you going to miss the most?" Like a dancer she leisurely lifted her hands over her head and then lowered them again until they rested outstretched on the top of the headboard. "The one from here, or the one on the back porch of the Wilson family cabin?"

He didn't answer, but looked her over as he'd done many times since they'd all moved here from D.C. last spring.

"Does the wine settle your stomach?" she asked.

"Not really."

He placed the half-empty glass on the coffee table. There was something different about him. She no longer had total control. He slowly walked toward her and then sat in the chair on her side of the bed. His eyes continued to run up and down her nakedness. When he finally looked into her eyes, he smiled, only slightly, giving only a hint of his perfect white teeth.

"When are you leaving?" she asked.

"Not sure, maybe tomorrow, the next day. Depends on Bucky...and you."

They continued to wrestle for control with their eyes. It had never been a contest before. The struggle intrigued her.

"Bucky? Who's Bucky?"

"You know Bucky. Big dumb guy that hangs out every night at McKey's. He's way behind on his powder tab—owes me big time. Bucky don't realize it, but Bucky boy is going to help me settle a big score before I leave town."

She rolled over on one elbow to face him. Eyebrows raised, she said with some excitement, "With the Preacher?"

Unable to hide her disgust, she angrily sat back up against the headboard.

"Why do you hate him so much?" he asked.

She got that old familiar look in her eyes. She laughed at him. But again, this time, he was not phased by the ridicule of her eyes and her laugh. Her expression took a sinister turn and she stopped laughing.

With a curled lip she jeered, "Because he's not on our side...and he knows it. He's dangerous."

Juice shook his head. "Your side? You and Bob? The Preacher's not on your and Bob's side?"

"No, no," she said with frustration. "Bob doesn't know what side he's on anymore than most people. He thinks he's on the side of goodness and of the people," she mocked. "He really believes the stuff he has to say to get elected."

"And you know better?"

"J.J., you and I will never be on the side of 'love your enemy and turn the other cheek.' That's mealy-mouthed hogwash! It makes no sense. It's for weak people, not for survivors, not for winners. But, Bob thinks he believes most of that stuff he spouts about doing good, about serving people. That's what makes him so easy to control. Cater to his needs, turn your back on his dalliances, tell him how wonderful he is—Bob's easy. But, the Preacher is about to neutralize him. Soon Bob will be of no use."

"So, you and the Preacher are the only two people in the world who know whose side they're on." Juice shook his head in confusion.

She nodded vigorously. "He knows. That's why he ripped your money to shreds. You should've known better." She laughed and ridiculed him. "At least you should have asked me before trying something so stupid." Again, he was not intimidated. She suddenly ceased her laughing.

Hatred dripped from her curled lip. "The Preacher haunts my husband. Since Bob lost to Linda Cabinet, the poor fool calculates everything by what the Preacher might say or think." She paused, "That's why I hate him. He's dangerous." She reached to grab his hand, but Juice sat up and pulled it away.

"We have to stop him, J.J. All my plans...Bob can be Senator...I can go back to where the real action is. He could be President...you could..."

"What? Be the President's pimp?" It was his turn to laugh, to ridicule. Juice raised his hands and shook her off. "Your battle, Jez. Your battle," he sneered.

She quickly recovered and resumed her own smirk. Slowly she turned her naked back on him and rolled over to retrieve a thick envelope from the drawer of the end table on the other side of the bed. She turned back and tossed it into his lap, then deliberately resumed her pose against the headboard.

He looked in her swamp-green eyes and without breaking his stare picked up the envelope.

"My reward?"

"You asked for traveling money."

"How much?"

"Twenty thousand dollars."

Juice sneered and tossed the envelope toward the love seat where he had carefully arranged his clothes. He pulled his chair closer to the bed and leaned forward until his face was just inches from hers. She smiled and tossed her blond hair aside in an effort to cover her sudden cold discomfort.

Abruptly, he reached out and roughly grabbed her opposite breast. She didn't flinch, but fought to control the fear and the erotic jolt that rushed through her. Something had come over him. There was something about the eyes.

"Jez," he hissed. "I said I need some serious traveling money." With a sideways motion of his head toward the love seat, he said, "That's chump change."

She coolly ignored the grip he had on her and said, "Create some chaos in the enemy camp before you go, and I'll make it an even fifty thousand dollars."

Without letting go, he stood and put one knee on the bed.

"You hate him as much as I do. You said you do."

He straddled her and with his other hand roughly grabbed the other breast.

"You're not afraid of him, are you?"

He squeezed both nipples, hard.

"Afraid of the curse he put on your sorry life?" She taunted him. "Stomach still upset, J.J., darling?"

He angrily twisted and pushed upward. She let out a shrill whimper. Her green eyes grew wide and she smiled at him. It was a new smile, something close to admiration, maybe even joy.

"Hurt the Preacher, J.J." Her eyes darted wildly over his face. "Don't just kill him. Break his heart. Break his heart, J.J. I'll help you."

He threw back his head and roared at the ceiling, a hideous laugh she'd never heard before. Her heart raced. When he gazed back at her, she looked into his eyes which had hauntingly turned to a misty green, as she quivered in her satisfaction.

She looked through him, through the green haze, past his eyes, and whispered hoarsely, "The Preacher, J.J., hurt the Preacher on your way out of town."

For the first time they laughed together, a macabre duet of evil—the wicked consummation of her merciless and sinister plot.

ESCAPE

29

THURSDAY, SEPTEMBER 5, AFTERNOON

"**G**ood afternoon, Officer. What can I do for you today?"

The greeting was flat, lacking sincerity. Her facial expression and tone of voice said she intended to do as little for him as possible. Diaz ignored it. This was the assistant director he'd raised hell with, demanding a doctor for Andre two days ago.

"Lucille, this is Charles Andrews. He's Andre Fitzgerald's attorney."

Lucille looked over the well-dressed and professional Charles Andrews. Again, her face betrayed her annoyance that a child would even have the privilege of having an attorney. She sighed deeply as if to say, "Let's get this over with."

"Ma'am, I have a court order releasing Andre Fitzgerald into my custody until Sunday when his new foster parents will return to town."

"Well, you'll have to wait until he gets back."

"Gets back? From where?" asked Diaz, suspicious by something new that had flashed across the woman's face.

"One of our probation officers volunteered to take him over to University Hospital, just five or ten minutes ago. He's pretty sick. Real bad flu," she said sheepishly.

"Let me guess." Diaz moved forward until his thighs touched the desk and then he leaned over it. "You were too busy to get him to a doctor before now? Right? That kid laid back there sick for three days until some probation officer volunteered to do your job for you. Right? You lazy...I'll be filing a complaint with the county commissioners about this. I might even have to have a little conversation with Mindy Martinez. Come on, Charles, we'll take him home from the hospital."

"No! You will have to bring him back here to process his..."

Diaz's stare shut her up. The two men turned and hurried back out the door.

• • • • •

"Hey, it's me," Bucky said into his cell phone. "Yeah, I got him, but the kid's pretty sick. Maybe I better take him to the hospital.... I know, man, but we could split town together next week...I know, man. It's just..."

The probation officer had a cool car. He had tilted the passenger seat as far back as it would go and Andre lay there with his eyes closed. Bucky was cool, too, the best of all the probation officers. He was nice to all of the kids, especially the younger ones. Even though Andre was not on his caseload, Bucky had been really good to him. He promised to take Andre out for pizza and a movie as soon as he was out of the youth center.

"Listen to me, man," Bucky said into the phone again. "This kid is sick.... Awright, but you better get him to a doctor or a hospital the first town you come to....I'm just saying....I know, but...I hear you, man. I know I owe you.... Yeah, big time, and we'll be even after this, right?"

Andre was in and out of consciousness. He kept his eyes closed. He was confused by the conversation. Who was Bucky talking to, a judge? Lucille? Lucille had argued when the probation officer insisted he go to a hospital. Andre opened his eyes. Bucky looked worried, nervous as he drove the car through the traffic.

"I hear you, but.... Listen, I'm taking a chance here.... That's right...I checked the boy out, he's sick and I'm not sure anyone will believe me when I tell them this sick kid jumped out at a red light and ran away."

Andre closed his eyes, but he was now on full alert.

"Nah, he's asleep. Probably unconscious from the fever. Look, J.J...."

J.J.! Andre's body tensed. *Bucky was talking to Juice!*

"I know you want to take your little brother back to D.C. with you...I just want you to promise me that you'll get him to a doctor in the first town you come to, okay? Well, yeah, I'm sure you love your little brother, but...yeah, I can understand you wanting to take him with you, but...."

Bucky's going to take me to Juice! Oh, Jesus, are you with me, Jesus?"

"I told you, man. He can't hear me, man...believe me, man, and he'll be surprised. He's zonked out. He's probably hallucinating, his fever is so high.... Okay, okay, J.J. I was almost to the hospital, but...I know, I got the address. Honk the horn and you'll open the door of the garage. You sure no one lives there anymore? Okay, J.J., then you and me will be even, right? No more threats about the money I owe you, right? And, you'll give me a supply of blow, right? When I deliver him to you.... Okay, I'll see you in fifteen minutes...I told you, I was headed to the hospital, but—Hey! Hey, kid! Come back here!"

Just as the light turned green and as Bucky took his foot off the brake, Andre opened the door and stumbled out into the intersection. He was dizzy, but he gathered himself and ran as hard as he could. It was a busy intersection. Andre cut across two lanes of traffic. Drivers just starting with the light now slammed on their brakes. Bucky opened his door and got out, but by then the other cars were rolling again. It was all the time Andre needed.

• • • • •

Horns honked, a man talking frantically on a cell phone stood in the middle of the busy intersection looking all directions, but Jacob and Maryann were oblivious as they made their way around the traffic jam and out of town. They both wore shorts, T-shirts and sandals. The back seat of the convertible was packed with new camping gear and outdoor wear. Jacob, like an excited kid, turned to look at it again.

"And you sure we can afford all of this?"

"I'm sure, Jacob. When we get back, we'll sit down and go over all of our finances, but having enough money will not be one of our worries. I've made a good living for eight to ten years, now. And, I'm married to a rising songwriter. Having enough money won't be a problem—investing and giving it away will be the real challenge for us."

"Until the past several months, I had no idea how hard you work. What's your secret? Why have you been so successful?" asked Jacob, genuinely impressed.

"You said it, hard work—and self-discipline. I spend a good deal of time listening to my clients, both current and prospective, and I try to sell them only what I think they need. I spend the same amount of time with the low-income folks as I do with the affluent ones. I'm honest, trustworthy and I never lie. I treat people right.

"I've done well, better than I had ever dreamed possible. Being an independent insurance agent is the only job I know where you can own your own business, with little or no start-up capital, and if you work hard and treat people right, within eight to ten years, it's possible to be making a six-figure income."

"And you love it, don't you?" smiled Jacob.

"I do. I love getting out and meeting people. I love the flexibility, being my own boss and setting my own schedule."

"How did you and Joe do such a good job of raising your children and balancing your two challenging careers?" asked Jacob, the admiration he felt for her was evident in his tone.

"That was another reason that I focused on the senior insurance market—retired people are usually home during the day. Plus, from the time each of the kids was six years old, they spent their afternoons at the Club. Joe and the children would come home for dinner at six. It was important for all of us to eat together every night. When Ruth got to be about twelve the kids wanted to go back to the Club with their dad almost every evening. And Ruth watched after her little brother like a mother hen."

"What about their homework?"

"They would do their school work along with all of the other kids during Power Hour at the Club. I have truly been blessed with responsible, self-motivated children."

"Sure," said Jacob. "I've seen that program in action. Mrs. White has that little library packed every afternoon. She makes learning fun for those kids. The Club is a wonderful place. It will always have Joe's mark on it—what a legacy."

Maryann laughed as she remembered, "I used to have to volunteer at the Club just to see more of my husband and children. But it did work out well for my insurance business. I would try to not schedule any appointments for late afternoon, so I could get home and fix dinner. In the evenings I did community work, made a call now and then.... What? Why are you looking at me like that? What?" She laughed self-consciously.

"I think you're just amazing. I love you, Maryann. So, you won't mind being married to a songwriter?"

She nodded her head in and out like a funky chicken imitation. "As Mark and Andre would say, 'Cool, Dude, bein' a songwriter is cool.' Plus, I only married you for your body." She ran her hand slowly up his thigh and played with the edge of his cut-offs.

• • • • •

Andre ran as hard as he could down the alley. He hurried through the big gate into an unkept backyard and hid under the steps of the old house. The sun was shining bright and it was hot, but Andre shivered uncontrollably. His head was spinning. The dark, damp hiding place seemed to be getting smaller. The fever, the fear, the run—they all crashed in on him at once. He thought of Mark and Ruth, of Jacob and Maryann, but it was his mother and Angela that he most longed for as the darkness began to swallow him.

RAPID
DESCENT

30

The immense orange ball slowly fell toward the darkening mountain skyline. Its rays shimmered and danced on the gentle waves, spreading its vibrant orange and red hues across the distant horizon and reflecting on the lake shore hundreds of feet below them. Jacob and Maryann hiked the steep, rugged path until they found the perfect spot—a grassy, tree-lined knoll, high on the mountain that offered privacy and a spectacular view. At daybreak, they would descend the mountain and drive home. They wanted the last sunset of this special weekend to be unforgettable. They built a campfire and laid one of the new sleeping bags on the grass between the fire and their mountain tent. Sitting side by side, arm in arm, they waited, a blanket covered their legs and bare feet from the brisk mountain air.

"I just love the way it slowly descends and then when it touches the horizon, it seems to just melt behind the mountains," said Maryann.

Jacob said nothing. He just smiled and observed the excitement in her face, the shimmering lake reflected in her dark eyes, the mountain breeze played with the dark hair that hung just above her eyebrows. This lovely woman, the epitome of public grace and demeanor, had been a creative and uninhibited lover. In one week of marriage Maryann introduced him to delights he had never imagined. The first night of their trip, she found lovemaking in the small tent too confining and insisted that the next two nights they find more secluded spots where they could make love under the stars.

Maryann was holding his arm with both of hers. She squeezed tighter and said, "Here it is! This is the moment. Let it burn itself into our memories.... There!"

Jacob could feel her tense as the sun touched the mountain's peak and then she seemed to relax completely as it did its disappearing act. The change from daylight to twilight was instantaneous. They sat in a comfortable silence for a long time, savoring the moment and their intimacy.

She reached over and stroked his cheek, gently turning his head towards her. They looked deeply into each other's eyes.

"I'm so happy," he said.

As she stretched up and gently kissed him, she licked a tear from his cheek and then flicked her salty tongue across his lower lip.

"Maryann, I hope we have a long life together. I want you to know that I love you more than life itself. If this weekend were all the time we are to have together, I have lived and experienced a lifetime here on this mountain. Every beautiful sunset I observe for the rest of my life will usher me straight back to this place in both my mind and my heart."

"Just to be sure of that," she smiled mischievously, "I have one more honeymoon gift for you."

"What, you carried a gift all this..." She silenced him with a feather-light touch of her finger to his lips.

"I've memorized a Bible verse for you, to help you remember this night," she said as she smiled and unclasped her hair. She reached under the cover and removed her shorts and panties, pulled the T-shirt over her head and slowly reclined against the mountainside, her dark hair cascading around her bare shoulders. The twilight and the flicker of the campfire did a finely-choreographed dance that rippled over her tingling flesh and as she beckoned him with her sparkling dark eyes, she whispered, "Let my lover come into his garden and taste of my fresh fruits."

• • • • •

I'm too old and tired for this, Casey Rivers said to himself. Then he whispered out loud, "Oh well, a job's a job." And he settled in the shadows to wait.

Fifty-eight-year-old Casey Rivers looked at least seventy. He was a small time gangster from Chicago who had spent more of his adult life in the penitentiary than out. His professional crime career included only two hits. He was no expert at this kind of thing, but he needed the money. His last stretch in the joint had lasted nearly fourteen years. When he got out last April, Casey was determined to go legit for the rest of his life, but, jobs were hard to find for someone with a violent record. He had received permission from the State of California to live with his older sister, a widow who lived on the South Side. Most of the available jobs were in fast food and telemarketing. Casey even had trouble landing one of those. His voice was too raspy for telephone work and he looked too old and hard to even take hamburger orders. He scared away the customers. He'd always had a thing against hard labor and now he felt terrible all the time anyway. There was no way he would do that.

Winter was approaching and he had to think about heading south. Maybe he would go back to California. He settled in behind the bush, with his back against the wall of the garage, giving himself a clear view of the driveway and the sidewalk that led to the house. He looked at his watch. Nine-fifteen. He gave himself till midnight. He was definitely too old for this. Casey could not remember the last time he'd felt good. He was chewing on the strongest cough drops he could find to stifle his smoker's hack, and they weren't working. He had a coughing fit, then muttered, whining to himself, "Damn! My back is killing me."

• • • • •

"See, I told you. I said you'd get some quality time. I only saw the fourth quarter, but based on what I saw, you could be starting before the season is over. You've just turned fifteen and you're holding your own with the seniors, on a *good* football team," Ruth encouraged her little brother.

"Yeah," said Mark, his mouth bursting with a huge bite of his Taco Supreme. "I played half of the second quarter and all of the fourth. The game was still on the line in the second quarter." Suddenly serious, he swallowed and asked, "Do you think I should concentrate on just one sport?"

"I don't know—what do you think?"

"I dunno, I like both sports, but I might do better if I chose one and concentrated on that."

Ruth knew better than to offer advice. This was Mark's dilemma to work out. She thought he had the potential to end up All-State with a full ride to college in either football or basketball. They drove toward home in silence for awhile.

Mark said, "Has anybody seen or heard from Andre?"

"No, Tod called the Club just before we closed at six tonight. Nobody has seen any sign of him since Thursday. He just disappeared a block from University Hospital."

"Man, it's been three days. If he would've just called me, I would've hid him until Mom and Jacob got home," Mark said defiantly.

Ruth just looked at her younger brother and she said, "I would have, too."

When she continued her silence, staring more at him than at the road, he said, "Don't worry. I'm not hiding him anywhere. I can't believe he hasn't called me. I hope he's okay."

"Me too." Ruth believed him. Mark had never been able to lie to her.

"Do Mom and Jacob know?"

"No, Evelyn and I convinced Mom not to take her cell phone and not to call. They'll be home sometime tomorrow afternoon."

"Are you okay with them being married? I mean, I wasn't surprised, but I was—you know?"

"Yeah, they did surprise us, didn't they? But," said Ruth in a reassuring tone, "it was a wonderful surprise. I'm so happy for Mom. She has been pretty lonely during the past couple of years. Mark, did you know that Daddy had told her several times that he wanted her to remarry someday."

"Really?"

"Really. When people love each other like Mom and Daddy did, the thing you want most for the other is happiness. If that's what you're worried about, that Daddy would be mad or hurt by Mom getting remarried, you can relax." She smiled over at him, marvelling at how grown-up he was becoming and how young he looked at the same time. For the first time she recognized that her little brother was really a man-child, suspended for only a short time between childhood and his quickly approaching manhood.

"Do you think I should call Jacob, 'Dad'?"

"Only when you're ready and if you want to. But, if you do, I think that Daddy would be pleased about that, too."

Mark nodded, satisfied. A few seconds later as Ruth turned into the driveway, he asked, "What time is it?"

"Almost eleven-thirty. Don't forget, we've got to be at church early tomorrow, so try to get some sleep."

• • • • •

The crunch of tires on the gravel and sand at the entrance to the driveway snapped Casey out of his stupor. *Awright, I can get this over with fast and go crawl into bed*, he thought.

Suddenly, the garage lights came on as the automatic door opener engaged. At the same time, the whole backyard was lit up by sensor lights.

"Holy shit!" he cursed and quickly crouched, but there were no longer any shadows around for him to hide in.

The car rocked to a stop, but only the headlights had cleared the door. Then it began to back out of the garage. Casey had been spotted.

"Nooo!" he screamed and lurched from his hiding spot, the automatic pistol with its silencer raised high.

That's when the pain in his chest hit him—hard. It was like nothing he'd ever felt before. He dropped the gun. Fear gripped him and with both hands he grabbed at his chest.

• • • • •

Casey was in prison garb, with leg-irons fixed tightly around his ankles. He thought how strange it was that there were no guards present to usher him into the van. No need—he knew this routine. With his head bowed, he climbed into the van and sat in the second of the three bench seats in the back. He leaned forward and rested his head on the seat in front of him. It felt more like cold concrete than a cushioned van seat. He was so tired, so very tired. The sliding door closed and the engine started. The van began to move and in an instant, Casey's pitiful life flashed before him.

Startled, Casey looked up. The steering wheel moved, but there was no driver. He looked around. There was nothing. No buildings, no streets, no people, nothing. The van was moving. He could feel its movement. But when he looked out of the windows there was nothing, just the overcast gray day everywhere. Fear had stalked Casey all his life. Now it grabbed hold like never before. He thought his beating heart would explode out of his chest. He screamed as the van accelerated. It was as if it was flying, but it seemed to be going down, like a roller coaster instead of up like a plane. The faster the van went the blacker it became outside.

It became pitch black and there was only the eerie red-orange light of the van's instrument panel to break the suffocating darkness. The van was going incredibly fast now and Casey could taste his fear, but he could not even manage a scream; only whimpers escaped through his gritted teeth. Suddenly, the van began to spin in a downward spiral and then there was no windshield. A hot wind hit him in the face just as the sides of the van were blown away and the seats vaporized out from under him. It was totally dark now. Casey could not see the end of his crooked nose but he knew he was being pulled down. The chains on his feet accelerated his descent and accentuated the spiral. First he felt the heat, then at the bottom of the spiral he saw the same red-orange glow. But this time it was off in the distance and closing fast. It was a ball of light, or was it fire? It was a lake of fire lapping against an invisible shoreline. The smell! Ugh, the smell. His ears were assaulted by horrible sounds.

Suddenly, Casey crashed to a stop. He was on his back. It must be broken, he thought. The bright lights of the backyard hurt his eyes. The pain in his chest was unbearable. The ground under him felt like a slab of wet ice. He saw two men in white above him talking to a young woman.

"Will he live?" she asked.

"Probably not," replied one of the men.

"Who is he, Ruth?" asked the other man.

"I don't know."

"And what's he doing in your backyard with a gun?"

"I don't know."

HOME AGAIN

31

They broke camp as planned at daybreak and hit the road for home. Clouds had moved in overnight, and a fine mist over the mountains made the colors even brighter. Mother Nature was giving her majestic jewels a gentle cleansing. It took only a couple of hours to make their way through the mountains and foothills. A steady rain had settled in across the gently rolling plains that would lead them home.

They stopped for breakfast and gas at a truck stop just off the interstate. After breakfast, Jacob grabbed two cups of coffee and waited behind the wheel of the car for Maryann. It would take them another five hours to get home. He searched through the case of CDs for music that she might like to hear. He selected *Deep Enough to Dream* by Chris Rice. He pushed "play" and looked up in time to see her backing through the front door of the restaurant, opening it with her hip. In her hands was the Sunday edition of the *Herald*. She seemed engrossed by something on the front page. As she stepped off the sidewalk and out from under the overhang, the rain seemed to rouse her from the paper and she quickly moved to the waiting car.

As she settled in, the paper upside down on her lap, Jacob was immediately confused by her sudden mood change. He asked, "Anything interesting happen in the real world while we were on the mountaintop?"

It was as if she hadn't heard him.

"Maryann?"

She turned to face him. Her look more than confused him. His heart began to race.

279

"What?" he asked almost pleadingly.

She looked down at the paper in her lap. Slowly she turned it over and right side up. Jacob first noticed the file picture of a smiling Bob Wilson. Then the headline reached out and grabbed him.

"Wilson Implicated in Secret Sex Ring." The subheading read, "Ex-Congressman Denies Everything, Says He Was Duped by Man He Tried to Help."

"Oh, my God. Tell me," he said.

Maryann reached down to the cup holder and removed the top from her coffee cup, taking a big drink, as if she needed something to sustain her before talking.

"Now I understand the hold Juice had over Bob Wilson. It all began in D.C. and continued here at McKey's." She shook her head in disbelief.

"What...?"

Maryann took another drink. "That no-good, lying, cheating scoundrel! Mindy Martinez is nailing his sorry ass to the wall."

"Who?"

Maryann pointed to the byline under the headline. "She's the reporter who has worked on this since May. She has to have the goods on him or the *Herald* wouldn't have gone with this story. They've endorsed him in every election—he was their boy."

Jacob slipped the Sebring into gear and backed out. As he turned off the CD player, he said, "I'll drive, you read."

"I've only gotten through the first several paragraphs and I'm already sick to my stomach." She took another drink of the coffee and began to read.

"With the presidential sex scandals of the nineties came revelations of the sexual escapades of presidents and politicians of all stripes throughout history. Current conventional wisdom is that politicians with serious aspirations will have to clean up their act and be on their best sexual behavior.

"It has been decades since the press has been willing to give the 'good old boys' a pass for philandering. In fact, many feel that in recent years the press has gone overboard, looking under every rock for any whiff of scandal. While the public has been open-minded about discreet single office holders and quite forgiving of divorce, the public nonetheless has grown tired of the extramarital affairs and scandalous behavior of many politicians. The public has grown especially unforgiving of the hypocrisy of philandering office holders who have won their elections under the banner of family values.

"Evidently the close press and public scrutiny of ex-Congressman and Senate candidate Bob Wilson succeeded in making him more careful when satisfying his extracurricular sexual desires. Wilson used his wealth and two successful restaurants to create an elaborate ruse to hide the activity that feeds his sexual dalliances. Wilson and his assistant manager, Josef Johnson, may also be guilty of numerous crimes including kidnapping, rape and even murder.

"It appears that McKey's, the Old Market restaurant opened last winter by Wilson and his wife, Cynthia, is more than a trendy, popular restaurant and night spot. It is similar to a restaurant owned by the Wilsons in Washington D.C. in more than name, cuisine and furnishings. Wilson purchased McKey's in D.C. the same month he was defeated for re-election to the Congress by Linda Cabinet three years ago. Three months later he purchased the building in the Old Market that now houses the local McKey's. He brought Josef Johnson from the D.C. restaurant to be the assistant manager. It seems Johnson had some very unique responsibilities, which he has ruthlessly carried out.

"Both restaurants, by all accounts and according to well-placed sources, have been quite successful. Both restaurants are also where Bob Wilson and a select few and trusted friends have had their sexual needs satisfied by beautiful young women, some of them still in their teens, who have been employed by Johnson as hostesses—all under the guise of providing unfortunate, at-risk girls with 'life skills' and career opportunities."

"Above the local McKey's are three upscale apartments, typical of many in the area. One apartment is reserved for Wilson's use. According to Wilson the apartment is a convenient location, close to downtown and to the airport. Wilson says he utilizes the apartment when business and social activities keep him downtown in the evenings, or when he has late arriving or early departing flights, rather than make the long trip to and from his main residence twenty miles west of town. According to several sources, the other two apartments are reserved for the attractive young ladies who serve as hostesses at McKey's. When Wilson is in D.C., as he frequently is on national party business, he stays at a condominium he owns just around the corner from the D.C. McKey's.

"The hostess' job at both McKey's is to greet and seat customers, always with a smile. On the surface, the hostesses appear to be very fortunate young women. Ask those currently employed in both locations and they will tell you how lucky they feel to be working at McKey's and for Mr. Wilson.

"According to current and former hostesses, Wilson pays them a fair salary and provides them with a rent-free apartment that they share with another hostess. McKey's provides them with attractive wardrobes and extensive 'life skills training' that includes such social graces as communication, dress and grooming. Since the girls work evenings, the job is convenient for those who wish to attend college or, a favorite fantasy of these young ladies, modeling school. Tuition to attend college or modeling school is also provided by McKey's. As many as three or four hostesses are employed at any time in both restaurants.

"And, the program appears to have worked well—for some. Several former hostesses credit McKey's and Bob Wilson for launching them in their careers. Interviews were conducted with three former hostesses in D.C. who are now college graduates and are holding good jobs. One of them now serves on the congressional staff of one of Wilson's closest political allies.

"But other former hostesses and restaurant employees in both cities tell a very different story. The three former hostesses cited above adamantly deny that as a part of their job they were supposed to be available to satisfy the sexual needs of Wilson or his associates. An extensive investigation that began last May indicates otherwise. The details are sordid and ugly and may even include murder. Police are now investigating a new angle in the mysterious disappearances of two former hostesses at the D.C. location and the disappearance and murder last May of eighteen-year-old Nadine Flemming. Her badly decomposed body was discovered last month along the River northeast of town."

It was a long story full of sidebars and related reports that covered several pages of the *Herald*. Maryann read every word as they drove home. Mindy Martinez had done a masterful job of pulling the facts together from dozens of interviews with former employees, hostesses and, off the record, disgusted "friends" of the Wilsons. The story revealed that Juice maintained a heavy-handed control over the young women. Obviously, Mindy had found Angela, who had told the reporter everything she knew.

As Maryann read, they found themselves on a roller coaster of emotion. With each sordid detail and new revelation her voice reflected their oscillation between anger and disgust and sadness. Finally, they had a clearer understanding of this past summer's disturbing events. When she finished they were drained and neither of them said anything for awhile. Jacob stared straight ahead unaware of how slow he was driving as a steady stream of cars passed him. Maryann gazed out of the passenger window but did not really see the farms and pastures and mile upon mile of cornfields ripe for the harvest that they passed.

Finally, Jacob sighed. "Those poor girls."

"That's what made it so...evil." She continued looking out the window. "Dangling nice clothes, a nice apartment over the heads of vulnerable, lost children—hiding behind a pretense of doing good."

"You're right, these weren't interns or spoiled little rich girls. These were poor kids, some of them running away from abusive homes."

She turned to look at Jacob. "He probably, in his heart, really believes he did those poor girls a favor. I can hear him rationalizing this whole thing to himself. 'Poor thing was already turning tricks. I took her off the street and cleaned her up.'" Maryann was animated as she talked, mocking Wilson. "'She only has to sleep with me... and occasionally one of my sick cronies.' I'll bet he told his church friends that he viewed the hostess program as a *ministry*. Can you believe he thought he could keep something like this covered up forever?"

Jacob shook his head and laughed sadly. "Can you imagine the jealousy felt by the other kids, the waitresses and bus boys? Trying to figure out why the hostesses were being treated so special? He was a fool to expect immature nineteen-year-olds, enchanted with their new status, their own beauty, to keep this whole thing a secret."

"That was his downfall," said Maryann. "Mindy had no problem finding plenty of former hostesses and employees who were willing to talk."

"Between that and Juice's greed—it wasn't enough for him to have this sweet sex deal—he had to run a gang and a drug business on the side. No wonder everything unraveled. Bob turned his back on Juice's drug activity because Juice managed Bob's harem so well."

"And now," emphasized Maryann. "Juice is a very convenient fall guy. Bob is blaming everything on him."

Jacob snorted in disgust, "Sounds kind of familiar—he's disappointed that someone he had tried to help betrayed *him*—at least they've finally got a warrant out for Juice."

Maryann picked up the paper and rustled through it. "I don't remember reading that they've arrested Wilson," she said incredulously. "What's that scum being charged with?"

"They probably haven't figured it out, yet. The police will begin their own investigation of Wilson. Mindy will have to protect her sources, but I'm sure she can point them to people who are more than willing to talk to the police."

"Who knows what they'll uncover," she said. "I can't wait to get Tod's take on all this."

"I've got a sick feeling that there's a lot more to this story, and that more surprises are in store for us."

Jacob's premonition deepened when late that afternoon, as they pulled into Maryann's driveway, they recognized Diaz's unmarked police car. As they walked toward the house they saw Nathan's bike leaning against the deck. Ruth was placing a large pitcher of iced tea in the middle of the kitchen table where Diaz and Nathan were already seated as Maryann and Jacob came tentatively through the door. Ruth's shaky smile and feeble attempt to greet them only intensified Maryann's already heightened maternal instincts.

"What's wrong, Ruth? Where's Mark?"

"Mark's okay, Mom. He's at a friend's house. Everything's...okay, but..." Ruth glanced toward the *Herald* on the table.

"We've read the paper," said Jacob.

Nathan stood up and stepped toward Maryann. "There are more

developments." He pulled out a chair for her and said, "You'd better sit down."

First Ruth told them the story of Andre's disappearance just as Charles Andrews had finally been able to arrange his release from the youth center. Juice had not reported to work at McKey's, or been seen anywhere around town since Tuesday. A warrant had been issued for his arrest on Friday, but so far nothing had turned up.

Maryann wiped a tear from her cheek and asked Diaz, "Does Juice have him?"

Diaz shrugged. "According to Bucky Paxton, the probation officer, he got away. Paxton is now in police custody, and he's cooperating."

"Police custody—why?" asked Jacob.

"Drug charges, possession of cocaine," said Diaz. "He got caught up in a big sweep over the weekend. Seems he has been a big customer of Juice's and owes him a lot of money. He claims that Juice tried to kill him last Thursday, the day Andre got away, so at least we know that Juice is still around."

"There's more to that story," stated Jacob.

Diaz nodded. "Probably, but Paxton's not the only one singing. Gerald Hampton, the manager at McKey's, came into the station first thing this morning after reading the stories in the paper and told us everything he knows. He hates Juice with a passion and resents the way he was duped by Wilson. He said that by the time he figured out what was going on, he didn't know what to do or where to turn. I don't think he's as innocent as he claims, but…when we showed the stories in the *Herald* to Juwan, he figured it was finally time to cut a deal. And even Anthony, who is still in the psyche ward at County, is talking. It's all coming down like a house of cards on both Juice and Wilson. Juice is going away for a long time."

"What about Bob Wilson?" challenged Maryann.

Diaz shrugged again. "Who knows? He's already retained an attorney. We're still trying to figure out what to charge him with, and we'll probably serve warrants on him tomorrow, maybe even later today. But…money buys a good defense—this one will have to be very creative as well."

Nathan said, "I just spoke with the senior pastor over at Community Church, Dr. Sam Nash. Sam said Bob is quite distraught."

Maryann could not hold back a quick burst of derision. "I'll bet!"

Jacob quietly took her hand as Nathan continued, "He's in deep denial and sees himself as the victim in all of this. Sam has asked me to go with him to see Bob, to try to get through the facade he's built around all of this. He may have a good attorney, but his public life is definitely over." Nathan made eye contact with Jacob. "He's going to go to prison for a long time."

"Good," said Maryann, as if it would be the last word.

"Mom, there's more," said Ruth cautiously.

"More? What do you mean? More?"

"Everybody is okay, but something very bizarre happened here last night. Mark and I had a close call." She turned to Diaz who filled them in.

Maryann and Jacob sat in stunned silence. Finally, Nathan asked, "Why, Tod? Any idea why Ruth and Mark?"

Diaz looked his old friend in the eye. "I'm not sure, Nathan, but I think it was a way to hurt you."

Nathan sat back in his chair as if he'd been slapped, confusion all over his face. "Hurt me? I had heard that Cynthia didn't like me, but...."

Diaz looked around the table and shook his head. "This situation is the most bizarre shit I've ever worked on. Here's what I've pieced together based on conversations this morning with Juwan and this character, Rivers—the hit man."

"He's able to talk?" asked Ruth.

Diaz nodded. "Barely. He almost didn't make it through the night, but this morning they had just taken him off the respirator when I got there. He kept saying something about having already been to hell and back. I don't know. Casey is an ex-con who worked as a dishwasher for a couple of weeks at McKey's earlier in the summer. Hampton fired him, but Juice hired him to do some work on the side."

"Juice hired him to try to kill my kids?"

"Not only that," said Diaz who next looked at Jacob, "Rivers is the one behind the skinheads, that shooting you prevented at the Children's Museum. Rivers knew those guys from prison and hired them. He thought it was funny that they didn't even realize that they had been hired by a black man."

"But, why?" asked Jacob.

"Because he hates you and Dennis, and especially you, Nathan."

"Then why didn't he try to kill me instead of innocent children— instead of Mark and Ruth?"

Diaz shook his head, the look on his face saying, *You're not going to believe this*. He took a deep sigh and said, "Because, according to Juwan, Cynthia Wilson told Juice that the way to really hurt you, Nathan, was not to kill you, but to destroy the things you love—the Club, the children, Jacob, Ruth, Mark, Maryann."

After they sat in stunned silence, Maryann was finally able to ask, "Cynthia Wilson? Tod, how do you know this? What do Cynthia Wilson and Juice…"

"They were sleeping together—regularly. And, evidently, not too discreetly. Both Hampton and Juwan told me that Juice and Jez were lovers. Both said they frequently utilized Wilson's apartment over McKey's. But, Juwan told me…" Diaz paused to again make eye contact with Nathan. "that Jez hates the preacher even more than Juice, and Jez was always helping him figure out ways to hurt you. If you go over to Wilson's house tonight…you need to be careful, my friend."

• • • • •

Later that evening, just before nine o'clock, Nathan found the new suburban area called Harrington Acres where the Wilsons owned one of the largest of the fine new homes situated on the far edge of the expansive development. Each house sat on at least a half-acre of ground and had wide driveways that wound their way up to three- and four-car garages. Nathan was not looking forward to this meeting. Somehow he and Dr. Nash would have to get through Bob Wilson's denial and break down the carefully crafted facade he had built around his duplicitous life, in order for him to see himself the way he really was. It was Bob's only hope to salvage any semblance of his soul. As Nathan slowly made his way through the quiet streets he sensed something was wrong. A terrible uneasiness enveloped him even before he saw the flash of the emergency vehicle lights, before he made the final turn onto the street where the Wilsons lived.

Two ambulances were backed up to the open garage doors and the house was surrounded by at least five squad cars. The mobile units of all four television stations were there. Reporters stood at the front of the driveway with microphones in their hands talking to the cameras. He saw Mindy Martinez talking to two uniformed officers. Yellow crime scene tape was stretched around the entire front lawn and a handful of curious neighbors, some with groomed dogs on leashes, stood to one side talking and shaking their heads. The house was a flurry of activity, with detectives and technicians scurrying about. Diaz broke away as soon as he saw the preacher.

"Who's dead, Tod?"

"Both of them. They're both dead."

"When?"

"Not long ago. I got a call a little after five, right after I left Maryann's—been here ever since."

With a sense of deep dread, Nathan asked, "How? What happened?"

"The crime scene team is still putting it all together. Looks like a murder/suicide. She's in the master bedroom, naked and cut up pretty bad—there is blood everywhere. It was obviously a murder of passion." The tired old cop motioned toward the back of the house. "We found the knife out back next to the pool."

"Sounds like he lost it, went berserk?"

"Looks that way. Our folks are going through everything now."

Nathan surveyed the scene and just shook his head.

Diaz continued. "They each had their own study. I spent over an hour in hers. It's full of pictures, scrapbooks, and articles about Bob from their days in D.C. She was obsessed with the Washington scene and with you, Nathan."

"Me? I don't understand..."

"She hated you—*passionately* hated you. She kept a daily journal of sorts. I read some of it. It's full of mumbo jumbo—some really strange stuff...very cryptic and almost impossible to understand. She was obsessed with power and influence. But you were mentioned a lot. She blamed you for Bob's, how did she say it...'fall from loftiness,' something like that. One section was really strange. It was like she had received orders from someone somewhere to destroy you, and that she felt as if Juice was an angel sent to help."

"Sounds a little demonic," mused Nathan.

Diaz shrugged. "Our people will sort through it and analyze it. They may need your help."

"And Bob?"

"Next to the knife, at the bottom of the pool."

"Drowned? He drowned himself?"

Diaz nodded. "He took one of those decorative concrete blocks out of the garden, used about four feet of rope to tie it around his neck and then jumped in. What a way to die. His hands were caught between the rope and his neck, like he'd changed his mind, was trying to untie the knot or something. Who knows?"

Nathan groaned softly and shook his head.

"Listen to this." Diaz turned back in his notebook a few pages and read;

> *Alas, my love is dead.*
> *With the black she defiled Father's weekend bed.*
> *For my miserable soul do not mourn,*
> *Better for me, I'd never been born.*

Diaz looked up. "What do you make of that?"

"He finally got through the denial, but...*Judas Priest.*"

"He's a goddamned poet."

"That he is, my friend, that he is."

FOUND, BUT LOST

32

MONDAY, SEPTEMBER 9, AFTERNOON

Jacob left the nursing home for the second time that day. He was mentally and physically exhausted. After their wonderful trip to the mountains, followed by the horrible revelations and dramatic events of yesterday, it had been hard to find the energy for the routine of a normal day. And now, it looked like his mother would pass at any time. It was a little after five when he parked Old Blue in front of the house and walked up the driveway. Evelyn's car was still there, but Maryann's was not.

"I hear you had a wonderful time in the mountains," Evelyn said as he entered the office. "Not my idea of a romantic weekend, but…" she teased.

They spent a few minutes talking about the trip, then about Jacob's mom and the latest news and rumors surrounding the scandal and murder/suicide. Evelyn took pride in knowing the latest inside stuff.

"Where's Maryann?" asked Jacob.

Evelyn waved her hand in gentle disgust. "You know Maryann. She's been gone a few days and thinks she has to work twice as hard now that she's back. She had a four-thirty appointment. She should be home anytime."

"Hear from Ruth?"

"Yes, she said she'd be by later to see what everybody's plans are for dinner. She assumed that with all that's going on, Maryann wouldn't feel like cooking."

"She doesn't have to work at the Club tonight?" asked Jacob.

"Club's closed," said Evelyn. "Winter hours began, closed on

291

Sundays and Mondays till next summer."

"Oh, that's right. Well, I'm going to go take a shower," said Jacob as he made his escape to the door. "See ya, Evelyn."

"Oh, I almost forgot," she called out to him, making him pause. "Mark said to tell you that the youth group from Antioch is conducting a prayer service tonight to pray for the safe return of Andre. It's at six-thirty."

Maryann was still not home when Jacob finished his shower. He dressed and fell across the bed.

• • • • •

"Jacob, Jacob darling. Wake up. Wa-ake u-up."

Jacob stirred from his deep sleep and reached across the bed, trying to find her.

Suddenly a hand grabbed his and yanked hard.

"Come on you sleepy-headed turkey, wake up."

Jacob sat up immediately.

"Andre? Andre! Oh, Thank God."

Andre was smiling from ear to ear, laughing and jumping up and down with excitement. Jacob stood and threw open his arms as Andre jumped into them. Jacob heard Mark and Nathan's duet of laughter as they peeked through the bedroom door.

"Where have you been? Why...? How...?" began Jacob.

"Mrs. Carlson. She hid me out till she was sure I wouldn't be goin' back to that place."

"Mrs. Carlson?"

"Isn't it glorious, son?" exclaimed Nathan. "That dear, precious widow found Andre passed out from exhaustion and a fever on the doorstep of your apartment the night he escaped. She took him into her house, put him to bed and called Dr. Mullins. She swore the good doctor to silence and insisted that he treat Andre for the flu. Thank God, it was not pneumonia. She hid him out until now, when she was sure Andre wouldn't be taken back to the youth center. Charles Andrews just got confirmation from the judge an hour ago. She called me and here we are."

"Where is Mrs. Carlson? I need to give her a big hug," said Jacob.

"Downstairs talking to Evelyn and Ruth," said Mark.

"Where's your mom?" Jacob asked excitedly. "Does she know?"

"No. She's not home yet," said Mark, who obviously could not wait to give her the news.

"What time is it?" asked Jacob.

Nathan looked at the big black sports watch on his wrist. "Just a little after six."

"After six?" Jacob said with concern. "She should be home by now. Evelyn said..."

"Mom called and said she had one more call to make. So, come on or we'll be late," said Mark.

"Late for what?" said Jacob as they moved out of the room together.

Nathan laughed his big laugh again. "The kids have already planned a prayer service for tonight. There's not enough time to call everyone, so we're going to surprise them with Andre and turn it into a praise service, instead."

"Maryann—but, what about Maryann?" asked Jacob as they turned the corner into the office.

"I'm calling her every two seconds on her cellular. Soon as she gets back in her car, I'll tell her to head to the church. Then I'll head over there myself. Go ahead, but she's mad at you, music-man," teased Evelyn.

"Me? Why?" said Jacob.

Evelyn said, "'Cause you gave out her cell number to someone. She knows the kids and I know better, so you must have done it. That's why she's not here. She was on her way home when a prospect called her on the cell phone, and asked her to come by. She said it's not far from here so it won't take long."

"That's strange."

"What? She'd go to the moon for a client," said Evelyn.

"No," said Jacob. "I don't even know Maryann's cell phone number."

"Well, you should know it." Evelyn quickly scribbled on some notepaper and handed it to Jacob. "Here it is."

• • • • •

Evelyn would be mad at me if she knew I was in this neighbor-hood by myself, thought Maryann. As she drove by LaTisha Johnson's old house she said a prayer for Andre and his poor mother. The next block was mostly well-maintained older homes. Maryann's anxiety eased a little—she already had two clients on this block.

"There it is," she said aloud. "Third house on the left with the yellow swing on the porch."

Maryann parked her Sebring just a couple of spaces from the front of the house and walked up to the front porch. She thought it was strange that the main door was slightly open. Flies are thick in early September. She rang the doorbell, several times. She called into the open door, "Hello? Anybody home?"

"You the insurance lady?" someone from inside the house called out.

"Yes, I am. My name is Maryann Be...I mean, Riddler. Maryann Riddler," she smiled at the sound of her new name.

"Well, come on in," a friendly voice rang out.

She stepped into the doorway. The stabbing pain on the side of her head was followed instantly by a flash of red and yellow, and then blackness engulfed her.

• • • • •

Maryann's return to consciousness was slow, hard and intermittent. At first she was lying on a floor, then she was being carried and didn't care who had her or where she was going. She was annoyed by the strange sensation of not being able to move her hands or feet, and the acrid smell of gasoline. She was dimly aware of the opening and closing of a car door. *What!* Suddenly, she was fully conscious and terrified. She was in the back seat of her own car with her mouth covered tightly by duct tape. Her hands and feet were bound by duct tape. Excruciating pain made the idea of sitting up impossible to contemplate.

The car began to move. Every bump and turn sent flashes of pain and brilliant streaks of red and yellow across her vision. *Why was the smell of gasoline so strong?* With great effort she shifted her head to look toward her feet. Before passing out again, she saw behind the driver's seat two five-gallon cans.

• • • • •

A crowd of about fifty had settled into the pews at the front of the church. Nathan stood to address the group.

"We are here to pray for the safe return of our young brother, Andre Fitzgerald." Nathan briefly told the story of Andre and his family, his evil brother, of his unjust incarceration, his subsequent illness and his escape. He talked about the spirit of the boy that had blessed them and made them all smile. Nathan spoke just a little about how sometimes it appears that God has abandoned the faithful and the innocent, and often we wonder where he is. "Brothers and sisters," Nathan proclaimed loudly. "I want you to know that we worship a God who hears and answers our prayers."

That was Andre's cue. The door to the side of the pulpit swung open and Andre marched through smiling from ear to ear. People spontaneously stood and erupted in applause. Nathan asked Mrs. Carlson to come forward. With one arm around her and the other around Andre, he told them the rest of the story.

Nathan then informed the gathering of believers about Andre's desire to be baptized. Since the Club was closed on Monday evenings, Nathan said there was no need to wait until Sunday and then proceeded to lead his congregation across the street to the Club.

People gathered around the baptismal pool, singing the praise songs they knew by heart. Nathan, Jacob and Andre, all in black baptismal robes, climbing down the ladder into the water, then moved a short distance toward the middle of the shallow end.

With one hand on Andre's back, Nathan raised the other high over the boy's head and boomed, "Andre Fitzgerald, do you believe that Jesus is the Christ, the Son of the Living God?"

"I do!" Andre shouted.

"Do you promise to love, serve and follow Christ the rest of your days?"

"I do!" he shouted even louder and the words echoed off the water and the walls of the large room.

"Andre Fitzgerald, as a preacher of the Gospel, I now baptize you in the name of the Father, the Son and the Holy Ghost."

While Andre held his nose, Nathan and Jacob lowered him back until the water covered his entire body and then together they lifted him and returned the smiling boy to his feet.

Nathan asked for God's blessings on Andre and the crowd broke into song as, arms entwined, the smiling Nathan, Jacob and Andre made their way to the side of the pool.

"Hold it! Stop!"

The singing stopped and everyone looked to the shouter.

Officer Diaz had stepped to the front of the crowd. He reached inside his coat, unbuckled his holstered gun and handed it to the closest adult. He quickly, almost frantically kicked off his shoes and removed his coat, tie and shirt.

"I'm coming in. It's my turn—would you baptize me, too, Preacher?"

• • • • •

Maryann came to again quickly, noting that the car was no longer moving. The smell of gasoline lingered, but the cans were missing and she discovered that she was alone. She looked out the back window. Down the street, she saw cars in Antioch's parking lot. She remembered the prayer meeting for Andre. She saw Old Blue parked next to Ruth's car. She tried to get her hands around so she could push down the front seat and open the front door, but the pain and a sudden attack of nausea drove her back down. She heard the explosion and forced herself to look again. The entryway of the church was in flames. Maryann tried to scream. She laid down, scooted herself into position on her back and with all the strength she could muster began to kick at the driver's door from the back seat. *Wait! Kick off my shoes. Use my toes to open the lock and then the door*, she thought just before losing consciousness again.

Juice tossed the second can, top off, through one of the stained glass windows and ran across the street. He dove into the yard and behind the bushes where he had hidden the high-powered rifle he'd stolen from the Wilsons. Hiding in the bushes, he took aim at the side door where he hoped the panic stricken parishioners would begin streaming out, including Riddler and Andre and maybe even the preacher, himself. He could see flames through the broken window. In the background he could already hear the first sirens. "Come on, come on," he coaxed and fingered the trigger.

• • • • •

"Are you decent?" Ruth yelled into the same locker room used by the Friday noon basketball crowd.

"No!" Jacob and Diaz yelled in unison. "But, I've never felt so clean," added Diaz with a broad and beaming smile that had not been seen before. He seemed younger, vibrant—somehow more alive.

A pair of old sweat pants came sailing into the room. "Here you go, Tod," called Ruth. "Sorry it took so long."

The other three had already changed back into their clothes.

"You guys go ahead," said Diaz.

"No hurry," said Jacob.

"Just take your..." Nathan's words were drowned out by the distant screams. Even from a distance, the panic was evident. Nathan bolted for the door with Jacob and Andre on his heels. Diaz struggled to slip into the sweatpants.

The screams got louder as they turned the corner and even before reaching the Club's front door they could see the flames reflected in the glass. Nathan groaned, the deep mournful groan of a man whose heart had just been ripped apart. He burst through the door and ran across the street through the shocked crowd and up the steps of his burning church. Sirens split the evening air as two fire engines turned the corner at the end of the block.

Andre started to follow, but saw Mark standing on the Club side of the street and staring, not at the church but at something else.

"Mark, what's wrong?"

"There's Mom's car, but she wasn't with us." He pointed across the street at the burning church. "Jacob's over there looking for her. He ran around to the back of the church. What if she was in there?"

"Come on!" said Andre as they took a step together into the street.

Maryann managed to open the driver's door with her bare toes and with a great deal of effort scooted out of the back seat. Eyes wide, she stood and paused to survey the scene. She saw the people from church, her friends, standing in the churchyard, crying and holding on to each other as they watched their church burning out of control. No one saw Maryann. The tight tape around her mouth cruelly stifled her pleas for help. She looked down at her bound feet and wondered if she could hop into the crowd. She felt as if she were about to pass out again.

"Mom!" screamed Mark.

Maryann spun to face her son who was now halfway across the street and running toward her. She saw Juice step out of the shadows with a pistol in each hand. She tried to scream beneath the tape and warn her son. It was the panic in his mother's eyes that made Mark stop and follow her gaze. A heinous grin spread across Juice's face. In the dusk of the setting sun, his eyes reflected the fire and changed hue as he took aim.

"Oh Lord!" screamed Andre as he jumped in front of his friend. "Open this fool's eyes so he will see why we are not afraid...."

Mark saw and felt the impact of the bullet crash into his friend before he heard the crack of Juice's gun. Andre was lifted off his feet and into Mark. Mark was knocked flat on his back. He was covered by Andre and Andre's blood.

"Noooo!" It was Ruth running into the scene from the church-yard. "Noooo!" Maryann tried to scream through the tape as she saw Juice take aim at her other child.

"Juice!" Nathan's booming voice was heard even above the arriving fire engines. Juice twisted to see Nathan standing at the top of the church stairs silhouetted by the raging flames behind him. Their eyes locked and the hatred that crackled was as palpable as the sound and the smell of the fire. "I'm here!" screamed Nathan.

Juice fired five rounds. Nathan did not flinch as the bullets whizzed by him and into his church, now hopelessly engulfed in the fire. Ruth stopped when the shots were fired. In the churchyard, some screamed, some fell to the ground, some began to run and a few, including Ruth, stood like deer trapped in oncoming headlights.

On the Club side of the street Diaz maneuvered, trying to find a safe angle that would allow him to fire his gun without hitting Maryann or any of the crowd in the churchyard behind her.

Maryann heard her son screech and she jerked again to see Mark's anguished face as he crawled out from under his bleeding friend.

Another shot rang out and a bullet ripped through the front edge of the convertible top of Maryann's car. Juice spun to see Diaz across the street in a shooting posture.

"It's over, Juice. Put down the guns! Now!" screamed Diaz. Juice looked wildly around and saw Nathan still standing. He saw Jacob running full bore at him, eyes wild. Juice dropped one gun and jumped to grab Maryann around the neck. He put his oversized pistol to her temple. "Stop! Or she's dead."

Jacob pulled to a stop ten yards away.

Juice's black warm-up jacket was soaked with gasoline and it made another assault on Maryann's fragile senses. She fought the nausea, and willed herself not to faint again.

"Throw that gun back over your head, cop. I mean it. Let me hear it hit the building. Now!" he screamed as he violently jerked and tightened his lock on Maryann's neck. "Now!"

Jacob choked on the howl that arose from his throat as he saw the terror in her eyes. She saw the helplessness in his.

Diaz threw the gun over his shoulder and Juice fired. Diaz fell, but did not cry out, grabbing at the hole in his left shoulder. Juice roughly threw Maryann into the back seat and pointed the gun at Jacob.

"Juice!" Nathan screamed as he ran, closing the distance between them. Juice fired wildly at his charging nemesis. A police car, siren blazing and lights flashing, turned the corner at the far end of the block. Jacob took a step and Juice turned and pointed his gun into the back seat. Nathan pulled to a stop alongside Jacob. As he backed in behind the wheel, Juice eyed them over his left shoulder while with his left hand he pointed the gun over his right shoulder into the back seat. "Stay there or I shoot!" With his right hand, he fumbled to find the key in the ignition and then started the car.

Jacob took his first tentative step, eyeing the angle of the gun, desperately trying to determine the flight of the bullet should Juice fire over his shoulder into the back seat.

"Nooo!" screamed Ruth as she bolted past him toward the car. She reached it and had her hand on the door handle as Juice hit the gas. For an instant Ruth looked into her mother's frenzied eyes. The tires squealed, the car jumped and Ruth was knocked to the ground, hitting her head on the curb. By the time Jacob and Nathan reached her, she too had been swallowed by the darkness.

33 MOM COMES THROUGH

"Nathan!" Jacob jumped to his feet when the preacher entered the hospital waiting area just off the emergency room. The two men grabbed each other in a desperate embrace and Jacob uttered a wretched plea, "Oh God, Nathan, oh God, this is awful."

Dennis came rushing into the room and blurted out, "Ruth? Is Ruth...?"

Jacob pulled away from Nathan and gathered himself. He said, "She's okay, just a hard knock on the head. They're going to keep her tonight under observation."

"Thank God," said Dennis, and then as if his legs could no longer hold him, he collapsed into one of the chairs. He looked back up at Jacob, "And...Andre?"

Jacob shook his head. "The doctor has been out to see me once. He says..." Jacob choked and barely uttered, "his chances are not...at all good."

Without saying a word, Nathan ushered Jacob back to his chair and made him sit down. As he, too, took a seat, Nathan asked, "How's Mark?"

"Physically, he's fine. Not a scratch. Mentally...he's got Andre's blood all over him.... That monster has his mother somewhere. Evelyn ran home to get him a change of clothes. Nathan, this is so horrible...."

"I know, son. Where's Mark now?"

"They took Ruth to a room. He went in there with her. I promised him I would come tell him as soon as I hear something about Andre...or his mom. Nathan, the church? How bad...?"

"Burned to the ground. It was an old wooden structure. It went fast. It's gone—completely gone."

Dennis began, "Nathan, I'm sorry…."

"You don't destroy a church by burning down a building!" The fury in Nathan's face quickly turned to resolve. "Anyway, it's not important right now. Where's Tod?"

"Right here," said the old cop as he turned the corner with a young uniformed officer. "I've been on the phone." He still wore the old sweat pants that Ruth had thrown into the locker room. He wore a hospital gown and had his left arm in a sling. "Johnny," he said to his young companion. "Go get your car and meet me at the door."

"You okay?" asked Nathan.

Diaz nodded and pointed to his shoulder. "Just a flesh wound, in and out of the muscle—there's no real damage. Most street punks can't shoot worth a damn." The tired old cop looked at Jacob. "Son, we'll do every-thing we can to find your wife. I promise you that. Johnny is going to run me downtown. I'll make sure every resource is on this—I promise."

Jacob could find no words. He only nodded.

"Nathan," Diaz said, and motioned with his head. The two men stepped into the hallway. Diaz asked a nurse for a place where they could visit privately and she ushered them into a small office. Neither man sat down. As if he still didn't want to take a chance of being heard, Diaz rasped in an intense whisper, "Start praying your ass off, Preacher."

"What? What do you mean?"

"I just got off the phone. Some of the lab work is back on the Wilsons."

"So?"

"Bob Wilson didn't kill his wife—Juice did. His fingerprints were on the knife and everywhere in that bloody room…."

Nathan moaned angrily, "God! This can't get much worse." He looked up. "I need some help, here, dammit!"

"Nathan, that trip across the street saved some lives."

"What are you talking about?" asked Nathan, still seething.

"You must have moved the folks from the church across the street to the Club before Juice arrived. He thought you were still in the church. We found a high-powered hunting rifle…the gun cabinet at the Wilsons was broken into. Anyway, we found one of Wilson's rifles in the bushes on the east side of the church. Looks like he was laying there all set to start shooting people as they ran from the church."

Nathan could say nothing as he contemplated the tragedy that could have been.

Diaz continued, "He's gone loony and we don't have a clue where he went. We found his car and Maryann's in the big garage behind LaTisha's house, the one old man Andrews built."

"Oh, God."

"There's more. In the next block we found the bodies of an older couple. Shot dead in their own house."

Nathan shook his head in confusion.

"Maryann's purse was found just inside the front door. Only clue I have is maybe Juice is in the old couple's car."

"Why did he take her hostage? Why didn't he...?" Nathan couldn't ask the obvious.

Diaz shook his head and said, "I gotta get downtown."

Stunned, Nathan moved back into the waiting room. Reverend Jill Thomas had arrived. They made eye contact and she motioned for him to join them in the circle of chairs.

"Jacob, I don't..." Jill struggled to find the words. "On top of all that has happened tonight, I don't know how to tell you this..."

"Maryann? They've found her? Is she..."

"No, Jacob." With both hands she reached over the large Bible that lay in her lap and grabbed his hand. "This is not about Maryann. I don't know anything about Maryann."

Nathan wished to himself that he didn't know what Diaz had just told him about Juice and about Maryann's life-threatening peril.

Jacob noticed for the first time that the Bible Jill was carrying was his mother's big family Bible.

She squeezed his hand, then said, "Your mom passed away, just an hour ago. I was with her. Shirley called me instead of you because..." Jill looked around the room, "of all that has been going on."

The shock on Jacob's face quickly turned to a peaceful smile.

"You okay?" asked Dennis.

Jacob laughed, "God, no! Not with all of this, but I'm happy for Mom. And," he looked at each of their faces, "when Ruth came to, just an hour ago, she told Mark and me about a vivid dream," said Jacob. "She said Mom had come to her, quoting some psalm about God being in charge and protecting us."

"Oh my, a gift of grace during this horrible time," said Jill. "Shirley said her Bible was right where you left it on the bed when you came up after work today. Did you put this in her hand?"

Jacob took an old photograph from Jill and shook his head. "No, I didn't put it in her hand."

"Well, it was in her hand when she died."

"What is it?" asked Dennis.

"It's a picture of my mom and dad, my real dad. And Maryann's mom and dad, must be nearly fifty years ago. Maryann has the same picture in her kitchen."

A cell phone began to ring.

"That's Ruth's purse. Someone's trying to call Ruth," said Jacob, pointing under the chair where Dennis sat.

Dennis quickly grabbed up the purse, flipped open the cell phone and handed it to Jacob.

"Hello...hello...who's there?"

"You want to know why your lady is still alive?"

Jacob went white and his heart nearly leapt from his chest.

"You want something. Money?"

Juice laughed scornfully. "That's right, I need some traveling money. Your lady tells me she has some, too."

"Let me talk to her."

"Not yet. I want the preacher. He there with you?"

Jacob looked desperately at Nathan. "Yes, Preacher Nate is here."

"Simple. Bring me the preacher and your old lady's money, and we'll make an even trade. Is the preacher willing to die instead of her? Can you get him to make the trade?"

"Yes."

"I thought so." Juice laughed again.

"Let me talk to Maryann."

"Sure, she's going to give you the combination to her safe. Says she has nearly twenty thousand in there. Do you believe that?" Juice's voice changed. "I got a gun to her head. Just get the combination and remember, I'm close enough to hear. So just the combination. Got it?"

"Yes."

"Jacob?"

"Maryann! Are you okay?"

"Yes, but he's crazy, Jacob. You do exactly what I say or he's going to kill me."

Juice leaned closer to the phone and said, "She got that right. You do *exactly* what she says. Double cross me like Jez did, she'll get the same treatment. Give him the combination."

In a shaken voice, Maryann said, "Write this down, Jacob."

"Okay...hold on." Jacob turned over the photo in his hand and with a pleading look on his face, Jacob made a writing motion with his hand. Nathan reached into the pocket of his old blue blazer and pulled out a pen and handed it to him.

"Okay. Maryann, I didn't know you had a safe. Where is it?"

"Listen carefully, Jacob," Maryann said desperately. "I never told you about the safe. I'm sorry. I'm sorry I didn't tell you about the money I have stashed there. But, listen, the safe is on the back wall of the walk-in closet at the end of the upstairs hallway."

"Maryann, you...I don't know...."

"Jacob! On the back wall of the walk-in closet at the end of the hallway. Okay? You'll see it, okay?"

"Okay," said Jacob confused.

"Here's the combination. Right three times to sixty-eight. Left two times to twenty-nine. Right to sixteen. I think it's sixteen. If it's not, I've got it written down on the base of the atlas."

"What, the base of the atlas? Where's the atlas?"

"Never mind, Jacob. I'm sure the last number is sixteen, anyway. Right three times to sixty-eight. Left two times to twenty-nine. Right to sixteen. Got it?"

Juice snatched the phone and Jacob heard a cry from Maryann.

"Got it, Jacob?"

"I got it," he said steely.

"Then you go get the money, bring the preacher and..."

"Where? Where do I come?"

"One step at a time. Shut up and listen," demanded Juice. "Get the money, bring the preacher and cross the Parkland Bridge. Then call your lady's cell phone. I'll tell you where to go next. You got it?"

"Yes."

"Let me talk to the preacher."

Jacob handed the phone to Nathan. Nathan looked around the

room and then lifted the phone to his ear and said in a steely voice, "I know who you are."

Juice erupted in laughter and said, "Then you know not to mess with me, Preacher. They call you over to the Wilsons' house last night?"

"Yes."

"You see what I did to Jez?"

"Yes."

"You and the money—an even trade for Jacob's sweet little bride, here. Deal, Preacher?"

"Yes."

"Put Riddler back on."

Nathan handed the phone back to Jacob.

"If you hurt her..."

"Shut up! You call me from the Parkland Bridge in less than an hour, or she's dead. Just you and the preacher. If I see or even smell any cops, she's dead. You got it?"

Before Jacob could reply, he heard Maryann say, "I love you, Ja..."

The sound of the smack and her sharp cry ripped a ragged tear through Jacob's soul. He screamed over Juice's deranged laughter, "If you hurt her..." The phone went dead. Jacob looked at it and completed the threat. "I'll kill you."

He looked around the group and then told them everything Juice and Maryann had said.

"We'd better go," said Nathan and he started to rise. "Jill, call Diaz!"

"Nathan, there's no safe," Jacob said. "There's not even a closet at the end of the upstairs hallway." Nathan sat back down. "She convinced him she had cash in a safe, to buy us some time, to keep him from..." Jacob could not finish.

"But, she's trying to tell us something," said Dennis. "She said something about an atlas?"

"Yes, I...a map. An atlas is a map!" said Jacob, excitedly waving the picture he still held in his hand.

"The combination to the safe!" said Dennis. "What's she trying to tell us, are those directions?"

Jacob said them again, "Right three turns to sixty-eight, left two turns to twenty-nine, right to sixteen." Slowly he repeated, "Sixty-eight to twenty-nine to sixteen."

"That's it!" shouted Dennis. "The Parkland Bridge. Juice said to call him after you crossed the Parkland Bridge. The Parkland Bridge is part of the 680 bypass. It leads right to I-29."

"Left to 29! Left is north, North to 16?" said Jacob.

"16 miles? Exit 16? Highway 16? What?" asked Dennis.

Jacob shook his head and waved the picture in confusion. "I don't know. Exit 16 or Highway 16, then where?"

"Oh, God help us figure this out," said Nathan. Something was missing. Suddenly, out of nowhere, a line from Bob Wilson's suicide poem popped into his head. He confused the rest of them when he said out loud, "With the black she defiled my father's weekend bed." Nathan's eyes got wild and pointed to Jacob. "There! There! Your dear mother was trying to tell us."

"What?" said Jacob, confused.

"The picture. Give me that picture," Nathan demanded and snatched the old photo from Jacob. He studied it. "Do you know where this was taken?"

"No," said Jacob as he took the photo back and studied it. "It looks familiar, but...Yes! Yes! It was taken in front of the Wilson summer cabin. Bob and I and his buddies used to party up there all the time when we were in high school."

"Did your mom and dad know the Wilsons?" asked Jill.

"Maryann's folks and mine, before my dad died, and Bob's parents—they were all close friends," responded Jacob excitedly. "She's giving us directions to the cabin, the 680 bypass to Interstate 29, to County Highway 16!"

"But, how would Juice know where the Wilson cabin is?" asked Dennis.

Nathan jumped up. "Because Cynthia Wilson was banging that punk at the cabin." Nathan moved toward the door. "Let's go!"

Jacob and Dennis jumped up. Dennis said, "I've got my wife's Explorer—I'll drive."

Nathan barked, "Jill, call Diaz. Tell him where we're going. Give him directions. Tell him to send in the cavalry! Hurry!"

As Jacob, Nathan and Dennis ran to the visitors parking lot, Nathan asked, "Can we get there in less than an hour?"

"Yes, it's only about thirty or thirty-five minutes from here," said Jacob.

They threw open the doors to the black Explorer.

"What's this?" said Nathan as he reached for a flat package wrapped in brown paper that lay across the entire back seat.

"Oh, just put those in the back. But, be careful, they are three matching mirrors Eileen bought for the guest bathroom," said Dennis.

As Nathan carefully moved the mirrors, his mind raced. The tires squealed as Dennis exited the parking lot. Nathan snapped his seat belt and asked, "Do you have a flashlight?"

Dennis pointed to the glove compartment. Jacob opened it, found the flashlight and held it up for Nathan to see.

"Got a gun?" asked Nathan.

"No."

"We've got less than a half-hour to develop a plan, boys," said Nathan from the back seat.

Jacob said, "It's been a long time, but if I remember right, there's a neighbor just up the hill, about a half mile. We should go in their road and park and walk over through the woods. We'll be above the cabin that way and will be able to get the lay of the land without tipping him off that we're there."

"Good," said Nathan. "Do you remember much about the cabin?"

"Yeah, we did a lot of drinking out there."

"Does it have two stories?" asked Dennis.

"No, it's one level...no, that's not right, it's two. It sits on a steep hill. You enter on one level, but it has a walkout basement."

"Is there a walk-in closet at the end of the upstairs hallway?" asked Dennis.

"Yes...."

"That's where he's keeping her," said Dennis.

"Right," said Jacob.

34 THE FIERY CLOSET

Maryann's head felt like it was going to split. Every movement sent a searing flash of pain behind her eyes, but she had to think. *God, help me to think!* She desperately searched the large walk-in closet. Other than three old dining-room chairs stored there, an old single bed mattress on the floor and a few hangers on each side, it was empty. One long pull-string hung from the only light in the ceiling. *Think, Maryann! God, help me think!*

Maryann used one of the chairs to search the wide shelves that ran high above the clothes rods down both sides of the closet. One was empty. On the other, in the back, she found a few old candles, an old disposable lighter and some pornographic magazines. She trembled to contemplate what kinds of things might have occurred in this place and wondered if some young hostess had ever been locked in this same closet. *Think, Maryann, think!*

Wide-eyed and agitated, Juice paced around the cabin, stopping to sling curses and threats down the hallway at Maryann. The cell phone and his gun lay side-by-side on the kitchen table. He'd opened the well-stocked refrigerator a dozen times, but could only stare and fight the nausea. He flicked the little kitchen counter television on, turned to all four channels and then turned it off again. The firebomb destruction of Antioch was already old news, nothing but late night movies and infomercials. CNN might be covering it along with Wilson's apparent murder/suicide, but no cable.

Maryann's heart pounded in her ears. It almost stopped when she heard him approach. She retreated to the corner of the closet. Juice threw open the door and pulled the string to the ceiling light. He moved in and out of the closet door, agitated. His eyes were wild. In a high-pitched voice that bordered on hysteria, Juice told her about his affair with Cynthia Wilson, how "Jez" had tricked him, and used him to get at Preacher Nate and then both of them turned on him in the end and refused to give him his traveling money. Suddenly he quit pacing and an eerily pleasant smile came across his face. He moved closer and the look in his green eyes raised the hair on her arms and the back of her neck. In a calm, almost reassuring voice, he told her the ugly details of Cynthia's murder. He took a step closer. From the kitchen the cell phone rang. The wide-eyed hysteria and jerky movements returned. Juice looked around as if he was not sure where he was or what to do next. He looked toward the kitchen where the cell phone continued to ring. Suddenly he backed out of the closet, slammed the door and Maryann heard him turn the lock.

Think, Maryann. God, help me think! She prayed desperately and rose from the corner of the closet.

Juice looked at his watch as he snatched up the cell phone. "Good, Riddler. You're ten minutes early."

There was no reply.

"Hello." Juice desperately spun around the kitchen. "Don't be messing with me, Riddler. Hello! Answer me, you stupid..."

Still no reply, but he heard some heavy breathing.

"Keep messing with me, Riddler, I'll shoot her right now. You hear me?"

"Hello, Juice."

"You!"

"That's right, it's me. I'm the one you wanted, right?"

"Where's Riddler?"

"Just me, Juice. Just me. Mrs. Riddler can drive my car home. It's just me."

"Okay, from the bridge you..."

"I'm already here, Juice."

"What? Where?"

"Here, Juice. I'm waiting for you on the front porch. Come let me in."

"How?" The doorbell made Juice jump.

"God told me, Juice, and he sent just me. Nobody else. Can you handle me and God all by yourself—without Jez? Let me in." Nathan rang the doorbell again.

Gun in hand, Juice cautiously made his way to the front of the cabin. Suddenly Nathan appeared in the front window, his face lit up and smiling.

Juice screamed and fired wildly at the image in the front window. Windows and mirror shattered, scattering bits of glass all over Jacob as he rolled from under the window, past the front door and off the porch. Nathan turned off the flashlight, took two steps and jumped off the right side of the porch where Dennis laid under the side window. As soon as Nathan was in place he nodded to Dennis who raised another mirror at the same instant Nathan again turned the light on his face.

"Juice," he screamed. "I'm here!"

A second time the window and mirror exploded. Nathan flipped off the light, but at that instant the yard lit up as four State Patrol cars, spotlights beaming, came streaming down the long driveway.

Jacob tried desperately to open the locked front door. Through the small window in the door he saw Juice, gun in hand, running toward the hallway. Dennis grabbed an old lawn chair and began to break out the rest of the front window.

Maryann heard the commotion and knew that help had arrived, but Juice was at the closet door and had no trouble breaking down the barrier she had created with the dining-room chairs. He came bursting through the door. "Let's go, bitch!"

The room was dark except for the small candle Maryann had placed on the shelf in the far back corner of the closet. He cursed when he reached for the pull cord that was no longer there. Maryann heard Jacob frantically calling her name. When Juice took three steps toward the light in the corner of the closet, Maryann made her move from beneath the mattress she had covered herself with. It almost worked.

Maryann screamed as Juice pulled her up by the hair. Once again, his arm went around her neck, his gun at her temple. Once again she could smell the gasoline on his black warm-up jacket. She saw desperation in Jacob's eyes as he came to a halt in the hallway,

Dennis and Nathan behind him. Highway patrolmen with bulletproof vests and shotguns came bursting through the front door. Nathan turned and held up his hand. The troopers quickly assessed the situation and stopped.

Juice calmly began to laugh, a low, evil chortle. He tightened his arm around Maryann's neck.

His eyes jumped back and forth between his three tormentors. His face suddenly seemed ravaged by an abrupt, unnatural aging.

"Juice, it's over," said Dennis calmly. "Let her go."

"YOU don't even know MY name!" Juice screeched.

The words "you" and "my" seemed to Dennis like he had been slapped in both ears, making them ring. None of them had heard the voice before.

"I know your name, fiend," said Nathan. "You've already got Jez and Juice. Let *her* go. She's not yours."

Juice flared at Nathan as if recognizing him for the first time. "I'm taking him *and* her with me," came the unearthly voice from deep within Juice. "And no power anywhere can stop us. No power! *We* are as strong as death."

"No, not both. In the name of Jesus you will not have them both!" boomed Nathan.

"Yes, yes, both burn with *me!*"

Jacob saw Maryann's hand go into her skirt pocket and bring out the lighter. Their eyes met. Juice was crazed and so focused on the crowd in front of him he didn't notice the three attempts it took for Maryann to draw a flame. She held it up to the jacket.

"It's over," Juice said in his normal voice again, "and I'm taking as many of you mother..."

Juice's arm and Maryann's blouse and the hair around her face erupted in flame. They both screamed and he released his grip. Jacob took two steps and yanked Maryann into the hallway. Even with his jacket in flames Juice began to calmly raise the pistol. Dennis bolted past Jacob and with a powerful forearm knocked Juice into the corner of the closet. Just as quickly he sprang back through the door and Nathan slammed it shut, locking the screaming madman in the fiery closet. Jacob extinguished the flames that threatened to engulf Maryann by pulling her into his own chest and frantically patting her hair with his hands. She collapsed as he scooped her up into his arms. Troopers quickly ushered the four of them down the hallway.

Juice's screams turned to laughter again and when the state troopers beat open the door, flames shot from the closet where the old mattress, the magazines and Juice burned. Plastered across Juice's face, for just an instant was a sick grin. And then he was engulfed in agony and the screams returned. Troopers scurried around the cabin and finally found two fire extinguishers that had long ago lost their charge. There was nothing they could do, but back away from the fiery closet.

Diaz arrived a few minutes later with the first group of volunteer firemen. He found Nathan and Dennis giving a report to an investigator from the State Patrol. Maryann, with an anxious Jacob by her side, lay in the back of the ambulance while medics tended to her wounds. Behind them the fire spread quickly. Like Antioch Church, the Wilson cabin burned to the ground.

EPILOGUE:
HOME AT LAST

FRIDAY, MARCH 7,
EVENING

As the lady next to him rose from her seat, Jacob smiled at the memory of Andre's infatuation with the Reverend Jill Thomas. This lady, too, was one pretty woman. She seemed nervous as she walked to the front of the auditorium, yet she moved with quiet dignity and grace. Nathan gave her a warm embrace and then turned the podium over to her. Her delicate, attractive hands quaked a bit as she grabbed hold of the podium, as if to brace herself against an imminent blast of wind. Then she smiled at Nathan and looked over the audience and in her clear dark eyes all could sense her serenity and her genuine spirit.

Jacob thought of all that had happened since that fateful night six months ago. Maryann's head wound and her burns were not as bad as Jacob had originally feared. She spent a few nights in the hospital but everything healed quickly, leaving no outward scars. Ruth suffered a severe concussion when her head hit the curb, but was kept in the hospital only two nights. Within a week she was back at the Club, more passionate than ever about the kids—her kids. Dennis seemed different following the final clash with Juice. He was the same efficient, dedicated professional he'd always been and yet, different...somehow different.

Jacob was happier than he ever imagined anybody could be. He awoke each morning full of wonder that Maryann and her children loved him. Following Christmas Eve services at Antioch, for the first time, Mark tentatively called him "Dad." Now it seemed to flow naturally from the boy, but Jacob's heart skipped every time he heard it. The new family quickly settled into the daily routines of the good life. And the music! The music poured from Jacob's soul. He turned the old apartment above Mrs. Carlson's carriage house into his studio, and hired an agent to negotiate with record companies and recording artists so that he could focus on the music alone.

Antioch had always been an exciting, vibrant, diverse family of believers. The loss of their beloved old building had brought them even closer, energized them, and more than a new building had begun to arise from the ashes. Parkland and the surrounding metropolitan community rallied around the congregation. Sunday morning services were being held in the Club gymnasium while the new building was under construction across the street on the original site. The Friday evening AA meetings, where Jacob now sat and pondered these events, as well as several other of Antioch's regular weekly meetings, were being held temporarily at Community Church, where the Wilsons had attended.

In a strange twist, the media frenzy that had examined every lurid twist and sick detail of the Wilson scandal had also focused attention on Antioch, its ministries and intriguing clergy team. Nathan declined most interviews and three invitations to write a book. Jill assumed the role of media spokesperson with her usual intelligence and grace.

Donations to rebuild came in from churches, businesses and individuals all over town and around the country. The congregation decided to build a church much like the original—a modern church about the same size as the old one. By the time they broke ground, only two months after the fire, more than three times the necessary funds had been received. Nathan sent letters explaining to donors that the building had been fully insured, but with their permission the additional funds would be used in Antioch's Welfare to Work Program and other ministries of the church. No one asked for their money back.

Of all the things that had happened, the most amazing had been Andre's recovery. He spent three weeks in intensive care and then twelve more in rehabilitation, confounding his doctors at every turn. At first, they said it was hopeless—they were sure that he would not survive. Then, if he did survive, they said, his mental capacities would be sadly reduced and he certainly would never walk again. Within six hours of coming out of the coma, no one had any doubts about Andre's mental capacities.

From the beginning Ruth had reminded everyone not to underestimate Andre. "He's a survivor," she said every day, "he'll pull out of it."

Nathan gave credit to Mrs. Carlson and her brigade of praying grand-mothers. "Prayer Warriors," he called them.

As he progressed through his rehabilitation, Andre took great pleasure in gift wrapping first his wheelchair, then his crutches, and finally his walker. With great fanfare, he presented each as a gift back to the doctors who had predicted he would never walk again. He beamed his patented smile when, two days before Christmas, he finally limped out of the rehab center, using only a cane. Nurses and physical therapists were seen wiping the tears from their cheeks, but Andre promised to return someday to make a presentation of his cane.

Early on during rehab, Jacob bought Andre his own guitar and Maryann bought him an electric keyboard. Jacob and Mrs. Carlson took turns coming every other day to give him music lessons. Andre was now a proud and talented member of the Antioch Praise Band. Last week, for the first time in Sunday morning worship, he had accompanied himself on the keyboard as he sang his first solo, his own delightful version of Jacob's first hit song, *The Redeemed.*

Recovery had not gone so smoothly for Andre's mother, LaTisha. Juice's death and Andre's initial diagnosis almost put her over the edge. She left the treatment center and spent her days and nights at Andre's bedside. The second day, Angela arrived from Springfield to join her in the bedside vigil. LaTisha was a mess, but she hung in there. One of the first things Andre did when he came out of the coma was plead with his mother to return to treatment and with his sister to return to Missouri, to the life she had begun for herself. LaTisha returned to the treatment center. After thirty more days she moved to a halfway house for women in the western part of the state, four hours away from Parkland. She wrote at least two letters a week. Andre eagerly read each one to Jill and Maryann. The letters became a journal of the progress she had made. Angela made several weekend visits to see her little brother. Over Christmas, Jacob, Maryann, Mark and Andre traveled to Missouri to spend a couple of days with Angela.

As Andre got better, so did LaTisha. She worried Andre would not want to live with her anymore. How could she compete with the nice home and the family life he experienced with Jacob, Maryann and Mark? She needn't have worried. Every Sunday, Andre asked the folks at Antioch to pray for his mother. As the time approached for her to leave the group home, his excitement grew. He went with Ruth and Jill to pick an apartment that was halfway between the Club and Mark's house, his primary criteria. Just as eagerly, he threw himself into finding furniture and furnishings.

At last, the time for her release came and last evening, Jacob and Maryann made the trip with Andre out to the group home and this morning returned with LaTisha. Tonight would be LaTisha and Andre's first night together in their new home. Andre was beside himself with anticipation. Monday morning, LaTisha would begin working at the Club as a receptionist under the tutelage of Antioch's aftercare program.

Finally, the pretty woman who held onto the podium at the front of the auditorium found the words and she began to speak.

"Hello, my name is LaTisha and I'm an alcoholic and a drug addict. Last week I celebrated six months of sobriety."

She smiled and basked in the applause and cheers of encouragement.

When it subsided, she said, "And today for the first time in my life, I feel like I've come home."

From all over the auditorium people yelled, "Welcome home."

Jacob nodded and said under his breath, "I know exactly how you feel. Welcome home, LaTisha. Welcome home."

To order additional copies of:

W H E N
SPARROWS
FALL

$24.95 US / $36.95 Canada
$4.00 Shipping & Handling

Contact:

 **B**OOK**PARTNERS**
INCORPORATED

P.O. Box 922
Wilsonville, OR 97070
Fax: 503-682-2057
Phone: 503-682-3235

www.bookpartners.com
E-mail: info@bookpartners.com